"I'M ABOUT TO
CRIPPLE THIS PLACE."

He swiveled his mike to his mouth, then reached into a pocket and switched his radio to the regimental command channel; the need for radio silence was over.

"Little A, Little A," he said, "this is 2nd Platoon, A Company, Alsnor commanding. The enemy's commanding brigadier and his aide are dead. Their operations control center is crippled; I've destroyed their computer and comm central. Oh, and we encountered no pickets."

Acknowledgment was prompt. Then feet ran up to the center, hesitated for a minute outside the door. Someone opened it and stepped in, the other one following. Jerym rolled out and to his feet, and went in after them, gun in hand again, firing. "Two more dead!" he snapped, and turning, was gone again. One of the last two had been a full colonel; and he suspected he'd "killed" the brigade exec. Now it was time to steal some armored assault vehicles.

THE WHITE REGIMENT

JOHN DALMAS

BAEN BOOKS

THE WHITE REGIMENT

A Baen Books Original

Baen Publishing Enterprises
260 Fifth Avenue
New York, N.Y. 10001

ISBN: 0-671-69880-X

Cover art by David Mattingly

First printing, June 1990

Distributed by
SIMON & SCHUSTER
1230 Avenue of the Americas
New York, N.Y. 10020

Printed in the United States of America

This novel is dedicated to

KRISTEN LYNN JONES
my favorite redhead

Born Dec 24, 1987

Acknowledgements

Jim Baen, for his encouragement.

Rod Martin, Elaine Martin, and Larry Martin for ideas and discussions that were central in developing the philosophy of the T'sel. For example, Larry came up with the insight that grew into the Matrix of T'sel. In my infrequent visits to Arizona, some marvelous evenings have been spent in the Martin living room.

Elizabeth Moon, for comments that have sharpened my writing skills. Elizabeth is the author of the outstanding *Paksenarrion* trilogy and such excellent shorts as "ABCs in Zero-G" and "Too Wet To Plow."

Bill Bailie, U.S. Navy (retired), for the benefit of his knowledge of electronics, ordnance, and a great deal more; and for our yak sessions that cover the spectrum and help ideas germinate and mature. And again for his friendship.

Staff Sergeant Phil Yarbrough, U.S. Army, eight years a ranger, for reviewing the manuscript and for the loan of material on military strategy and tactics.

Also my respects to the elite forces, notably the U.S. Army Special Forces, the Ranger battalions, and their equivalents in the other services; and Air Force, Navy, and Marine fighter squadrons. These organizations in particular provide roles for warriors; may their careers be spent in training.

And finally my respects and appreciation to all branches of the United States armed forces.

Prologue

Summer Solstice, the Year of Pertunis 736

Head tilted, Lotta Alsnor looked critically at herself in the mirror, yet hardly noticed the freckled face and carroty hair, the skinny arms and legs. She'd dressed herself in what she thought of as her prettiest dress, a yellow print with small white flowers, that Mrs. Bosler had given her for Equinox. She'd worn it almost every weekend since, at Sixday mixers where you got to visit with the staff and the older children. Mrs. Orbig had showed her how to clean it—it was a kind you sprayed with a special cleaner, then rinsed with water and blew dry. At home she hadn't cleaned her own clothes. Her mama hadn't taught her, probably had thought she was too little. Things were different here, a lot, and of course she was seven now.

Lotta frowned. The dress didn't have as much body as when it was new. Mrs. Orbig probably knew how to fix that too, she told herself. She'd ask her. Her eye noticed a small scuff on a white shoe, on the toe. Taking a tissue from her desk, she knelt and spit on the place,

1

wiped it as shiny as it would get, then threw the tissue away.

With a final glance in the mirror, she hurried out of the room she shared with two other little girls and an older girl, then down the hall, the stairs, through the vestibule and onto the side veranda, where she stopped to wait.

Sunlight was hazy yellow on flowerbeds and lawn; insects floated among clustered blossoms. It was seldom this quiet. Summer Solstice was the first holiday since Equinox long enough for children from far away to go home. Lotta couldn't, of course. Pelstron was 1,600 miles* away, and her daddy didn't make enough money to buy the ticket. That didn't bother her though; she took it for granted. And her mother had written that they'd be able to fly her home for Harvest Festival.

A bee reconnoitered the bank of butterflowers at the veranda's edge, and Lotta wondered what it would be like to be a bee. Wisdom/Knowledge was her natural area; in a few years she'd be able to meld with a bee and find out. She gave the insect her full attention, intending that it happen now, that she suddenly slip inside it. Thus she didn't notice Mrs. Lormagen come out on the veranda.

Mauen Lormagen watched the rapt child for a minute or so without speaking. "Good morning, Lotta," she said at last, and the child turned and looked at her.

"Good morning, Mrs. Lormagen." The little girl's gaze was steady and direct. Mrs. Lormagen was old—forty-nine she'd heard someone say—but still pretty. She taught dancing as part of the T'sel. You knelt; meditated space, time, and motion; then practiced the forms; and finally you danced. Mrs. Lormagen could stand on one foot, put her leg out in front of her, her

---

*In this book, customary units of measurement, as well as the twenty-four-hour clock, are used for convenience in visualization. However, Confederation calendar units are used here instead of months.

foot higher than her shoulder, and hold it there without falling down. Lotta could put her leg out like that too, either leg, but couldn't keep it there without holding on to the balance bar. She liked dance next best to meditation class, and Ostrak sessions with Mr. Bosler; actually she liked all her classes.

Mrs. Lormagen was going with them on the picnic, and Lotta realized now that the woman was wearing rough slacks, a plain shirt, and casual beach sandals. Of course. The boat's seats might not be clean, or the picnic benches. For just a moment the little girl considered running back upstairs to change, then dismissed the thought. She *liked* to wear her yellow dress.

Mr. Bosler came out then, and Mrs. Bosler. Each carried a large wicker basket covered with a towel. The Lormagens' grown son Kusu was with them. Lotta knew that Kusu was too old, twenty-two, for her ever to marry. Twenty-two was fifteen years older than seven, more than three times as old. Although . . . when he was thirty-five, she'd be twenty. But someone else would marry him by then. Kusu was beautiful: he was tall and had muscles, and blond hair with some red in it, but not nearly as much red as hers. And he laughed a lot. His area was Wisdom/Knowledge like hers, and he was home from the Royal University.

Kusu grinned at her, a flash of teeth, then hopped off the veranda and loped across the yard toward the boathouse, where the oars were kept. Mr. Bosler grinned at her too. He was sixty something, she'd heard, and didn't have much hair; none at all in front. He led them across the yard to the dock, where they got in one of the larger rowboats, and Kusu came down with two sets of oars, one for himself and one for Mr. Bosler. When everyone was seated, they pushed away from the dock and started rowing.

Lotta watched the oars push them through the water, making little whirlpools at the end of every stroke. Mr. Bosler was strong too, though not as strong as Kusu of course, and they rowed in perfect unison, as if they practiced together.

"How're you doing on the selection of your doctoral research?" Mr. Bosler asked over his shoulder.

"I've decided to open up the project I talked to you about," Kusu said, "and establish its feasibility. You and I are pretty sure it's feasible, but Fahnsmor and Dikstrel are positive it's not, so what I'm proposing is a study of the nature of hyperspace."

He laughed. "It's remarkable how long we've used hyperspace travel without anyone knowing or wondering about things like that. I'm sure that neither Farnsmor nor Dikstrel got the real Sacrament when they were little, but they're at Work, on Jobs. And educated when they were, they don't have the faintest idea of what research is about. They want a study plan with no room for the unknown, so I'll give them what looks like one, and we can be surprised together."

Lotta wondered what Fahnsmor and Dikstrel were like. Fahnsmor she pictured as tall and lanky, Dikstrel as short and pudgy, and wondered if they really were. She knew the difference between imagination and reality, but she also knew that people sometimes knew things subliminally they didn't know they knew, and called what they knew imagination to account for it.

"You haven't been home for a few deks*," Mr. Bosler said to Kusu. "Have you heard the idea your dad's been playing with recently?"

"I guess not. Something in addition to translating the T'swa history of the old Home Sector?"

"Right. There's been a frequency increase, the last dozen years, in disorderly pupils in the public schools.

---

*In the Confederation Sector, the year is divided into ten parts, known as deks. Each world has its own calendar based on its orbital period. The Standard Year and Standard Deks, used in interplanetary records, commerce, and Confederation government, are the year and deks of the principal planet, Iryala.

It's not conspicuous, but teachers and school administrators have definitely noticed it. Varlik had a survey done on sample schools, and more than seventy percent of disorderly students belong in the same slot in the Matrix of T'sel."

Lotta saw Kusu's eyebrows arch. "Warriors," he said.

"Right. An unprecedented bunch of little warriors have gotten themselves born, with nowhere to fight." Mr. Bosler grinned, his mouth and eyes both.

Lotta knew a child at home like they'd been talking about: her older brother Jerym. He'd gotten in trouble at school for fighting. Once he'd told her he was going to be a T'swi when he grew up. She hadn't had the T'sel yet then, so she'd thought that was a dumb thing to say. The T'swa were born, not made; she'd already known that. Now she realized that T'swa meant different things to different people—a human species that lived on the planet Tyss, and the mercenary warriors from there. And that a long time ago, in the Kettle War, Mr. Lormagen, Kusu's father, was called "the White T'swa," which was wrong grammatically—T'swa was plural or an adjective—but that was how people said it on Iryala. Kusu was even named for a T'swa: Mr. Lormagen's sergeant on Kettle.

"What's Varlik's idea?" Mrs. Bosler asked. "Or was getting the statistics it?"

"Tell her, Mauen. He's talked to you since he has to me."

"He's proposed to Lord Kristal that regiments of children be formed and trained. Like the T'swa mercenary regiments: starting with six- and seven-year-olds."

Jerym's too old then, way too old, Lotta thought. Ten.

"Who'd train them? T'swa?" asked Mrs. Bosler.

"The first ones trained would be a cadre unit. T'swa would train them. Then the cadre unit would train the white regiments."

"Would they be mercenaries like the T'swa? If they were part of the Iryalan army, they could easily spend their entire career without fighting."

"He's thinking in terms of having them trained under the O.S.P. He doesn't think it would work to have the army do it; they'd want it done their way. Then, when an actual regiment finishes training, they'd become part of a special branch of the Defense Ministry. The Movement would hire them from Defense as a mercenary unit, and contract them out to warring factions on the trade worlds."

"Wouldn't they be competing with the T'swa?"

"Not really. The trade worlds would hire twice as many T'swa regiments if they were available."

They were just about to Gouer Island. Most of it was woods, but the end they were coming to was grassy, like a lawn with shade trees. The grass was even short like a lawn. Lotta could see two sets of outdoor picnic tables, far enough apart for privacy, and a big, open-sided shelter with tables of its own, in case it rained. Kusu had stopped rowing, and crouched ready to grab the dock. Mr. Bosler dabbed with his oars to guide them in. Lotta reached down, unbuckled her white shoes and took them off, along with her socks, so they wouldn't get dirty on the island. But her main attention was on the grownups talking.

"We can use the profits from the contracts to open more schools," Mrs. Lormagen was saying. "With the teeth taken out of the Sacrament, society needs a new and better glue. Or it will when the various centrifugal factors have been operating for a while."

Lotta understood almost all the words they'd been using, and being a Wisdom/Knowledge child, she knew pretty much what they'd been talking about, even what Mrs. Lormagen meant about glue: People who knew the T'sel liked other people more.

But Mr. Lormagen wouldn't have to worry about contracting his regiments out. They'd fight for the Confederation; she had a feeling about that.

The boat slid alongside the dock; Kusu grabbed one of the posts it was built on, and tied up to it. Lotta was the first one off, running barefoot up the dock to explore.

One

Excerpt from *Historical Abstract of the Home Sector*, translated from the Tyspi, with commentary by Sir Varlik Lormagen. Until otherwise authorized, distribution of this book is restricted to The Movement. The material summarized here was compiled and refined over several millenia by T'swa seers. An entire monastery of the Order of Ka-Shok was occupied with the task for more than a millenium, and the work is continually being updated.

The ancient home of humankind was dubbed "the Home Sector" of the galaxy by early investigators. . . . This civilization, an empire consisting of fifty-three planets, was destroyed by a megawar more than 21,000 years ago, the principal source of destruction being His Imperial Majesty's ship *Retributor,* an immense warship designed to destroy planets.

Rumors of the emperor's intention to build the *Retributor* undoubtedly caused the confrontation between the imperium and its antagonists. Otherwise the megawar might never have happened, for the imperium was decaying, and the opposition, usually factionalized, might well have resigned itself to awaiting the empire's self-generated dissolution. As it was, rebellion and mutinies, more or less coordinated, broke out on a number of worlds, involving powerful forces both loyal and in rebellion.

When *Retributor* sallied forth under the command of its mad emperor, it did not spare worlds already ravaged. They too were "punished"—literally blown apart. And when the emperor blew himself up with his ship, only one subsector of his empire—eleven inhabited or previously inhabited worlds—remained intact. Of these, eight had been totally depopulated, or so nearly depopulated that humans did not long survive on them. What was left of the empire's population, once nearly 600 billion, was at most a few score million, probably fewer, scattered on three planets. And those millions diminished further before they began to increase.*

Eventually they did increase, but they had lost every trace of civilization and history. After a long time, civilization re-emerged, and eventually, on the planet Varatos, a culture arose that reinvented science. In time there was hyperspace travel again. By 19,000 years after the megawar, the other ten surviving planets, two of them populated, had been rediscovered, and those without humans had been colonized.

The eleven worlds found themselves surrounded by a vast region of space without habitable planets. They didn't know why, of course. In fact, it seemed to them that they occupied an aberration—a region with habitable planets in a universe where there seemed to be no others. Science provided no convincing rationale; by that time it was in serious decline. . . .

Of course, there were the survivors—refugees, our ancestors—who fled early in the rebellion in a fleet of eight large merchant ships, and came to the sector we live in now. But they are not the subject of this work. [Translator]

In the year 742 Before Pertunis, the eleven worlds became a religious empire—the Karghanik Empire. The statutory structures within the empire are largely but not entirely uniform. Actually, the "empire" consists of eleven somewhat autonomous, single-system sultanates, mutually engaged in political and economic rivalries. Neither the empire nor its sultanates are true theocracies. In each, the religious hierarchy shares power with a secular aristocracy.

The imperial worlds are tied together by a complex network of political treaties and trade agreements administered largely through an artificial intelligence known as SUMBAA.* It is probably only through SUMBAA that the Karghanik empire has survived in the face of rivalries and especially of distance. Each planet has its SUMBAA; the SUMBAA for Varatos serves the imperial adminstration.

The empire has a fleet and army more than sufficient to its rather modest needs.† Its ships are manned by a mixed crew from all the worlds of the empire, the mixes and proportions being based on recommendations by SUMBAA. The higher command strata are filled largely by officers from Varatos, the Imperial Planet. Army and marine units, up to battalions, are each from a different world, each with its own officers, and no imperial battalion is stationed on its home world. Divisions never contain more than two battalions from the same world.

---

*SUMBAA is our Iryalan acronym for Sentient, Universal, Multiterminal Bank, Analyzer, and Advisor—our translation of their name for it. They have their own acronym. We do not know very much about SUMBAA. It was designed to program itself, with the potential for self-expansion, and has grown beyond, perhaps far beyond, the understanding of the people who designed it. And their ability was considerably above that of the empire's present-day computer scientists, let alone our own. [Translator]

†It seems probable that any one of its fleet combat teams—three vessels working together—could defeat the entire Confederation fleet as now constituted. [Translator]

Each world has its own flag, and also its own several warships and planetary forces under its own command, partly for purposes of home-planet security and partly for reasons of prestige.*

The monastery named Dys Tolbash stood on a narrow side ridge that descended from a much higher ridge to the east. The building, long and proportionately narrow, was constructed in the form of three uneven steps, accommodating it to the sloping ridge crest. It seemed almost to have grown out of the ridge crest. The lower step stood on an outlook, below which the crest slanted down abruptly like the edge of some rough plowshare, to the boulder-cluttered valley at its foot.

A tower stood at each corner of each step, eight irregular towers in all, overlooking the desert valley two thousand feet below and the two ravines whose craggy walls formed the ridge sides.

It was summer, a season of furnace heat on Tyss, a heat scarcely moderated by the elevation of 3,400 feet. In the west, the evening sun squatted on the horizon, and the temperature had fallen a bit, to 121°F. Master Tso-Ban didn't know that—there was no thermometer at the monastery—and he'd have given it no importance if he had known. At the moment he was climbing the stone stairs that slanted up the outer north wall of a tower.

His tower was at an upper corner, and therefore one of the two highest. At the top step, he paused to scan the rhyolite outcrops and the bristly scrub that broke their starkness here and there. In the pale sky, a car-

---

*Their weapons too seem generally superior to our own, and apparently their naval armament is far superior. We can expect it to take two to three generations before we will have caught up in the technology of space warfare. If we decide to. First our culture will need to adjust sufficiently to the changes we are leading it through. [Translator]

rion bird rode an updraft, tilting, watching, silent. A lesser movement caught Tso-Ban's large, still-sharp eyes. A rock goat, male and solitary, stood browsing with careful tongue among the leaves of a fishhook bush.

The old T'swa monk turned then and entered the top of the tower, a small cell with thick stone walls on three sides, open to the north, away from the sun. On the others, wide eaves-shaded windows gave access to whatever breeze might come. The only furnishings were two pegs in the wall, and a stone platform a foot high, padded with a hide over which a straw mat was spread. On one peg he hung his waterbag, on the other his unbleached white robe. At his age, the skin he exposed was no longer the black of a blued gun barrel, but a flat, faintly grayish black. Seating himself on the platform, he arranged his legs in a full lotus.

In seconds his eyes lost focus; in seconds more they saw nothing, though they did not close. It took a moment to find his unwitting connection, a man who never imagined that someone like Tso-Ban existed, or the planet Tyss. Unfelt, Tso-Ban touched him, and in a sense, in that moment, was no longer on Tyss, in a tower in the Lok-Sanu foothills. His attention was on the bridge of a warship, the flagship of a small exploration flotilla, outward bound from a world named Klestron.

Tso-Ban was a player at Wisdom/Knowledge, and had taken the Home Sector world of Klestron as his psychic playground. For some time, the Sultan of Klestron had been his unknowing connection. The sultan, an ambitious man, had decided to gamble, to send out a flotilla of three ships, with orders not to return until they'd found a new, habitable world. This action was quite unprecedented, by imperial standards illogical and arguably illegal. So of course it attached Tso-Ban's interest.

The sultan had given command of the flotilla to a brevet admiral, Igsat Tarimenloku, making him its commodore. Tarimenloku wasn't brilliant, but he was loyal, a devout son of Kargh, and a friend of the sultan, insofar as the sultan had friends.

Tarimenloku had become the T'swa monk's new connection. Tso-Ban could have used the ship as his connection, but far more information was available this way. In trance he became almost one with Tarimenloku, perceiving through him and with him, sensing his emotions, his surface thoughts, and in a general way his underlying intentions. But always there was a certain separation, Tso-Ban remaining an observer.

It was ship's night in the command room, the light soft, free of glare. Others were there, but Tarimenloku's—and with it Tso-Ban's—attention went to them only now and then. Mostly the commodore watched his instruments, which after a bit told him that in real space there were a major and a minor nodus adjacent to his ship's equivalent location in hyperspace. If he emerged now, he'd find a previously unknown solar system near enough to examine.

It would be better though to be nearer. Tarimenloku tapped keys, changing course, moving "nearer" to the major nodus and "farther" from the minor. He touched a key, and a bell tone alerted all personnel of impending emergence—a standard courtesy and precaution—then touched two other keys. Together his three ships emerged into "real-space," Tso-Ban sharing the commodore's moment of mild disorientation. And there, only 1.8 billion miles away, was a system primary, as he'd known there'd be, at 277.016° course orientation, with a gas giant barely near enough to show a disk unmagnified, at 193.724°. His survey ship, small, totally automated, crewless except for a dozen maintenance personnel, began scanning to locate the system's planets and compute first-approximations of their orbits, radioing its data to the flagship's computer as well as storing it in its own. The troop ship followed, its marine brigade inert, unconscious in their stasis lockers.

Tarimenloku's main screen showed the alien vessel almost as quickly as his instruments found it, showed it newly emerged at a distance of only twelve miles. Looking like a disorderly stack of scrap metal and rods welded together, it was presumably a patrol ship. The commodore stared, alarmed: Clearly it had perceived him in hyperspace with a most unusual precision, to have merged so remarkably near and on a matched course: Clearly the alien had technology well beyond his own. The alternative explanation was coincidence, and the odds of that were too small to compute.

Suddenly, on the screen, he was looking into what seemed to be their bridge, the first of his species, so far as he knew, to see an intelligent alien life form. The screen showed creatures vaguely humanoid, with thick leathery skin and vestigial horns, and somehow it seemed to him they were larger than men.

If there'd been any doubt of their technical superiority before, this dispelled it. Their instruments and computer were sufficiently sophisticated that in seconds they'd remote-analyzed the flotilla's electronics sufficiently to beam video signals compatible with Klestronu* equipment.

Then a voice came out of his speaker, seemingly a computer simulation of human speech. But the words—they certainly sounded like words—meant nothing to Tarimenloku. There was about a sentence-worth of them; then they stopped. After a pause of two or three seconds they were repeated.

"I do not understand you," he answered, and repeated it three times.

DAAS, his computer, spoke to him. "Commodore, there is an alien electronic presence in my databank, scanning."

Tarimenloku's brows knotted and he set his exit controls. "Gunnery," he said quietly, "do you have a fix on the alien?"

"Yes, commodore."

"Have you identified his control structure?"

"Yes, commodore."

Klestronu adj. *Of, pertaining to, or derived from Klestron or its inhabitants.*

"Fire bee-pees one through four."

As soon as his systems screen told him the pulses had been fired, he touched the flotilla control key with one hand and the exit key with the other. His three ships flicked back into hyperspace.

Then he keyed his microphone to confidential. He'd better record right now his justification for what he'd done. (Second thoughts were already pressing his consciousness, and he pushed them away.) It wouldn't do to have the alien reading, and surely recording, the contents of his databank uninvited; simply to try could be considered a hostile act. (But there was a subliminal awareness that the alien might have had no hostile intention at all.)

He had no idea how much damage he'd done to the alien ship. It seemed possible he'd destroyed it. Hopefully he'd at least prevented it from pursuing him.

"DAAS," he said to the computer, "what was the nature of the data being scanned?"

"Sir, it first found my vocabulary. Then it began to read verbal data files indiscriminately."

Another thought occurred to Tarimenloku, a thought that left a moment of bleakness in its wake: After the alien's failed attempt to speak to him, it might have been taking data for a linguistic analysis, for communication. If so, his action might have made a dangerous enemy for the empire and humankind, of beings who initially had not been hostile. He hoped he'd destroyed them, and that their government would never know who'd done it.

One more thought occurred to him; he wasn't sure whether it was trivial or important: Who had they thought he was when they tried talking to him in that unfamiliar speech?

One thing was certain. He wouldn't return to real space for three imperial months at least—best make that four or five—regardless of any interesting-looking nodi that said "system."

Two

The day of graduation was clear but not hot. A breeze ruffled the flags, of Iryala and the Confederation, that flanked the temporary platform where the dignitaries sat.

There was a sizeable grandstand facing south—away from the sun in this southern hemisphere. On it sat more than two thousand people—mostly relatives of the cadets plus press representatives from their home districts. Photographers occupied the uppermost row. The broadcast media had not been invited, so of course had not come; the Crown wanted the event known but not to seem particularly important.

A sound began from the other side of the nearby classroom building, high-pitched voices calling cadence. In the grandstand, the susurrus of conversations thinned, almost stilled. The cadets began to appear, nearly six hundred preadolescent boys in parade uniforms marching around the corner of the building in a tight brisk column of sixes, all straight edges and sharp corners, to enter and bisect the exercise field. Approaching the

15

platform, alternating companies peeled off left and right,
diverging. Their cadet major's boy-alto voice called a
command. They halted, and crisply, in perfect unison,
turned to face the dignitaries. Six columns had become
six rows, aligned so precisely, they didn't need to dress
ranks. Another command and they semi-relaxed at parade rest.

Now attention went to the platform.

The dignitaries numbered eight. In the center sat
Emry Wanslo, Lord Kristal, who was personal aide to
His Majesty, Marcus XXVIII, King of Iryala and Administrator General of the Confederation of Worlds;
and Colonel Jil-Zat, a uniformed T'swi who could almost have been carved from obsidian. To Jil-Zat's left
sat his three principal training officers, T'swa like himself. On Kristal's right were Varlik Lormagen and two
officials from the Office of Special Projects.

With the boys at parade rest, Jil-Zat got to his feet
and stepped to the microphone. "Cadets!" he said. His
voice was a resonant bass. "Congratulations! You have
my respect and joyous admiration, which is not news to
you. We know and understand each other well, and we
will be together for your advanced training on the other
worlds.

"More than that I need not tell you." The black face,
the large T'swa eyes, shifted to the grandstands. "So I
shall direct my words to our guests. This ceremony is to
honor 594 young warriors on the completion of their
basic training. A very special training. For five and a
half years they have been learning to live and fight in a
very famous tradition, the tradition of Kootosh-Lan. A
tradition which is the gift of Tyss to the Crown of
Iryala, expressing our thanks for the Crown's recognition, thirty-one years ago, of Tyss as a trade world
under royal protection."

Jil-Zat paused, shifting to another theme.

"What are these young warriors about? What are *we*
about, their cadre? Why this training? This school? Any

of the cadets could tell you, but I am on the program and hold the microphone, so I will.

"Every person is born with a purpose. These young men were born to be warriors. And they have had the good fortune to find a special place, a home, a small society of warriors. As warriors, their training is very unlike that of soldiers. Their basic training has taken far longer, been much broader, much deeper. They have learned to be a very special kind of human being."

While Jil-Zat talked, Varlik Lormagen's eyes had been examining the front rank, the mostly twelve-year-old faces. Boy faces, most of them tanned, a few fair and freckled. Very different from the black, combat-seasoned faces of his old Red Scorpion Regiment, long dead. But they were cousins now in philosophy.

"Each of them," Jil-Zat was saying, "has mastered all his lessons, and all the skills so far addressed—mastered them very thoroughly. There are no marginal graduates. You can be proud of every one of them, as I am.

"Those of you whose sons these are, I congratulate for agreeing to their enlistment. Many of you, I am sure, felt misgivings at all this. Misgivings which I trust have long since been relieved by your occasional visits here to witness your sons' physical and spiritual growth."

Misgivings, yes, thought Varlik Lormagen. *But relief, too.* In the conformist culture of Iryala and the Confederation worlds, there'd never been a decent niche for the would-be warrior, nor any good way of dealing with a warrior child whose innate drives had been aberrated by life there. These parents had been given a respectable, an honorable way of dealing with their intentive warrior by allowing him to enter early a subculture of his own.

". . . Their training on Iryala," Jil-Zat went on, "is over now. But they have six more years elsewhere. Three on Terfreya—"

Good, Lormagen thought. *I'm glad he didn't use its nickname.*

"—and three on my own world, Tyss." The black face flashed teeth. "Where, I might add, they will live in the only cooled barracks ever built there. We value these young men, and will not waste them. We require a great deal of them, but we treat them well.

"I consider it a privilege to be their commanding officer. . . ."

When Jil-Zat had finished, Lord Kristal spoke to the boys, beginning with a message from the King. It was neither rhetorical nor in the least hortatory; these boys, Lormagen told himself, didn't need rhetoric or exhortation. The speech was shorter than the guests might have expected, but long enough.

When it was over, the cadet major threw back his head and yelled, "Dismissed!" The boys didn't break ranks as they usually did, like an air burst. Instead they turned toward the stands and sort of spread out, waving at parents and siblings, waiting for them to come down rather than storming the stands themselves. Lormagen wondered if that was per instructions or grew out of the boys' own wisdom. Increasingly, these boys had been living the T'sel since they'd come here, and it was counter-productive to instruct needlessly; let wisdom function.

Together, the dignitaries walked toward the central building, led by Jil-Zat. In the Kettle War, Lormagen remembered, Jil-Zat had been a nineteen-year-old commanding officer of mercenaries, of a virgin T'swa regiment, the Ice Tigers. He wondered what rough trade world or resource world that regiment had finally died on, and how Jil-Zat had come to survive its destruction.

Ice Tigers! An interesting name for a regiment from Tyss, nicknamed "Oven," where few had ever seen even artificial ice.

At the building, most of the dignitaries dispersed to rooms or duties. A courier had been waiting for Lord Kristal, and handed him a package presumably containing a message cube. Lormagen and Jil-Zat waited while His Majesty's representative opened it.

"Colonel, may I use your computer?" Kristal asked. "Privately? This is from His Majesty's staff chief."

Jil-Zat gestured at his office. "Be my guest."

Even in the T'sel, courtesy oils human relations, Lormagen thought to himself. As Marcus's representative, Lord Kristal hadn't needed to ask. Kristal closed the door behind him, and Lormagen turned to Jil-Zat. "I hadn't thought to ask before," he said. "What exactly became of the Ice Tigers?"

Jil-Zat smiled. "We took considerable casualties around Beregesh, as you will recall. From there we went to the planet Ice—appropriately enough, considering our name. We'd been hired by its government, which was dominated by the fur ranchers' cooperative. In effect, the co-op *was* the government. They had been trying to suppress the free trappers, whose response had escalated from lobbying to sabotage to guerrilla warfare.

"It became a very interesting and enjoyable campaign. The trappers had scraped enough money together to hire what was left of the Ba-Tok Regiment, a short battalion actually—we were two somewhat short battalions ourselves—and we had some very good combat before the trappers faced reality and agreed to bargain. By that time we'd cut the Ba-Tok down to barely company size, and the locals themselves, both sides, had taken severe casualties."

The colonel chuckled. "Actually, I claim some credit for the peace agreement coming as soon as it did. I had exerted such influence as I could on the co-op's executive board, and they decided it was time to ease their unreasonable position. While Major Tengu of the Ba-Tok was influencing the Union to modify their more extreme demands.

"To directly influence our employer's political positions is not our contractual function of course, but it's the sort of thing we often do, where it seems likely to shorten a conflict to an ethical result."

Lormagen nodded, remembering Kettle.

"From there, the lodge contracted us both out to a mercantile consortium on Carjath, that had joined forces with a dukedom in revolt against a king. Operating combined, we comprised an overstrength battalion. It turned out that the consortium had seriously underestimated the king's support and overestimated the duke's." Jil-Zat chuckled again. "Intelligence organizations are as apt to mislead as they are to enlighten, and that was an extreme example."

His office door opened, and Jil-Zat cut short his account as Lord Kristal stepped out. "Thank you, Colonel," Kristal said. "Varlik, we need to talk."

They excused themselves, and the two Iryalans went to Kristal's room.

"The T'swa ambassador carried a report to His Majesty from Tyss," Kristal said. "From the Order of Ka-Shok. One of their monks has been studying a world in the Karghanik Empire, an ambitious world called Klestron. Not long ago, Klestron's sultan sent an expedition out of the imperial sector. Not to explore immediately neighboring space, but to scout far inward for habitable worlds. An unprecedented act." Kristal paused meaningfully. "Recently they reached Garthid space, which means they may be headed more or less in our direction. The expedition consists of a flagship—a cruiser, well armed of course—plus a survey ship presumably heavily instrumented, and a troopship carrying a brigade of 8,000 Klestronu marines. The lodge master thought we'd want to know."

Lormagen pursed his lips thoughtfully. "The Garthids may send them home. They might not grant passage to a naval flotilla."

"They've already met, and the Klestronu flagship attacked the Garthid patrol vessel without warning; attacked, then fled into hyperspace. And its commodore doesn't plan to come out until hopefully he's beyond retaliation."

"The Garthids may have gotten message pods off," Lormagen pointed out.

"True. In which case the entire Garthid Sector could be waiting for the Klestroni* to come out of hyperspace.

"Meanwhile the Klestronu commodore doesn't realize how *vast* Garthid space is. At the time, he was thinking of staying in hyperspace for deks. It will have to be a lot of deks—probably more than a year. So he'll probably emerge still in Garthid space. If he does, he may well encounter another patrol ship, or several of them, and could be destroyed."

Beneath black brows out of sync with his white hair, Kristal's eyes were calm and steady. "But if—*if* he continues long enough, it's possible he'll reach our sector. Should that happen, it's hard to say what the result might be."

Lormagen nodded. He could think of several unfavorable scenarios. The Crown Council assumed that outside forces would discover the Confederation Sector sooner or later, perhaps posing a threat to the independence, even the safety, of the Confederation and its people. But large-scale upgrading of military technology required first that the Confederation be led out of the millenia-long "hypnotism" imposed on it by the deep psycho-conditioning of the Sacrament. A process which wouldn't be completed for at least another couple of generations and couldn't safely be rushed.

Neither man commented on that; it was understood.

"I'm going to recommend to His Majesty that should the Klestronu expedition actually land their marines on a Sector world, we rush elite troops there, troops whose quality they're unlikely to match, and hit them on the ground. We have no prospect of defeating them in space."

"We'll need to call on the T'swa then," Lormagen said. "They have the only troops that fit the requirement."

Klestroni noun, plural; singular Klestronit. Persons native to or inhabiting Klestron.

"True. And we won't hesitate to. But their regiments are scattered, engaged on various trade and resource worlds, on contracts they'll feel bound by. That is, after all, how Tyss gets almost all its exchange. And we don't know if, let alone where or when, we'll need them. The T'swa seer will be able to tell us if the Klestronu flotilla is destroyed or turns back. Or when they emerge from hyperspace safely away from the Garthids. But he can't tell us where. He hasn't the technical knowledge.

"The odds are, of course, that the Klestronu expedition will never reach the Confederation Sector. The Garthids will stop them, or they'll emerge from hyperspace somewhere away from us. But we need to prepare. We'll want elite troops on standby, with transport on hand and ready, as a quick response force."

Kristal's eyes, though calm as usual, held Lormagen's now. "Varlik, several years ago you suggested a test, of the suitability of raw adolescents with warrior profiles for an elite force, and His Majesty decided against it. That's what I'm looking at now. A regiment of teenaged would-be warriors; 'intentive warriors' as the T'swa say. Youths in their mid- and late-teens that we can train intensively for two or three years, or for one if that's all the time we have. Even at hyperspace speeds, it will be quite awhile before the Klestroni can arrive."

Lormagen frowned slightly, remembering why the Council had earlier recommended against such a regiment: *Most of the kids would be misfits, the youthful troublemakers of Iryala. With two or three, seldom more, in a school, they haven't been a serious problem. More in the nature of nuisances. But gather two thousand in one place. . . .* He looked at Kristal and nodded. "It can be done. But we'll need to hire T'swa as cadre; some battle-wise veterans, the survivors of retired regiments. There shouldn't be any shortage.

"And recruits will be a lot easier to identify as teenagers; we can start by winnowing through school and court records for youths with particular behavioral problems, then check their personality profiles. They won't train up to T'swa standards, but they should prove a lot more satisfactory than any army regiment we have. I'd want certain recent equipment designs put into manufacture for them."

Kristal smiled. "I doubt there'll be any problems with upgrading infantry equipment. I'll tell His Majesty what you've said. Sometime within the next several days you can expect a request to present preliminary plans to the Council. Agreed?"

"Agreed." Lormagen felt excitement growing in him. He already knew who he wanted as regimental commander.

Kristal glanced at a wall clock. "Well then, it's time for lunch. Let's go down to the dining room."

As they left, Lormagen felt ideas stirring not far beneath the surface of his consciousness. He'd stay over tonight, and try them out on Jil-Zat this evening.

Three

Farmland had ended several minutes back. Now rolling forest passed beneath the troop transport, a patchwork of late summer yellows and reds interrupted by occasional meadows, fens and marshes, lakes and streams. Narrow ribbons of road showed here and there, still summer green and seemingly without traffic.

Jerym Alsnor sat twisted in his bench seat to watch, feeling uncomfortable at what he saw. It was utterly different from the tailored industrial city of Pelstron where he'd lived all his seventeen years, and he felt sure that this unpeopled backwoods was where he'd be unloaded.

The Blue Forest Military Reservation they'd called it, back at the assembly center. He didn't know about the *blue*, but *forest* certainly fitted.

When he'd signed up, it had seemed the solution to everything, and an opportunity for adventure. But he'd also signed away his options, his freedoms, shaky as they'd already become, and now he was afraid he'd done the wrong thing. Again.

Ahead, buildings appeared, not of a town. Small buildings, looking somehow institutional. He felt deceleration: This was it—the Blue Forest Reservation.

Others had been looking too. Until then the floater had been remarkably quiet. Now a murmur began, and the recruits on the middle banks of seats got up, coming over to look out the windows, elbowing each other. Jerym might have felt hostile at the crowding, the encroachment, but his attention was too much on the buildings and their grounds. They weren't a kind of buildings and grounds he understood.

The transport began settling, sinking faster than his stomach liked. Its crew, in blue-gray uniforms, came down the aisles with batons, ordering the youths back to their seats, those who'd gotten up to see, whacking a few who lingered. The recruits obeyed, much more docile than might have been expected; they were in unfamiliar circumstances, felt exposed and vulnerable, didn't know what to expect.

Besides that, they didn't know each other. Under the circumstances not many had struck up conversations. Almost all were loners, misfits, had hardly known others like themselves, maybe two or three, excepting those few who'd been in reformatory. Then, at the assembly center, they'd been hurried, crowded, told to shut up, keep the noise down.

As Jerym watched, things on the ground acquired detail. Most of the buildings were single-storied; some were shed-like, a few mere roofs without walls. Men stood by, seemingly waiting for them, men in green field uniforms. Black men. *T'swa!* Jerym realized with a start. He felt a gentle landing impact, and one of the crewmen shouted orders. He got up tense, feeling a wash of desperation, sure now that he'd done the wrong thing in signing up. He'd never make it in this place. He'd have to find out how you got out of here; there had to be a way.

Colonel Dak-So, a subcolonel actually, watched the recruits shuffle down the ramp, a hundred of them.

He'd never seen anything quite like them till yesterday's batches. Their postures were bad, their auras gray and murky. His noncoms herded them into a crude semblance of ranks. Supposedly they were intentive warriors. *Suppressed* intentive warriors. He regarded them like a sculptor regarding a new medium. *It will be interesting*, he thought.

Colonel Carlis Voker watched from a window as the semi-column of recruits slouched by, herded by T'swa noncoms. He was keeping aloof till they were broken in a bit. They'd accept the alien T'swa more readily than they would an old white geezer like himself, he thought; be a lot more impressed by them. They'd had too many old geezers telling them what to do.

They were born to be warriors for a reason, he thought, *one we're beginning to see now*.

These were the fourth load in today. With the floaters from Vosinlak and Two Rivers due before supper, there'd be 1,200 of them by lights out. The rest would come in tomorrow, which would keep Supply humping. After all the recruits got boots that fit, he'd send most of his supply people home to the army, which they'd no doubt find a big relief.

Tonight would undoubtedly be as crazy as last night. Or maybe not quite. Last night the T'swa had discovered what kind of raw material they'd been presented with, and after their initial surprise, had handled things with quiet, nicely-gauged force.

If these young men were what their tests and interviews said they were, Voker did not doubt at all that they'd leave here the best fighting men the Confederation had ever produced. (He wasn't counting the cadets, who were still preadolescent, nor the T'swa, who were from a trade world.) But it would take some doing. He had no doubt of that either.

Jerym Alsnor was almost a good-looking kid, would have been handsome except for the cast of chronic resentment and evasiveness on his face. He was tall and still growing, shoulders wide but not yet well muscled. His features were strong and regular, his brown hair close cropped by an army barber at the assembly center in Farningum. Though measured in mere hours, that seemed quite a while ago. Now he stepped onto a small, glass-topped platform, feeling foolish in his green fatigues. He didn't need a mirror to know how poorly they fitted. And the paper slippers he'd been given looked even more ridiculous. He was glad no one he knew could see him like this.

An overweight, red-faced corporal scowled and snapped at him. "Pay attention, recruit! Put your heels against the rounded heel plates and stand still."

Jerym did, thinking where he'd really like to put his foot.

"Now keep your weight evenly on your soles and heels." The corporal eyed a blinking red light on the small instrument screen. "Didn't you hear me, recruit? I said *evenly!*"

The light stopped blinking.

"All right," grumped the corporal after a moment. "Go over to that bench and sit down by the last guy. Someone'll call off your name and number."

Walking to the bench, Jerym glanced again at the numbered tag hanging from his neck. *Jerym D. Alsnor, SR-0726-401, BVLN.* Oh-seven-two-six dash four-oh-one. Easy enough; the first four numbers were his birth year. He sat down.

"How'd you like that fat sack of shit?" asked the guy next to him, thumbing toward the supply corporal. The name label above the youth's left shirt pocket read *Esenrok*.

"Like?" Jerym said. "I'd like to kick the snot out of him."

Both of them spoke quietly. They'd seen one recruit sass a sergeant when they'd been getting their uniforms. A very large, calm T'swi had grabbed the poor sucker and frog-marched him pantless out the door, the guy's right arm up behind his back and a big black fist bunching his green field shirt at the collar. It happened so quickly and quietly, you could have been looking the other way for five seconds and missed the whole thing.

The recruit on the other side of Esenrok gazed at him and Jerym as if they were a pair of children. He was older than they, probably nineteen. "Be glad the boots'll fit better than these greens," he said.

"What makes you think they will?"

"They're who's going to train us, make fighting men out of us, and they don't care whether our uniforms fit good or not. Not now anyway. They probably like it this way; keeps us from acting too smart. But our boots? Our boots have to fit or our feet'll go bad."

Jerym eyed the guy's name label, *Carrmak*, and felt like asking what made him so damn smart. But it didn't seem like the time or place; a T'swa sergeant was standing by the door.

Army guys kept coming to a door and calling names and numbers, and guys would go through the door and out of sight. To get their boots, Jerym supposed. In a few minutes Carrmak went, then Esenrok. Finally they called his name, and Jerym too went through the door. Another army corporal looked at his dog tags to make sure, handed him a pair of boots with treaded soles, and told him to put them on and fasten them. Then prodded and pinched as a last check of their fit, as if he didn't totally trust the computerized fabricator that had just tailor-made them.

"Okay." He pointed. "Out that door and wait."

Jerym went, glad to be rid of his paper slippers, and stood around with the others, waiting for someone to tell them what to do next. Conversations began. A couple of guys—their labels read Warden and Klefma—took off, to find out what would happen. The rest of them speculated on the subject, then two more decided to try it. About three minutes later, two T'swa arrived, a corporal and a sergeant, and had them line up. Each T'swi had a clipboard.

"All right," said the corporal. "When I call your name, raise your hand and say 'Here, sir!' "

He began to read, alphabetically. Here and there, hands popped up and voices answered; a "here, sir" was shouted for every name. When the roll call was done, the sergeant, who'd simply watched, walked along the line of recruits, looking at the names above their shirt pockets. Then he stepped back and gave an order, his deep voice soft but easily heard.

"Barkum, Desterbi, Lonsalek, step forward."

The platoon stood silent, hardly breathing, sensing that something was wrong. The T'swa were large and powerful men from a high-gee world, and their expressions were unreadable, now at least. Uncertain, the three recruits stepped forward. The sergeant walked up to them, opened their shirts and looked at the dog tags dangling from their necks.

"Barkum, why did you answer for Mellis and Thelldon?"

"I don't know. To keep them out of trouble, I guess."

"You have been told how to address a sergeant. Answer my question again. Properly this time."

"Sir! To keep them out of trouble."

The T'swi turned to the next recruit. "Desterbi, you answered for Klefma. Why?"

"Sir, the same thing. To keep him out of trouble."

"Lonsalek? Why did you answer for Warden?"

"Sir, to see what would happen."

The T'swa sergeant nodded, and when he spoke, his voice was conversational. "In this regiment you should not lie to each other, and you very definitely do not lie to your officers." He pointed. "You three stand over there, with your noses touching the wall. Lonsalek wanted to see what would happen. You will find out."

Unexpectedly he whistled then, loud and shrill, one long blast and two short, the sound somehow intimidating. A moment later two more corporals came trotting up. Again the sergeant pointed. "Take these three to temporary detention." The two T'swa went to them, grasped their collars from behind, and shoving, marched them off. None of the three showed any inclination to resist or argue. The sergeant scanned the rest of them. "Corporal, take them to their barracks. They are to remain there till I give further orders."

The sergeant turned and left. "Platooon!" the corporal called. "Atten*tion!*" Each recruit came to his version of attention, all promptly, some sullenly. "Riiight face!" They responded appropriately to the unfamiliar command. "Forwaaard, march!"

They started off, stepping on each others' heels at first, muttering till they got the hang of it. *Column right* and later *column left* they managed more or less. *Platoon halt!* was no problem at all.

Then he herded them inside the long, one-story building, where they sat down on their new bunks. No one said anything till he was gone; then Esenrok spoke. "If we'd of jumped the son of a bitch, we could have beat the snot out of him, T'swa or not."

Jerym looked at Esenrok, saying nothing, thinking to himself he wasn't having anything to do with a crazy idea like that.

Again it was Carrmak who answered. "I doubt it. The first three or four that reached him, he'd have broken their necks. And everyone else would have backed off."

"What makes you so damned expert?" Esenrok snarled, getting to his feet.

Carrmak grinned mockingly. He was one of the bigger recruits in the platoon, probably the hairiest, and looked the oldest. "You don't believe me, go call him in. When he comes in, try him and see, you and everyone else that wants to. I'll watch. Maybe I'm wrong."

Blond Esenrok, seventeen, stood perhaps a little short of medium height. He was stocky, still with some baby fat, and so far his pale hair hadn't spread to chin or upper lip. He sat back down, flushing darkly.

"When do they feed us?" someone asked after a minute.

"*What* do they feed us?" someone else threw in.

Another looked at the wall clock. "It's 1740. I'll bet we eat at 1800."

Mellis and Thelldon came in then, grinning. Mellis looked younger than almost anyone else in the platoon, though at sixteen he was as big as most. "Hi, guys!" he said. "So they finally sent someone to bring you home."

Home! Jerym thought. *He'd called this place home!*

Thelldon was looking around. "Where's Barkum?" he asked.

"In detention," someone answered. "For lying to a corporal. Him and a couple other guys. For answering up for guys that took off. Like you and him." He indicated Mellis.

Mellis looked worried, Thelldon upset. "Shit!" Thelldon swore.

"What are you guys going to do?" someone asked. "The T'swa are sure to be looking for you."

"Wait here, I guess," Thelldon answered. "See what happens."

"Not me," Mellis said. "I'm getting out of here. I'm finding a road and leaving."

He went to the door, paused to peer around outside, then left.

Jerym and several others got up and went to doors and windows to look out. He saw newcomers being marched to other barracks, still wearing their civilian clothes. It seemed like a long time ago that he'd stuffed his civvies into a bag, tied a tag on it, and given it to a white sergeant. He wondered if he'd ever see it again.

He wished he was back home, arguing with his father.

Four

The autumnal equinox was nearing, and when the recruits had finished eating, it was nearly night. Stars had washed up the sky from the east, and some of the brighter spilled down the west into the final gray of sunset.

In the barracks, the young would-be warriors were getting to know one another, clustering, choosing buddies. Would-be leaders were making themselves known. Esenrok was one of them, trying to establish himself by his husky aggressiveness.

The recruits had been told to stay in barracks till otherwise ordered. Esenrok, with three others, huddled briefly in a corner, talking in undertones. When they'd finished, he walked to the middle of the floor. Most eyes moved to him, as if their owners knew that something was about to happen.

"Guys," Esenrok said quietly, "listen up. I've got an idea. We'll go raid the next barracks and start a fight." He turned and looked at Carrmak. "Anyone doesn't go is yellow."

Carrmak grinned at him. "Just call me butterflower," he said.

Esenrok didn't know how to reply to that, so he ignored it. "Who's game?" he asked.

About a dozen were on their feet instantly, eager. Others began to get up one by one, not willing to stay out of it, but not enthused. They were worried about what the T'swa might do.

"Come on, Alsnor," Esenrok said to Jerym, and Jerym got reluctantly to his feet. He'd sworn off fighting. He was very quick, and by Iryalan standards very good. He'd been in juvenile court twice for damaging guys; once more, in the civilian world, and he'd go to reformatory. He wasn't entirely sure that didn't apply here.

Within half a minute, everyone was standing except Carrmak and Thelldon; then Esenrok gave instructions. He and five others would run in the door, start dumping over bunks, and run out when the guys they were raiding started for them. The others would be waiting outside, ready.

When the last of Esenrok's raiders was out, headed for the neighboring barracks, Carrmak and Thelldon stood in the door watching. Carrmak leaned against a door post with his hands in his pockets and chuckled. "That Esenrok's a crazy little turd."

Thelldon shook his head, watching the platoon begin to bunch up by the corner of the next barracks in the row. He was bothered by his failure to go with them. "I'm already in trouble," he explained to Carrmak. "And Sergeant Dao told me to stay here till someone came for me. I'm not going to get in any more trouble till I find out what they do to you. I don't know what to expect from these T'swa; they're not like anybody else I ever knew."

He turned to Carrmak. "How come you didn't go?"

Carrmak laughed. "I'm the strategic reserve."

Thelldon looked at him, at his grin, not sure what he meant. Carrmak's hands were out of his pockets now, opening and closing. Yelling snatched their attention. Then fighting erupted at the other side of the massed platoon.

The first few of the other platoon galloped around the corner of the barracks after the raiders, and ran into the waiting enemy before they knew they were there. Jerym grabbed one of them by the shirt, punched him between the eyes and decked him. Someone else hit Jerym in the mouth with a long left, and he slugged the guy hard in the gut, then twice in the face. Someone barrelled into both of them, and Jerym lost contact. More guys were pouring, yelling, from the raided barracks, and briefly, with the advantage of momentum, they drove the raiders back.

For a minute the fighters were almost too packed to swing or fall down. Then the mass of brawlers began to open up a bit, and Jerym, engaged with a heavier, stronger youth, was thrown to the ground. The guy was on top of him, trying to punch him, but Jerym had hold of his sleeve, pushing on the guy's chin with his other hand while thrashing wildly, trying to buck him off. He lost his grip on the sleeve, and a fist slammed hard above his left eye. Then someone lifted the guy off and threw him aside. It was Carrmak, whooping, louder than any of the others. Jerym got to his knees, squinting one eye against a trickle of blood, transfixed by what he saw. Carrmak seemed incredibly strong, irresistible, throwing guys aside as if they were empty uniforms, and suddenly the opposition began to back away, those who weren't too tightly engaged. A boot struck Jerym's head a grazing blow.

Shrill T'swa whistling cut through the yelling, and disengagement became general, both platoons hurrying back to their barracks, some youths pausing to help the fallen. It was Thelldon who grabbed Jerym and jerked him to his feet. They ran.

Inside was an exited babble. Noses bled, and mouths; eyes had begun to swell. But most had no visible wounds, or at worst scuffs or scrapes. Almost all of them were exhilarated, flushed, bright-eyed. In a minute or so, Sergeant Dao came in alone, and the babble stilled. Esenrok made no move; the T'swa were legendary, and suddenly each recruit remembered what he'd heard or read of them.

Also Dao had presence, a kind of warrior presence that few men could match. Even, it seemed to the recruits just then, even more presence that most T'swa. If they'd never heard of the T'swa, they'd still have backed off from this man.

Dao said nothing for several long seconds, just smiled, a smile not unfriendly, even slightly amused. There was something unnerving about it. Then, mildly but loudly, he said, "Atten*tion!*"

Instantly backs straightened, arms dropped to sides, feet came together. "Outside for roll call!" They shuffled out the door and formed ragged rows. Their squad leaders were waiting, looking hard and untouchable. Dao took his place in front of the platoon, and in the darkness, without a light, called roll himself from his clipboard. Thelldon wasn't the only absentee who'd returned. Klefma and Warden were back too.

"Has anyone here seen Mellis?" Dao asked.

No one answered.

"I presume some of you would like to eat tomorrow," Dao said calmly. "Or if not tomorrow, hopefully the day after. I will ask again: Has anyone here seen Mellis?"

"Sir," said someone, "he said he was going to find a road and leave."

"Thank you."

A corporal trotted off in the darkness.

"Now. It is not acceptable that you fight among yourselves. Platoon, atten*tion!* Riiight face! Forwaaard march!" Again feet stepped on heels; youths muttered curses. The platoon moved. "Column left!" They turned onto a drill field.

Dao walked backward now, watching them. "When I say 'double time,' " he instructed, "you will begin to jog, following me and keeping up with me at all times. Now!" He turned, calling over his shoulder: "Double tiiime, march!"

They began to jog, crossed the drill field, turned onto a grassy road, passed the motor pool with its parked hover vehicles, came to a gate in the mesh fence that surrounded the camp, and continued down the road into the woods. Jerym became aware that his eyebrow wasn't bleeding anymore.

It was much darker on the forest road, and easy to stumble. A hover truck came up behind them on its silent AG drive, and a lamp on its cab shone a broad beam above them, reflecting off the tree crowns ahead, helping them see the road. Dao turned, running backward, facing them. "You are the Second Platoon, Company A, First Battalion," he called. "I am your platoon sergeant; I give orders and you obey them. I now order you to keep up with me. Any who do not will be dealt with appropriately."

He turned his back on them and speeded up, trotting briskly. After a few minutes, Jerym's legs were tiring badly. He wasn't used to running any distance. His lungs labored to get enough oxygen; his breath rasped in his throat. A few guys had slowed to a walk, falling back or peeling off to the sides. Dao did not ease up. The column, strung out a bit now, turned off on a lesser road, and it seemed to Jerym that they may have slowed, just a little.

But not enough. Soon his legs seemed too heavy to run farther. His strides slowed. He turned aside, one of the outer ranks breaking to let him through, and he stopped beside the road, bent forward, hands on thighs, mouth gaping as he gasped for breath. The truck pulled past, paused, and a T'swi reached out to him. Jerym reached back. The T'swi clamped onto his wrist and hoisted him onto the truck. The man's hand startled Jerym: The palm felt tough as a boot sole.

There were a dozen or so other recruits on board ahead of him; in the darkness Jerym couldn't make out who. He remembered Dao saying that those who didn't keep up would be dealt with, but just now he didn't care. He was sure he couldn't have run another step.

A minute later he decided he'd quit too early: Dao had slowed the platoon to a walk. Jerym moved to climb down, but the T'swi gripped his arm. "Stay," the T'swi said, and Jerym stayed. They followed the platoon, and three or four minutes later it began to jog again, but more slowly now, without any more dropouts. Twelve minutes more of jogging brought it back into the compound, headed toward the messhall, but the truck swung away with its cargo of stragglers and went to a shed.

"Everyone off," said the T'swi, and Jerym climbed down with the others, sure that he wasn't going to like what happened next, wishing fervently he'd hung on for another minute, out there in the woods. He could have, he thought, for one more minute or maybe even two. The truck drove away.

A light came on in the shed, and two T'swa herded him and the others inside. Jerym saw that Esenrok was there. Stacked on the floor were crude packs, bulky and shapeless, simple sacks sewn shut at the top and strapped to a pack frame. "Each of you put one on," a T'swi ordered. "Help each other if you need to."

Jerym grabbed one and lifted. Heavy! As he struggled into the straps, he decided the bag was full of sand. "All right, outside!" the T'swi ordered, and fifteen recruits left the shed. The two T'swa had them form ranks and checked their packs, adjusting straps as needed. Then they began marching. They passed the messhall, lit up now; Jerym wanted to go over and see what was happening inside. Then they were through the gate again. *It's better than running*, he told himself, but it didn't reassure him.

His mouth had swollen where he'd gotten hit in the brawl, and he was pretty sure his split lip was going to canker if he didn't get some powder for it.

* * *

Pitter Mellis was tired and hungry, and worse than either, he had to admit he was lost.

He'd hung around another barracks, another platoon, talking with the guys there, until a bell rang, brief but loud, shocking in its unexpectedness. Then a T'swi had called in that it was time to eat. Mellis had thought about going to the messhall with those guys, but was afraid that if he did, he'd be caught. So he'd hung out in the latrine. It had seemed a safe place. If anyone looked in on him, he'd say he had diarrhea.

But if he was still there when the guys who lived there came back from supper, it would look peculiar. So he'd watched out the window till he saw guys start to come out of the messhall. Then he'd left the barracks; it was getting somewhat dark.

He'd already noticed where the gate was, and that a guard was posted there, so he'd gone to the far side of the compound, scaled the eight-foot fence, and jumped off. His ankle turned when he'd landed, and at first it worried him, but it walked off in half a minute and didn't bother him anymore. To avoid getting lost, he'd circled the compound on the outside till he'd come to the side with the gate, then angled to hit the road that came out of it.

He'd begun to feel unsure of himself. Maybe he ought to go back in; it might be a long way to any-where, and he was getting hungry. On the other hand, it might only be a few miles, and he'd told the guys in his barracks that he was leaving. What would they think of him if he came dragging back in, saying he was hungry?

So he'd started down the road. By then it was crowding full night, and moonless; soon he couldn't see much. Then, after a bit, there'd been light, like a distant floodlight, paling the tree crowns where they overhung the edges of the narrow roadway, and he'd heard a sound behind him like running feet. Startled, puzzled, he'd left the road, scuttling back into the woods where it was really dark. He'd gone sixty or eighty feet, groping in blackness, hands in front of his face to protect his eyes from brush. Once he'd stumbled and fallen. Then he turned and watched, but couldn't see enough to tell him much. Running men passed with a tramping of boots, followed by a floodlight on what seemed to be a truck. When they were past, he groped his way back to the road and went on.

Occasionally it curved. Several times there'd been crossroads, forks, junctions, with signs, but he'd had no way to read them. Finally the road had come to a large meadow and appeared to stop there. It had seemed to him, though, that it must continue on the other side, that it was simply too dark to recognize a grass road on a meadow. So doggedly he'd started across. If he didn't find where the road went into the woods on the other side, he'd told himself, he'd just follow the edge of the meadow back to where he'd entered it.

But it was hilly there, humpy rolling country, and the meadow seemed to go on quite a distance. Seeren, the major moon, had come up more than half full, making it easier not to stumble, but it didn't show him any sign of the road. The meadow had bent right, then pinched out, and when he'd tried to backtrack, it had pinched out that way too, ending at a marsh. Anxiety spasmed. *How could that be?* he asked himself. He'd backtracked still again, and again it had pinched out, where it had pinched out the first time, he suspected.

He stood confused and defeated, utterly forlorn. Finally he decided to lay down and sleep till daylight. By daylight things would look different, he told himself, and he'd find his way out of there.

He'd never tried to sleep on the ground before. It was lumpy and hard and cold. He wondered if he could sleep. Lying there, he was soon shivering, and after awhile wondered if it would get cold enough to freeze to death.

"S-s-s-st!"

He sat up, staring in the direction of the sound.

"Recruit!"

It was a T'swa voice, deep and furry. *Shit!* he thought, *how could that be?*

"It's time to go back. On your feet, recruit!"

Mellis got up. *I would have been all right here,* he told himself now. *And gotten unlost in the morning.* But he didn't try to run. He was too tired and too hungry, and mostly he was glad to be found. The T'swi led off as if he knew just where he was going, and it occurred to Mellis that the man must have followed him all the way from the compound, letting him go, letting him get lost.

Jerym didn't know how far they'd hiked. Walked and occasionally jogged with forty pounds of sand on their backs, following close behind a T'swi and followed by two others. He remembered reading that T'swa could see like cats in the dark. Their eyes were big enough, that was certain.

They climbed one long steep hill that he thought must be the highest around there. His legs felt utterly exhausted by the time they reached the top, and he heard someone call out, "I name you Drag-Ass Hill." Somehow Jerym knew they'd climb Drag-Ass Hill many times before they left this place.

It seemed to him they'd been on the road for at least a couple of hours. His shoulders were sore from the packstraps. Seeren had come up, and her light made it easier to see.

"Fuck this shit!" a loud voice said up front, and someone stepped out of ranks onto the roadside. Jerym recognized the voice. It belonged to a guy named Romlar, a big, heavy, round-faced kid.

"Here. Give me the pack." That was a T'swa voice. Then Jerym was past them. A minute later, Romlar caught up, packless. Five minutes later they came into the open, the moonlight unscreened by trees. The gate was just ahead. Somehow they'd circled; there must be a network of roads in the woods, Jerym decided, and the T'swa knew them.

He wondered what would happen to Romlar.

They walked to the shed and got rid of their packs. A T'swi told Romlar to come with him, and the two of them left. One of the other T'swa took the rest of them to the messhall. Inside, a single panel glowed in the ceiling, and there was a big electric urn, its red light bright, with cups stacked by it upside down.

"Hot thocal," said the T'swi. "It will help you sleep."

The only thing I need to sleep is my bunk, Jerym thought. The hot cup hurt his split lip. The thocal tasted good though; good enough that he had a second cup. Unless he lay on his stomach, even his sore mouth wouldn't keep him awake, he was sure of it.

He wondered what was happening to Romlar. It didn't seem like a good idea to quit on something the T'swa gave you to do.

Five

Jerym woke up needing to go to the latrine, badly, and groaning softly, got out of bed. It was the two cups of thocal, he told himself. The wall clock glowed at him: 0320. His legs were stiff and sore, enough that he limped.

Mellis was there, on a commode, slumped with his head in his hands. He wasn't doing anything, just sitting there, his pants up.

"Anything the matter?" Jerym murmured.

The head raised, shook a negative.

Jerym went over to the long, trough-like urinal, thinking that Mellis looked as worn out as he'd been himself, four hours earlier. When he was done, Mellis was still sitting there, his head in his cupped hands again.

"Where've you been?" Jerym asked.

Briefly Mellis told him. "And now I'm so damn hungry!" He almost keened it. "I haven't eaten since before we got on the floater, back in Farningum, and the damn T'swi made me run half the way back. And then, when we got back, he gave me a shovel and told me to dig a hole. Six feet long, six feet wide, and six feet

42

deep! I'd have told him to go fuck himself, but I was afraid what he might do."

He looked up at Jerym. "I found out. There was another guy there from our platoon, a big guy, already digging. Real slow. The guard called him 'Romlar,' and when Romlar got his hole about ass deep, he quit."

Mellis shook his head, remembering. "There's some posts there, with chains on them, and the T'swi said, all right, come here. And started to chain him to a post. So Romlar started to fight him."

Jerym listened, engrossed.

"The T'swi never hit him or anything," Mellis went on, "just kind of grappled him around, and the next thing I knew, Romlar was laying there chained to the post, all curled up, swearing and crying. Actually crying! My eyes must have been as big as a T'swi's. The T'swi told him to let him know when he was ready to start digging." Mellis shook his head. "He said it as friendly as could be, even after Romlar had been calling him all kinds of things and trying to punch him.

"It took me quite a while before I got my hole dug, and when I was done, the T'swi pulled me out and had me fill it back up again. That's all; just dig it and fill it back up. Romlar was sitting up with his arms wrapped around himself, and I could hear his teeth clattering. It must be close to freezing out there now. The T'swi brought me here, and then I suppose he went back to Romlar."

Amber's balls! Jerym thought. *They're ruthless!* "You ought to go to bed," he said. "No telling what they'll have us doing in the morning."

Mellis nodded and Jerym gave him a hand, hoisting him to his feet. At Mellis's bunk, the younger boy asked for a boost. He had an upper bunk, and said he was so tired, he didn't think he could make it himself. Then he peeled out of his pants and shirt, and Jerym helped him climb up. After that, Jerym went to his own bed and lay awake for several minutes, thinking about his night and Mellis's, before falling asleep again.

* * *

He woke up to wild ringing that jerked him to his feet. There were groans and scattered curses as guys got up. Or pulled their covers up, trying to drown out the noise. A door opened, and a T'swi yelled in that they had three minutes to get dressed and outside.

The clock above the door read 0600.

Three minutes didn't even give a guy time to go piss! Jerym grabbed his shirt from the floor where he'd dropped it, and put it on, then his pants, his socks, his boots. Six-oh-two. That's when he noticed Romlar still in bed, asleep, face dirty, mouth open. The arm that was out of the covers showed he hadn't taken off his shirt. A booted foot stuck out too. Carrmak walked over, grabbed the bed by an edge, and dumped Romlar out.

"Hey! Fat boy!" he called. "Rise and shine! You've got about one minute to get up and outside."

Romlar lay on the floor, half wrapped in sheet and blanket, not moving. Spittle had dried at the corners of his mouth. A sort of half snore, half snort, came from it.

Tunis! Jerym thought. *What he doesn't need is to get in more trouble.* "Let's help him," he said to Carrmak. Carrmak grinned and nodded. Together they hoisted Romlar up, and half walking him, half dragging him, took him out between them for morning muster.

Six

The morning was not the physical ordeal Jerym had half expected. After reveille, they'd had almost half an hour to use the latrine, clean up, and make their beds before breakfast. They had another half hour to eat; after that they waited by their beds.

Then a T'swa corporal had them pull their bedding off and showed them how to make a bed in the military manner. After making their beds several times to train in the proper technique, they went to the drill field and learned to salute and do left, right, and about face; then practiced standing at ease, attention, and parade rest. After that they learned to march, both in close-order drill and on the road. Sergeant Dao told them that in this regiment, saluting and close-order marching would not often be done—they were primarily for ceremony—but they needed to do them well.

T'swa cadre, in platoon formation, gave a demonstration to show how close-order drill looked—sharp and precise—and that warriors didn't consider it beneath them.

They drilled these things till noon under the unrelenting eyes of T'swa, then ate dinner.

They were gone when the transports brought in the rest of the recruits. The T'swa had taken them out on a road march, nothing particularly strenuous—no running, no packs—a brisk three-hour hike on roads of grass, through the forests and meadows and smells of near-autumn. It wasn't at all bad, and much of the stiffness in Jerym's thighs wore off. The only ones in the second platoon who had difficulties that day were Mellis and Romlar, especially Romlar. Both kept falling asleep on break, and of course had to wake up brief minutes later.

That evening they watched recordings in the company messhall, of army and T'swa and "Birds," in the Kettle War. The real stuff. Dirt flew, and pieces of trees, and guys got killed—even blown up! Jerym got a nervous stomach watching, from pure excitement. Most of the best of it, Captain Gotasu told them, had been recorded by an Iryalan who'd been with the T'swa, a guy named Varlik Lormagen who'd been called the White T'swi.

"You," Captain Gotasu said—Gotasu was their company commander—"will be the new White T'swa. When we have finished training you. It will be harder for you than it was for us, because we began at age six or seven, and learned and trained for almost twelve standard years before we went to war. But we will help you. We will help you find out that you can do far more than most people would believe possible. We will push you nearly to your limits—sometimes you may think we've pushed you beyond them—and you, and we, will watch those limits grow."

He paused. "And when you have completed your training, you will know, and we will know, that you are warriors to be proud of."

When Gotasu finished, there was silence, but every recruit in the company had been affected by what he'd said. He dismissed them, and they returned to their barracks with only time to get ready for bed before lights out. There was no horseplay; lights out meant quiet. And they'd been warned that the next day would see their training begin in earnest. Orientation was over.

Seven

The young chauffeur opened the door for Lord Kristal, who got out easily despite his eighty-one years.

The Durslan estate at Lake Loreen was one of Kristal's favorite places, although he got there infrequently. And this was one of its pleasantest aspects—mellowed by late afternoon sunlight slanting soft through trees and autumn haze. The changes since he'd arrived there as a pupil, seventy-five years earlier, had been modest and graceful.

The greatest change was an addition. Despite some architectural innovations, the new building, the Research Building, might almost have stood there as long as the others, for generations, fitted as it was among great *peioks* that shaded the lawns and had begun to spill bronze leaves across them.

It was the Research Building where his interest lay today, but the limousine had delivered him to the Main Building. He took this for granted. Even among the alumni, even—especially—for a representative of the Crown, there was protocol to observe. But it was simple, common courtesy really, and with friends a pleasure. He went up the steps to the veranda, where Laira Gouer Lormagen waited, with Kusu, to greet him.

When she'd embraced her guest, she took his hand

and stepped back. "Emry," she said, "I'm the only Gouer family representative here today, the only one who hasn't flown off to Durslan Hall to help prepare for Harvest Festival. But it's my husband's research you've come to see"—she half turned and put her hand on Kusu's sleeve—"so I'll wait till dinner to claim you for a talk, if your schedule permits dinner with us."

She left them then—she'd seen the test already; it wasn't pleasant—and the two men walked the winding, eighty-yard sidewalk to the research building, exchanging pleasantries. Kristal knew in general terms what the test had shown, but he wanted to see for himself. In the actual presence of an event, a useful cognition might be triggered, if not then, perhaps later. Especially in someone of his training and experience. And a relevant cognition was needed here. Although he was at Service instead of Wisdom/Knowledge, over the years he'd shown occasional flashes of exceptional perceptivity.

Kusu did not defer to Kristal's elderly legs; he knew His Lordship better than that. Instead of the elevator, they climbed the curving main stairs to the second floor and walked to Kusu's lab. The equipment there was meaningless to Kristal. In his school days there'd been no science, no such thing as research, and hadn't been for a very long time. The Sacrament had seen to that, as it had seen to other things, and they'd lived off the genius of ages long past.*

*Even at the time of this story, the Sacrament constrained them, though in practice it had become an empty ritual. Roughly thirty percent of the people on Iryala, an aging thirty percent, had received the ungelded Sacrament, and in the Confederation sector overall, the percentage was considerably higher. Thus many things could not be said or done openly. Science and research could not be publicly discussed except in the most carefully oblique way. For example, what might more accurately have been called the Bureau of Research and Development was named simply the Office of Special Projects.

To have done otherwise would have been to trigger widespread psychosis and disorder.

To Kristal, the most nearly familiar thing in the lab was a cage containing five pale olive sorlex, the Iryalan mouse. They looked up at him with eyes like tiny black beads, their noses twitching.

"How are the others?" Kristal asked. "Did any survive?"

"The last two died while I was talking with you on the comm," Kusu answered. "This morning I tried it with three meadow soneys I live-trapped; something with substantially more body mass. They only lived about an hour. And a feral cat I caught last night. It was worse than the rodents; by that time I'd attached this microwave emitter"—he touched a black apparatus on the side of the box—"so I could put it out of its frenzy. That's what I'll do with these, too, assuming they respond like the earlier sets."

"And sedation doesn't help, you said."

"Depending on its strength, it eliminates or reduces the intensity of the frenzy, but so does exhaustion, and they die just as quickly. Even when I put them to sleep before teleporting them."

"Are you having post mortems done?"

"On the sorlex and the soneys; they weren't microwaved. I've gotten the results, and they're not very informative."

Kristal nodded. "Well, let's see it operate."

Kusu raised the cage lid and reached in. The sorlex investigated his hands. He took two of them out on one palm and stroked them reflectively for a moment with a finger. Then, kneeling, he put them in a glass box that sat on a waist-high platform, part of a much larger apparatus, set a timer, closed a switch, and took Kristal to a vacant table at the other end of the room. There was nothing on the table except an electrical cord plugged into a receptacle.

"It'll be a few seconds yet," Kusu said. Suddenly, after a moment, the glass box was there, and inside it a virtual blur of movement, the two sorlex racing frenziedly about. They caromed off the sides, off each other, launched themselves upward with remarkable leaps to bounce off the top. After ten seconds, Kusu plugged the electric cord into the microwave emitter on the side of the glass box, flicked a switch, and the sorlex stopped at once, to lie unmoving.

For a moment the two men stood looking silently at them, then Kusu spoke again. "The cultures I teleported—bacteria and yeast—are still growing normally, as if nothing had happened." He gestured at several potted plants on a window sill. "So did the saragol. And the horn worms. And finally the sand lizards. The lizards acted a little strangely afterwards, for a few minutes—scurried around enough more than usual to notice—but they gave us no reason to expect anything like this.

"If teleportation had killed the other life forms, too, I'd set this work aside and go back to theoretical studies. Maybe I will anyway. But . . ." He gestured. "Only the mammals."

"Hmh!" Nothing stirred in Kristal's mind, and obviously not in Kusu's either. "I suppose the box couldn't have anything to do with it?"

"It didn't harm the lizards. Besides, I didn't use the box when I teleported a set of heavily sedated sorlex. They were asleep when I sent them across, and they died anyway.

"And I can't teleport things *into* a box, because the nexus won't form on the other side of a solid wall. I couldn't teleport them into the next room, for example, except through line of sight, say through the open door."

Kristal's brows raised a millimeter. "I hadn't realized there was that limitation."

"I hadn't either, till I tried it. The teleport didn't grow out of well worked out physical theory. The possibility ocurred to me in an intuitive leap while I was studying some topological ideas the ancients apparently had played with but not done much with. So the research has been heavy on intuition and trial. And without adequate theory, a result like this can be a major block."

"Hmm. So what's your next step?"

"I don't know yet. I had Wellem up here for this morning's tests. He's much more at Wisdom and much less at Knowledge than I am, which can be useful when you hit a barrier like this. But he had no cognitions either; not yet anyway."

Kristal looked again at the sorlex, then back at Kusu. "Well," he said, "this feels like a good time to look in on him. It's been some two years. And his work is invariably interesting. Even when there isn't language to describe it."

Eight

Newly turned fifteen, Lotta Alsnor was becoming a rather pretty young woman, her once-carrotty hair now auburn red, her old freckles mostly gone, her complexion faintly tanned, with pink highlights. Small, fine-boned, she would have been slight, had it not been for ballet and gymnastics and the strong-slender muscles they'd given her.

She stepped into the mail room after lunch. She seldom received mail, seldom went in to look. When there was something for her, she usually knew it. Almost invariably it was a letter from her mother.

Today it wasn't. She looked at the return address and headed for the veranda to read it. At Lake Loreen, autumn was considerably less advanced than in the Blue Forest, and today was almost summery. Slim strong fingers tore the end of the envelope, withdrew and unfolded the paper inside. She read:

Dear Little Sister,
    I hope that getting a letter from me doesn't give you heart failure. I wish you were here. I'd show you

around and we could talk a lot. In fact, I'd send you a cube instead of this letter, but I put all my bonus in the bank, and I don't want to wait till we get paid. I've never sent you a letter before, unless you count the three-line notes at Winter Solstice that were all Mom could get me to write. But I never felt like I had anything to write about before. It's as if all my life I've been waiting for something to happen. Now it has, and you're the one I want to tell it to.

It's funny how you've been my favorite person in the family, considering that since we were little kids, I only got to see you once or twice a year for a few days, and we never spent much time together even then. But I always thought of us as being more alike than most brothers and sisters. Even when you were still at home, when we were really little, I could tell you stuff and you didn't go and tell Mom or Dad. You were different. And when you'd been away and came back, even that first time, you were more different that ever. You were still you, but you'd changed, and I was impressed. It was as if you'd outgrown the family somehow, but you were easier than ever to be around.

Now I've left home too, not for the reformatory like Mom and Dad worried I would, but for the mercenaries. Has Mom written and told you about that? It isn't the army, although the government is doing it. It's under something called the Office of Special Projects. I'm at a place in the Blue Forest, getting trained. And our cadre, the guys training us, are T'swa! Real genuine T'swa!

I got put out of school right after you were home last, and got in trouble on the job I got, which I didn't like anyway, because this guy gave me a hard time and I knocked three of his teeth out. I had to pay to get them fixed and had to borrow part of it from Dad. But I only got charged damages, no amends, because the judge said the guy had provoked it. Then a guy came to my apartment one evening and talked to me about joining the mercenaries. He told me I'd been selected because my school personality profile said I'd make a good one. The pay isn't too bad—it's the same as the army—and I get my meals and a place to live, and he offered me a signing bonus of DR300. When I agreed, he offered Dad 300 for his signature of approval because I'm not eighteen yet.

As far as I know, all the guys here, all the recruits that is, are pretty much like me. They always got in trouble at school and things like that. There's even a few guys who came here from reformatory.

So here I am. I've been here two weeks now, and you're not the only person that changed a lot being away from home. This isn't a bad place. It's way out in the country, in the forest. At first I thought I wasn't going to like it. You wouldn't believe all the stuff they make us do. Sometimes I can hardly crawl from the shower to my bunk at night. But most of the time I like it, and most of the time I like the T'swa. And sometimes I hate it all, for a few minutes, but when I'm hating it, I know I'll like it again pretty soon. Strange, huh?

They make us do stretching exercises for twenty minutes in the morning, right after our run. Next week they're going to give us rifles; so far we haven't even seen any, but in a few weeks we'll learn how to shoot them. My intestines get excited thinking about it! So far all they've given us to carry are packsacks with sand in them. To build our strength. We hike with them and do pushups with them on our backs. When we get stronger, we'll do our chinups with them too. A few guys do already. You start doing them with sand after you can do twenty without any. I'm up to twelve.

The T'swa say they're going to make White T'swa out of us. There was a guy named Varlik Lormagen that they called the White T'swi back in the Kettle War. But we'll be the first *regiment* of White T'swa.

I hope you'll answer this letter, Little Sister who's not little anymore. Actually, you're the only person outside the regiment I really want much to be connected with. Not that I don't appreciate all that Mom and Dad did, and put up with, but the guys here feel like my real family to me, except I don't have any sister here. You're my sister, and you're too far away to suit me.

I'll probably send you a cube when I've been paid. There's hardly anything around here to spend money on, and talking is faster than writing.

With love,
your brother
Jerym

Nine

Company A formed up its ranks wearing raincoats. Ponchos weren't needed: The rain was light, a thin cold drizzle with sporadic, half-hearted showers, and they'd already had their morning run with sandbag packs.

Jerym felt a beginning of wetness down the middle of his back, spreading. He suspected what was wrong, and who'd done it.

"Atten*tion!* Riiight face! Forwaaard march!"

They marched down the broad grassy gap between company areas and across their battalion drill field. There the platoons separated, 2nd Platoon going to the A Company gymnastics shed. The shed consisted of four walls, a stanchioned ceiling, and a wooden floor, with simple heating by matric converter panels in the side walls below the ceiling. Sets of parallel bars in rows alternated with rows of horizontal bars. The trainees hung their raincoats on hooks by files and positions, and stood at ease by them.

Jerym took the opportunity to look at his as he hung it up. A blade had slit the back beside the center seam

57

for about eight inches. He was satisfied he knew who'd
done it, and decided to be open in his revenge.

"First and third squads to parallel bars," called Sergeant Dao. "Second and fourth to horizontal bars."

The youths dispersed to their equipment, and under
the eyes of their cadre, did several minutes of stretching exercises. They'd been there for more than four
weeks; the general routine was familiar. Then, after
drying and chalking their hands, they began their training routines on one apparatus or the other, boots and
all, swinging at first, then doing kips; muscle-ups; kidney
swings; planches if they could; handstands with help as
needed. . . . Changing apparatus halfway through. They
spent nearly an hour at it. Near the end, a number of
them, with cadre permission, returned to handstands,
working on stability, a few even doing handstand
pushups. Two did them on the parallel bars.

They'd already done several sets of ordinary pushups
beside the road, wearing the sandbags, during "breaks"
on their morning run. Almost all of them exercised with
zest, with an eagerness to move on to new and more
difficult things, impatient with their own failures, and
with T'swa restraints that actually were quite permissive.

Then Dao whistled piercing blasts in a now familiar
signal. The trainees hurried to their raincoats and put
them on. Another set of blasts sent them outdoors,
where the rain had stopped for the time being, although the eaves still dripped. They formed ranks, and
at Dao's command marched to the next shed, where
they stretched some more, then practiced tumbling, again
for nearly an hour. And again there was no complaining
or timidity, no malingering, no holding back. By now
their bodies all were very flexible, though not as flexible as they would be. But for reasons of size, coordination, and strength, some made slower progress than
others on the exercise routines. Still, they all progressed
more rapidly than typical Iryalan youths would have,
for they'd been born on the stage of life to be warriors.

                    *   *   *

Because of the weather, mail call was in the messhall at noon, just before dinner. There was a letter for Jerym; he glanced at the return address, then tucked it in his shirt and got in the chow line. After eating, they had half an hour to lay around. Many of the trainees catnapped.

The rain seemed to be over. The clouds had thinned, and vague sunshine brightened the day a little. Jerym, in his field jacket, sat on one of the benches at the end of the barracks. With a finger he opened his letter, and read it grinning, shaking his head, chuckling.

"Your ma?" Romlar asked. He was standing on the stoop looking down at Jerym, had been waiting for him to finish. Jerym looked up and shook his head. Though scarcely taller than Jerym, and still the heaviest youth in the platoon, Romlar was no longer "fat boy."

"My sister," Jerym said.

"Huh. You got a letter before."

"Twice before. One from my ma, and one from my sister earlier."

Romlar didn't leave, but said nothing more for a moment. Then: "I'll never get a letter. Everyone in my family is mad at me. Ma used to be all right till I got sent to tronk—reformatory. She gave up on me then. Said I'd never be worth nothin'. Then the guy come to see me there, and told me I could come here, and I did."

"You like this better than reformatory?" Jerym asked. Romlar never looked happy.

"Yeah. No comparison. Reformatory wasn't much worse than school, for me, but this—ain't bad." He went quiet again, but still didn't leave. Jerym got up to go inside.

"What did your sister write about?"

Jerym took both of them by surprise with his reply: He held the letter out to Romlar. "Here. Read it if you want."

Romlar stared for a moment, then hesitantly took it and read, lips moving, commenting only once. "She talks about Varlik Lormagen, the White T'swi." He looked up at Jerym. "And his wife. How'd she get to know them?"

"Lotta goes to a special school. Mrs. Lormagen teaches dancing there."

"Special school. Your folks got money then."

"No. She got to go there kind of like we came here. Some guy came around when she was a little kid—six years old. He said her tests showed she was eligible. It doesn't cost my folks anything."

"Huh." Romlar stared at nothing. "If I wrote to your sister, do you think she'd write back to me?"

The question seemed strange to Jerym, and he almost said no. What he did say was, "The only way to find out is write to her. You want her address?"

"Not now. This evening maybe. I'll get a tablet and pen, and an envelope."

The big trainee turned and went back into the barracks. Jerym followed, wondering if Romlar really would write to Lotta. He also wondered if she'd be mad that he gave Romlar her address, then decided she wouldn't. Whether she'd write back was something else.

Ten

It was an evening without any kind of training, an evening off. In the 2nd Platoon barracks, several trainees were involved in a contest to see who could do the most handstand pushups. Two others were practicing stability by walking on their hands.

Jerym came in with a new raincoat under his arm, unfolded it and hung it in his "wardrobe"—his half of a fifty-inch rod by the head of his bunk. Then he walked to the middle of the long low building and spoke loudly. "Listen up, guys," he said. "We've got an asshole in the platoon. I just went and got a new raincoat because someone cut a slit in the back of my old one."

The place went quiet, a quiet no one broke for a few seconds. Guys lowered themselves from handstands to watch expectantly.

"Maybe the seam just split," Markooris said.

That was Markooris for you: *Don't think anything bad till you get shivved.* "Nope," Jerym answered. "It was cut. Right next to the seam. I showed it to the supply sergeant, and he agreed."

61

"Who do you think did it?" Esenrok asked, looking brightly interested.

"Well, you're the leading troublemaker, but it was too sneaky for you." Jerym looked around. "Who's the sneakiest guy in the platoon?"

Several of the trainees turned their eyes toward Mellis's bunk. He'd shown a penchant for practical jokes, till he'd put feces in Romlar's boots one morning just before reveille. He'd made the mistake of telling people in advance what he planned, and after it happened, someone told Romlar, who'd beaten him up for it. Badly. No one, not even Mellis, had told the T'swa who'd worked him over.

"Hey, Mellis," Jerym called, "why do you suppose everyone's looking at you?"

"I didn't cut your fucking raincoat!"

"What you mean is, you've gotten smart enough not to talk about the shit you do."

Mellis dropped from his bunk and confronted Jerym. "You can't prove I did it, because I didn't. So stop talking about me like that!"

Mellis's indignation seemed too convincing to be feigned. "Okay," Jerym said, mildly now, "maybe you didn't. But considering the stuff you have done, you shouldn't be surprised if people jump to conclusions."

Mellis glared. He was the youngest in the platoon, but nearly as tall as Jerym, though slimmer. "You're all mouth, Alsnor," he said. "You think you . . ."

That was all he got out. Jerym punched him in the face and knocked him down. Mellis rolled to his feet, and Carrmak and Bressnik got between them. "Back off, both of you! Remember the rules!"

"He hit me in the mouth!" Mellis almost screamed it. Blood ran down his chin.

"Mellis," Carrmak hissed, "if you want to get the platoon in real trouble, keep yelling that someone hit you!" For a moment he glared, then the glare faded and his voice become patient. "You're the one that got this platoon on probation. You're sixteen and you act like eight. Alsnor backed off on what he said, but you couldn't leave it at that.

"Now, we've got rules here that we all agreed to. After Romlar beat the snot out of you, what was it Sergeant Dao told us?"

Mellis only glared. Carrmak went on.

"He told us if we had any more fights, it'd be speed marches for us, running and walking alternate quarter miles from 2230 till midnight, rain or shine. That makes eight miles with sandbags." He paused, held Mellis's eyes for a moment and added, "Three nights for every fight."

He turned on Jerym. "Alsnor, I'm disappointed in you. You had no business jumping on Mellis the way you did, and with no evidence. You're usually smarter than that. If we get stuck with three midnighters, you're as much to blame as anyone. More!"

Carrmak blew noisily through pursed lips then. Jerym said nothing, holding knuckles that bled from Mellis's teeth, thinking that Carrmak was right.

"Okay," Carrmak said, "I don't suppose it'll work, but we'll try covering this up. Maybe the T'swa will appreciate the effort and let it go this time." He paused, frowning thoughtfully. "Alsnor, you hurt your knuckles uh . . . How *did* you hurt them?"

"Cleaning his rifle," Esenrok put in, then raised both hands as if to fend off the looks he got. "Really," he said. "He pulled the slide back and it slipped, and his knuckles were in the way!"

"Unh! It sounds about as likely as a blizzard on Kettle." Carrmak looked around. "Anyone here got a better idea . . . ? No?"

The faces around him were glum. "Okay." He turned to Jerym. "You cut your knuckles cleaning your rifle. Just now. We all heard you when you swore, and we saw your hand bleeding. And you—" he said, turning to Mellis, "you hurt your mouth taking a shower. Slipped, almost fell, and bit your lip. Desterbi, you and I saw it happen.

"Alsnor, go to the dispensary, right now."

Jerym nodded, and left at a trot. Carrmak turned back to Mellis. "You go over in ten minutes. If you go now, at the same time as him, there's no way the T'swa will let us get away with this. Go bleed on a towel. We've got to make this look good, or as good as we can. Desterbi, we'll all three have to wet our heads in the shower just before Mellis goes over."

He scanned the others, his eyes stopping at Esenrok. "Esenrok," he said, "you don't look as gleeful as you usually do when there's trouble. Anything you need to tell us?"

Esenrok's head jerked a sharp negative, but he didn't meet the older youth's eyes. Carrmak nodded. "Okay. We'll write this off to experience. We don't need to be geniuses, but we need to act halfway sensible." He raised his voice then. "These T'swa, and Colonel Voker, and whoever it was up the line that decided to set this place up, are giving us a chance to *be* something. Something I think we all want. And none of us ought to forget that.

"But it's up to us to make it work. Let's don't make 'em decide to give up on us and shut this place down."

The army medic on night C.Q. at the dispensary said nothing worrisome when he treated the lacerations on Jerym's hand, nor later when he treated Mellis's split lip. The platoon decided maybe—just possibly—they'd gotten away with it. Carrmak lay on his bunk, reading, when Romlar came over to him.

"Carrmak."

"Yeah?"

"I want to take you on again."

Carrmak looked at him exasperatedly.

"We'd do it according to the agreement," Romlar

went on. "No hitting in the face. No marks for the T'swa to see." His voice was earnest. "You're the champion around here. You've got to give people a chance to challenge you. And I'm a lot stronger than I was. I think maybe I can take you now."

Carrmak shook his head, though not in refusal or negation. "When you're just fooling around," he said, "it's easy to not hit in the face. But when two guys are trying to prove something . . ."

Romlar shook his head stubbornly. "I promise I won't hit in the face if you don't. Even if you do, I won't."

The others had turned to them, watching, listening. Carrmak recognized a situation here. He was the leader because these guys respected him. If they began to question his character and didn't recognize a leader anymore, one that had more than a teaspoon of brains, they could end up in the kind of trouble 4th Platoon was in these days.

"Okay," Carrmak said. "On these conditions: Rassling only; no punching. And that gives you a better chance, because you outweigh me. Also we wait till tomorrow night. The T'swa seem to have bought our lies, but they could still roust us out tonight for a midnight dance with the sandbags. And if you and I had been fighting, we'd never know whether it was us to thank for our troubles, or Alsnor and—whoever."

Romlar saw the logic of Carrmak's conditions and agreed, serious as always.

At 2130 the light blinked in the barracks, and guys started getting ready for bed. At 2145 the lights went out. Jerym lay with his eyes open for a bit, thinking about the evening. Someone had told him what Carrmak had said to Esenrok, and how Esenrok couldn't face him. It looked as if he'd accused Mellis wrongly, all right. He wasn't going to accuse Esenrok of it though. *Carrmak was right,* he told himself. *I've run off at the mouth too much already tonight.*

He closed his eyes then, thinking about the fight tomorrow night between Carrmak and Romlar. Second Platoon got leaned on less by the T'swa than any other in the company, maybe in the regiment, and that was because of Carrmak. In 2nd Platoon, the toughest guy was also the smartest, the most sensible. He hoped Carrmak won.

Not that he didn't like Romlar; he did. There was something about the guy he both liked and respected, though he couldn't put his finger on it. It wasn't Romlar's brain, that was for sure. Maybe it was because he stood by his principles, right or wrong.

Jerym's thoughts turned to his scuffle with Mellis; that had been childish. Maybe he'd apologize to Mellis tomorrow. If he did, Mellis would probably act like an asshole and throw crap on him. If so, he'd take it. If he *had* accused Mellis wrongly, why, whatever shit the twerp might throw, he had coming.

It seemed to Jerym that he'd just gotten to sleep when the lights came on and Sergeant Dao's voice called out:

"All right, 2nd Platoon, everyone on your feet! I am a man of my word: You will make a speed march tonight. You have ten minutes to use the latrine, dress, and form ranks."

Jerym rolled out with tight lips. It was his own mouth, he told himself, that had brought this on.

At breakfast, Sublieutenant Dzo-Tar and Captain Gotasu sat across from each other, speaking Tyspi, while Gotasu's executive officer, Lieutenant Toma, listened with interest. Dzo-Tar was the leader of 2nd Platoon. "So," Gotasu said, "you have put 2nd Platoon on company punishment. It has been our best platoon; perhaps the best in the regiment. Has there been some change in dynamics there?"

Thoughtfully Dzo-Tar chewed a mouthful of eggs and

bacon. *Company punishment*. Even the concept was foreign; they'd had to borrow it from the Confederatswa. "The dynamics appear to be unchanged," he answered. "The same trainee, Carrmak, remains dominant, but there are limits to what he can do. And at this point it would be harmful, I believe, to invest him with formal authority as trainee sergeant. It would set him apart, cut him off from them, perhaps even endanger him. Dao agrees."

He sipped his joma. "Among ourselves these problems never arise. Too many of these young men are not sane. There is great and admirable energy here, but it pulls and thrusts in every direction. In the absence of the T'sel among them, and with warrior appetites, they need policing. And we cannot depend on them to police themselves. Also," Dzo-Tar added pointedly, "it is time to begin teaching them the jokanru."

Gotasu nodded. "And we cannot, while they are like this. The regiment will never become T'sel warriors until they have the T'sel, and we have no means of bringing them to it, at their age." Thick black hands and blunt fingers dwarfed the table knife as he applied jam tidily to another slice of toast. *We are warriors, not the caretakers of delinquents*, he thought, then reminded himself that that was no longer true. They *had been* warriors. After the Daghiam Kel, Ssiss-Ka, and Shangkano Regiments had finally been decimated in the Long War on Marengabar, the lodge had offered their survivors this opportunity to teach Iryalan warriors. Most had accepted.

"Perhaps Voker will have a solution," Gotasu went on. "He has the T'sel now, but he gained it only after the Kettle War, when he was already in his middle years. So clearly, age is no prohibitant. I will bring up this matter of the T'sel in staff meeting this morning.

"Meanwhile, have you contemplated assigning a sergeant to live in the barracks with 2nd Platoon?"

"Not yet. I know the 1st and 4th have gone to that, and it has helped reduce the trouble there. But the 2nd is not that unsane, and such an assignment would largely eliminate Carrmak's influence." Dzo-Tars's voice and face were calm, matter-of-fact. "In the final analysis, the solution lies in the T'sel, not in repression. We would do the Confederation a disservice to train repressed savages in the warrior arts."

Eleven

Second Platoon had completed their three midnight speed marches, and on top of that, no training was scheduled for the evening. This, Romlar claimed, made it a good night for Carrmak to meet his challenge.

Carrmak agreed.

These matters were settled outdoors; the barracks had too little unoccupied space, too many sharp corners and hard edges. At the same time, for an entire platoon to go out and watch the fight would bring attention and the T'swa, so by nomination and the drawing of koorsa straws, five members were selected as judges. Then the two principals and five judges slipped outside by twos and threes, across the drill field to a space behind one of the gymnastics sheds. Despite the fair breeze, it was a reasonable evening for fighting. It wasn't raining, and Seeren, nearly full, shone blurrily through the overcast, a lamp in the sky. The temperature was mild for deep autumn.

Romlar was exceptionally strong, and he made a contest of it, but Carrmak's skill and explosive quickness were too much for him. They fought to three pins, and when it was over, shook hands and headed back for the barracks, Romlar telling himself that Carrmak was a good guy. If Carrmak ever got in trouble, he wouldn't let him down.

Carrmak didn't notice that some of the platoon weren't there till after he'd showered. "Where's Alsnor?" he asked, looking around. "And Esenrok? And Warden and Thelldon?"

It was Bressnik that answered, uncomfortably. "They've been planning a footrace—Esenrok and Alsnor—and they decided to do it this evening. Esenrok said we needed something to replace fighting, something that wouldn't get us in trouble with the T'swa."

He's got a point there, Carrmak thought, and frowned. "*Planning* a footrace? How come I never heard about this? And Esenrok runs like a damn yansa; there aren't three guys in the platoon that can beat him. Alsnor can't. How'd he get talked into this?"

"He might win if the race was long enough," Bressnik said. "Esenrok's pretty shortlegged."

"How far?"

Bressnik said nothing. It was Desterbi who answered this time. "They're running down the main road to the reservation boundary and back. Since the T'swa quit posting a gate guard, there's no reason why not. And it's not even against the rules."

"To the boundary . . . How would anyone know it was fair? If Esenrok got out of sight ahead of Alsnor, he could turn back short of the line and say he'd been there. While Alsnor, being honest, would go all the way. And he knows what Esenrok's like." Carrmak glanced around at the others. "Okay. What aren't you telling me?"

"We don't have to tell you nothing," Mellis countered.

"Shut up Mellis, or I'll slap the snot out of you, even if it gets us six more nights of sandbagging. Bressnik, what's the story?"

"Thelldon and Warden figured to borrow a hover car from the motor pool. Warden knows how to drive."

Carrmak clapped a hand against his forehead. "Borrow? You don't *borrow* a hover car. Not legally. The word is *steal*."

Bressnik talked doggedly on. "They'll drive out and wait at the boundary sign till both guys have gotten there. Then they'll come back and put the hover car right where they got it from. And if they'd had any trouble getting one, like they were locked or something, they'd have been back long before this; they left right after you guys went out to fight."

Bressnik paused, suddenly unsure. "Tunis, Carrmak," he said, "it'll be all right! The T'swa will never know. They don't post guards any more. It's not like the first few days, when there were guys wanting to run away."

Carrmak shook his head. Sometimes he wondered about the T'swa. "Let us hope. If they find out about this . . . How come I never heard about it?"

Mellis answered this time. "Esenrok said not to tell you. He said if you knew, you'd stop it."

"So you guys are taking orders from Esenrok now. That crazy son of a bitch. Second Platoon'll go from the best to the worst in the regiment."

"It's not that bad, Carrmak," Markooris put in. "It's going to keep us out of fights."

Carrmak had a strong feeling that it *was* that bad. *Tunis! Let's steal a car to keep from getting in trouble!* When Esenrok got back, he was really going to work him over. And Alsnor! Sometimes the guy seemed like the sanest one of the bunch, and sometimes he didn't have the brains of a weevil.

The road crossed the boundary in a meadow. A little half-ton utility truck sat parked by the sign, with Thelldon and Warden in the cab, waiting. The clouds had thickened, burying the moon, and the breeze had picked up. It was darker, and getting cold. Now and then Warden would start the propulsion unit and turn the heater on long enough to warm the cab. Thelldon fell asleep, and Warden was getting drowsy himself, but

that was all right. When the runners came, they were
supposed to slap the cab and yell their name.

Warden saw the first snowflake when he got out to
urinate. Turning his back to the wind, he relieved
himself, and was getting back in when he saw someone
coming. "Thelldon!" he said sharply. "Wake up! One of
'em's here!"

He recognized the chesty figure. Esenrok loped up,
yelled his name as he slapped the front of the cab, then
turned and started back.

"Huh!" grunted Thelldon sleepily. "Didn't even take
time to crow about getting here first."

"Maybe he just wants to get home as quick as he can.
It's starting to snow."

"Snow?! Amberus! It was almost warm when we left."

"It's not now." Warden peered through the windshield and saw another couple of flakes drift past. *If it
never comes down harder than that, there won't be any
problem,* he told himself, but even as he thought it,
they began to fall more thickly.

Jerym hadn't tried to keep up when Esenrok moved
ahead of him at the start. For the first several miles
though, the shorter youth was content to stay just a
dozen or two yards ahead, seemingly as a matter of
principle. Pacing himself to last the distance, Jerym
realized. Pacing had to be Esenrok's biggest concern.

They knew the road well by now, day and dark, and
at the five-mile crossing, Esenrok had speeded up,
satisfied that he'd have no difficulty with the distance.
Jerym saw him glance back, but made no attempt to
keep pace. *Let him think I can't,* he told himself. Then,
when he'd been unable to see Esenrok for a minute or
so, Jerym too speeded up, to stay within striking distance, keeping a sharp eye ahead. Twice, in the next
mile, he glimpsed Esenrok at the edge of visibility in
the darkness ahead, and eased off just a bit. He was
pleased at how well it went, how smooth his strides
felt, and how fast.

It was getting darker; the clouds, he realized, were thickening.

When he reached the edge of the boundary meadow and hadn't met Esenrok on his return leg yet, he realized how close he'd stayed. Grinning, he wiped sweat from his eyebrows. He heard Esenrok's yell at the truck, and seconds later saw him coming back. They were about sixty yards apart, and he wasn't more then eighty yards from the boundary himself. Here was his chance to psych Esenrok.

The shorter youth didn't seem to notice him till he was twenty yards away. Then his head jerked up.

"You're looking tired, Esenrok!" Jerym called. "I'm gonna run you into the ground!" Then they were past each other.

Jerym didn't look back to see whether Esenrok speeded up or not. He knew without looking. Grinning, he yelled his name twenty yards before he slapped the truck, yelled it as loudly as he could.

The sight of Jerym startled Esenrok out of a reverie of what he'd taunt him with when they passed, perhaps a quarter mile ahead. Jerym's gibe stung him, and he speeded up, swearing mentally. The son of a bitch actually thought he could catch him! He'd show him! He hadn't begun to tap his reserves yet!

Jerym's voice reached him clearly when he shouted his name. Tunis but that had been quick! He'd have turned, be headed back strongly now. Esenrok speeded up just a little more. His legs might be short, he told himself, but they were strong and tough and fast. He felt the light impact of his boots, the smooth pull and thrust as he jerked the road past him more than four feet at a stride. *Let Alsnor match this pace!* he thought grimly.

Warden watched Jerym's form disappear in the darkness. "Well," he said, "we might as well head back."

"Just a minute. I've gotta take a leak."

Thelldon got out and stepped behind the truck, out of the wind. A minute passed. Warden opened his door. "What in Tunis' name is taking you so long?"

"It didn't want to come out in the cold for a minute. It's doin' all right now though." Seconds later, Thelldon came to the door on Warden's side. "You said you'd show me how to drive."

"Me and my mouth. Okay, c'mon." Warden slid over and Thelldon climbed in. When Thelldon was settled behind the wheel, Warden pointed. "That's the starter."

"I know. I watched you. And I push on it, right?"

"Right."

"And this is the heater switch?"

"You got it."

"And I push on this lever to make it go forward. What do I do to go backward? Pull it toward me?"

"You don't need to go backward. We're headed the right way."

"But suppose I did? If I'm learning to drive, I need to know."

"All right. Before you go any direction . . . Start it. I'll show you."

Thelldon started it, then turned the heater on all the way. "Set it at low," Warden told him, "or you'll cook us out of here."

He turned it down. Then Warden showed him the drive mode control. "The indicator's at neutral, see? That's where you want it before you shift into a drive mode. Next . . ."

Pointing, Warden gave him the instructions, which were simple enough, and Thelldon backed up a dozen feet. It was jerky and so was his stop, but not bad at all for the first time. Then Warden had him drive ahead slowly. There were lots of snowflakes now; in the headlights they seemed to slant into the windshield. When the truck approached the meadow's edge, Warden reached over and turned the power off. The AG let the vehicle down with a barely perceptible bump.

"What'd you do that for?" Thelldon asked.

" 'Cause the road is narrow through the woods. I took responsibility for this thing when we stole it, and . . ."

Thelldon interrupted. "Borrowed it," he said.

"Whatever. Get out and change seats. I want to be sure I get it back in one piece, and before the T'swa know we took it, or they'll kill us both."

Thelldon got out and started around to the other side. *The T'swa wouldn't kill us,* he told himself. *Maybe work us to death, but they wouldn't kill us outright.* When he was in again, Warden restarted the vehicle and drove ahead into the forest.

With visibility limited, Warden took his time. It was several minutes before their headlights found a runner, loping down what looked like a white tunnel through the forest, while a suicide charge of snowflakes swooped headlong at their windshield. Without slowing, Jerym swerved to the edge of the roadway and they passed him. Eighty or a hundred yards beyond, Warden blew the horn, long and hard.

"What'd you do that for?" Thelldon asked.

Just ahead was a curve. Warden rounded it, and the headlights showed them Esenrok not more than forty yards ahead. He too swerved to let them by, and Warden, passing him, blared the horn again.

"He heard me blow before," he explained, "and he'll think it was when I passed Alsnor. He'll think Alsnor is right behind him. Shake the arrogant bastard up a little."

Thelldon nodded. Warden and Esenrok had fought a couple weeks earlier. Esenrok had won, and he'd crowed about it. A guy shouldn't crow like that. Not about a buddy.

As the truck passed, horn blowing, Esenrok felt a pang of anxiety. As much as he'd speeded up, Alsnor was gaining on him, or at least holding his own. Again he added speed; he was not going to let Alsnor beat him.

Soon Esenrok was breathing heavily. Within a mile he was laboring, his legs tiring. Badly. Despite himself he slowed a little, and wondered how much he'd added to his lead.

The snow had begun to stick on the grass of the roadway, coating it with wet whiteness. He tried to ignore it, even though his boots weren't gripping the road as well anymore. Once he slipped, sprawled heavily, and lay there for ten or twelve seconds, chest heaving, melted snowflakes mingling with the sweat on his face. Then he got back up and began to run again. Slower, hobbling briefly. He was almost weeping with frustration, and after a minute speeded up once more, as much as he dared. Alsnor would be having trouble too, he told himself. If he hung tough and kept pushing hard, he'd still come in ahead.

Jerym wondered how far behind he was. The footing slowed him some—his boots didn't grip as well—but it wouldn't be any better for Esenrok. The snow was about three inches deep and falling more thickly than ever, when he saw Esenrok not more than thirty yards ahead, running with the choppy, labored stride of someone badly tired.

When he passed him, Jerym did not taunt. It didn't even occur to him. He loped on by without saying a thing, only glancing back briefly a few strides past. Esenrok's head was down; Jerym wondered if he'd even seen him. Surely he'd notice his tracks though; he was bound to.

On an impulse—the kind of impulse a T'swi does not ignore—Sergeant Dao put down his book and went to the door to look out. It was snowing, hard, and where there was grass, the ground was white. But it wasn't snow that had touched his psyche.

He put on his field jacket and left the neat hut he shared with the other noncoms assigned to 2nd Platoon.

Left for the 2nd Platoon barracks. It was dark of course, except for the latrine windows. Quietly he opened the door and went in, and quietly walked down the long aisle between the rows of bunks. One, two, three, four bunks were empty. And Carrmak he sensed was still awake, despite the stillness of his blanketed form.

There was no sound from the latrine, and he did not bother to look in. It would have disrupted his night vision for the moment, and he did not question his ears, or the less standard, less precise sense that was similarly important to him.

He'd just turned when footsteps sounded on the stoop. The door opened and two youths came in, quietly they thought, starting toward their beds. Dao's soft voice stopped them in their tracks.

"Thelldon, Warden," he murmured, "come into the latrine. I want to talk with you. Carrmak, you come too."

Carrmak was on his feet and starting up the aisle before the other two, who stood frozen for a long moment. They had to pass Dao to enter the latrine, all but Carrmak keeping as far from him as the aisle allowed. Dao followed them through the door.

"Sit!" Dao said, gesturing at the row of commodes. They sat. Dao's eyes settled on the one he judged most vulnerable. "Thelldon," he murmured, "I want to hear your explanation." To Thelldon it sounded as if Dao already knew what they'd done.

"Sir, we were monitoring the race."

"Ah-h?"

"Yes sir. Esenrok thought that races could replace fighting."

"Umm."

"But Alsnor didn't trust Esenrok, so Warden and me, we went to monitor the race. And that's it. Really."

"I see. Where did you go to monitor it?"

"To the reservation boundary. We wouldn't ever have taken it otherwise."

Dao never blinked, never asked "taken what?"

"And we, Warden that is, parked it right where we got it from. In the exact spot. You can see for yourself."

"That won't be necessary. I'll take your word for it. Where are Esenrok and Alsnor?"

"They're still down the road, running. On their way back. We wanted to get the truck back as soon as we could. The last we saw of them was—" He turned to Warden. "Where? About a mile and a half, two miles from the boundary?"

Warden had been staring at Thelldon in shock. What in Tunis was making him run off at the mouth like that? At Thelldon's question, he shrugged. "Something like that," he answered.

Thelldon nodded. "About a mile and a half this side of the boundary. Esenrok was maybe a hundred, two hundred yards ahead. They've probably come another couple of miles since then."

Dao nodded calmly. "Thank you, Thelldon. You and Warden get ready and go to bed. I will talk with Carrmak now."

The two left. Dao looked at Carrmak without speaking for a moment. He could hear the sibilance of Warden's furious whispering to Thelldon in the sleeping quarters.

"So. Foot races to replace fighting? There is something to be said for that. Did you approve their taking a vehicle?"

Dao's face showed only curiosity, but Carrmak was sure that inwardly the sergeant was chuckling. "Sir, I didn't know about it," he said. "I was—out fighting."

"Fighting? Indeed. Put on some clothes, Carrmak, and come with me. I will trust Esenrok and Alsnor to arrive without my attention. They've gotten used to the roads after dark."

Glumly: "Yes sir."

Dao waited while Carrmak pulled on pants, shirt, and boots, pressed the boots shut, and slipped into his field jacket. They left together. Thelldon and Warden had shed boots and shirts. Now they headed back for the latrine. Barkum, whose bunk was next to the latrine door, joined them in the underwear he slept in.

"Tunis!" Barkum swore. "Carrmak's in real trouble now. And probably the rest of us." He paused. "I'm surprised Dao didn't take you guys along too."

"Where's he taking Carrmak?"

"I don't know. But he knows that Carrmak was in a fight tonight. I could hear 'em talking. I knew someone would see a vehicle was missing. Boy! I hope they don't do to us what they did to 4th Platoon."

The prospect seemed so grim, Warden forgot to continue reading Thelldon the riot act.

Outside, Dao felt uneasy, as if there was something else that needed to be taken care of. But the feeling came without direction, so he led Carrmak through the slanting flakes toward A Company's messhall. There'd be privacy there, and they had things to talk about.

They were almost there when they saw the glow of flames inside it, through the windows. The door opened and two youths slipped out, not seeing Dao and Carrmak at first. Dao rushed. One turned aside and fled. The other hesitated for just a moment, rattled, and when he did run, Dao cut him off and tackled him, his big hard body slamming the trainee to the ground. Dao was on his feet in an instant with the young man under a thick arm, feet foremost, and ran with him into the messhall.

Benches had been piled against one wall; paper and boxes burned beneath them. Carrmak was already slinging benches away from the blaze, benches that hadn't caught fire yet. Dao thrust the arsonist stumbling, then sprawling, in the direction of the kitchen.

"Get a fire extinguisher!" he bellowed, then pitched in with Carrmak. In half a minute more, all the benches not already on fire had been removed from the pile, leaving several burning. Behind the benches the wall was aflame, but the fire was not yet large. The arsonist arrived with a ten-gallon pot half full of water which he slung at the wall. He hadn't known where the fire extinguishers were. Dao did, and in another minute the fire was out.

Then Dao and Carrmak turned to look at the arsonist. He did not return their gaze.

When a tired Jerym arrived through seven inches of snow, the barracks was as quiet as if nothing had happened. He closed the door behind him and announced his arrival and victory, as agreed. Heads raised in the darkness, and— Someone got off Jerym's bed, someone large and black.

"Congratulations on your victory," Dao said. There was nothing sardonic in his voice except in Jerym's imagination. The sergeant stepped into the middle of the aisle, his voice taking them all in now. "There will be no celebration. You will all go back to sleep. Alsnor, come with me."

Jerym followed Dao out the door feeling as if he'd been slugged in the stomach.

The snow was falling more thickly than ever, the carryall's headlights penetrating it less than thirty yards, a cloud of white pluming behind. A mile from the compound they saw Esenrok lying in the road, white with the wet snow that stuck to him.

He was conscious, saw the headlights and raised his head. The moment that Dao stopped, Jerym was out, helped Esenrok to his feet and into the carryall. Esenrok began talking as soon as he was in.

"I'm all right," he said. "I was just resting. I'd have made it." He turned to Jerym then, "You told!"

Somehow Jerym let it lay, not answering.

"No," said Dao. "I was waiting for Alsnor when he came in. I already knew the story, stolen vehicle and all. Now lie down on the seat and be quiet."

Esenrok subsided and Jerym got in front beside Dao, who restarted the vehicle and turned it back toward the compound. When he pulled up in front of the dispensary, Esenrok was already asleep, and only semi-wakened when they took him in. He was soaked with sweat and melted snow.

Twelve

Colonel Carlis Voker had been away from Blue Forest for more than a week. His older sister, Meg, had been dying of *glioblastoma multiforme*. She'd served as surrogate mother to Voker after their mother had died; he'd been seven and she twelve. Now Meg was gone. He'd personally sprinkled her ashes in the Rivertown memorial garden, on a bed of candle flowers, as she'd once said she wanted.

From Rivertown he'd taken a commercial flight to Landfall the day before, and an OSP floater had brought him to the compound at Blue Forest after breakfast. He'd sensed that things had gone badly here, had noticed and identified the feeling while flying up, though what specifically had happened was not part of the perception.

His secretary, the only OSP civilian employee at the compound, gave him a cheery enough good morning, then told him Colonel Dak-So wanted to talk with him at his earliest convenience. Voker thanked the man and went into his freshly dusted office, scanned the originator/subject headings of the communications backlog on his terminal, and decided that whatever Dak-So wanted to talk about had priority.

He pressed a key on his commset. "Lemal," he said, "tell the colonel I'm ready to see him."

His joma maker was hot—he heard it chuckle—and he drew a cup, adding cream from the small refrigerator. Then he walked to the window and stood looking out at the snow—there'd been none at Landfall—wondering what the trainees thought of it. A minute later his secretary's voice spoke from the communicator: "Colonel Dak-So to see you, colonel."

"Send him in."

Dak-So entered, half a head taller and a hundred pounds heavier than Voker. In the T'swa manner, he did not salute. Although Voker was retired army, the relationship between these two was far more T'swa than army. Voker waved at a chair, and while Dak-So sat down, took one himself. "So," he said, "tell me about it."

"Carlis, trainee behavior has deteriorated since you left. I should say has continued to deteriorate." He catalogued some of the more extreme examples, beginning with a gang attack on Lieutenant Ghaz of 3rd Platoon, F Company*, and ending with the attempted arson of A Company's messhall by two members of C Company.

Voker nodded, lips pursed. "And the training: How is it going?

Dak-So chuckled. "The *training* continues to go very well. We are developing a regiment of tough, increasingly self-confident savages who tend to do to each other what should be reserved for opponents. They are

_____

*Made not with intent to kill or maim, but "just to see what would happen." Twelve trainees plus Lieutenant Ghaz and Corporal Toka-Ghit were treated in the infirmary; three trainees were flown to the army hospital at Granite River. All in all a remarkable demonstration of the value of T'swa training.

not the sort of person we recommend training in jokanru, for example."

Voker sat with eyes steady on Dak-So, saying nothing, listening.

"I remember," Dak-So continued, "when my regiment was virgin, newly shipped out, and I a nineteen-year-old battalion commander. I was amused at the large number of administrative staff in the military forces on Carjath. I could see the reason, of course: They did not know the T'sel. Like most armies, they consisted largely of personnel at the level of Work. A level at which there is a tendency to be orderly. But even so, they were sufficiently aberrated that a large staff—record keepers, guards, military police and the rest—were necessary. You are thoroughly familiar with that sort of thing, of course.

"By contrast, rather few of your intentive warriors are at Work. Most of them alternate between Fight and Compete. And become unruly and self-destructive when brought together like this. Fortunately, under the duress of discipline, they are at Contests much of the time, instead of Battle."

Dak-So stopped, giving Voker a chance to speak. The colonel only nodded, an invitation to continue.

"I wish to review some things for you," Dak-So went on. "Most of it you already know, but itemizing will connect it and establish its relevance."

"Go ahead."

"On Tyss we grow up with the T'sel, from nurselings. Each of us is born with an intended area of activity, with its own natural rules and rights, so to speak. As you are here, of course. On Tyss it is infrequent, and thus rather quickly conspicuous, when someones tries despoiling others of those rights. When one knows the T'sel, respect for rights and for reasonable rules is natural and does not have to be enforced. Thus guards are not necessary, nor military police. While far fewer records are required when people behave reasonably and have no impulses to cheat or steal."

Voker nodded and sipped his joma.

"Those of us born to be warriors are trained by our war lodges to high competence. We develop not only the skills of combat but the wisdom of combat, including what a warrior may do without the universe penalizing him. Thus pleasure in war is possible for us throughout our careers.

"Do you know our service history? Those of us training your regiment?"

"The basics," Voker answered. "You're remnants of three regiments. In the recent war on Marengabar, you were contracted to opposing sides and fought each other. You're old 'enemies,' in a manner of speaking. And you fought long and bloodily. But of course, you were never really enemies at all."

"Exactly! The T'swa warrior has no enemy. He only has those against whom he makes war. Opponents, in a sense. Also, your term 'playmates' applies."

It occurred to Voker that most people would consider that impossible. Or insane.

"We were contracted to train warriors for you," Dak-So went on. "And of course we will honor that contract. But unless your young trainees can be brought to know the T'sel, it seems that heavier and heavier discipline will be needed. And when they have been trained, you will have something dangerous on your hands, which can only be destructive to you."

Voker said nothing, sipped joma, listened.

"Unless, as I said, they can be brought to know the T'sel. And I do not know how that can be done, with youths their age. Perhaps you do. On Tyss we grow up with the T'sel, and learn simple personal procedures to stay attuned to it. Among your people, the T'sel is relatively new. Relatively very few know it, or even know of it. Some of you—you are one—come to know it as adults."

"I was in my forties."

"And the procedures by which that was done—can they not be applied to your trainees?"

Voker nodded. "We looked at that. And foresaw problems. Our procedures require talented, very skilled operators who know the T'sel. People in very short supply, compared to the overall need. And the procedures were designed for use in a calm, controlled environment, not among a disorderly concentration of troublemakers. So we decided to go at it the way we have, and see what we could accomplish.

"It's been my experience that in any large number of people, there are some who respond well to hard challenges. And I knew that a few leaders would arise within the ranks who'd try instilling sanity from inside. But apparently they're not enough, with the overall dynamics so aberrated.

"I've considered giving the natural leaders authority—make them trainee sergeants. We'll need to do that sooner or later anyway. But with these kids—it's not time for that yet. The leaders would lose the kind of influence we need them to have, inside influence on viewpoints and attitudes. And anyway, part of what they need is a willingness to behave rationally without coercion."

He paused thoughtfully. "So it's time to try something further. Including Ostrak Procedures."

He smiled ruefully at Dak-So. "You people have the better system. It's more effective and much easier to start people from birth in a T'sel society. For example, I'm not as wise in the T'sel as you are, who grew up with it. But Ostrak Procedures, used on adults, make dramatic changes in just about anyone they're used on. When delivered by masters working in reasonable environments. We do our best by starting with selected small children, like the cadets we shipped to Backbreak last summer. Generally you don't need to use the procedures as much when you start with six-year-olds.

"So I'll see what can be done about getting these yahoos introduced to the T'sel.

"I'm optimistic that something can be arranged; it's a matter of the wise investment of resources. The Crown has a long-term program to bring all Confederation worlds to the T'sel, and our qualified Ostrak operators are fully committed to projects that are part of it. Is the regiment important enough to pull some of them out and assign them to a project here? Considering the uncertainties in it? Including the uncertainty that this regiment will ever be needed?"

"The decision is His Majesty's to make. I'll discuss it with Lord Kristal." Voker got up. "Meanwhile I'll see what else we can do." He grinned. "I've had to deal with yahoos most of my life, and I've got forty years of army experience. Experience that I can look at now from the viewpoint of the T'sel. Let's assume we'll get some kind of help from the Crown.

"Meanwhile you and I are going to provide a groundwork. This afternoon. . . ."

Thirteen

After the noon meal, the entire regiment crowded into the assembly hall, the first time they'd been there. The first time they'd all been inside anywhere together. Their cadre was with them—more than four hundred commissioned and noncommissioned T'swa officers. (But not administrative and service personnel—clerks, cooks, mechanics etc.—almost all of whom were Iryalan army people on detached service to the Office of Special Projects.) When the trainees were seated, a man white like themselves walked out on the podium, an old man of scarcely medium height and compact build, his gray hair thin and as short as their own, his face lined and leathery. He appeared to be in his sixties.

The chatter thinned to murmuring.

He ignored the lectern, which had been left at one side, and positioned himself front and center, where he stood for a minute without speaking, as if examining his audience.

Then: *"At ease!"* he bellowed, and the room went silent till he spoke again. His voice seemed quiet now, but it filled the hall. "I am Colonel Voker. I am your commanding officer."

He paused, then bellowed once more: "Who likes it here?"

There was brief lag followed by a few tentative *me*'s, then the hall erupted with cheers. He'd expected them, but their vehemence surprised him, though he didn't let it show. He gave them half a minute, then bellowed again, this time using the microphone in his hand in order to be heard over their cheering. "AT EASE!!!"

It took several seconds before he had quiet.

"Good!" He looked them over again. "Each of you is a would-be warrior. We knew that from your personality profiles. So I expected you to like it here. There's no other place in the Confederation that's worth a damn for warriors."

He paused then. "And I want you to like it here." Again he paused, then raised an admonishing finger. "But on my terms! T'swa terms! It will have to be on my terms!"

It seemed as if somehow Voker looked at every one of them at once. And spoke to each of them, not simply all:

"You've come a long way since you got here. You've come a long way—and you've still got a *long* way to go. I have no doubt you can make it . . . Most of you. But I will not hesitate to kick any one of you out, or any one hundred of you."

Abruptly he switched modes, from genial to hard. "Third Platoon, Company F, answer 'Here Sir!' "

Forty trainees, standing in ranks in the back of the hall, shouted "Here Sir!" in response. They were clothed in stockade uniforms, faded and patched. Their heads were covered by bags with eye-holes, and they wore handcuffs to assembly. In addition to their regular training schedule, they'd been sleeping on the ground in squad tents and doing two-hour midnighters nightly, all on beans, rice, bread and water, supplemented with raw cabbage and poor quality apples.

"Third Platoon, Company F, you are very lucky. Tell me you're lucky."

Their answer boomed: "Sir, we're lucky!"

"Right." Voker's voice was casual now. "And here's the reason you're lucky: If anything like what you did happens again, the people involved will be out of here the next day. In an army prison. That is not a threat. It is a *promise!* We are sparing you that."

The hall was very quiet. He left it that way for several seconds before he spoke again. "We are not trying to break you. We want to *make* you. Or more accurately, we want to help you make yourselves. Into White T'swa." He paused for emphasis. "And T'swa— *would never, do, the kind, of stupid shit that many of you have been doing!* They have too much pride to act like a bunch of savages.

"Last night two men from First Platoon, C Company, tried to burn down A Company's messhall. 'For something interesting to do,' they told us. One of them is no longer with us. He's on his way to Ballibud Prison. The other one helped put the fire out. He is here with us now. Tonight, immediately after supper, he will begin to repair the damage done to the messhall. When he has finished repairing his damage, he will make amends to the Regiment by starting a swimming pool. With a shovel. His contribution to it will be a three-yard span across the shallow end, a span 200 feet long and four feet deep. He will dig from 2300 hours to 0100 hours each night, or longer if his guard feels he hasn't worked hard enough.

"After I told him the conditions of his remaining, he thanked me for letting him stay. Because he is not basically stupid. I doubt that any of you are. He simply did a seriously stupid, destructive thing."

Voker paused again and pursed his mouth. "Now. I am going to ask you a question, a question for each of you. And I want you to answer honestly to yourself. If the answer is yes, I want you to stand up and remain standing. Don't think honesty might make you look bad. It won't."

He could feel the silence, the uncertainty. The tension.

"Would you, any one of you, like to leave here? And return to civilian life? If you do, we'll arrange it."

No voice spoke. No one stood. Not Pitter Mellis, not anyone.

"Good.

"In a few minutes, Colonel Dak-So will speak to you, and when he's done, you'll begin to realize a lot of things. But that'll be in a few minutes; I've got a few things to tell you myself yet. And show you.

"You're training has just begun. You've learned to do some of the basics. Among other things, you've learned to follow orders and to do some things as part of a unit. You've begun to toughen physically; you've begun to develop the needed strength. Soon you'll begin weapons training.

"But there are a lot of things you haven't begun to learn, that make the key difference between a unit of soldiers and a unit of T'swa warriors. I was a soldier for years myself, and proud of it, but a warrior—a warrior is something else."

He paused. "Trainees Coyn Carrmak and Varky Graymar, come to the front of the hall."

Neither man froze for more than a second, then each pushed his way to the aisle and walked to the foot of the podium, where they stood side by side, seemingly calm.

"Your first sergeants consider you the best fighters in your companies." He turned to the regimental sergeant major. "Sergeant Kuto, do you have the straws?"

A stocky T'swi answered. "Yes sir!"

"Fine. Bring them to me."

The T'swi did. Voker arranged them in one fist and turned to the trainees. "Each of you draw a straw. The short straw wins. Carrmak, you first. Step up here."

Carrmak stepped onto the podium and faced the colonel.

"Draw."

He did.

"Graymar, your turn."

Graymar, a bit taller and slimmer than Carrmak, also drew.

"Show your straws to Colonel Dak-So."

They did. "Colonel Voker," Dak-So said, "Carrmak's straw is shortest." He held them up.

"Fine. Carrmak, over here." He stepped to the center of the podium, Carrmak following. Then Voker spoke to him so all could hear. "You and I are going to fight," he said.

Carrmak looked carefully at the old colonel, a lot smaller and so much older than he. Voker took a jokanru stance.

"Are you ready?" Voker asked.

Carrmak flexed his knees, raised his fists. "Sir, I am ready."

Voker's left fist jabbed out, and the youth moved to counter. Carrmak wasn't sure what happened next—none of the recruits were—but in a second he was on his belly on the floor, left arm angled upward and twisted back, his wrist in Voker's grasp, Voker's knee on his kidneys.

The colonel spoke without getting up or letting go, still lecturing. "This is a warrior skill," he said. "In combat, I would have done it a little differently: I would have dislocated my opponent's shoulder and followed with a death blow."

Then he let go and stepped back. Carrmak got to his feet. "Thank you Carrmak, Graymar," Voker said. "Your cadre say you're both more than just tough. You have the making of outstanding warriors. Return to your seats now."

They did. The silence of the trainees had changed. It was swollen with attentiveness.

"How did I do that?" Voker asked. "What do I have that you don't? Besides long training and experience? Obviously it's not youth. Nor strength. Nor superior quickness. Those I lost years ago; I'm seventy-six now. For one thing, I have jokanru, the close combat techniques developed by the T'swa. You just saw one of those. They are more than physical; they are mental and spiritual. And they are very useful to a warrior.

"But they are far less important than something else the T'swa developed. Something called—the T'sel." Voker's voice shifted, still casual but louder. *"Remember that word! T'sel!"* He spelled it for them.

His voice softened then, though it was heard clearly in back. "It is the T'sel that makes the T'swa what they are. With the T'sel, much becomes possible that otherwise would not be.

"You have met challenges here already. Successfully. Challenges of the body, challenges of tenacity and endurance. You are *beginning* to discover, *beginning* to realize, how good you can become. Now we have a new challenge for you, a challenge of the mind and spirit, the attainment of the T'sel.

"It is not a challenge that requires great effort, only a willingness to look at things in a new way. It is a challenge that I expect each of you to meet. Without the T'sel, you will never be T'swa."

Voker turned then and looked at Dak-So. "Colonel, talk to them about it," he said, and joined the other regimental and battalion headquarters officers in a short row of chairs on one side of the podium. Dak-So got up and stepped to the center. A large screen lowered behind him. The lights went out.

Fourteen

Light filled the screen, and a chart appeared. At the top, Jerym read the words: MATRIX OF T'SEL; below that was a bunch of stuff. He hoped it wasn't going to be like school.

"This," Dak-So said, gesturing with a light pointer, "is not the T'sel. It is an introduction to it." His eyes were faintly luminous as he scanned the room. "Trainee Alsnor!"

Having the regimental executive officer call his name hit Jerym like a jolt of electricity, knocking the breath out of him. After a moment he managed to answer. "Yes Sir!"

"Trainee Alsnor, when you were a child, what did you dream of being? Some day."

A picture flashed in Jerym's mind, one he hadn't remembered in years. He'd been about seven years old, sitting in the living room watching a story about a war. Probably some fictional war set on a trade world somewhere—he couldn't remember much about it. But it had had T'swa in it; actors made up like T'swa, they had to be, and he'd thought it was really great.

He'd told Lotta—she was watching it with him—he'd told her that when he was big, he was going to be a T'swa!

"A mercenary, sir!" he answered.

"When did you first dream about being a mercenary?"

"When I was—" He flashed to an earlier time. When he was really little. Could he have been only two or three? It seemed like it. His parents had been watching—Watching reruns of some of the same cubeage Captain Gotasu had shown them in the messhall, the second day he'd been here! He'd been playing with something—what it was didn't come to him now—but much of his attention had been on the screen. And he'd known then what he would someday be.

"—two or three years old, sir!" And hadn't recalled it since! He'd been into playing "soldier" after that, by himself and with other kids in the park, which older people didn't like. Some parents hadn't liked their children playing with him at all, because they usually ended up playing war. And he'd played warrior in his mind when the weather was bad or before he went to sleep. He'd never been someone else in his dreaming, either. He'd always been himself, grown.

"Thank you, Alsnor." Jerym realized then that he'd stood up when his name was called, and sat back down. Dak-So continued.

"Did any of the rest of you dream of being a warrior or mercenary or soldier a lot when you were children?" A general assent arose, not loud and boisterous, but thoughtful, contemplative. It occurred to Jerym that the others, or most of them, were recalling as he had.

"Then perhaps it is real to you that a person, every person, begins life with an intention, a purpose to be something more or less specific. Be it athlete, dancer, warrior, farmer . . . Something.

"Now look at the screen."

Jerym had forgotten the screen. He gave it his attention.

	FUN	WISDOM/ KNOWLEDGE	GAMES (CONTESTS)	JOB (SERVICE)	WAR (BATTLE)
PLAY	Play just for fun	Study as play; learning unimportant	Games as play; winning unimportant	Job as play; reward unimportant	War as play; victory unimportant
STUDY	Study for fun; learning secondary	Study for wisdom &/or knowledge	Study for advantage	Study to enhance job accomplishment	Study for power
COMPETE	Compete for the fun of winning	Compete to be wisest or most learned	Compete to win	Job as a challenge	War as a contest
WORK	Work at playing	Work at learning	Work for advantage	Work for survival	Soldiering
FIGHT	Fight to control pleasure	Fight to control wisdom and knowledge	Fight to subdue	Fight for monopoly	Fight to kill or destroy

"There is a row across the top, in capital letters, defining categories of *purposes* from Fun to War. The words here, of course, are in your own language, Standard. The originals are in Tyspi, my language, and the translations, being restricted largely to one-word headings, are not precise. In fact, they differ slightly in different translations. But they provide a useful approximation.

"Any human activity can be fitted into one of these categories.

"So. In which of them does Warrior fit?"

A number of voices answered: "War."

"And a farmer?"

"Job."

"What of a dancer?"

There was less unanimity on dancer; some said Job and a few Games, but more, after hesitation, said Fun. *Of course it's Fun*, Jerym thought. *If we're talking about purposes.*

"Very good. And on the left we have a capitalized series from Play to Fight. Now consider a possibility. Consider the possibility that a person is *born* to follow one of these purposes, from Fun through War. Depending on his environment and personal history, he will pursue that purpose if possible, at one of the levels from Play to Fight. Though he may also Work at Job, in order to survive. In many cultures, as a small child, he will be at the top, at Play. Often to move downward over the years until, usually from the level of Work, sometimes from that of Fight, he falls off the chart with his purpose abandoned."

Dak-So paused. "Look the matrix over. At what intersection of columns and rows do T'swa warriors fit?"

Answers started popping almost at once, building toward a consensus for War at Fight. Jerym felt an elbow nudge his arm, and Carrmak, grinning next to him, murmured "War and Play."

Jerym's eyes found the intersect of War and Play,

and was irritated with Carrmak. Victory unimportant? Tell that to the T'swa!

"Tell me," Dak-So said, "when you have had fights lately, what are called 'fights,' how many of you tried to kill or destroy your opponent?"

No one spoke up.

"We have here a confusion because of words," Dak-So said. "This chart, this translation, has a column headed War, but with a subheading Battle, to better cover the full meaning in Tyspi. So for the sake of discussion, consider what you were doing as 'battling.' Did you battle to kill, or did you battle for pleasure? Or as a contest?"

The answers began quickly, divided between pleasure and contest. Jerym couldn't see much difference.

"Excellent! I will not tell you why the T'swa battle. Not now. I will point out, though, that when we have asked you why you have started fights, or done other destructive acts, no one has said to injure or destroy. Mostly the answers have been something like 'for fun,' or 'to see if I could take him.' Or 'to see what would happen.' Injury and destruction occurred, but they were not the purpose of the acts."

"Sir!" someone called. "Can I ask a question?"

"Ask."

"I read once that you guys, you T'swa, fight for money. That it costs a lot of money to hire a T'swa regiment. Wouldn't that put you at Work on the chart? Or at Job?"

"We do not make War to get money, although we receive money for it. Money is not our purpose, it is only a means. Most of it goes to our lodge, to finance the training of other boys such as we were, helping them fulfill their purpose. To make possible our way of life—the more than eleven years of training, the warring on various and interesting worlds with various and interesting conditions. And to care for us when we are unable.

"Let me mention that what you are doing, training as

warriors, falls under the concept labeled here as War. A warrior delights in good, intelligent training. You may wish to examine whether you enjoy yours or not.

"Now, are there other questions?"

There were; more than thirty minutes' worth. Then Dak-So cut them off and they left the hall by companies, for more training.

From the assembly, Voker went with Dak-So to the T'swa colonel's office. There Dak-So poured them each a glass of cold watered fruit juice, the favorite T'swa drink.

"Carlis," Dak-So said, "despite your rather limited contact with the trainees, I must say you know them very well. Our presentations to them took hold better than I'd expected."

Voker grinned. "They're my people, Dak. I've dealt with them—coped with them, handled them, what have you—all my life. For most of that time, forty-one years, I was one of them. Lived as one of them, thought like they do, and had the Sacrament like all my generation, though in me it somehow didn't take the way it normally did.

"But you were right this morning. We do need to deliver the T'sel. If we can. What we did this afternoon was a start. It set things up, and I expect it to reduce the disorders considerably. But there's a lot of aberration there."

After they left the assembly hall, Jerym was too busy to think any more about the Matrix of T'sel or what it might mean to his life. When they finished training that evening and went to their barracks, each bunk had a printout of the Matrix of T'sel on it.

He put his on his shelf. He'd look at it when he wasn't so tired.

After showering he went to his bed. Next to Carrmak's. The lights were still on, and Carrmak was lying on top of the covers, looking at his copy. Jerym, before he lay down, saw Carrmak purse his lips and nod at whatever he'd just read, his eyebrows arched. Tomorrow, Jerym decided, he'd look his over during dinner break.

Fifteen

The novice, Itsu-Ta, stood in the darkness outside the little tower room, looking at the marvelously star-rich desert sky, admiring it. Itsu-Ta was *Homo tyssiensis* of course, and to his large T'swa eyes, night was some-what less dark than it might have been to a man from, say, Iryala. He was from the Jubat Hills, from Tiiku-Moks, where the sky was to some extent obscured or closed in by trees, and not infrequently cloudy. The monastery of Dys Tolbash, on the other hand, was on a ridge crest, and he on a tower of the monastery, with the night sky a vast, bottomless, scintillant bowl.

It might almost have drawn him into it—his full attention or even his soul—but he was on the tower for a purpose, and not free just then for wandering in the spirit. So he satisfied himself with looking, and enjoying the gentle winter breeze on his nearly naked body. (The temperature had slipped to about 85°F.)

He stepped back into the tower room; there was no wall on the north side, where the sun struck briefly only in summer, near sunrise and sunset. Master Tso-Ban sat there with his legs folded, had sat for sixteen hours unmoving, scarcely breathing, his heartbeat only sufficient for the tonus necessary to an upright posture.

Yet his attention was fully occupied.

Itsu-Ta could have eavesdropped; he had the ability. Although he was only a novice, he had been born to Wisdom/Knowledge, had been nurtured in it, had drilled its techniques for most of his eighteen years. But to eavesdrop on a master uninvited would have been discourteous, and more, it might have distracted Tso-Ban. Itsu-Ta's function this night was simply to give Tso-Ban's passive body a little water from time to time, water spiked with fruit juice as sustenance.

Tso-Ban's spirit was in a ship in hyperspace, on its bridge, with Tarimenloku's watch navigator. (The commodore himself was sleeping.) It seemed that the Confederatswa were very interested in whether the ship might emerge in Confederation Space. Which had provided Tso-Ban with a very interesting challenge, and, incidentally, Tyss and the Order with useful Confederation gold dronas.

So from the monastery library, Master Tso-Ban had memorized, imprinted, the galactic coordinates of a number of reference points in Confederation Space. Then by long and patient monitoring of ship's data, and its subliminal analysis, *he'd gradually managed to visualize as a chart the ship's—the computer's—galactic model, with its coordinates!* He'd had no one to instruct him, even unwittingly: Tarimenloku and his officers operated by long-conditioned automaticities, and relied heavily on the ship's computer. Tso-Ban's feat had been one of the outstanding accomplishments of millenia of Dys Tolbash's monks.

Then, after fixing his purpose, he'd meditated long, until the two sets of coordinates finally had reconciled for him. The project had kept him thoroughly engrossed for a number of deks. Now, with the coordinate models reconciled, he was monitoring in order to get a fix on the ship's course in hyperspace, as related to the Confederation's galactic chart.

Because the night was cool, Itsu-Ta did not attempt to give Tso-Ban another sip just then. Instead he assumed his own lotus posture on a mat on the stone floor, and re-entered a sort of reverie, monitoring the condition of Tso-Ban's body.

Dawn was still an hour away when Tso-Ban roused, and with him Itsu-Ta. The master yawned, stretched hugely, took a swig from the water bottle, bowed slightly to Itsu-Ta who bowed back, then began to descend the steep outside stairs that zigzagged down the side of the tower.

Tso-Ban had completed the challenge. The course the Klestronu flotilla was on would not take them into Confederation Space or even very near it. And with that knowledge, his interest in the flotilla faded. He'd had enough for now of a ship in hyperspace. A ship that had been in hyperspace for months and promised to be there for another year or more, if it didn't emerge prematurely to destruction by Garthid weapons.

Perhaps he would return to his off-and-on interest in the sapient sauroid hunters on another world he'd encountered. There were humans there, too, unknown to the Confederatswa or the Karghanik Empire, and sapient ocean life forms as well, but the sauroids interested him most.

Sixteen

The enemy leaped from behind the tree, blast hose raising, and Jerym half turned, crouching, rifle at hip, squeezing off a burst as he pivoted, then threw himself prone onto the wet leaves (the snow had melted) while his "assailant" fired a crashing burst of sound before evaporating into its constituent photons.

From behind them, a T'swa voice announced, "Trainee Alsnor: you expended most of your burst before your line of fire reached the enemy. Your last round scored a superficial wound, right pelvis, insufficiently severe to prevent enemy from firing effectively. Enemy blast hose caused severe casualties to your squad."

Scowling, Jerym got to his feet and turned the point over to Esenrok, wishing he knew where the projectors were. Esenrok bagged the next holo and gave way to Romlar, who got off his burst on target but too late.

When they reached the end of the course, Esenrok clapped Jerym on the shoulder in mock friendliness. "Remind me to get transferred to another squad, Alsnor. Before we get into combat somewhere and you really get your squad wiped out."

Jerym turned to him, eyes blazing. "Off my back, asshole! Yours was right in front of you. Mine was around to the side."

" 'Mine was around to the side,' " Esenrok said in a mocking falsetto. "Come off it, Alsnor. You're a fucking crybaby . . ."

Jerym was on him then, a hard punch catching Esenrok full on the nose, blood splatting. For a moment they grappled furiously, heels striving to trip, before Jerym got Esenrok's feet off the ground and threw him, crashing on top of him.

That's when it ended. Their squad leader, Sergeant Bahn, grabbed Jerym by the shoulder, sending a wave of numbness through him, and then, by his jacket collar, jerked him backward to his feet. Esenrok scrambled to his, attempting to get at Jerym, but Bahn caught the swinging fist with his free hand, Esenrok dropping to his knees at the pressure.

"Alsnor," Bahn said, "go to the stand and sit down. I will speak with you later."

Jerym, shaking with emotion but saying nothing, picked up his rifle and left with the squad, all of it but Esenrok, all equally silent, walking toward the small stand where they'd receive a critique of their performance.

Bahn gripped the stocky Esenrok by the shoulder and started walking him toward the company's aid man, another T'swa sergeant, leaving Esenrok's rifle where it lay.

"My rifle!" Esenrok objected.

"It will be seen to," Bahn replied equably. "And you will receive company punishment for taunting a squad mate."

Esenrok, whose nose was bleeding copiously, squealed with indignation. "Me? Company punishment? He slugged me! Sucker-punched me!"

"He did not sucker-punch you. He will receive company punishment too, but it will be less severe than yours. Had you not taunted him, he would not have struck you."

Esenrok shook loose from the burly T'swi's grip on his shoulder, screaming, "Next time I'll shoot the sonofabitch!" With startling suddenness, shocking power, a T'swa fist grabbed Esenrok's jacket front and jerked him close, disregarding the blood. Esenrok went limp with the wave of fear that washed through him.

Bahn replied almost gently. "Trainee Esenrok, let me clarify some things for you. You started the fight with Alsnor, with your mouth. Thus you will receive the more severe punishment. Now, with that same uncontrolled mouth, you have earned something more severe, perhaps expulsion, for threatening to shoot a squad mate."

In a state of shock, Esenrok said nothing more, stumbling numbly to the aid man, propelled by Bahn's thick hand. A T'swa corporal, one of the cadre not assigned to a specific platoon, trotted over, picked up Esenrok's rifle, and put the partially expended clip into one of the large pockets in his field pants.

Lieutenant Dzo-Tar and Sergeant Dao, waiting near the stand, had heard Esenrok's screamed threat, and watched Bahn handle him.

Dzo-Tar turned to his platoon sergeant and spoke in Tyspi. "In your view," he said, "should we get rid of that trainee?"

Dao shook his head, eyes still on Bahn and Esenrok, who were with the aid man now. "I recommend that at this time we do not. True he is 2nd Platoon's principal troublemaker, but if the Confederatswa procedures the colonel has spoken of prove efficacious, Esenrok should become an excellent warrior. He has valuable leadership qualities."

He looked at his lieutenant then. "Interesting how Voker's and Dak-So's lectures ended almost entirely the challenge fights and vandalism, while fighting in anger has increased. Has the captain heard anything further about when the procedures will begin?"

Dzo-Tar's eyes moved to the trainees seating themselves on the stand. "He mentioned nothing further this morning. Apparently it is still scheduled for sometime this week."

That evening before dismissal for supper, Dao addressed the platoon in ranks. Jerym was there, and Esenrok, the latter with a bandage on his face and no rifle.

"There was a fight in 2nd Platoon today," Dao said. "But there will not be a midnighter tonight. We'll save them for you, for later. The captain has learned this afternoon that visitors will arrive tomorrow. They will interview certain of you, and we have been asked to see that you get a full night's sleep in preparation.

"Alsnor, Esenrok, I want to talk with you. The rest of you are dismissed."

The platoon broke ranks and hurried into the barracks. Jerym and Esenrok still stood there, not looking at each other, Jerym's expression morose, introverted, Esenrok's sulky, defiant. Dao, on the other hand, seemed genial despite what he was about to say. "Alsnor, I have not yet decided what the penalty will be for your behavior today."

He turned to Esenrok then. "Esenrok, Lieutenant Dzo-Tar will discuss your case with Captain Gotasu. You will be informed of the captain's decision at second muster tomorrow morning. I have spoken for you incidentally. Like Alsnor, you have certain admirable qualities that particularly commend you as a warrior-to-be. Unfortunately you have shown a severe propensity for causing trouble, not only for yourself but for others." The large T'swa eyes had drawn Esenrok's to them. "Therefore the captain may decide you are not worth it. Or he may decide to give you another chance.

"Meanwhile there is tonight." Dao looked them both over. "I am going to handcuff you two together, left wrist to left wrist. Very awkward, I know. At supper you will eat with me at a separate table, handcuffed, and—you will not feed yourselves. You will feed each other. If you do not work out an effective, cooperative system, you will go hungry. Tonight you will put your mattresses together on the floor of the dayroom and sleep there, again with your chains on. I shall sleep there too. And if you fight, at any time, I will handcuff you together, all four wrists, on the opposite sides of a tree, and you will spend the night there in your greatcoats.

"This is a test of you both, but especially, Esenrok, of you." He looked at them with an almost kindly expression. "Are there any questions?"

Both youths stared wordless at the ground.

"Very well. Go and clean up now. And remember that tree."

Company A's dayroom was a small building lined with bookshelves. Beyond that it had a drinking fountain, chairs, small tables, and at one end a latrine. Nothing more. Jerym and Esenrok, manacled together, had managed jointly to lay their mattresses side by side with their blankets spread over them, and to get their boots off. But there had been no hint of reconciliation. Dao eyed them speculatively.

"Before you lie down to sleep," he said, "there is something I require of you. First, place two chairs facing each other, four feet apart."

Sullenly they did. Then Dao removed their handcuffs. "Sit down," he said, and still sullen, they sat.

"Now I will give you instructions, and the sooner you carry them out to my satisfaction, the sooner you lie down to sleep. Also, do not forget the tree. Alsnor, I will ask you to tell Esenrok something you like about him. It must be genuine, neither untrue nor sarcastic."

Jerym sulked.

"Esenrok, I will ask you to do the same to Alsnor. You must look at each other while you do this, and the one who is complimented must thank the other." He looked from one to the other. "Alsnor, begin!"

Jerym took a deep breath and let it out. "Esenrok, you—You're the best sprinter in the platoon."

Esenrok could scarcely grind the words out: "Thank you."

"Another," said Dao.

Jerym grimaced. "You are . . . You fired the fifth highest score on the target range."

"Thank you."

"Another."

Jerym shot a scowl at Dao, then turned back to Esenrok, saying nothing for several seconds, as if he couldn't think of anything. Then: "You had a good idea about running races instead of fighting. If we'd done that earlier, we wouldn't have had all those midnighters."

Again Esenrok thanked him, and again Dao called for another.

"You can do more chinups with a sandbag than I can."

"Thank you."

"You— Got more guts than sense." Jerym turned quickly to Dao. "That's a compliment! Around the barracks that's a compliment!"

Esenrok's blush was visible beyond the tape on his face, but gradually he grinned. "Thank you."

"Very good," Dao said. "Now it is time for Esenrok to have a turn. Esenrok?"

His first took only a few seconds. "Uh . . . You beat me in the race."

"Thank you."

"Again."

"You . . . You never snore."

"Thank you."

"Again."

"For a long-armed guy, you can do a lot of pushups."

"Thank you."

"Again."

"And you . . ." Once more Esenrok grinned. "You got an awful good straight right."

Jerym blushed. "Thank you," he answered, then a grin began to creep onto his face too.

Dao added his own grin. "I have one more instruction for you." They looked at him. "Take your mattresses back to the barracks, and go to bed there. I will return the handcuffs to the master-at-arms."

No one said anything when Jerym and Esenrok came into the barracks, jointly carrying their mattresses one atop the other with their bedding on top. They made up their beds, then went outside together.

"They gonna fight, you think?" Romlar asked.

Carrmak shook his head. "For one thing," he said, and fingered his nose, "when your nose is broken, you don't want anyone bumping it. And Captain Gotasu is likely to ship them both home if they get into it again. Very soon anyway. Neither one of them wants that."

Outside, Jerym and Esenrok strolled toward the dayroom, which normally would have been dark by then, but Sergeant Dao hadn't turned the lights out yet.

"Esenrok," Jerym said, "I never should have slugged you like that. I'm—sorry."

Esenrok stopped. "Sorry doesn't fix this," he answered, touching his nose gingerly. "But look. I've always had a big mouth. I know that. And a lousy temper. And I've told myself more than once that I was going to quit mouthing off." He shrugged. "But it seems like I don't remember it when I need it."

Jerym nodded. "My mouth hasn't been my problem, but slugging someone has. The last time, the judge told me, 'Once more and you go to the reformatory.'"

Esenrok nodded. "They told me that when I was fifteen. So I quit slugging guys, pretty much. After that's when my mouth got really bad." He spread his hands to Jerym, as if to say, what's to do? "You know, there's a lot of us here like you and me."

"Yeah. Shit!" Jerym's mind went to the Matrix of T'sel, and wondered where he was on it. "This is the first place I ever knew of for guys like me. And you. I mean, you know, a place for us. For warriors I mean . . ."

"I know what you mean. And you're right." Esenrok looked worried now.

The lights went off in the dayroom, and the door opened. "Just a minute," Jerym said. "I got to say something to Dao." He loped off. Esenrok waited, curious, till he came back.

"What was that about?"

"I told him . . ." This time it was Jerym who spread his hands. "I told him you hadn't really meant it when you said you'd kill me, and that he should tell the captain that. I told him it was just a way of talking. A way of saying how mad you were. I told him that's the way we are here." He shrugged. "Maybe when we're T'swa it'll be different."

They turned and strolled together toward the barracks. "You know," Esenrok said, "maybe I did mean it when I said I'd kill you. I was crazy. You know?"

Jerym nodded. "I know. But maybe the captain doesn't. And anyway you didn't shoot me. And when I—hit you—you had your gun."

Esenrok stopped walking, stared at nothing. "Huh! I guess I did, didn't I. Well." He turned to Jerym and grinned ruefully. "I'm not as bad as I thought I was!"

He put out his hand and they shook, making it a contest of strength. When, after half a minute, neither had won, they both laughed, let go, and went on to the barracks.

Dao had paused beside a tree and watched the scenario between the two trainees. When he went on, it was not to the rows of neat huts that comprised noncoms' country. Instead he went to officers' country, a hutment scarcely different from that of the noncoms. (For they all were T'swa.) Lieutenant Dzo-Tar would be interested in the reconciliation of Alsnor and Esenrok, and what it said about the young men.

These Iryalans still surprised him from time to time, refining his knowledge of them.

Seventeen

Youths in field uniforms hustled out the door to form ranks in the freezing gray morning. Briefly Sergeant Dao regarded his watch, then looked up. "Atten*tion!*" he called, and the ranks stiffened. "Report!"

The T'swa squad sergeants didn't need to take roll. A glance had served. "First squad all present, Sir!" snapped Sergeant Bahn, and the sergeants of the second, third, and fourth squads followed suit. Dao about-faced easily but crisply, and saluted Lieutenant Dzo-Tar. "Second Platoon all present, Sir!"

For the purpose of training these Confederatswa, the T'swa had adopted army-style protocol, a major but easy adjustment for them. In T'swa units, roll call might be taken if there'd been casualties or if personnel had been dispersed, but otherwise never. "Sir" was seldom used except in the presence of foreigners who expected it. And when they did salute, it was in the Confederation style, because they lacked a salute of their own.

Similarly, in most situations, Sergeant Dao spoke for Lieutenant Dzo-Tar because Voker considered it good tactics with these trainees. Let the platoon sergeants be the immediate authority; let the platoon *leaders*, the lieutenants, be a step remote, each ruling through his sergeant, with whom the trainees would then feel more rapport.

The T'swa had no problem with this; they accepted Voker's experience and judgement.

But at morning roll call, the platoon got its day's orders from on high, from Lieutenant Dzo-Tar. They'd come to expect this. During the day, Sergeant Dao would enforce, interpret, and modify those orders as circumstances required.

"Men," Dzo-Tar said, "the uniform of the day will be winter field. The following men will remain in barracks after breakfast and receive specific orders later. Alsnor, Bressnik, Carrmak, Darrmiker . . ." He read off a dozen names including Romlar's. Then Dao dismissed the platoon, and they went in and washed up for breakfast. Jerym was optimistic that whatever this special duty was, it would prove to be good. Because the others named were all trainees in good standing with the cadre. He was the only one of them currently on a shit-list.

After breakfast, the rest of the platoon went off on their morning run. According to Markooris, who'd passed by the drill field where the company had been forming up, it looked as if 2nd Platoon was the only one with men held out. None of the twelve waiting in the barracks even speculated out loud what this might be about, but they remembered what Dao had said the day before about visitors and interviews. They hung around, read, played cards, practiced walking on their hands, even managed not to scuffle or get into other trouble. After a little, Carrmak and Jerym got into a situps contest, but they'd only gotten up to 517, with the others loudly chanting the count, when a T'swa corporal came in and called six names, including theirs. It was cold out, about ten or fifteen degrees, Jerym thought, with a breeze, so they put on field jackets before they left.

The six of them were led to the Main Building, the administration building. There'd been a lot going on there lately, buses pulling up with civilian workers, trucks with building supplies, and Jerym wondered now if that had anything to do with them. The corporal left them in a room with chairs and sofas, and a bunch of books spread on a table. All the books seemed to be about the planet Oven—Tyss—or the T'swa or the T'sel, and there was a big Matrix of T'sel on a wall, with a lot more writing in the boxes than there'd been in the version he was familiar with. Jerym went over to look at it, but was too fidgety to do more than scan.

After five or ten minutes a civilian came in with the T'swa corporal and took the six of them on a tour, showing them where they'd be going, describing briefly what to expect. They'd be led individually to one of a number of small rooms along a hall—a hall that smelled like fresh lumber—where someone would interview each of them privately. The civilian used the terms *interview* and *interviewer,* instead of the unfamiliar *session* and *operator* which might worry the trainees.

Even so, Jerym wasn't sure he liked the sound of this. He'd been interviewed by psychologists at school and before going to court, and while nothing bad had happened, he'd felt exposed, endangered by their questions.

The civilian told them that when they came back out of the interview rooms, someone would lead them to a room where they'd be given a snack. The snack room seemed small to Jerym, with six tiny tables, each having a single chair. If, their civilian guide said, there was more than one of them in the snack room at the same time, they were not to talk about what had happened in the interview. From the snack room they'd be led to a room with a bunk in it, where they were to lie down and rest—sleep if they felt like it. Afterward they could go back to their barracks. They were to say nothing about any of this to the others. They could say they'd been to the administration building and been interviewed, but that was all.

That was the end of the tour. They went back to the waiting room curious and apprehensive. They didn't wait long though, any of them. The civilian came back to lead them, one by one, to the hall with the fresh lumber smell, where he'd knock at the assigned door, then leave them there.

After Carrmak, Jerym, and the other four had been led from the barracks, Romlar napped in his bunk. He hadn't even watched out the window in hopes of seeing where they were being taken; he'd know soon enough. That had been 0730; it was 0930 when the corporal came in again and took the rest of them. They saw the same waiting room as the earlier six, the same everything. Bressnik was in the snack room when they passed, with a glass of something and a sandwich.

Romlar felt good about it. It wasn't anything he could put his finger on; he just felt good. He didn't even feel restless about not being out training, though he, like the others, had developed a strong appetite for it. (Physically he was a very different Romlar than had fallen out on the run and on the sandbag hike, that first night at Blue Forest.)

The civilian made sure he knew not to talk about what happened to him. He wondered what that would be. He wasn't nervous about it though, or not much anyway. He was pretty sure he could wad the civilian up in a ball, if it came to that. Or just about anyone except the T'swa and Carrmak. And that gray-haired little colonel!

Back in the waiting room he browsed a book by Varlik Lormagen, about the T'swa. He remembered the name, Varlik Lormagen. The White T'swi. Alsnor's sister knew Varlik Lormagen. It occurred to him that he'd never written to her, never even gotten her address from Alsnor.

The book was mostly about T'swa warriors on Kettle, in the war, but there was also stuff about their home world, Tyss, and what it was like. There were lots of pictures to help make it seem real. While he was looking at it, the civilian came in and led Lonsalek away, and Markooris, and then Presnola. The next time he came in, he called: "Romlar!"

Romlar got up, and now his stomach was nervous after all. He wished he'd had a chance to talk to Carrmak and find out what they did to you here. But Carrmak wouldn't have told him, because they made such a big deal out of not telling.

The civilian led him down the hall to one of the doors, and knocked firmly.

"Send him in," a voice answered. It sounded like a female voice, and came from a little grill. The civilian opened the door and motioned Romlar through. Romlar stepped in, ducking his head a bit as if he thought he was too large, too tall for it, and the door closed behind him with a firm click. Romlar didn't notice the thickness of the door, or of the carpet, and couldn't know about the sound insulation between the wall panels. What he did notice was—the girl. Just a young girl! Fourteen or fifteen, he thought, on the skinny side, with red hair and a pretty face. And green eyes! He had a sudden impulse to turn and leave, run out. He'd always been afraid of girls. At school, girls had made fun of him, and if you ever hit one of them, forget it! You'd be put away.

She smiled at him. "Artus Romlar?"

"Uh, yeah." Even at home, not many people called him Artus: his mom and dad, his teachers— That was all. Here the guys didn't even know that was his name; here people called you by the name above your pocket, your last name.

"My name is Lotta," the girl said. "Sit down please, Artus." Across the desk from her was a chair with a cushioned seat. He sat down on it.

She was still smiling. Her teeth were pretty—small

and even. "Do you like it here at the Blue Forest Reservation?" she asked.

"Yeah."

Her green eyes were direct, steady, comfortable. "Good. What do you like best about it?"

"Uh, I don't know . . . I like the T'swa pretty good. They work our tails off. And they never get mad at us."

"Okay. Is there anything else here you like a lot?"

"Uh, yeah, I guess so. I like the guys really good. And the training. I really like the training."

"Sounds good. How do you feel about yourself these days?"

The question startled him, and for several seconds he didn't know what to answer. "Uh— Oh, pretty good I guess." It seemed to him that that was true. And that it hadn't been true before he'd come to Blue Forest.

"All right." She paused, drawing his attention out of himself, to her next words. "Now if you could change one thing about yourself," she said, "what would you most like to change?"

The question snapped his attention back inward. He couldn't think, couldn't possibly answer. Then he heard his own voice saying, "I'd like to not be stupid."

"All right," she answered. "Tell me about a time you felt stupid."

Romlar nodded slowly. "My first night here. A T'swi told me to dig a big hole. Because I fell out on the run, and then I quit on the sandbagger—the sandbag march—and told them they could go *F* theirself. And after I dug awhile, I quit digging and told him that again. And the T'swi was going to chain me to a post until I would dig some more, so I tried to fight him but he was so strong I could hardly believe it, and he knew just what to do. And it was cold and I was sweaty, and all I could do was lay on the ground and shiver, because I was cold. And I— I cried. And I felt so damn stupid, because all I needed to do was run a little farther, or hike a little farther, or dig a little farther, and I wouldn't have been laying there on the cold ground, chained to a post."

A six-inch-high shield sat on the desk, and behind it from time to time her fingers moved on a flat keypad, silently and unobtrusively. Her gaze, however, never left Romlar's face. It was as if her hand operated on an independent circuit from her eyes and tongue. "Okay," she said. "Was there an earlier time when you felt stupid?"

It came to him at once, but he wasn't sure he ought to tell her. Then he heard himself saying: "I was— I asked this girl in school to go to a music program with me. I asked her because she'd always talked nice to me and she wasn't too pretty. She said she couldn't because she was supposed to go somewhere with her family that night. But somebody told me later that he'd heard her laugh about my asking her. She said she wouldn't go out with somebody as stupid as me; that I'd probably try to rape her."

Romlar looked at the redheaded girl to see what she thought. She was just gazing at him, quietly and steadily. "I got that," she said. "What's the earliest time you can remember feeling stupid?"

The question stopped him. The earliest time. He sat dumbly, shaking his head. Nothing came to him. "The time with your father," she prompted. "When he held you up by the ankles."

Her words were like an unexpected blow. His buttocks began to burn, and the back of his legs, to sting, to hurt. He didn't want to remember, wanted to get up and run out of the room, but his body wouldn't move. "I was . . ." he heard himself start. "I was—just a little kid. Maybe two." He had no idea what this was going to be, but a feeling of dread had crept through him. "And—" He paused. The images were slow to form, the events conceptual at first. "I guess I must have broke something. Something valuable. My father came in and he was really mad. And I was scared. Scared! He grabbed me by my feet, my ankles, and held me up with one hand and started beating on my ass and legs as hard as he could."

Romlar had begun weeping, tears overflowing, spilling down his cheeks. "And he yelled at me and he yelled at me and yelled, 'You damn stupid little animal! You stupid little animal! Look what you did! Look what you did! You stupid little animal!' And he kept on hitting me and hitting me and yelling like that, a big strong man, and I was just a little tiny kid and he kept hitting me and hitting me!"

By the time he'd finished the account, Romlar was blubbering the words brokenly, and when he was done, lapsed into violent, bitter sobs. Not only were tears rivering down his cheeks; his nose was running, and he was slobbering. The girl sat there and didn't say anything till he tapered off and looked across at her. Her gaze was as steady as before, and she handed him a box of tissues. "Thanks for telling me about it," she said quietly. "And it's all right for you to cry in here. We kind of expect it, and it's all right. This is all just between you and me."

He nodded, mopped his face, blew his nose. This girl wouldn't talk about him to people and say he was stupid, or that he'd cried. He knew that. He was sure of it.

She had other questions, and there was more weeping. It seemed as if, when she asked about something, it came to him. When she needed to, she prompted him, as if seeing his memories before he was able to. And Romlar didn't think of it as weird, didn't wonder how she knew those things.

After each time he cried, he felt better, as if he'd never have that grief again. Finally she asked him about a time he'd been happy, and he told her about rassling Carrmak. And the time when Esenrok slapped his shoulder and told him he was okay. And some other times, on the playground, and when he was little. Even a couple of times when his father took care of him and dished them up ice cream, and told him stories about being a boy on the farm.

By that time Romlar could laugh, not something he did very often, and the girl laughed with him.

"Well," she said when he was done. "Thanks for coming in. We'll talk together again soon." She must have pushed a button because someone knocked on the door—it didn't sound very loud—and she talked into a little microphone, telling them to come in.

The civilian at the snack room gave him juice and a sandwich and the first ice cream he'd had at the compound. Then another civilian took him to a little room with a cot—he was starting to feel drowsy already—and when he lay down, he fell right to sleep.

Eighteen

Eight imperial months previously, Commodore Igsat Tarimenloku had awakened with a decision: to reenter real space. It was a reasonable mistake; so many mistakes are. It happened like this:

He'd long since convinced himself that his spur-of-the-moment attack on the strange patrol ship had been imperative, the only justifiable action. Still it had no doubt put himself and his flotilla at serious risk, so to be safe, he'd remained in hyperspace for six standard months, long enough to clear any conceivable politically unified sector.

With this decision in mind, he'd spent a few minutes in his shower, then went to his private dining room. After a disinteresting breakfast, he went to the bridge and informed the crew on watch there of what he was going to do.

This emergence was not done carelessly. After activating security systems—emergence wave detector, command room alarm, automatic shield and targeting responses—he *entered real space at a point where their instruments showed no nodi, no sign of a planetary system*. There should be no patrol there.

121

When they'd emerged, though, there was a system in the vicinity, if you consider the vicinity to extend more than 85 billion miles, more than five light days, from the primary. Still, it was surely far enough.

They'd been recording in real-space for less than two minutes (DAAS, the flagship's computer, gave him the figures later: one minute, 29.27 seconds) when the alarm began to beep its response to an emergence wave.

Instantly, or as close to it as human reflexes allow, Tarimenloku touched the flotilla control and exit keys. And at the moment of disorientation heard/felt the shrieking of what had to be a ruptured matric tap. Not the flagship's, or he'd never have heard it, would have ceased to exist. As it was, his head rang with it.

The monitor screen showed the hyperspace blip of only one other ship, the troopship. Clearly it was the survey ship that had been destroyed. Fortunately, he told himself, it had been manned by only a handful of maintenance people. Thank Kargh for all blessings! But actually he didn't feel fortunate at all. He felt shock, and loss, and threat. And being a senior commanding officer, did not let any of these interfere markedly with his functioning.

It was after the ringing in his head had moderated that Tarimenloku conferred with his executive officer, Commander Dimsikaloku, and they'd sorted it out.

Their reconstruction of the situation, admittedly conjectural, had it that the hostile patrol ship had been stationed in real-space at some distance outside the system, detected them from there, and shifted at once into hyperspace for the "short" jump (in terms of hyperspace "distances"). That would account for its quick arrival. To have detected the flotilla's emergence wave, the patrol ship had almost surely been on the near side of the system and outside the Oort Belt, which might have been coincidence, or . . . Or maybe the system was ringed with patrol ships! *Maybe it was the aliens' home system!* That would explain the prompt hostility and the distance from the primary! They wanted strong security at the maximum practical separation from the home world!

And it had emerged at a separation of twelve miles again, like the patrol ship in the earlier system. Interesting.

But this one had begun shooting virtually on emergence; there'd been time (milliseconds at most) for only the briefest identity scan. And it appeared that they'd known the intruder was himself, the one who'd attacked a patrol ship eight months and some eighty parsecs back. Message pods must have preceded their arrival here, and patrol ships were on orders to attack without further attempt at communication.

Dimsikaloku had favored turning back then, taking home the information that an alien civilization existed here, the probable location of the aliens' home system, and what they'd inferred about alien technology. But the commodore had decided against it, a position easy to disagree with. He'd justified his stance—more to himself than to Dimsikaloku, because the rank was his—by pointing out their mission orders: The sultan had sent out this expedition—a politically risky decision—because he was intensely interested in the possibility of worlds to expand to. And as yet they had found none. Furthermore, the danger here could be minimized by remaining in hyperspace long enough to *ensure* they were out of the hostile sector.

All that had been more than eight imperial months earlier, and even now, Tarimenloku had every intention of staying in hyperspace for another three. Though it was hard to conceive of a politically unified sector even approaching that volume of space; the problems of communication, administration, and control would be impossible.

Just now though his attention was on a most unusual major nodus. The apparency was of quadruple primaries near enough for a four-way tidal sharing of plasma, a situation which seemed physically impossible.

He slowed, tempted to emerge long enough for a quick data recording. Not nearly what his survey ship might have given him, but enough to excite the astronomers back home.

It was that slowing that exposed their pursuer and stunned Tarimenloku. A second hyperspace blip showed briefly on the monitor, very briefly, but unmistakably. They were being followed! Then the pursuer reacted to their slowing by slowing himself and disappearing from the monitor.

And suddenly all the rationalizations for the prompt, close appearance of the alien ship in real-space, eight months earlier, came into doubt. It could well be the same ship they'd fired at fourteen months earlier!

And obviously the aliens' instruments could perceive farther in hyperspace than theirs could. Which had allowed the alien to follow without being noticed.

The commodore did something then that he'd never heard of before; something his chief science officer agreed theoretically might work. He sent a distortion bomb in the hyperspace "direction" of their shadow, their follower. Then, having given the two time to approximately coincide, he changed course by fifty degrees in the plane of the ecliptic, and briefly, seconds later, by thirty *from* the plane of the ecliptic.* The purpose was

---

*Hyperspace is not actually a space. It is a field enclosing a ship, generated by the ship's hyperspace generator and fully occupied by the ship. In this limited sense, hyperspace is analogous to the warp field enwrapping a ship at sublight speeds, with the additional similarity that in either case the ship has no momentum as gauged against external fields. However, a ship riding its warp field travels through space, while a ship in hyperspace is in a sort of limbo: It can be said to be nowhere. Its field can be said to move, taking the ship with it, but in a sense they aren't moving through anything.

Yet in an equally valid sense it is moving, with a movement that can be quantified and perhaps actually measured—a matter of dispute—through a sort of quasi-topological "reverse side" of real-space. Thus different ships separately "in

to lose their pursuer. Several times during the watch, Tarimenloku slowed sharply again, and several times changed course. There was no further sign of pursuit, which was somewhat reassuring but by no means proof of anything.

Meanwhile they were well off the course they'd been on, the one prescribed by admiralty staff. (And the one described by Master Tso-Ban, who was no longer monitoring.) But this seemed substantially safer. It could not be extrapolated by their ex-pursuer, if in fact they'd rid themselves of him, and it was consistent with mission orders as drafted by the sultan, which included the line "with due regard to a successful return."

Of course, they had no locational objective anyway.

_____

hyperspace" (more properly in separate hyperspaces) can communicate with each other by simple radio, with the transmission times a complex function of their "hyperspace positions" relative to each other.

   Suffice it to be aware that a ship in hyperspace can stop abruptly or turn without inertial effects, though guaged within the specific hyperspace field, inertia is normal.

Nineteen

Rifles slung, A Company double-timed down the road, carrying the almost ever-present and now even heavier sandbags. They trotted through a cloud of fog—their breath—and nine inches of new snow. It was the coldest day they'd seen here, for some the coldest they'd ever seen.

Still, the gills of their winter field uniforms were open, the earlaps of their helmet liners were tucked up, and some had stuffed their finger mittens into their waist pockets. Standing in ranks that morning, they'd felt glum about the subzero cold, but exertion had soon warmed them.

"How cold d'you think it is, Carrmak?" Jerym asked.

"Ask Bahn. Maybe he's heard."

"Bahn," someone else called, "how cold is it?"

"It is exactly as cold as it is," Bahn answered cheerfully. There were groans.

"I think my nostrils may have frozen," Markooris called out. "They feel funny."

"That feeling in your nostrils is the hairs." Bahn said it without puffing. "When it is cold enough, the moisture on them freezes and they stiffen, tugging on the membrane."

"Where did you learn that?" Jerym asked. "Not on Oven, I'll bet."

"On Hemblin's World we fought in very cold conditions. And I never heard of anyone's nostrils freezing, although all of us froze the outside of our noses."

"Does it hurt? To freeze your nose?" someone asked.

"You do not even notice when your nose freezes. The ears though, and fingers and toes, you definitely notice."

"How do you know when it happens then?"

"Others tell you. It is visible; your nose turns gray. After it thaws, the skin splits, and a scab forms."

Lieutenant Toma, who was leading A Company this morning, speeded the pace a little, as if to say that having breath enough to talk so much, they had breath enough to trot faster.

Jerym thought of the T'swa, from such a hot world, having to fight in polarlike weather. He couldn't imagine them complaining though. Which made him think of Mellis, who complained a lot. Mellis wasn't with them today; he was getting interviewed—one of the last in the platoon. Maybe now he wouldn't hassle people to tell him what went on there. Some of the guys had been interviewed twice already—Romlar for example, and himself—and Esenrok was having his second this morning.

He wondered if Mellis would still be a whiner when he came out. Interviews changed you. You could feel it in yourself and see it in other guys. In Romlar more than any of them. Romlar still seemed a little stupid— that hadn't much changed—but he was cheerful now, talked more, seemed less introverted. He even talked differently—more grammatically.

Ahead someone farted, loud and long, to a mixture of groans and laughter. "Bressnik!" someone yelled, "back to the end of the line with you!" "Gentle Tunis," said someone else, "it's making my eyes water! They'll freeze on a morning like this!"

First Platoon turned off on a side road. After half a mile more, Sergeant Dao led 2nd Platoon off on another, a road Jerym was sure they'd never been on before. It crossed an easy hill, then sloped gradually down until, after a mile or so, it ended in a small opening, where they halted. Around the opening was sparsely wooded swamp, dense with underbrush.

Dao ordered them at ease, and they all stopped talking. "Now," he said, "you will apply your lessons in reading maps and compasses, to find your way over unfamiliar ground. You will travel by fire teams. Your squad sergeants will give each team a map. A course is marked on it, with bearings you will follow. Each course has five or six legs. All but the last leg end at a marked and numbered point where you will find an instruction to follow. The last leg will end at a point on a road, where you will be picked up and transported by vehicle to the compound for dinner. Do not be late, or you will go hungry."

Their squad sergeants took command then, instructing. Each man was to be the compassman on at least one leg. Then they left, group by group on different bearings, disappearing into the thick brush. There were only four in Jerym's team; Esenrok was getting interviewed that morning. As team leader, Carrmak led the first leg.

The damn brush was not only thick; it was about seven or eight feet tall and loaded with snow. But in the subzero cold, it didn't melt on your clothes, didn't even stick on them. Jerym quickly discovered why the trees were so sparse: A forest fire had killed most of the old stand, and in time most of the killed trees had fallen over, lying at different angles to the ground. Their snow-covered trunks had to be climbed over, crawled under, or bypassed, their uptilted root disks gone around. Jerym couldn't see more than fifty feet through it, which was about as far as they got before Carrmak called a halt.

"I need something or someone to guide on." He pointed. "Alsnor, you'll be the next compassman, and the next compassman will always be the guide-on." He pointed. "Go through there till I tell you to stop."

Jerym went, wearing his mittens now, parting the snowy brush with them, until Carrmak called for him to halt. He did, turning to look back. Carrmak was peering down the compass sight. "A couple steps that way," Carrmak said gesturing. "There! Right on!" Then he came with the others to where Jerym stood. "Tunis!" Jerym swore. "This is slow going! I hope this course isn't very long, or we won't get anything to eat."

Carrmak shrugged. "Takes as long as it takes," he muttered, raising the compass. "And according to the map, the legs are only a quarter to a half mile long." He pointed. "Through there," he said, "and this time I'm not going to do any yelling. We'll do it right—pretend we're sneaking through enemy territory. So go about fifty, sixty feet and stop. If you can't see me then, backtrack till you can."

Thinking that if the T'swa wanted them to keep quiet, they'd have said so, Jerym led off again. And again. It was tricky climbing over blowdowns with a bag of sand on his back; it kept overbalancing him, wanting to dump him on his face.

It was a slow quarter mile before they hit the first check point, hit it right on—a post with a small, snowcapped box, and a small sign hung on it. Carrmak read the instructions aloud and took a coded tag from the box, evidence that they'd found the checkpoint. Then they went on, Jerym with the compass now, and Romlar as his guide-on. He almost missed the next checkpoint; they were only about fifteen feet off line, but on the wrong side of an uptilted root disk. It was Romlar that spotted it.

Romlar turned out more than just lucky, Jerym decided. He turned out weird! It was his turn next as

compassman. And instead of sending Markooris out as
guide-on, Romlar flicked a glance at the compass, shoved
it in a pocket, and bulled off through the brush. He
couldn't possibly have picked out a useable mark to go
to. Jerym looked at Carrmak, who opened his mouth to
call to Romlar, then changed his mind and followed
him. Romlar never slowed, never took the compass out
of his pocket, just kept going.

Halfway through his leg, which was a somewhat longer
one, they came out of the swamp, the brush now replaced by sapling growth. The saplings weren't *that*
thick, and they were vertical, not a tangle, while here
the fire-killed older trees were mostly still standing. So
the visibility was better and the walking easier; Romlar
speeded almost to a jog. And hit his checkpoint dead
on, grinning, pleased with himself. It was at the margin
of unburned forest, into which they could see a lot
farther. So Markooris didn't need a guide-on, either,
though he used his compass. Here there was always a
visible tree on line ahead, or near enough on line to
correct course by eyeball.

Each time Markooris took his next shot, they'd jog to
the guide-on he'd chosen, usually a hundred feet or
more. It was a half mile leg, and at the check point they
found a snow-covered stack of slender logs—big posts,
really, nine or ten feet long and about eight inches
thick—roughly 120 to 150 pounds each. The instructions said each man was to carry one of these logs to the
final checkpoint. Added to sixty pounds of sand, that
was a lot.

This was the kind of difficulty most trainees enjoyed
best, even reveled in. They tipped the logs up, Carrmak
helping the others get theirs balanced on the shoulder
which didn't have the rifle slung on it. Then he shoul-
dered his own. This last leg was Carrmak's again. They
lumbered off with their burdens, Carrmak pausing as
infrequently and briefly as possible for compass shots.
At each pause, each trainee lowered one end of his log

to the ground, resting for a few seconds while Carrmak found another guide-on.

Before long they came out of the woods into a meadow, and saw the final post eighty yards ahead, with a T'swi waiting nearby on the road. Carrmak began to run with his cumbersome burden, the others galloping after. Jerym almost whooped, then remembered Carrmak's injunction against noise. When they reached the post and the grinning Sergeant Bahn, they let the logs roll off their now-sore shoulders, panting, sweating copiously. Breath and sweat had frozen crusty on their eyebrows, collars, and the rim of their helmets.

"I radioed when I saw you coming," Bahn said. "A bus will be here soon."

They stood waiting in the cold sunlight, and for a minute or so, no one spoke. Then Carrmak said to Bahn, "If you T'swa had to go from there to here, through all that brush, and you'd never been here before, how would you do it?"

Bahn's eyebrows rose. "We would walk or run. As you did."

"Would you use the compass?"

"If necessary."

Carrmak looked intently at the sergeant. " 'If necessary' isn't the kind of answer I'm looking for. *Would* you use the compass?"

Bahn smiled slightly. "No, we would not. We would simply—go from there to here. Walking or running."

Carrmak thumbed toward Romlar. "That's what he did, on his stretch: just barrelled off through the brush. I thought you ought to know he can do that."

Jerym looked at Romlar, whose face was flushed but grinning.

Then the bus came and picked them up. After awhile it had a load of guys and took them back to the compound.

Jerym made a point of walking with Carrmak from the barracks to the messhall. "What in Tunis's name," he asked, "made you ask Bahn how they'd have done that course?"

"Read Lormagen's book on the T'swa," Carrmak answered, "or just look at his cubes. On Kettle, the army set the T'swa down in the jungle, jungle they'd never seen before. And there weren't any maps or roads or anything. But the T'swa ran around all over the place, zigzagging and circling, hunting Birds and fighting them, and always got back to their rendezvous, their rally point. Never got lost. When Romlar started off like he did, I was going to stop him, but then I thought, no, I'll let him go. If the T'swa can do it, then probably some other people can too. Let him try."

"But if he'd gotten us lost," Jerym objected, "we would've missed dinner."

"Big deal. We've learned something—that Romlar can do it. And now the T'swa know. And Romlar feels good, the kind of feeling good that'll stay with him."

Jerym nodded silently. He'd learned something just now, too: A way of looking at things, of considering importances. And a little more about the kind of guy that Carrmak was.

Second Platoon's noncoms had their own table. It was round, but wherever Dao sat was the head. Bahn sat down next to him and mentioned what Romlar had done. When Dao had finished eating, he went to the officers' table and told Lieutenant Dzo-Tar, while Captain Gotasu listened. From the A Company orderly room, Captain Gotasu phoned Colonel Dak-So, who told Colonel Voker, who phoned the civilian in charge of scheduling interviews. All in all it was no big deal, but it was the sort of thing they were watching for, expecting to see from some of their intentive warriors.

When the company fell in for its afternoon training, Dao ordered Romlar to stay at the barracks. Someone would come to take him to an interview.

Twenty

Romlar settled himself on the chair, glad it was the red-headed girl again who would interview him. He suspected that was how they did things—always gave you the same interviewer. And he didn't think of her as "just a girl" any more.

"Cold out there," she said, glancing up as she arranged her notebook. "Did you train outdoors this morning?"

"Yep."

"What did you do?"

Grinning he told her, including how he'd done his leg of the course. Mentally, psychically, he was far lighter than when she'd first seen him, much happier, far more confident.

She grinned back at him. "Marvelous," she said. "I love it!" Then she moved to another subject. "We got a lot taken care of in our first two sessions. Now at the end of our last one, I asked if you still thought of yourself as stupid. And you said—" She paused as if inviting him to finish for her.

"I said yeah, I guess I was, but it didn't bother me anymore."

"Right. How do you feel about that now?"

"The same. I know I'm not as smart as most of the other guys, but that's all right. I'm me. I do some things better than most of them."

"Good. So tell me a use for stupidity."

"Huh! Well— I can't think of any."

"Okay. Then imagine a use for stupidity."

"Imagine? Well, uhh— If you're stupid, you don't get asked to do some stuff."

"All right. Now give me something more specific than that."

"Uhh . . . Well— People don't ask you to figure stuff out. They know you can't do it very good."

"Good. Tell me something else you don't get asked to do if you're stupid."

"You— You don't get asked to do some things that are really important."

"Okay. Another."

"You don't . . ." He stopped, eyes suddenly blank, face expressionless, mouth slightly open, and sat like that for a long minute.

"Um-hm?" she nudged.

He'd begun visibly to sweat. "You don't get asked— You don't get asked to decide things that other people's lives depend on." He'd said it in an undertone, little more than a whisper.

"All right," she replied calmly. "What else don't you get asked to do?"

For a moment he trembled, vibrated might be a better word, then began to jerk, then rock back and forth, rotating from the hips in utter silence. She watched him quietly for a minute, not nudging him with what she saw. Instead she simply repeated the question: "What else don't you get asked to do?"

He croaked the words: "To lead."

And with that her serious work began. Per instructions, ordinarily she tried to keep sessions to about an hour, two at most. This time it took nearly three before she had him through all of it, alert again and in good spirits. Actually very good spirits. And ravenous! She wrote him a chit to give to the cook at the project's small dining room; the snack room wouldn't be adequate to his needs. After that he went to one of the nap rooms and slept for more than an hour, dreaming swift eventful dreams he couldn't afterward remember.

After the session, Lotta Alsnor went to a small office at the end of the hall, and knocked.

"Who is it?"

"Lotta."

Wellem Bosler was in charge of the project. Because of the shortage of fully qualified people, he'd selected the best of his advanced students, his and others', and had coached them intensively for a week before bringing them here. And because their experience was limited and some of the cases promised to be especially demanding, he'd come with them to supervise, and to bail them out when necessary. One of the things he did was call up and look over each session record before any further session was scheduled with that particular case. So far everything had gone remarkably well, and his operators had quickly gained confidence in their ability to do the job here.

Lotta was the second youngest, and the most gifted if not the most skilled.

"Come in, Lotta," Bosler said.

She did. "Wellem," she said, "I'd like you to check out the session I just gave Artus Romlar."

He called it up, and his eyebrows raised as he scanned. When he'd finished, he looked up at her with a grin. "Marvelous, Lotta. I'm proud of you. Talk about the unanticipated! If I'd had any misgivings about your readiness for this job, and I didn't, this would lay them to rest." He paused then before adding, "You need to get him back after supper, you know."

She nodded. "I thought—you might take him after supper. I'm afraid I might get in over my head."

"Ah. But I want *you* to take him, and if you do get in over your head, *then* I'll take over. Okay?"

She nodded. "If you think it's safe for him that way."

Wellem Bosler grinned. "Even if you screw up to the maximum, we'll have him in good shape before morning."

Then he outlined briefly the approach he wanted her to use.

Twenty-One

Wellem Bosler's office was tiny but adequate. Much of its space was occupied by a work table on which sat a computer, the repository of session reports. With Voker and Dak-So there, seated on folding chairs, the room was crowded.

"So you've got a preliminary evaluation for us," Voker said.

"And a very positive one." Bosler paused to sip carefully the scalding joma that one of his runners had brought for the meeting. Usually he was too busy, too preoccupied, to have joma, or to remember to drink it when he had it.

"We're getting very good results, even though my team is green. Or was green. By working with one platoon at a time, and by starting with its dominant trainee and the people closest to him, we're largely avoiding the problems of the individual's barracks mates getting on his case before he stabilizes. For a day or so after a session, and particularly during the first few hours, the individual is susceptible to being sharply introverted and invalidating what happened to him."

He grinned. "It's a little like a new painting: You need to let the paint cure before you handle it much. Then, once a person's stabilized, he's pretty much immune to self-doubts. The nap helps with that, the nap and the dreams."

"Will they know the T'sel when you've finished with them?" Voker asked. "Or is this treatment too abbreviated?"

"Let's just say they're more sane, and stably sane, than the great majority of humankind. That's the bottom-line result; a regiment of sane warriors. Some will know the T'sel. All will have considerable T'sel wisdom,* and this will increase bit by bit after we're done with them. They'll cognite on things, and grow, in the process of living."

His eyes shifted to Dak-So. "As for the ancillary abilities that are general among your own warriors— useful degrees of psychic awareness, like the ability to orienteer without a compass, that sort of thing—they've already begun to crop up. I don't know how frequent they'll be. Don't look for them to be general though. Just take what develops."

"When do you expect to finish here?" Voker asked. "Or is it too soon to predict?"

"In about a dek and a half. It depends somewhat on how well the two new teams do; they'll carry out their first sessions here this afternoon. I didn't train them— one team's from the school at Kromby Bay and the other's from Ernoman—but I know the people who did train them; know them well. I anticipate that they'll do as well as my team. Six to eight more weeks should finish our work here."

"Ah." Dak-So turned to Voker. "I would like your decision on whether to train our young warriors in jokanru, and if so, when. I have had thoughts on the matter."

---

*Wisdom, as defined by T'sel masters, is appropriate action, and knowledge of appropriate action.

"Let's hear them." Voker looked at Bosler. "We'll take our discussion somewhere else—get out of your way."

"Fine. Today's interview reports won't start coming in for another hour, but I need to review administrative procedures with the new teams."

The two officers left, talking as they walked down the corridor. "Are you satisfied with the kind of results Wellem described?" Voker asked.

Dak-So nodded. "Yes. They're not what we might prefer, but combined with their warrior intentions and their young strength and level of training, they will be superior to any troops I foresee them facing, given comparable equipment. Unless of course, as mercenaries they face my people."

"Good," said Voker. Apparently the Klestroni were going to miss Confederation space after all, but presumably someday they would meet. Then there'd be the matter of equipment. T'swa seers had assured the Crown that the Karghanik level of military technology was not inordinately superior to their own, for planetary warfare. In fact, the empire had stagnated technologically, not as badly as the Confederation had under the Sacrament, but badly nonetheless.

As for Iryalan regiments fighting T'swa regiments, that could be addressed in contracts or treaties—Kristal would work it out.

"Okay," Voker said. "Let's hear your plans."

"I have prepared a limited menu of close combat skills and drills," Dak-So said, "that young men like these can master quickly at an effective level. They do not constitute jokanru, but they are based on it. They emphasize aggressiveness and force, with less reliance on refined technique. The practitioner would be no match for someone trained in jokanru, someone reasonably well conditioned. But with their strong, flexible, gymnast bodies, these young warriors would quickly destroy ordinary soldiers in unarmed combat.

"And jokanru is less a combat tool than a matter of

developing the complete warrior, mentally and spirtually as well as physically. The time required for it would be difficult to justify, when we have only three years to complete their training.

"What I propose can be completed in far far less time than full training in jokanru. I recommend we train the entire regiment simultaneously, during mud season. By then the trainees will have completed their basic training in other skills, and also the Ostrak operators will be done with them, even if they progress more slowly than Wellem envisions. Further, the more advanced gymnastics training they'll have had by then will have increased their flexibility."

Voker nodded. "Not to mention their strength. And frankly, what you've described is the sort of thing I'd envisioned for them anyway. How long will this training take?"

"I foresee three weeks of very intensive full-time training. If necessary, we can add a week to it. Then, when they're done, we'll begin their training in battalion and regimental actions."

"Fine," Voker said. "That'll give us time to get the necessary equipment made: bags, dummies, whatever. I want a list as soon as possible."

By that time they were standing at Dak-So's office door. "Can I see what techniques you have in mind for them?" Voker asked.

"Of course. I made photocopies."

They went in. A minute later Voker came out, examining a thin sheaf of papers, nodding as he scanned. These kids would love it. They were going to be a hell of a regiment.

Twenty-Two

The evening of Winter Solstice was clear and still, moonless and moderately cold, but inside the main building were warmth, light, and noise. Most of the benches had been removed from the big assembly hall, stacked in an adjacent storeroom. Scattered tables, surrounded by slowly eddying trainees and T'swa, held food in quantity, delicacies, mostly prepared by the regiment's cooks but partly flown in. Here and there, mingling with the military, were young civilians about the age of the trainees—the Ostrak people—and army personnel on detached service there.

"You were right," Esenrok was saying to Jerym. "No liquor. I suppose they were worried about the guys that haven't been defused yet, getting drunk."

Jerym chuckled. "I'm pretty sure they weren't worried about the T'swa. I wonder what a T'swa would be like, drunk."

"Huh! I can't imagine one ever getting that way. But if one did, I suppose he'd be as mild as if he were sober. Just not as well coordinated."

"Yeah, I expect you're . . ." Jerym stopped. A slim,

141

red-haired girl had walked up to him on his right,
looking at him; he turned and stared.

"Lotta!"

"Hello, Jerym. You've changed. And grown."

He reached out unbelievingly, and they held each
others' hands between them. "It's been a year last
Harvest Festival," he said. Then, "What are you doing
here?"

"I'm an interviewer."

"An inter. . . . You must be one of the new ones."

"Nope. I've been here for three weeks, working seven
days a week from eight in the morning till 21 or 2200 in
the evening—more than half around the clock. Otherwise I'd have looked you up."

He stared, then recovered and turned to Esenrok,
who stood watching and curious. "Esenrok, this is my
sister, Lotta. She's— Well, you know as much about
that as I do. Lotta, this is a buddy of mine, Esenrok.
Eldren Esenrok, isn't it?"

"You've got it." The blond trainee and the red-haired
girl saluted each other formally, but grinning, hands
raised to the sides, shoulders high, palms forward. "Jerym
never told me he had a good-looking sister."

"I do though," Jerym said. "And right now I've got
first claim on her time. We've got some catching up to
do."

Esenrok shook his head. "And I thought we were
friends. Ah well. Glad to meet you, Lotta."

Jerym led her away toward a bench that had been
left down, then spotted someone and steered her off in
that direction. "There's someone else I want you to
meet," he murmured to her. "I showed him one of your
letters, and he said he wanted to write to you. But he
never did. Too shy."

Romlar's back was to them. He turned at Jerym's
touch. "Hi, Alsnor. Oh! Hi, Lotta! I see you found
him."

"Hi, Artus. Yes, he brought me over to introduce
us."

Jerym's jaw had dropped, then he turned to Lotta. "You interviewed Romlar?"

"That's right. We're good friends."

Jerym looked from one to the other. "Well, then, let's you and I go sit somewhere and talk. You two have had hours to talk lately!"

"Go ahead," Romlar said. "But, Lotta, when you're done, I want a chance to ask *you* some questions. So far it's been all one way."

"Sure," she said, then left with her brother, stepping into the corridor to escape interruptions.

"I guess you know Medreth," Jerym said. "My interviewer."

"Medreth was yours? We've been at Lake Loreen together since she was eight and I was six."

"You guys don't—" Jerym's grin was lopsided. "No, I guess you wouldn't. Share confidences about interviews."

Lotta laughed. "Wellem would skin us alive if we did. No, it's never done."

"When you're at home, why haven't you ever done for Mom and Dad what you guys have done for us?"

Her eyebrows rose. "Consider the questions," she said, "the kinds of questions we ask, the things we ask you to do. Can you picture Dad or Mom sitting still for them? Especially from one of their kids!"

He laughed, imagining.

"Actually I have done some," she said, "in a sneaky way. Nothing ambitious, nothing formal, but it helps."

They talked, about home, parents, life in the regiment, for about twenty minutes before Voker's voice overrode the lively hubub of hundreds of conversations. *"At ease, men! At ease!"* The noise level dropped abruptly. *"At ease and face the podium!"*

The brother and sister stepped inside to watch and listen. Then His Majesty, Marcus XXVIII, strode out from the wings without the customary fanfare and attendants, a tall, lean, vigorous man of sixty-seven in a white dress uniform. The final murmurs of conversation stilled instantly. The trainees hardly noticed the man a step behind His Majesty on his right.

The king stopped just back from the podium's front edge and looked the silent audience over. "Good evening, gentlemen!" he boomed, without electronic augmentation, and they responded instantly, almost in unison, as if drilled in it.

"Good evening, Your Majesty!"

He waited three or four seconds, then continued. "I had several other invitations for this evening. The most tempting was to spend it with my grandchildren. But I understand you don't have too many evenings off, so I decided to take this opportunity to see you instead."

There were a few tentative hurrahs that grew into somewhat ragged, audience-wide cheering. The trainees were in a state of low-grade shock.

"You men, you trainees, are a first in the Confederation—a regiment of warriors. You will not be the last such regiment, but you are the trailbreakers. It has not been easy for you, in more ways than one, but you are proceeding very well, and as you continue, you will do better and better."

He paused, once more scanned them deliberately, then boomed again: "What do you think of your T'swa cadre?"

The question released them from their awed bemusement, and they began cheering at the top of their lungs, the cheer shifting gradually to a chant of "T'swa, T'swa, T'swa!" This went on for the better part of a minute, until Voker's voice came over the loudspeakers: "That's it, men. At ease." The chant stumbled and stopped. "Thank you," Voker said.

"And now—" His Majesty went on, "now I want to introduce someone to you—the man who first proposed we form such a regiment." He half-turned to the man who'd followed him onto the podium, and gestured at him with a white-gloved hand. "The man who told people what the T'swa truly were like, the man who was called 'the White T'swi,' Sir Varlik Lormagen."

Again the crowd erupted with sound as a grinning Lormagen stepped up beside the king. After half a minute, Lormagen raised his hands overhead, so that the cheers faded. He too was a man in his sixties, taller than average and husky, recognizably the same man they'd seen on the old cubes from the Kettle War. When they were quiet enough, Lormagen spoke, using a microphone clipped to his collar.

"I want to tell you just one thing," he said. "I'm proud of you, every last one of you."

Again they cheered. Voker might have interrupted them, but the king looked toward him as if anticipating that, and still grinning, shook his head, then waved to his audience and left the podium with Lormagen. Cheers followed them into the wings and out of sight.

After that the crowd began to eddy again around the tables, bemused at first. But soon their conversations were even livelier than before.

When the cheering was over, Pitter Mellis worked his way to a door and walked down the corridor to a latrine. It was crowded, the commodes occupied, the urinal lined with men, with others waiting. He turned and left, going to an exit and out into the cold. It was only 200 yards to the barracks; jogging would be better than waiting.

No one was at the barracks when he got there, and he went quickly to the latrine, seating himself on a commode. After a minute he heard the barracks door open, heard footsteps coming his way, several sets of them. Others, he thought, had gotten the same idea he had.

But the men that peered in at him were strangers.

"What are you guys doing in this barracks?" he demanded.

They looked at Mellis, then at each other, and came into the latrine, two, and then four more. When he started to get up, reaching to pull up his pants, they rushed him, grabbed him. He opened his mouth to yell, and a hard blow to the gut drove the wind out of him. One arm was free, and he swung it wildly, cursing. Someone hit him hard on the nose, breaking it, another slugged him in the kidneys. His head snapped back at that, so that a blow at his chin struck his throat instead. Then, pants around his ankles, he was dragged bleeding and choking through the barracks. At the door their leader stopped them, measured his victim and hit him a heavy blow to the point of the chin, slamming Mellis backward off the stoop, unconscious. They left him lying there in the snow.

After the king had left the podium and the cheering had stopped, Lotta promised Jerym to see him again when she had a chance, and began to circulate, talking with other trainees. Jerym headed for a table, where he put hors' d'oeu'vres of several kinds on a plate. A moment later he spotted Romlar again and worked his way to him.

"So you know my sister."

"Yep."

"How'd you know she was my sister? By the name?"

"I didn't know her last name. At first, to me, she was just a girl named Lotta. But the last interview I got, it came to me: 'This is the Lotta that's Alsnor's sister.' So I asked her, and she said she was.

"But she asked me not to say anything. She said she'd surprise you at Solstice.

"You know," he added, "the King made us out pretty special, and maybe we are. But without the T'swa training us, we'd be nothing, and what those interviewers are doing is as important to this regiment as the T'swa are. We need the training, but we need the Ostrak Project just as much."

Jerym nodded, thinking that the changes in Romlar might be bigger than anyone else's in the platoon. And Lotta had been Romlar's interviewer.

*　　*　　*

Esenrok, with one of the hot, non-alcoholic drinks in his hand, saw Sergeant Dao standing beside the main entrance to the assembly hall, and went over to him. "What do you think of that?" Esenrok said. "The king came to see us." He peered at the big black man curiously. "Does the king know the T'sel, do you suppose?"

"I have heard that he does. And perceiving him as I did, I am sure of it."

Perceiving him as you did. Esenrok wondered what the T'swa might perceive that he didn't. "How old are you T'swa when you get the Ostrak Procedures?"

"We do not get the Ostrak Procedures. They are something originated on Iryala, I believe, for persons who did not grow up with the T'sel in a T'sel environment." He gazed at Esenrok for a moment before continuing. "It was a man named Ostrak who brought knowledge of the T'sel to Iryala, you know."

Esenrok hadn't known, and it occurred to him to wonder why. He was about to ask Dao—the sergeant knew so much else, he might know the answer to that too—when a hoarse croak interrupted them from behind, from the door they stood beside. He turned and stared; Dao reached and grabbed the form there as it teetered.

"Mellis!" Esenrok said, staring. "What in Tunis happened to you?" Mellis's cheeks, nose, and ears were waxy gray from frostbite. Blood smeared his lower face and shirt, frozen blood granulated with snow.

Others nearby, having heard Esenrok's exclamation, were turning to look.

"They trashed the barracks." Mellis barely mumbled it; his jaw didn't move.

"Bahn!" Dao bellowed. "Here!"

The crowd nearby began to form a vortex through which Bahn pushed from not far off. "Take Mellis to the infirmary," Dao called to him, then started off himself with Esenrok at his heels. A few others followed till Dao told them to go back.

The barracks was a mess. Mattresses and bedding were on the floor, slashed and torn. In the latrine, washrags had been flushed, and the overflowing commodes had flooded the place. Windows had been broken. Glow panels, dislodged from the ceiling, lay trampled and bent. Esenrok felt rage begin to swell, then saw Dao's calm, and felt the rage ebb.

First Platoon, occurred to Esenrok; it was the 1st on whose barracks he'd led the raid that first night. But he rejected the thought immediately. First platoon had been interviewed too, most or all of it; it wouldn't have been them.

These thoughts flashed while he followed Dao, striding back through the barracks and onto the stoop, where the big T'swi looked around. The latest snow had been a week earlier, and was trampled beyond tracking. Beside the stoop, it was stained red where Mellis had lain bleeding. Dao stood unmoving for a moment, frowning, lips pursed, then started for the main building at a lope, Esenrok close behind.

Within five minutes, groups of T'swa were fanning through the compound. Two barracks and several T'swa cabins had been vandalized. Six men were busy vandalizing another barracks. They'd left two sentries outside. These yelled, then fled at the T'swa's approach. Two T'swa peeled off in pursuit, and surprisingly ran them down.

The culprits were manhandled off to the main building, into the assembly hall, and up front. The regiment had been formed up as units, and stood waiting. The Ostrak teams and army service personnel stood curious in the rear of the room. Voker and Dak-So stood at the front of the podium, with the king and Lormagen to one side, observing, faces unreadable.

Mounting the podium, Dao reported quietly to Voker and Dak-So. Bahn had already reported on Mellis's condition: A broken nose, bruised larynx, dislocated jaw, concussion, frostbite. And hypothermia; it was surprising and fortunate that he'd regained consciousness.

Voker questioned the six captives then. They denied knowing anything about Mellis. While they were denying it, some T'swa frog-marched four more captives in. Sergeant Major Kuto informed Voker that all ten were from 3rd Platoon, F Company. And that only four regimental personnel remained unaccounted for, also from 3rd Platoon, F Company. He'd hardly said it when two more culprits were brought in, one unconscious across a T'swa shoulder.

Voker gazed coldly down at the second group of captives. "Trainee Mellis is in the infirmary," he said, "with multiple injuries, hypothermia, and frost bite. Who did it?"

One of the second group straightened and looked up at the colonel with glittering eyes. "Sir, we did! We couldn't let him spread an alarm."

Voker's gaze turned thoughtful. "I see. What is your name?"

"Trainee Jillard Brossling, sir!"

"Brossling." Voker seemed to taste the name. "And why did you vandalize barracks, Brossling?"

"Sir! This was our opportunity. Everyone—almost everyone—was here in the main building."

"Ah. And why did you wish to vandalize barracks at all?"

"Sir! It was something warriorlike to do. And we chose platoons the T'swa favored—their pet dog platoons!"

"Mmm." Voker turned to Sergeant Major Kuto. "Sergeant major," he said mildly, "have the criminals, under T'swa guard, erect a squad tent to live in. Have them do it barefoot, so they won't take too long. The rest of 3rd Platoon, F Company, will erect a barbed wire enclosure on X-posts around the tent. When the tent has been erected, the criminals will be given their boots and sleeping bags and will sleep in the tent on the ground, manacled. The rest of 3rd Platoon, F Company, will stand sentry shifts around the fence. Between sentry shifts, the remaining members of 3rd Platoon will also repair and clean up the vandalized huts and barracks tonight. The building engineers will supervise the work and see that 3rd Platoon has the materials for the job.

"The platoons which were vandalized will occupy 3rd Platoon's barracks tonight, and the overflow will move into other F Company barracks. While there, they will carefully abstain from doing any damage whatever."

He turned his gaze back to the culprits. "We'll decide in the morning what to do with you. But know now that you will be required to make up the damage, make heavy amends, and petition the rest of the regiment to be accepted back into it when the amends have been satisfactorily completed. You are responsible for what you did, and it is a responsibility you cannot avoid. If we send you to Ballibud, it will not be before you have met that responsibility."

Twenty-Three

All his adult life, Wellem Bosler had made a point of getting enough exercise to keep his body functioning well. Here, for several weeks, he'd let it slip. Now he'd begun jogging and walking about the compound in the dark of pre-dawn morning. Sometimes it was snowing; more often the sky was clear, starlit, and cold.

The detention section—sixteen youths from 3rd Platoon, F Company—had been digging on the intended swimming pool at night, breaking the hard-frozen earth with sledge hammers and long-handled chisels, throwing the larger chunks out by hand, the smaller with shovels. But they'd be sleeping exhausted in their squad tent, their jail—*tronk* was their slang for it—well before he came out.

Not much, good or bad, surprised him about human beings, but the tenacity and morale of the detention section had. They trained hard all day, then dug till past midnight, yet the few times he'd made a point of strolling out to watch them dig, before he retired in the evening, they seemed to be in good spirits, vying to see what pair could move the most dirt.

151

Third Platoon, F Company, had been the most aberrated in the regiment, the result of two dominant individuals who were reasoning psychotics. Second and 3rd Squads were the most aberrated in the platoon. Third would be the last platoon to undergo the Ostrak Procedures, and the fourteen men in the detention section, all from 2nd and 3rd Squads, would be the last individuals.

Yet Voker had left Brossling with them—Brossling, their ringleader and chief troublemaker. The wise, tough old ex-soldier and the tough but crazy intentive warrior, had come to an understanding: Brossling would ramrod the amends project and maintain discipline, and Voker would grant them the privilege of not having a pair of T'swa corporals bossing the job, would let them do it on their own.

Usually, when T'swa whistles rousted the trainees out of bed, Bosler jogged back to the Main Building for a hot shower and breakfast. This morning though, he stopped to watch, from a little distance, one of the platoons go through reveille, heard its squad sergeants reporting in their mellow T'swa voices. And recognized one of the trainees, even at forty yards in the predawn: Artus Romlar. Bosler himself had done the last two interviews on Romlar; the procedures needed were beyond Lotta's training and experience.

That had been a week earlier. Romlar needed a few weeks to settle out before they did anything further with him. Then perhaps . . . Bosler turned and jogged toward the Main Building. Romlar had received three times the attention of any other trainee, but he had a potential unique in the regiment. He'd been born to a particular role, one they understood only vaguely. Which didn't necessarily mean he'd get to play it, or that he'd succeed if he did.

The trainees had eaten dinner—the midday meal— and had a half hour to loaf around before forming up for training. Jerym lay on his bunk, booted feet on the floor, looking at his hands. Before signing up, he'd never even seen hands like them, their palms and fingers callused like boot leather, with hard ridges and pads on the pressure points.

"I never thought I'd be doing what I did this morning," he said, to no one in particular.

"You mean giant swings?" Esenrok asked. "I knew you were ready. What impressed me was Romlar doing 'em. Remember when he was 'fat boy?' Less than four deks ago, for Tunis' sake!"

Romlar had entered the barracks just in time to hear Esenrok's comment, and paused to raise the foot of Esenrok's bunk with one big paw, lifting it chest high, Esenrok on it, before setting it gently back down.

Jerym had watched the little interplay. He really didn't feel that much changed himself, but Esenrok and Romlar now . . . Romlar especially; he still didn't say a lot, but somehow or other he was definitely no longer stupid.

He explored his calluses with a finger, remembering the hard T'swa palm that had hauled him onto the straggler truck, that first, late summer night when he'd fallen out on the run. Give him another dek or so and he'd be able to juggle hot coals.

Giant swings for Tunis' sake!

At 2000 hours, Artus Romlar stopped at the Charge of Quarters desk in the Main Building. CQ was an Iryalan soldier on detached service, good at obeying orders and not bad at thinking for himself.

"What's your purpose here?" the man asked. Seated as he was, Romlar loomed above him, not threatening but impressive, almost T'swa-like in his size, his physical hardness, his sense of calm strength.

"I've come to see the civilian interviewer, Lotta Alsnor."

The CQ touched keys at his console, his eyes on the display. "Do you have an appointment?"

"No. She'll see me."

The soldier, a buck sergeant, looked Romlar over.

"What's your name?" he asked, and Romlar told him.
For brief seconds the sergeant hesitated. He knew how
little free time these project people had, and this request was irregular. But then somehow he shrugged,
and keyed the console again. The button in his right ear
told him her room comm was buzzing. After three or
four seconds he spoke to his collar mike. "Lotta Alsnor?
This is Charge of Quarters. There's a trainee Romlar
here to speak with you. Do you want to see him?"

After a few seconds he touched a couple of keys,
looking up at Romlar again. "She'll be down," he said,
and gestured with his head. "Have a seat over there."

Romlar did. A few minutes later Lotta came down
the stairs, wearing coat, mittens, and fur cap. Romlar
got up and met her at the door.

"This is a surprise," she said as they stepped out into
the cold.

"I didn't know whether it would be or not. The way
you looked into my mind in interviews."

She grinned. "Those were special situations. A special environment, and the stuff I was helping you pull
out to look at was pretty powerful, easy to see."

They began to walk, nowhere in particular, beneath
bare shade trees, stars glinting through the branches.
"What brought you over?" she asked.

"I wanted to say goodbye. Now, when we had an
evening without training."

"Goodbye?"

"Yes. You're leaving, you know. Within the next day
or two. Maybe three or four."

She didn't ask how he knew. "For where?"

He shrugged big shoulders. "That's not part of it—
part of what I know. Where you came here from, I
suppose. Lake Loreen, you said at Solstice."

A move was news to her—they were extremely busy
here—but she didn't challenge him. If he was wrong, it
didn't matter. If he was right . . . He might be; she
wouldn't be astonished at it. "It was nice of you to want
to tell me goodbye," she said.

He grinned, shrugged. "I'm not sure why I did, really." His tone changed then, became softer. "That's not true. It's because I've got a crush on you. I suppose everyone does that you interview. And I wanted you to know how I feel.

"When you've gone, you're not likely to be coming back, and next fall we're supposed to go to Terfreya for a year, and then to Tyss for another one." He chuckled. "That'll be something, training on Tyss. No frostbite there! Tomorrow we'll be out in twenty inches of snow and probably below zero, with explosives and fire jets, learning how to clear fortifications.

"From Tyss I'll go somewhere to fight, to some trade world or gook world." Again he chuckled. "And never see you again. It's the sort of thing that, on the cube, they'd make out to be sad, and me heartbroken. But somehow or other . . ."

He shrugged, grinned, and with a hand on her arm, turned her, facing him. "Anyway I need to let you go now. I imagine you need rest as much as we do." Her face was clear, her features fine-boned, her eyes shadowed but somehow penetrating in the night, looking into him. "And thank you," he said, "for what you did. I feel as if I'm on the track now. Whatever that is, and wherever I'm going on it."

"It seems that way to me too, Artus. That you're on the track."

He walked her back to the Main Building—they hadn't gone a hundred yards—and said goodbye to her inside the door. From there he walked to the barracks and got ready for bed. It wasn't lights out yet, but near enough, and someone had turned the light intensity way down.

Before he closed his eyes, it occurred to him that he really didn't know why he'd gone to see Lotta. He did have a crush on her, true enough, but that was only part of it.

Then it struck him: *I was demonstrating*, he thought, *showing off my precognition*.

He wondered, as he drifted toward sleep, if this

precognition would prove an isolated occurrence. It seemed to him that for a warrior to get precognitions useful in battle would take the joy out of combat.

It also seemed to him that the universe wouldn't be wired that way.

Twenty-Four

"Come in," said Wellem Bosler, and Lotta Alsnor entered.

"Unless there's something you don't like in the session record," she said, "I've just completed Forey Benster. I'm ready to start three new cases tomorrow."

Which makes this the ideal time for it to happen, she added silently, *if Artus was right. It's unusual to turn over a full slate of operants on the same day.*

Bosler nodded and gestured her to a seat. "Tomorrow I've got a different kind of assignment for you."

He looked at her curiously then, as if he'd picked up on her inner reaction. Which, she thought, he no doubt had. "You've always been good at melding with non-human life," he said, "mammals, birds, insects, plants. You've done more of it than anyone else I've known, of any age."

He leaned his elbows on his desk, fingers interlaced beneath his chin. "I suppose you know what Kusu's been working on, and what he's run into."

"You're referring to the teleport, and what's happened to the mammals he's tried to put through it."

"Right. Theoretically there shouldn't have been any problem, but the theory was pretty sketchy, pretty incomplete. So when the mammals came out insane, at first he tried to tinker his way through it. When that got him nowhere, he went back to the theory, to expand and strengthen it. Which he did, appreciably. But when all's said and done, it made no difference in the apparatus or the results, and it didn't give him any leads."

Bosler straightened. "Today he called me. He's decided he needs a study on what, subjectively, happens with a mammal's mind when it teleports. And asked me who I'd recommend to work with him. I told him you. He wasn't surprised."

Lotta's look was steady and direct. "I can already see some procedural problems."

He nodded. She didn't elaborate.

"You wouldn't be offering me this assignment," she said, "if you didn't think it was important enough to cut your staff here by one. But what makes it urgent? Is there something I'm overlooking? He *could* wait till we're done here."

"True, he could. And I can't specify why it seems urgent. The initial sense of urgency was his, and he can't rationalize it either. But the feeling I get is that he's right; it is urgent." He paused. "Although not so urgent that it calls for reckless action."

She made a face at Bosler, then nodded once in decision. "I'll do it. It does sound really interesting. Is there anything more you and I need to say about it before I leave?"

Bosler shook his head. "Anything out of the ordinary in the session?"

Lotta laughed. "Most people would say so. Actually it was pretty routine."

"Good. I'll call Lemal and have one of the OSP floaters ready for you tomorrow after breakfast. Say 0800. You'll be at Lake Loreen for lunch."

"Right." She got up. "I'll see if Jerym is still up.

We've only visited once since I've been here." She stopped with a hand on the door. "Oh! There's something you should know." Then she ran down for him her brief conversation with Romlar the evening before. "And that was before Kusu called you," she added.

"Hmh! Interesting." Bosler grinned. "I'm not too surprised, considering. But it's good to know."

When she'd gone, he shook his head. The T'sel certainly saved a lot of teenaged anxieties. That fifteen-year-old girl—woman—was more mature and stable and intelligent than ninety-nine point nine nine percent of the middle-aged population on Iryala, and bringing the population at large to anything approaching Lotta Alsnor's level wasn't going to happen overnight. Or in a generation, or even several.

Twenty-Five

Wearing white winter field uniforms, A Company worked quickly in the bitter, midwinter dawn. They'd eaten breakfast—cold field rations—in their sleeping bags. Afterward each man stuffed his bag in the small sack provided for it, and each pair struck their tough if fragile-looking two-man winter tent, separating its velcroed halves and stowing them in their packsacks. They did more with their mittens on than looked possible, taking them off almost not at all. Their winter equipment, of recent issue, was designed with mittens in mind.

When their packs were ready and their snowshoes clamped on, they donned their new helmets. The optical visors, face shields were pivoted into the *up* position, headphones snug over ears, microphone tucked out of the way. Every man could hear his platoon leader and sergeant, and talk to them if necessary. Sounds from the environment—squad mates, wind, the hiss and occasional clack of snowshoes—were also mediated electronically, could be amplified by a simple finger adjustment or reduced in the din of combat. But they took some getting used to, and some of the trainees still felt cut off by them. The visors none of them much liked yet. They weren't supposed to ice up or fog, but on days like this they did when they were down, even if lowered only to the end of the nose.

They'd just spent their second night in the field; this would be their third day on this exercise, in thirty-two inches of snow. The first two days had been on the march, on snowshoes, at first making as much speed as conditions allowed. It was undesirable to sweat heavily; there was a limit to what the gills in their winter uniforms could vent.

On most of the second day they'd kept to the most difficult and unlikely terrain: a series of steep, timbered recessional moraines; burned-off swamp forest, thickly brushy; fens where the snow, supported by sedge and heath, had not settled but lay more than forty inches deep, so that even wearing snowshoes, the scouts and lead men sank to their knees.

(Covert troop movement was often feasible for mercenaries. A substantial part of the mercenary market was on resource worlds, the so-called "gook worlds," where off-surface equipment, including reconnaissance aircraft, were generally prohibited for military use by the Confederation. This was true even when the combatants were, or more often had the support of, rival Confederation commercial interests. It was one of the strictures installed more than seven centuries earlier by Pertunis, in the Charter of Confederation, to reduce the ravages of war. While on the trade worlds, the national governments had planetary compacts, though they were not always strictly adhered to, which prohibited the use of aircraft in one or more military roles.)

The T'swa had begun assigning trainees as acting officers and noncoms, with the cadre observing and coaching. Mostly Carrmak had served as A Company commander, although others had worn the hat. On this exercise it was Romlar, who no longer feared to lead, and who, as acting squad leader and platoon leader, had discovered both taste and talent for leadership.

The exercise was to attack an enemy encampment, hopefully by surprise. Of course, there was no assurance that the camp would still be where the map showed it, nor that the enemy wouldn't have learned of their coming and have an ambush set. Enemy patrols could be expected. Certainly pickets would be posted, and presumably fields of fire would have been cleared.

The map was in part a fiction: It showed things that weren't there in reality, but for the sake of the exercise must be treated as if they were. The first two days the company had followed a marked route with no other rationale than to give them a variety of difficult terrains. However, for this third day the map showed no marked route; the commander was to find his own. Using his map, and information from his scouts, Romlar moved his company out. The men were free to talk as they went, but softly, and there wasn't much talking. They'd done plenty of drills on scouting, picket duty, and reconnaissance, training each man to stay highly aware of his surroundings, so their attention was mostly outward.

Romlar's orders were to be in position to attack by midday. Supposedly another company was to approach by a different route and attack at the same time: 1200 hours. Romlar suspected it was an imaginary company, pretended for the purpose of the exercise. If it wasn't there, A Company was to attack by itself. After the enemy was destroyed, Romlar was to march his company to a rendezvous by 1530 hours.

For the most part he followed the crest of a broad ridge that ran for miles, generally about fifty or sixty feet above the country flanking it. Which on the map was marked liberally with wetland symbols, much of it with the subsymbol for brush, and also with occasional small round ponds that suggested fen pools, roofed thickly with ice in this season.

It seemed apparent to Romlar that the planners intended him to stay on the ridge crest. The required time of arrival seemed to demand it. The side slopes would be much more difficult, and slower, to showshoe on, and on them he'd have been more vulnerable to attack, though less to detection. While if he traveled through the adjacent brushy flats, with their real and imaginary fens, he'd arrive too late to make the attack.

It was a design for ambush, and on a hunch, he marched the company faster than he might have, sweat or not.

After more than two hours, the point radioed back that they'd come to a stringlike fen not shown on their map. All the map showed was the creek that flowed through it. Romlar ordered the company to stay put, and with Jerym, his trainee first sergeant, moved up to see for himself. Lieutenant Toma followed, observing, saying nothing.

The scouts lay back a bit from the fen, close enough to observe it but keeping back among the trees and behind the sapling fringe. They were nearly invisible in the snow, white hoods hiding their helmets; even their rifles were white. Romlar took off his snowshoes, then crawling, slipped slowly forward between his scouts and down to the edge of the fen, where he could see better. Jerym followed, and Lieutenant Toma.

Jerym judged the fen to be 250 to 300 yards across, with no visual cover except for isolated patches of tattered cane grass, head tall, dead leaves fluttering and rustling in a light breeze. The nearest way around was a mile to their right, where the fen ended in evergreen forest. He watched Romlar scan the woods on the opposite side with white binoculars.

Toma spoke while Romlar scanned. "What will you do?"

Romlar didn't answer till he'd put his binoculars away. "Go around," he said.

"How near are you to the enemy encampment?"

"According to the map, two and a half miles plus a little bit, if we cross here."

"Going around will add considerable distance and take additional time. Consider whether you'll be in position to attack by midday."

Romlar didn't even glance at Toma. *He's not interested in advice,* Jerym told himself.

"I allowed for the time," Romlar said. "There's no cover in the fen, and if we were attacked there, we couldn't move fast in the loose snow. We'll go around."

The T'swi said no more, and the three of them backed away into the woods, to their snowshoes. Back with the company, Romlar changed its course. In something less than half an hour they'd flanked the fen and were at the creek. There was a sag ice on it, something they'd run into before and learned about the hard way. It had frozen over in autumn, then the ice had gotten snow-covered. Afterward the creek had fallen, leaving an air space beneath the ice, which had sagged. Insulated by the thick snow atop the ice, the new water surface had probably not frozen thickly enough to carry a man. It looked like a good place to fall through and soak your feet, maybe even lose a snowshoe—serious incidents on a day of minus fifteen or twenty Fahrenheit and with snow up to your ass.

Romlar had scouts cross, moving carefully. When they'd checked the forest on the other side, he had the company advance, spread out, a few at a time, not crossing in bunches. It slowed them, but not critically.

After they'd crossed, Romlar had them form a column of twos again, Toma not questioning, letting him function, and they moved out once more, angling now to regain their old line of travel.

Romlar spoke quietly into his throat mike. "Rear guard, be alert and keep well back. Flankers on the left, stay wide. I suspect there was an ambush laid at the fen, across our old line of march."

"Yes sir."

He moved them fast. Thirty minutes later they hit snowshoe tracks headed from the encampment toward the fen, and Romlar adjusted their direction of march, following the trail toward the encampment. After a bit they heard rifle fire not far ahead. His scouts reported contact with pickets. Romlar ordered 1st and 2nd Platoons into a skirmish line and sent them forward, leaving immediate tactics to their platoon leaders. Shortly the volume of fire increased, now including blast hoses. The T'swi with the enemy pickets reported that the pickets all were casualties. The T'swi with Romlar's scouts reported light casualties. First Platoon reported sighting the encampment in a meadow. A minute later, 4th Platoon's lobbers could be heard thumping. The rocket launchers weren't loud enough to hear.

Romlar had ordered 3rd Platoon to backtrack down their trail aways, to form a crescent facing their would-be ambushers from the fen, who'd probably be coming at a run. Ahead, an imaginary force at the encampment was counterattacking 1st and 2nd Platoons, and the T'swa informed him that the company which should have been helping in the attack on the encampment seemed not to have arrived. Romlar wasn't surprised. He had 4th Platoon concentrate their fire, lobbers and rockets both, on "the counterattack" instead of on the encampment. Minutes later the T'swa reported the counterattack broken, with heavy enemy casualties. Fourth Platoon then began bombarding the encampment again.

Romlar then called 2nd Platoon back and ordered them to join 3rd Platoon, to move toward the fen in a broad crescent, horns forward. The T'swa with 2nd Platoon had tagged twelve of its people dead or disabled, including Carrmak as platoon leader. Esenrok, as platoon sergeant, was unwounded and took command. Overall command of the two platoons fell to 3rd Platoon's leader, a trainee named Kurlmar.

About nine hundred yards back, Kurlmar stopped his advance at the top of a mild slope, the steepest locally available. The assumption was that the enemy, pressed for time, would follow his old, straight-line snowshoe trails, rather than detour and break new ones. Nonetheless, Kurlmar separated two squads from each end of his line, half his force, and sent them well to the sides, with orders to send scouts out farther, just in case.

Six minutes later he saw enemy movement in the forest to his front, and gave the order to fire. The enemy began to advance, moving from tree to tree as much as possible. Blank ammunition from rifles and blast hoses ripped the forest with their racket.

It was quickly apparent that the force they faced was a full company. Kurlmar's outlying squads too began firing; enemy troops were moving to flank him. He was tempted to withdraw, but instead called for reinforcements.

By the time Romlar arrived with 1st Platoon, most of the 2nd and 3rd had been tagged by their T'swa as casualties, but the enemy had suffered substantial casualties too. (Fourth Platoon had been left to watch for an attack by whatever [imaginary] enemy might have survived at the encampment.) A few minutes later the T'swa called the fighting off, and everyone, dead, disabled, and operational, mushed to the enemy encampment. There the cadre took command and led them all on a forced snowshoe march back toward the compound, fifteen miles away on snowburied roads.

Twenty-Six

It was midafternoon at Lake Loreen, but dark enough that Kusu Lormagen had the lights on in the lab. Thunder muttered, and sleet rattled on the windows. He sat at his desk reading a thin sheaf of papers, while Lotta Alsnor watched from a tall lab stool. When he'd finished, he looked up at her.

"You're convinced then," he said.

"Right. A ported mammal goes berserk because teleportation reactivates every terror, every pain, every rage it ever felt. Or inherited, so to speak. Its whole case turns on, all at once, full force and out of context."

Kusu grunted. "Even those that were sedated and unconscious . . ."

"Right. Beneath that unconsciousness, an absolute mental frenzy broke out.

"Since then you've exposed mammals to each of the constituent fields, separately and in partial combinations, without severe effects. Mostly they didn't even notice. The most logical conclusion is that it's the actual *transfer* that activates their cases."

She paused for emphasis. "The point is, that if you

167

teleported a mammal without a significant case, it would come through sane and safe."

He smiled at her. "Can you provide me with a mammal like that?"

She nodded. "As near as need be, yes. Me."

Kusu laughed. "Serves me right for asking." Then, more seriously: "You haven't proved your thesis though. The evidence is highly suggestive, but by no means conclusive." She said nothing. "I know," he went on. "You're volunteering to be the proof.

"But consider: It's not vital that we teleport humans. Or any mammals. Teleporting manufactured goods, foodstuffs, mail, almost anything else you want to name, will make this far and away the biggest technical advance since the invention of hyperdrive."

Lotta shook her head. "Human teleportation is where the biggest potential lies,' she said. "And you've got a made-to-order experimental subject: me. Use it."

" 'No significant case,' " he said. "How do you know what the level of significance is?"

She shrugged. "The evaluation is subjective, obviously. But it's the only informed evaluation you're likely to get."

"Why shouldn't we test it with someone else who knows the T'sel? Me for example."

"Why don't you answer that?"

"Sure. Because you feel significant uncertainty about your evaluation. You don't want someone else to risk their life on it, or at least their sanity."

Lotta nodded. "Certainly not *your* life. It might take quite awhile before someone else could digest your logbooks and interim write-ups and figure out what to do next."

Kusu laughed again. "What makes you think I know what to do next?"

"You know several things you could do next. You're just not sure which to choose."

"True. Well. To paraphrase a famous Pertunian principle: When you don't know what to do, grab an option, at random if you have to, and do it. So. Supposing we subject you to some constituent fields, one at a time, and you can evaluate subjectively what each of them feels like. To a human, not a sorlex or soney. A human that knows the T'sel. And after light tranquilization, just to hedge our bet."

She shook her head. "We know tranks don't help. The rest of it I'll go with."

Kusu smiled. "It's a deal. It'll take some time to build a port big enough for a human. We have the design and some of the components, but others are still being built. You draw up a set of safety precautions for my approval, and meanwhile I'll expedite the hardware."

She nodded. "I'll have a draft of the safety proposals for you in the morning."

"Good. Oh! And one thing more: Be sure they include having Wellem standing by. If you come through like the sorlex did, maybe he can bail you out."

Twenty-Seven

Kusu watched while Wellem Bosler and the Institute's physician fastened Lotta to the table with a rubber body sheet. *When she agreed to draw up a set of safety proposals,* Kusu thought, *she went all the way.*

The jury-rigged teleport was not a single unit. Made of metal tubing, the gate itself resembled a door frame without a wall, with a ramp to accommodate the gurney. Modules sat on a lab bench and on a small wheeled work table, with cables to the gate. But it had passed a series of tests without problems of any kind—a series that ended with the successful teleportation of horn worms and sand lizards.

Lotta lay patiently while the fastenings were secured. She hadn't expected to be uneasy, but she was. And so, she sensed, was the student technician who stood at her head, waiting to push the gurney.

When they'd finished with the fastenings, it was Bosler who spoke. "Are you ready?" he asked her.

"Ready," she said. Her speech was thick; she wore a rubber mouthpiece to protect her tongue and cheeks from her teeth, a mouthpiece too big to spit out.

With the physician, Bosler walked a dozen feet past the gate, to stand beside the target site. He could *feel* Lotta's unease, and the physician's, and the student's. And Kusu's most of all. Each had its own flavor, distinguishing it from the others, including his own. None was severe, but the tension was there, and as sensitized as he was just now, it was palpable to Bosler.

He looked at Kusu and nodded.

Kusu threw a switch. A red light came on beside the gate. Bosler turned his gaze to Lotta. Hers too was on the light. Her face was calm but the tension remained. The red light switched off, and the green one beside it flashed on. He saw her eyes close as the technician rolled the gurney up the ramp, onto the platform—

And into the gate.

It was the length of the gurney that made it conspicuous: The foot end began to appear in front of Bosler while the rest was still on the runway. The effect was startling and disorienting: Lotta's feet and legs were a dozen feet from her torso. Then all of her was there. Her eyes still were closed, her face relaxed as before.

His nerves settled. "You made it," he said quietly.

"I know," she answered, and her eyes opened, her face turning to him. "Now if you'll let me loose . . ."

Twenty-Eight

Equinox was well past, and the snow, still twenty inches deep, had been settling wetly beneath the springtime sun. That noon, A Company had reached a "village"—a set of buildings crudely framed—only to find signs informing them that it had been "burnt" by "the enemy" when he'd left. Then, by snowshoeing hard all afternoon, they'd reached a meadow with supposedly an "enemy camp," arriving between sundown and dark. The "enemy" wasn't there, and when "he'd left," of course, he'd "destroyed his camp and taken his supplies with him."

It had been a tough bivouac. They'd been out for five days and four nights, breaking camp each morning and carrying it with them. Once a radioed message from regiment had routed them out at midnight, and they'd moved in darkness. On top of that they hadn't gotten their scheduled resupply, and had been on half rations. They'd been drizzled on and snowed on, and definitely preferred the snow. One morning they'd been ambushed, and one night their camp had been assaulted.

In turn they'd ambushed or assaulted other companies twice, once in the night.

In general they'd enjoyed themselves enormously.

Of course, while the T'swa had set things up to seem as real as readily feasible, the casualties had been assigned by umpires, not bullets, and after each encounter were reinstated as alive, combat-effective, and ready to march.

They had cadre with them, but the T'swa had kept apart, saying nothing except as umpires when the company encountered a real or imaginary enemy force.

Carrmak set pickets out, and the company pitched their winter shelter tents in the adjacent woods. (The trainee company commander now was always either Carrmak or Romlar.) The command tent was somewhat larger than the standard two-man size—made with four panels, longer and differently shaped, sheltering Carrmak; Jerym as his EO, his executive officer; and the trainee first sergeant, Orkuth, from 3rd Platoon. They'd carried the panels and framing in their own packs, T'swa style, rather than having someone else carry them.

It was dark in the tent, but not utterly dark. The only artificial light was the tiny red dot of the power light on the command radio, on the floor by where Carrmak would sleep. But Seeren was at the end of her first quarter, wouldn't go down till around midnight, and the thin fine fabric of the tent roof glowed faintly with her light. *Like daylight for the T'swa's big cateyes*, Jerym supposed. He spread his insulating ground pad beside his rifle, unrolled his sleeping bag on top of it, opened the bag and laid down on it. His clothing was warm enough for now; he could crawl in the sack later, when it got colder.

They'd spoken very little in the tent. There wasn't a lot to say. Jerym lay with his eyes open for a little and heard someone's stomach growl. His own answered. They'd eaten the last of their field rations that morning, and his attention kept returning to his hunger. His last conscious thought was to wonder if it would keep him awake.

*   *   *

The moon was still up, the tent faintly lit by it, when he was awakened by the command radio: "Able Company, this is regiment, over. Able Company, this is regiment, over." It rolled Jerym onto his knees, instantly intent. Stripping off his mittens, he fumbled the orders recorder out of a pocket on his officer's pack. The voice had been Gotasu's. Carrmak, kneeling, picked the radio up. "This is Carrmak commanding Able Company, over."

"Able Company, I have map coordinates for you."

Jerym thumbed the *record* switch on his recorder.

"In quadrangle J-2-7-M-5-3. Coordinates are: X:2113, Y:1797. Again, X:2213, Y:1797. Over."

The pale oblong of Carrmak's face turned to Jerym. "It's recorded," Jerym murmured.

"Recorded," Carrmak said into the radio. "That's in our present quadrangle, coordinates X:2213, Y:1797. Over."

"That's right, Carrmak. Take Able Company and proceed to those coordinates at once. You will find vacant defensive positions dug in there—bunkers and trenches. You will occupy them by not later than 2400 hours, midnight. And wait for further orders, prepared to defend them if attacked. Over."

"If attacked," Jerym thought to himself. *"Further orders." They're apt to leave us sitting there for a day without food, or have us get ambushed on the way. Or the defensive positions might have enemy in them when we get there.* A real enemy could hardly be more unpredictable, a fact in which he found much satisfaction.

"Got that," Carrmak said to Gotasu. "Able Company will occupy dug-in defensive positions at X:2213, Y:1797, not later than midnight, prepared to defend against possible attack. Over."

"That is correct, Able Company. Regiment out."

"Able Company out."

Jerym looked at the time glowing green on his recorder, then thumbed it off: 2141 hours and seven seconds—they had just less than two hours and twenty minutes to get there. How far, and what was the terrain like? He took out the mapbook,* switched it on, called up the quadrangle, and tapped in the coordinates as the display lit up.

A tiny white square appeared, with a hard white center dot, defining the exact coordinate point and the limits of coordinate precision. They fell within a pale yellow square, a field, surrounded on the holomap by the pale green of forest. This was a part of the reservation they weren't familiar with. But the terrain was gentle, which was encouraging, given the time limit. Jerym called up a distance scale with its two ends on their destination and their present position, then held the map board so Carrmak could see it.

"There's a crossroad within the square," he said. "The dug-in positions are probably to defend it. It's 7.12 straight-line miles from here."

"Good," Carrmak said. "Orkuth, roust out the company. Tell them they've got till 2150, eight minutes, to break camp and be formed up for the road. Alsnor, decide on a route and show it to me."

Deciding the route was easy. One of the roads that crossed the coordinates crossed the meadow they were in, a nearly straight shot. Call it seven and a quarter miles, allowing for the few curves in it. The only alternative was to go through the woods, which would slow them to no advantage unless they swung far enough from the road to avoid possible ambush. That would

---

*So-called. The new "mapbook" is a computerized holographic atlas 12 × 10 × 1 inches—about the size of the standard army field mapbook. Based on high elevation, computer-enhanced holography, it gives a realistic display of the topography and, at the largest scales, of tree heights. The computer adds contour lines. The broadest vegetation categories are differentiated by color. At larger scales, the classification becomes progressively more detailed, the finer types being outlined and defined by symbols.

add distance, and time they didn't have. On snowshoes they'd have to push hard as it was, after having hiked all day, almost without food and only an hour and a half's sleep; no sleep at all for the guys on picket duty.

He showed Carrmak the route. Carrmak agreed, and they struck their tent, assembled their packs. Around them was activity, crisp and meaningful, with acting sergeants giving quiet orders.

It was a beautiful night. Seeren, seeming perfectly cut in half, was partway down the western sky. The air was absolutely calm, and still felt somewhat above freezing; the snow was doomed, Jerym thought. His mittens were in his parka pockets; the parka itself was open and the hood thrown back. The snow seemed to give off light of its own; visibility was no problem at all. It seemed to him that, outdoors, the T'swa could hardly see better than he could on a night like this.

When Carrmak sent the point out, and the flankers, Jerym's wristwatch read 2149:49. Two minutes later, Carrmak gave the order to march. They had almost exactly two hours and eight minutes.

The snow on the road was undisturbed, except for a slight hollowing caused by wind swirl from some hover truck before the thaw had started. But the warm weather had settled it so much, their snowshoes didn't sink in at all. They'd have no trouble reaching the crossroad by midnight, Jerym told himself, unless there was an ambush waiting for them.

Within the first hundred yards, the swinging stride, the soft crunch of snowshoes on spring snow, the moonlit snowscape, combined to produce a dreamlike clarity in Jerym's mind. His thoughts, what there were of them, seemed remote and out of time. He'd become a mobile observing unit; any computing was subliminal. Along the road, the forest canopy was mostly of deciduous trees that let the moonlight through, with here and there tall evergreens, their thick tops variously oval or pyramidal or ragged blacknesses. Occasionally he saw the small round blobs of yarpu roosting asleep in the

treetops. And twice smelled urine and excrement somewhere nearby, beneath some evergreen, some koorsa
tree whose top had been homesteaded by a burly,
twenty-pound stinkpig who'd spent days or even weeks
there feeding on buds, needles, and inner bark, reliev-
ing itself repeatedly onto the snow beneath.

Time did not pass for Jerym. He floated through it
without effort, neither tiring nor hungering. Yet at any
point he could have told you without looking what time
it was and how far they'd gone and how far they had to
go. He saw the ethereal tracery of branches against the
night sky, the glint of stronger stars between them,
those that could override the moonlight.

The condition lasted until, at 2341, they reached the
crossroad. The defensive positions were a circular series
of six-foot-deep foxholes with firing steps on both sides,
connected by narrow, four-foot-deep crawl trenches.
All dug by machinery in some past summer.

But snow-filled, they weren't evident, would have
been hard to find except for the mounds of four snow-
covered bunkers spaced along the circle. Carrmak had
pickets posted, then set the men to digging out the
snow with their trenching tools. They worked furiously;
it was to be finished by midnight.

They'd cleared the foxholes and were working on the
crawl-trenches when, without warning, the first explosions occurred in the middle of the circle, sending dirt
and snow flying. The ground jarred with them, and the
sound, unexpected, was stunning. The explosions went
on, one after another and several at once, within and
outside the circle. Between the explosions, Jerym could
hear the violent hammering of blast hoses spraying the
area. Their tracers seemed to float lazily, yet their blast
slugs, slamming into the parapets, ripped them, throwing chunks of frozen dirt into the foxholes and onto the
men that crouched in them. The noise, the violence,
were shocking.

Yet after half a minute, the trainees crouched less
low, gripped their rifles less tightly, checked to make

sure there was a round in the chamber. When the barrage ended, an assault seemed likely.

A minute later it did stop, and they got onto their firing steps, ready. Though still somewhat deafened, they could hear the sounds of other, similar barrages miles away, before those too ceased. Then a bull horn sounded from a silent floater overhead, and they recognized Gotasu's voice:

"That's it, gentlemen, end of exercise!"

None of them got out of their holes though; they hadn't gotten it from their acting company commander yet. Then Carrmak crawled out of the bunker and gave them the word: "Able Company, fall in!"

They scrambled out and formed up ranks while the floater landed, unloaded Captain Gotasu and Lieutenant Toma, and left. The field was humps and craters now, brown mixed with white. Jerym wondered if the "shells" they'd been bombarded with had been explosive charges buried in the field long in advance. Or if the T'swa had such confidence in their own marksmanship that they'd used actual lobber rounds, dropping them safely, near but not too near. Most of the churned-up ground was toward the center of the circle or outside it by at least fifteen yards.

Gotasu looked them over. "A Company," he said, "you've done very well on this bivouac. Your trainee officers and noncoms have done very well. We are now twenty-one miles from the compound. We will march there tonight." He paused. "And the cooks will serve you a very good breakfast. Meanwhile, if the platoon sergeants will come to the vehicle, there is a carton of hardtack, with a packet for each man."

Gotasu waited while the hardtack was distributed and devoured. A packet held three ounces; it took about a minute to eat it. He looked at Carrmak then. "Commander, consider the war over, the enemy vanquished. You need not put out scouts nor fear attack. Move your troops out."

Twenty-Nine

Company A, still hungry and almost without sleep, hiked hard and fast, marching into the compound soon after sunup. It was the first night in nearly four deks that it hadn't frozen, and they arrived sweating. Breakfast was toast and jam, baked omelets, juice, and buttermilk. Delicious, and enough but not enough. They got only one large serving each, to avoid the risk of getting sick. The mess sergeant, a somewhat overweight Iryalan, announced that at dinner they could eat all they wanted. And here, dinner was at noon.

After showering, the trainees crashed. It was the first time in more than five deks of training that they'd been allowed to sleep during normal training hours after a night exercise.

The alarm bells were used to waken them at 1145, the first time the alarms had sounded since their first week. It gave them fifteen minutes to get ready for dinner. The meal was steaks and baked potato, with mixed vegetables barely cooked, and corn fritters. There were seconds, even thirds. Dessert was hot fruit cob-

bler with ice cream. Then they were ordered to the
assembly hall.

While the trainees filed into the rows of benches,
Voker and Dak-So came onto the podium and stood
waiting. When the regiment was seated, Voker grinned
and spoke:

"Good afternoon, warriors!"

The response was deafening. "Good afternoon, sir!"

"I'm up here to say I'm proud of you. When you came
here, I knew you were going to be good. As I watched
you, those first rough deks, I never doubted, in spite of
all the trouble you made for yourselves. All I had to see
was the way you trained, the spirit you put into things,
to know you were going to be as good or better than I'd
originally expected."

He paused, looked them over, then continued. "Now,
though you've been here for less than six deks, you're
already better, as individuals, platoons, and companies,
than any other light infantry in the Confederation. Unless you count the T'swa, and they're determined to
make you as nearly their equal as possible in three
years. T'swa pride doesn't let them do anything less
than their best, and I know yours won't either.

"You've all just come in from a tough, wild five days.
Your companies have reconnoitered each other, ambushed each other, assaulted each other. And last night
we exploded a whole lot of takite and other good stuff,
giving all of you the sound and feel of gunnery, and
plowed up a lot of dirt doing it. Then marched you back
in on almost empty stomachs, for distances of fifteen to
twenty-three miles. In the last five days and nights you
hiked about a hundred and seventy miles on snowshoes
and short rations, most of it with full winter packs, and
some of it in tough terrain. That would have killed a lot
of troops, and had most of the rest of them bitching
their heads off."

Again the old man looked them over, then nodded
emphatically as if approving what he saw. "You've completed a phase of your training," he went on, "the

phase in which you've operated solely as platoons and companies. This spring and summer you'll be working as battalions and as a regiment. And between now and then . . . We'll talk about that later—before we're done here today. I think you'll like it.

"Now I'm going to turn this meeting over to Colonel Dak-So. He's the man in charge of delivering the training, and he's got things to talk to you about. "Colonel," he said turning, "they're yours," and took a seat to one side.

"Thank you, Colonel Voker." Dak-So flashed a quick grin at the regiment. "You *are* good," he said. "You are tough, enduring, strong, and growing smarter. Even wiser! And wiser is very important to a warrior. We have given a number of you responsibilities as acting officers and noncoms, and you have shown growth and skill in carrying these out. I have no doubt that the rest of you could function in those posts, too, because all of you are warriors. But some men have a special, innate talent to lead, and we will take full advantage of that."

He stood silent for a moment then, drawing their attention more strongly. "I mentioned wisdom. Your company commanders have, on occasion, discussed further with you the Matrix of T'sel. You have shown by your responses and questions that you have rather largely absorbed its principles and made them yours. That is very reassuring, because without them, a warrior is not complete. I now want to look at some principles with you which heretofore you have been introduced to only casually."

Again Dak-So paused, his eyes settling on Artus Romlar. "Trainee Romlar," he said. "What is the most important thing a warrior must be able to do?"

Romlar stood. "Sir, a warrior has to do the right thing at the right time."

"Good! And Trainee Brossling, how does a warrior know what the right thing is?"

Brossling got easily to his feet. "He just knows. He either knows or he doesn't."

"Good. Now Brossling, both you and Romlar got in trouble early on, doing the wrong things at the wrong times—" He paused, grinned, went on. "Although you exeeded Romlar in that. What made the difference in your early performances and your recent performances?" He cocked an eyebrow at the trainee C.O. of F Company, earlier the regiment's number one troublemaker.

"Sir," Brossling answered, "most of the difference comes from getting our heads straightened out. The colonel made us see our responsibility and make it up to the regiment. You T'swa never let us run over you. And the Ostrak Procedures took it from there."

Dak-So raised an eyebrow again and nodded. "Excellent. You may sit down now . . . All right. A wise warrior knows correctly. An unwise warrior knows incorrectly. You might say there is a state of knowingness and a state of false knowingness.

"And the difference is what the Ostrak teams call one's 'case.' When you, with their help, unloaded the heavier and more active parts of your cases, you became far more able to know correctly.

"Incidentally, some might say there is also a state of *un*knowingness. Such a state only seems to exist. Knowingness and false knowingness are very often at a level below awareness, hence the appearance of unknowingness. Even so, our knowingness or false knowingness drives our decisions."

His eyes sought again. "Klarister, how many times have you been killed since you've been here?"

Klarister rose. "Twice sir," he said. "Twice that I got tagged for. Last night they weren't tagging us, but if that had been a real barrage, intended to hit us instead of miss, it might have been three times. Seems likely."

"Ah. And how many cadre are we here?"

"T'swa? Uh, probably three or four hundred I'd guess, sir."

"Four hundred twelve. We are almost the totality of the able-bodied survivors of three regiments—of nearly fifty-four hundred men originally on our rosters. Thank you, Klarister." His gaze took in the entire assembly then. "You do know, I trust, that most warriors die violent deaths, mostly while still more or less young."

His eyes stopped on another trainee. "Benster, doesn't that worry you?"

Benster stood. "Not particularly, sir. I'm a warrior. Because I want to be. The danger is part of it; you can't have the game without the risk."

"But getting killed!? . . ."

Benster grinned. "Call it recycled, sir. Lotta, my interviewer, helped me see lots of times I got killed, died in bed, what have you. Old and young, what have you. Seems like I keep coming back."

"Ah! Seems! And suppose that what you saw during your interviews was all hallucination, somehow an outgrowth of suggestion."

Benster shrugged, the grin undimmed. "I suppose that possibility has occurred to most of us. But what it comes down to, sir, is that if we recycle, death isn't that big a deal. And if, when we die, that's the end of it for us, then we won't miss it, because we'll be dead. So we might as well live the life we're here for, and enjoy it."

"Thank you, Benster, for a good exposition." Benster sat down, and Dak-So's eyes moved again, stopped.

"Trainee Alsnor, Benster mentioned his interviewer, his Ostrak operator, Lotta. As I recall, she is still a young girl, perhaps fifteen or sixteen. Suppose she was in danger, Alsnor. In immediate danger of being murdered. How would you respond?"

Jerym's face was stiff. "Sir, I'd do anything in my power to keep it from happening."

"I'm sure you would, Alsnor, I'm sure you would. Be seated please, and thank you." Dak-So scanned the assembly again. "The operator we talked about, as some of you know, is Alsnor's sister. I did not ask him that question to make him uncomfortable. I wanted to make something real to all of you: That there are circumstances which tend to carry strong polarity with them. Even when a warrior is neutral about his own survival, prepared to accept death, there may be matters about which he has strong preferences. Things he wants and rejects, must have and must not have.

"As a warrior or a workman, a father, an athlete— whatever roles one plays in life, one can be appraised by the excellence of his performance. Aside from whether he wins or loses. And the excellence of that performance is a reflection of his decisions.

"T'swa warriors for millenia have been humankind's most successful warriors, but sometimes we lose engagements, even wars, and the great majority of us die in battle. We always intend to win, we always intend to survive and see our friends survive, and most often our actions are such as to bring about victory and survival. But these actions are not compulsive. They are not burdened with a sense of 'must have' or 'must not have.' We are perfectly willing to lose, or to die, or to see our friends die, if that is what transpires."

The T'swa major paused. "I do not insist that you agree with me on this. If you do, that is fine. If you don't, that is fine too. And in either case it is all right to change your mind. But I will tell you that to the extent you have strong preferences and strong aversions, to that degree you will make decisions which do not conduce to high performance as a warrior.

"In fact, strong preferences and aversions are likely to result in losing that which one strongly wishes to keep. And in experiencing that which one despises.

"Feel free to disagree with me. I've told you these things not with insistance, but because I want you to be aware that T'swa warriors hold such a philosophy. Nonpolarity is a key to what we are like."

Again Dak-So paused to scan them. "Very well, enough of that." He turned to Voker. "Colonel, your regiment."

Voker stood, stepped forward, grinned. "Feel the floor with your feet!" he ordered. Genially. The wooden floor resounded with the clomping of field boots, the room changing auras with the release of tension.

"Was the floor there? Did you feel it?"

"*Yes!*" came an answering roar.

"Good. Look at the person on your right! If you're on the extreme right, look at someone else . . . Good! Now tell that person hello! . . . Good! Now stand up! . . . Good! Now stretch! Hard! . . . Good! Now sit down again, and I'll tell you something I believe you'll like to hear."

They sat.

"Tomorrow you will begin to learn unarmed combat. You have three weeks to learn it. You will train at it all morning and all afternoon. In the evening you will study various other things, many things. But during the daytime you will learn to fight with your hands and feet.

"For a week after that, you'll receive training with and against the knife, and improve your skill with the bayonet."

He felt their incipient cheer, and held up a hand, postponing it a moment. "Do you like that idea?" he asked.

Their enthusiasm came bellowing out, the most deafening cheers yet. He let it continue till it started to weaken, then cut it off with a single motion. "Good. The people who analyzed your civilian records and tests told us you were intentive warriors. It's obvious they knew what they were talking about.

"This afternoon, however, you will clean your barracks to the satisfaction of your company commanders, and they will be hard to satisfy. This evening—" He grinned again. "This evening there will be a holo show here from 1915 to approximately 2100. How would you like to see, um . . . 'For Love of Thora'?" I understand it's a good cube."

There was applause.

"Or would you rather see 'A Crown Prince on Ice,' a cube about a T'swa campaign?"

Hands beat, feet drummed, throats roared. After some seconds he cut them off. " 'A Crown Prince' it will be then. But I warn you, it's an old cube from before the

Kettle War, and the T'swa in it are figments of an uninformed imagination. Considering your experience, you'll no doubt look at it as comedy.

"Now, when I dismiss you, leave the building in an orderly manner. You are free till 1430. At 1430, you will start cleaning your barracks. Dismissed!"

Voker and Dak-So watched the trainees file out, talking as they went. *They are good young warriors, progressing very well*, Dak-So told himself. *Given three years training, they will be very good indeed.*

Thirty

Commodore Igsat Tarimenloku took the bit in his teeth and pressed the two keys. His Reverence's ship *Blessed Flenyaagor* emerged into real-space with its troopship companion. Everyone was at his battle station, but nothing happened except that they continued at emergence speed in the now star-bannered blackness.

He hadn't really expected an attack. For the last two hours in hyperspace, he'd stopped, speeded, stopped again, with no sign of a bogey. And it was inconceivable that they were still inside the hostile sector they'd been in before. But as the first minutes passed, he felt the gradual ebbing of tension, leaving him slack, letting him know how tense he'd actually been.

He'd emerged in a system whose primary was a singlet, a Type F main sequence star, visually a small disk blazing intensely some 800 million miles away. His flagship couldn't evaluate the system for a habitable planet nearly as quickly as the lost survey ship would have, but if any planet had parameters promising enough to call for close examination, he'd know it within the hour and close on it within a day or so. And depending on the outcome of each subsequent phase of observations, he'd determine its critical habitability parameters within a few days more, at most.

Thirty-One

Lord Kristal walked a trifle carefully; his arthritis was flaring up a bit. "We could have done this by cube or beam of course, and saved me the trip," he said. "But I like to see things live when I can. The touch of reality can make a difference."

The new peiok leaves were out and half expanded, sheltering the lawns with springtime's delicate green. The last time he'd been to Lake Loreen had been— That long ago? Early autumn—more than half a year. Then the leaves had shown the first touches of autumn color: yellow, bronze, scarlet.

"I'm glad you came down," Kusu answered, and grinned. "For a milestone of sorts."

They entered the Research Building, and Kusu turned right at the foot of the stairs, stopping at the elevators where he pushed a button. *Hmh!* thought Kristal. *He noticed the knees. Otherwise we'd have walked up. Not much gets by this young man.* The doors opened and they stepped on.

"Is Wellem around?" Kristal asked. "And your parents?"

189

"All three, and Laira and Konni. I'm under orders to bring you to lunch if at all possible. If you want to get with any of them singly, I don't suppose there'll be any difficulty with that either."

The elevator stopped and opened, and it was the roof they stepped out onto, which did not surprise His Lordship. It would have to be the roof; the thing didn't work through walls. A girl was there, a young lady with red hair, standing by the parapet. She turned toward them as they stepped out, as if she'd been watching something and heard the elevator doors open. The "something" had no doubt been the *oroval* which now was running up a branch of a peiok tree, its long tail undulating behind.

And there, sitting on an AG sled, was one of the three teleports Kusu had built.

Kristal returned his attention to the girl. "You must be Lotta Alsnor," he said. "The first person to teleport."

"Yes sir," she answered. "You're right, as usual."

He bowed slightly. "I understand you have other talents—qualities and skills that go beyond boldness. Please accept my admiration."

He turned to Kusu then. "Ernoman you said. There's an ocean between here and there. A horizon and—What? A hundred degrees of curvature? You said it only works on line of sight."

"I was wrong. And I hope you don't ask me to explain it. One of the problems with inventions that grow out of an intuitive leap is that you may not really understand how they work. And draw wrong conclusions from incomplete observations. Besides that, weak understanding can make things pretty tough to explain, let alone debug and modify. I can teleport objects to Offside Base on Seeren if I hit a limb at a tangent, more or less. It's as if it slides around the circumference then. But if I just aim as if to teleport something on a straight line with Seeren's mass in between, nothing happens. It just sits here; it doesn't go to the intervening mass or anywhere else. It either goes to the coordinate destination, or else it stays.

"On the other hand, something like a tree trunk is no obstacle."

Kusu raised a hand slightly, shaking his head. "None of which makes sense, I know, any more than the exclosure limitation does. Theoretically and apparently the object being teleported doesn't traverse the intervening space. It simply ceases to be at one set of coordinates in real space, and instead and instantaneously it's at the other, through their intersection on the back side of reality, so to speak. No physical movement seems to be involved, and hyperspace isn't generated.

"Sense or not though, it works the way it works. And we seem to be making progress on theory; some, anyway. I've had two grad students working on it for several deks now; they're each taking a different approach, and I'm taking a third. We brainstorm usually once a week. But how long it'll be before we understand it remains to be seen."

Lord Kristal's eyes left Kusu, moving to Lotta. "And you, I understand, are to make a real trip, the first long jump, so to speak."

He turned to Kusu. "To Ernoman. Hmh! I'd like to go with her. A step behind, so she'll have the honor of being first. Will you send me?"

The request took Kusu completely by surprise. Lord Kristal had been brought up in the T'sel, but even so . . . "If Your Lordship wishes. There may still be a risk though."

Kristal ignored the warning. " 'Your Lordship?' " he parroted. "When did I stop being Emry to you, Kusu Lormagen?"

Kusu laughed. "Never. But at the same time, you've always been Your Lordship to me, too. Considering all the things you've done and how long you've done them, and how well." *Personal aide to the king,* he added silently, *and to the king before that. The man who sees*

*to things, all kinds of things, takes care of things,
without arrogance, upsets, or unwanted notice.*

Kristal had turned to Lotta and spread his hands.
"What can I say to someone who butters me up like
that?" He grinned, showing still sound teeth. "Lotta,
will you accept my company on a brief but long trip?"

Entering his playful mood, she curtsied. "Your Lordship, I'd be honored."

"Hmmph! 'Your Lordship' again!" He looked at Kusu.
"I believe I'm being put in my place. Are any preparations needed, or can we go now?"

"I'll power up and we'll give it half a minute." Kusu
stepped to the teleport, pressed a switch, and they
waited without speaking. Kristal felt his stomach knot a
bit, and was mildly surprised at it. After perhaps twenty
seconds, a green light came on. "It's ready," Kusu said.

The nobleman and the girl went to the ankle-high
platform, then Kristal gestured. Lotta stepped onto it.
"Ready," she said. Kusu pressed another switch and
she was gone. In her place was what seemed a rectan-
gular hole in the local reality, a door with the gate for
its frame. Through it, seeming both in and beyond it,
they could see Lotta's back. Then she stepped aside,
disappearing, and Kristal found himself looking onto
another roof. Farther off he could see a blurry section
of parapet and, blurrier still, what seemed to be an
evergreen tree. Obviously the teleport was not much
good for tele*viewing*.

Then Kusu looked at Kristal. "If you're ready," Kusu
said, and gestured. "Just step through."

His Lordship stepped onto the platform too, and
through the gate. He hadn't known what to expect,
hadn't thought about it. For him, it was like a mild
twitch, a whole-body twitch. Then he was on another
roof, and it was evening. Lotta Alsnor was standing five
feet away, beside a young man His Lordship had never
met. Beyond the roof, the trees were not peioks, and in
the distance, a row of mountains stretched with snowy

upper slopes. It was early evening instead of late morning.

"Well. I seem to have arrived." He gave his attention to the young man. "I don't suppose you expected me. I'm Lord Kristal."

"I'm Rinly Barrlis," the young man said. "You know my father, I believe."

"So I do. So I do." He looked at the nearby teleport, an apparent duplicate of the one he'd just used, and then at Lotta. "I seem to have no business here, beyond arriving, and I do have people to talk with at Lake Loreen. Is there any reason I shouldn't go back directly?"

"No sir. I should go right back too."

He turned to young Barrlis. "Will you do the honors, Rinly?"

"Of course, Your Lordship." He powered up the teleport, and in less than a minute, Kristal was back with Kusu. Lotta followed a few seconds later, and handed Kusu an envelope which he put in a pocket. The test was over. And somehow it all seemed quite natural to His Lordship, not epochal at all.

It was a half hour short of lunch, and Kristal saw no point in interrupting the mornings of busy people, so he and Kusu sat on a sunlit bench, looking out across the lake. A light breeze blew, cool enough to make the old man glad of his jacket. Wavelets chuckled against rowboats tied to a dock.

"You've teleported objects to Seeren," Kristal said. "What seems to be the feasibility of sending persons to other systems? Persons without a burden of case, of course. Is there any possibility they'd arrive frozen or asphyxiated?"

"There shouldn't be. The last thing I sent to Seeren was an airtight box with three sand lizards. They arrived there alive and well, which says something about temperature, at least. There's a problem though, in sending anything to other *systems*. Actually we key a set of conventional coordinates into the teleport's computer.

The computer converts those to operational, topological coordinates, using an equation."

He paused. "Are you familiar with mail-pod astrogation?"

"Not really."

"Well, to teleport outsystem, the math we use is analogous to that used in mail-pod astrogation. It guides the pod to an imprecisely predictable location within the target system, where it emerges from hyperspace. From there, the pod homes on a beacon off the target world, normally mounted on the local Postal Outsystem Processing Center, which is parked on a gravitic coordinate outside the radiation belt.

"But there's always an error of location, an inaccuracy, in the point where the pod actually emerges from hyperspace. A targeting error. At distances like, say, from here to Rombil or Splenn, a typical error is around a hundred thousand miles; an extremely minute error over a distance of several parsecs. But in teleportation we'd like accuracy within yards—close enough that we can correct by eye to as near as need be, which could be at the entrance of a specific building.

"That's the ideal, of course. At the very least we'd want to land things safely on the planet's land surface."

Lord Kristal's expression was thoughtful. "What needs to be done to attain that accuracy?"

"The most basic approach would be to develop a new math that better fits the topological problems involved. The *quickest* approach though, and the one we can be surest of, is probably to refine the targeting equation. I've started a pair of astrophysicists working on it— members of the Movement of course. They fly down from L.U. on weekends and use the teleport to get data."

"Hmm. Can someone see the roof and the teleport here from the other side? The destination side?"

"No. It's a one-way gate and a one-way view."

"What do you think are the short-term prospects of succeeding?"

"Assuming that 'short term' isn't too short, the prospect of putting things down on a land surface on the target planet seems fairly good. From there, for a while, we may have to settle for providing our passengers with a beacon, so a shuttle can find them and take them by air to where they want to go."

Kristal nodded thoughtfully. "Good. Because now that we have this"—he thumbed back toward the Research Building, where the teleport stood—"I have a feeling we're going to need it."

Thirty-Two

The reality generators, in a coincidence of factors, had brought forth against the Lok-Sanu Range a desert storm, a rain of rains to rend the night, drowning and nurturing, carving and smoothing. It boomed and banged, lightning pulsing, stabbing mountain ridges, punctuating a darkness otherwise absolute. Wind whoomed. Rain slashed in sheets against thick walls and stubby towers. Torrents, rock-laden, snarled and rumbled down deep ravines.

Inside his tower-top cell, Master Tso-Ban sat in trance, unaware of the misted spray, the ruptured rain which swirling gusts brought in beneath the eaves and through the open side to wet his skin with unaccustomed coolness.

His awareness was elsewhere—much farther even than Iryala. In fact, he lay as a sellsu, in a cool ocean current, on a world as wet as his own was (usually) dry. Rose and fell gently, slowly, on oil-smooth swells fathered by some distant storm, his flippers gently stroking to hold him in place. Floated among his pack listening to a poem, a favorite ode among the sullsi, told this night by a master bard who phrased the well-known tale in words and meter of his own. A human maiden, Juliassa, daughter of a chief, had found a sullsit chieftain, Sleekit, left by the tide sick and dying on a beach. She'd cared for him, brought fish to him, protected him from saarkas. Had even learned to speak the sullsit air speech, so they could share stories, until he was well and strong enough to fish and fight again and travel with his own.

And how, with the help of the far-listening serpents who call themselves Vrronnkiess, the sullsi, people of the waves, had gone to war to save Juliassa's people from the big-ship humans who'd come to enslave them. (Two verses were given to explain enslavement, and another for war.)

The bard was describing the gathering of the packs, when Tso-Ban felt himself drawing out of the sellsu he'd melded with, a sellsu who'd been aware of him as a psychic presence, a visitor silent and benign, and by now was used to him. For just a moment, Tso-Ban was aware of his tiny tower room. Then, unexpectedly, he was with—

Tarimenloku! Nearby! Quickly but gently he melded, and found himself looking at a screen, the bridge's version of a window, looking at a world, his own world, Tyss, a tan ball with a visible area of blue flecked with white. The Klestronu flotilla was parked 50,000 miles out, beyond the radiation belt.

Tso-Ban stayed unnoticed with Tarimenloku for hours—till after sunup. Because Tyss was technologically so backward, at 50,000 miles the ship's instruments failed to perceive that it held people. Instead, from those instruments he reluctantly decided that this planet was not habitable. Most of its surface he judged too hot for human life, while in the polar regions it was utter desert. Closer examination would not be worthwhile.

Although it was the most nearly habitable world that Tarimenloku had found in the systems he'd examined. In a sour mood he moved his two ships away from Tyss, accelerating in a warp field toward a point far enough from any gravitic nodus that he could generate hyperspace safely. Meanwhile his astrogator was taking data on the nearest other stars, deciding which to visit next.

Gently Master Tso-Ban disengaged, woke his body from its trance, then stood and stretched, and stepped outside. Desert rocks steamed beneath the newly risen sun. He would go and notify Master Deng before his exercises. This unexpected visit by the Klestroni was something the Confederatswa would want to know about.

Thirty-Three

It was a lovely late-spring day—one might say presolstice summer—when Lord Kristal called Wellem Bosler. Bosler didn't answer. Reception referred the call to Laira Gouer Lormagen, who wore the coordinator's hat at Lake Loreen. She paged Bosler while Kristal waited, and when there still was no response, told His Lordship that Bosler must be at the *ghao,* a small, rather Pagoda-like building on the islet in Gouer Cove. The ghao had no commset. She'd go herself and see if he was available.

There was a wooden causeway to the islet, giving quick access. She found the red light glowing on the door of Bosler's inner sanctum, warning her away.

Kristal knew that much of what went on at the ghao was not to be interrupted short of serious emergency. And while his business, which was the Crown's business, was extremely important, it was not immediately urgent. He told Laira this, and asked her to have Bosler call him back at his earliest opportunity. And that Kusu was to sit in on the call if at all possible.

Within The Movement there was a large amount of

mutual respect. That, not rank, was the basis of their operation, for all of them knew the T'sel. Although there was rank, and one gave orders as needful. But usually it was only necessary to make known what was wanted, what needed to be done.

It was the better part of an hour before Kristal's commset chirped. When he switched it on, his screen was split, showing both Bosler's face and Kusu's.

"Ah, good!" Kristal said. "Wellem, this is mainly for you, but Kusu needs to be in on it too." Then he read them a message to His Majesty, a message that had just come by pod from Tyss, from the Grand Master of Ka-Shok. One of their seers had discovered the Klestronu flotilla in the Confederation Sector, parked off Tyss. It was looking for habitable worlds, and decided that "Oven" didn't meet their criteria of habitability.

"That was twenty-eight days ago. It could already have landed on some other world, and it might not be known on Iryala for weeks."

"But the Ka-Shok are monitoring it again?"

"Right. But there's still that twenty-eight-day communication lag. That's one reason I'm calling you. Can you meld with their monitor? You or anyone else you know of on Iryala?"

Bosler frowned. "I've never melded with anyone as far away as the next room. Very few can meld without eye contact, and of the few who can, it's generally with someone they know and have strong affinity with." He paused thoughtfully. "When we're done with this conference, I'll see what I can come up with. I have an advanced student who might, just conceivably, work out. Meanwhile I recommend you check with the other institutes."

Kusu spoke then. "Why didn't the Ka-Shok have one of their seers connect with you, Emry? Or with Bosler? That'd take care of the lag."

"They recognize the situation. But they're communicating by message pod, so there may be technical reasons. On the other hand they may simply have chosen not to. I don't try to understand the Ka-Shok; I believe the word is 'inscrutable.' Wellem?"

Bosler shook his head. "They have reasons, I'm sure. Which can be as trivial as curiosity about how we'll handle the situation, or as profound as"—He gestured. "As curiosity about how we'll handle the situation."

Kusu grunted. "Did the Ka-Shok alert the warrior lodges?"

"It wasn't mentioned," Kristal answered. "They may have, of course, but they may not have. The war lodges are rather like the Ka-Shok in that respect: They look at things in their own way, with their own sense of importances.

"But even if they had alerted the lodges, it could easily take a dek or more to get a troopship from Tyss to wherever it was needed. Assuming they had a regiment available at the time. Or a fledgling regiment they were willing to send short of graduation, which seems very unlikely. But then, this is not the sort of thing that's come up before.

"And Kusu, that brings up what I need to talk with you about. How ready is the teleport for the interstellar transfer of humans?"

"Umh!" Kusu's response was a grunt, almost as if he'd been elbowed in the stomach. "You're talking about people who've been through Ostrak Procedures of course. We're not nearly ready. Haven't been looking at the problem as urgent. The people working on it didn't even come down last weekend. Family activities."

"When *can* it be ready?" Kristal asked.

"I don't even have a respectable guess for you; I haven't been following their progress very closely lately. I'll get in touch with them today, get a status report for you, and tell them we have an urgent need. That's the best I can do. That and start an independent analysis of the problem myself, when I have their report."

"Hmm." Frowning, Kristal pursed his lips. "If you had to guess, are we looking at a dek, two deks? A year?"

"Possibly as soon as a couple of deks. If all we have to do is get people onto a planet's surface. Getting them on the right continent is something else."

"Is there any reason I can't have the teleport from Ernoman?" Kristal asked. "For Blue Forest? How long would it take to build another?"

"You're welcome to the one at Ernoman. And I can have another one ready within about a week. Meanwhile if you can get some qualified people sent here from L.U., we can start building a large one for teleporting smaller teleports to places. Along with small floaters—things like that."

"Good. You asked for qualified people. Give me some names and I'll see what I can do."

Kristal's fingers quick-stepped on his keyboard while Kusu named. There weren't many. *We've got too few scientists in The Movement,* Kristal told himself. *And in the culture at large. And too few highly qualified technicians.*

The long-term job was to transform the Confederation from a calm but stagnant, firmly aberrated order to a sane one, from quasi-religiously imposed conformity under the Sacrament to consensus under the T'sel. The recognized priority need, toward that goal, had been for human services—the delivery of Ostrak Procedures on twenty-five Confederation worlds and two key trade worlds. All of it very quietly, covertly.

The job had been more dangerous when virtually the entire population was under the Sacrament, although caution was still important. But so was acceleration now, because with the Sacrament defused, the problems of slow but accelerating centrifugal forces in society would surely assert themselves. And strain the fabric of a confederation that had long depended on the Sacrament, the canons of Standard Practices, common origin, and basic cultural similarities to compensate for vast distances, slow communication, and little personal contact. The first signs of strain were evident already, small but unmistakeable. So The Movement, under

Crown leadership, was trying to shorten the job from centuries to hopefully not more than three generations, with the hump to be crossed within fifty years.

Now the Klestronu expedition was complicating and crowding the timetable.

Bosler spoke when Kristal had finished writing the names he'd been given. "If you're considering teleporting the regiment from Blue Forest," he said, "we need to run them through more Ostrak Procedures. Some might arrive safely, but I've examined Lotta's analysis of the experimental animals, and I can almost guarantee a dangerous fiasco if we send our young warriors as they are."

Kristal bobbed a nod. "Right. Which leads to my next question: Can you get them all processed in, say, a dek?"

"It's barely conceivable. Two or three deks seems more likely. It depends on how much need we'll have for advanced procedures. There aren't many operators qualified to use them; not on Iryala. They're scattered all over the sector."

His Lordship's gaze was steady. "Do what's necessary. I'll back you. But don't disrupt other work more than you need to. Kusu, I'll get you the people you need to make the larger teleport.

"Meanwhile I'll have the teleport at Ernoman flown to Blue Forest. Wellem, I suppose you'll have to establish the hard way what case levels can be teleported safely. If you want to, use trainees for your tests."

His Lordship straightened. "We'll talk again at 2000 hours, or sooner if necessary. Any questions you need to ask right now?"

There weren't.

"Good. At 2000 then."

Kristal cut the connection. Each of the others began at once to jot down a working plan.

Thirty-Four

When she stepped into the Main Building, Lotta smelled fresh lumber again. Of course. The Blue Forest Reservation was on loan from the Army, which had used it at intervals over the centuries. The Main Building had been built not only as reservation headquarters, but as an officers' dormitory, and the new interview rooms, like the old, would have been made by subdividing offices and sleeping rooms.

Her team got brief instructions in the lobby, then went to find their sleeping rooms.

The one she'd been assigned was a virtual duplicate of the one she'd been in before, but instead of two beds, it now had two double bunks and two large dressers, and the couch was gone. A narrow metal cabinet had been added in the bathroom. She unpacked and put her things away, then the four of them found their supervisor's office, knocked, and were let in. Eight empty folding chairs were crowded in front of a desk.

Two people were there ahead of them, both middle-aged: a woman behind the desk, and a man standing.

Lotta had never seen either of them before. "You're from Lake Loreen?" the woman asked.

As senior in operating qualifications, Lotta answered for her team. "Yes ma'am."

"Good. We'll start when the others arrive." Gray eyes examined them briefly. "You're Lotta Alsnor?"

"Yes ma'am."

"Were all of you in the previous project here?"

"We four were. Two of the other Lake Loreen team weren't; they're brand new Intern-Twos."

There was a knock. The other four entered and took seats.

"All right," the woman said. "We'll get started. I'm Meteen Voranis Kron, your supervisor." She gestured at the man. "This is Jomar Kron, my husband and your bail-out operator." She grinned. "The ideal is not to need him. We were here in Iryala, vacationing from Rombil, and Wellem tabbed us for this emergency project; we're old students of his. Which of you are the new I-Twos?"

A boy and girl of fourteen or fifteen raised hands.

"Congratulations." Her eyes took in the rest of them then. "I suppose you all got a technical briefing before you left Lake Loreen."

"Yes," Lotta said, "from Wellem over the comm. But it was short and pretty general."

"I'll give you another. You can ask questions afterward.

"There'll be eight teams of us—fifty-three operators plus eight bail-outs. Wellem is in overall charge, of course. Jomar and I are Masters. We've spent the last five days here with Wellem, setting things up.

"We selected a sample of twenty trainees, stratified by case level, to send through the teleport. Ran them through 'a space-time loop,' as Kusu calls it, bringing them back to the same place and same time they'd left. The level 5s weren't phased by it. Which was expected, but we had to know for sure. They knew something had happened, but that was all. The 4s were disoriented and more or less spooked, but they weren't a serious problem. We snapped them out of it with two or three minutes of 'Look at That.'

"The 3s came out either scared stiff or semi-comatose, but at least we could get through to them. Took a little while though to get them back to normal. Had to give them each a session."

Meteen smiled slightly. "We almost didn't send a 2 through; we could assume he'd be worse. But would he be manageable? It was worse than we'd thought. He came out totally berserk—it was a good thing we had a couple of T'swa on hand to control him—and for a little bit we thought we might even lose him, it was that bad.

"And of course, we don't have any 1s or zeros here. The earlier project took them all at least to 2s."

Again she smiled. "We sent a T'swi through too, just for the record. All he had to say was, 'Interesting.'

"So—" She paused and looked them over again. "We have a lot for you to do. The 5s don't require any processing, but there are only three of them in the regiment. We need the whole 2,000 at 5. That's our job, ours and the other five teams. Sixty-eight percent are 2s, which any operator in the project can upgrade to 3s. Another twenty-seven percent are 3s, which most of you can handle. Roughly five percent, a total of ninety-one, are 4s. They'll require Experts, which we're short of." She scanned them. "Lotta and Bart— Which one of you is Bart?"

He raised his hand.

"I presume you're aware that Wellem has raised you to provisional E-Ones. Congratulations. He says you can handle it, and if he says so, you can.

"Granted it usually takes only one session—seldom more than two—to take a 4 to Level 5. But we've got nearly 2,000 men here who'll need a session or two from an Expert or higher. And aside from supervisors and bail-outs, we've only got eleven E's or higher in the project.

"And we can't have the bail-outs doing routine sessions. They have to be available when an emergency comes up. While the supervisors will have their hands more than full, supervising.

"Wellem's gotten agreement from a number of E's to come and help out when the 4s start to pile up on us. You may not appreciate how few Es and Ms there are on Iryala, planet-wide, or on any world; not nearly as many as there'll be ten years from now. For too long the need for lower-level operators has had the institutes sending most of us out when we'd reached journeyman."

She scanned them again, grinning now. "So you journeymen—that's Feelis and Norla and Rob, right?—as much as we need you to process Level 2s and 3s, in the evenings you'll be training instead, under Jomar. We plan to make provisional E-Ones out of you, to help with the 4s. It'll be a crash course, but we're depending on you.

"Any questions?"

There weren't.

"Fine. The exception to that is tonight. All of you will be giving sessions this evening." Meteen got up and gestured. "You'll find the summary and instruction for your next trainee on a shelf in the ready room, above your name. Now I'll show you what session rooms are yours. You'll be there no later than 1845 this evening, and familiarize yourself with the case summary. A page will bring your trainee to you at 1900. You'll get another one at 2100, unless the first one gets into something that takes unusually long to lead him through."

They left the small office then. To Lotta's surprise, she had the same session room as before. She still had time to look up Bosler, if he was available.

Bosler was tied up, so she waited till supper and caught him on his way to the dining hall. They got their food and sat down side by side; their conversation was casual until they'd finished eating.

"So," he said then. "What is it you need from me?"

Lotta's gaze, as always, was direct. "I'd like to give a

session, sort of, to Artus Romlar. Tomorrow evening would be a good time."

Bosler's eyebrows raised slightly. "Romlar's a 5. In fact, he's already been through the teleport. Unfazed. I have no session lined up for him at all."

She nodded. "Right. I'd like to give him one anyway."

" 'Sort of a session,' you said. What do you have in mind? An Expert-One is pretty limited in what they're qualified to do with a 5."

"I know. I want to do a meld with him."

Wellem Bosler wasn't often surprised. He was now. "Before I ask you why," he said, "let me remind you that that's tricky business with a 5. For an E-One certainly; especially a provisional. If he was a Level 3 or 2, it would be pretty safe; most 2s wouldn't even be aware of a meld, and most 3s probably wouldn't know what was going on—feel a bit spooky perhaps, or exhilarated. While a 7 and probably most 6s have enough stability to deal with it easily. But a 5's got a lot of power freed up, Romlar especially. The meld could easily get out of control. Then we'd have to bail you both out, and it could take awhile." He eyed her curiously. "What do you hope to accomplish?"

"I'm not sure. But you know what he is, what his potential is. And you said you wanted to get him in session again before he left Iryala."

"Hmh! I did, didn't I. I've had so much to do, I'd lost track of that. But—"He smiled slightly. "I was talking about me, not you. Supposing that's what we do? I'll give him a session—get him up to a 6—and maybe you can meld with him then. Will you settle for that?"

"I'd like to have you give him a session. But meanwhile, I'm asking to do a meld with him myself. As he is."

"Hmm." Bosler frowned, contemplating the suggestion. Ordinarily he'd have said no, out of hand. But ordinarily the matter would never have come up. And Lotta Alsnor had more native talent than perhaps any student he'd ever had. Including Meteen Voranis. Someone like that needed as free a rein as possible, when their intuition spurred them.

And when someone as sane and talented as Lotta asked to do something crazy-sounding, he couldn't help but wonder if she was giving birth to a breakthrough of some sort.

Although he still couldn't see what a meld would accomplish. Melds were not in themselves therapeutic.

"All right," he said after a slow minute. "I'll speak with Meteen about it. If she's willing to spare you, you can have him tomorrow evening. I'll have her alert Jomar, in case you get into trouble. And you be sure your monitor is on before you start, so he can keep half an eye on you."

She nodded soberly. "Thanks," she said. She got up and took her tray to the wash belt, then left, wondering if she really had any business doing what she'd proposed. She caught herself half hoping Meteen would refuse.

Thirty-Five

Romlar came in and closed the door behind him. "Hi, Lotta," he said cheerfully, and sat down. "I hadn't expected to see you again."

She smiled. "I hadn't expected to be here again. How have things been going?"

"We're doing battalion exercises now. And good old 2nd Platoon's been hogging the command posts. Coyn Carrmak and I have been switching off as battalion commander and battalion EO. And Jerym is A Company exec under Eldren Esenrok, when it's not the other way around."

"Well! Congratulations! Did you have a good supper this evening?"

"Always. Almost always."

"Good. Did you get enough sleep last night?"

"Yep."

His aura reflected good health and good spirit. "All right. We'll start the formal interview then. I want you to sit back and relax. Get nice and loose. You can close your eyes if you'd like."

He did.

"All right. Now just let your mind relax too. Let it drift if it wants to. And if you feel anything strange happening, it'll be all right. Just let it happen and ride along with it. It'll be no big deal."

He didn't nod, didn't move, just let himself go. For almost all his life, it would not have been possible except while falling asleep; resentments, worries, and thoughts had tended to crowd his mind. Now letting go was easy. An idea drifted through and he watched it pass, was aware of watching it, then aware of its absence, all very relaxed and unimportant.

Then something else was there that for a moment he couldn't identify. His awareness sharpened a little with curiosity. Of course! [Hello, Lotta! What are you doing?]

[It's called a meld. Our minds join.]

[What do we do next?]

[Relax and let things happen. Or not happen.]

His awareness softened again. Another thought came to him. His thought? Or hers? He decided it didn't matter. After that, for a while, nothing seemed to be happening, and he lost track of time. There was time, but he had no real notion of how much was passing. His main awareness was of a sense of intimacy and dormant power, power that was his and that he hadn't recognized before.

Then he saw his own face, as through Lotta's eyes, and the thought was there, her thought, that it was time to separate. [All right,] he thought back to her. And felt her withdraw slowly, gently, till his mind was alone.

Alone but not the same. He was aware of himself at a depth beyond anything he'd experienced or suspected. In spite of so little having happened.

He opened his eyes. "Thank you," he said. "Thank you very much." And when he left the room, it seemed to him he was bigger, had expanded, was seeing the floor from a foot higher than before.

* * *

Wellem Bosler awoke gradually, uneasy in the dark of his small room. It struck him then why. [Who,] he asked, [is in my mind?]

[Lotta, Wellem.]

[Huh! Where are you Lotta? Physically I mean?]

[In my room.]

[You can meld at a distance then.]

[I thought I could. After I melded with Artus. I felt such power when we were together, he and I. So did he. Wellem, you need to have a session with him. To know where he's at. At what level. He's not just a 5; not now anyway.]

[All right. And I need to do an eval on you, to find out what level you're at now. You've changed too, I'm sure of it. Huh! I've melded with Konni, and with others a few times, and never got any personal change out of it. Never before heard of anyone getting any.]

She didn't respond, seemed relaxed. After what might have been a minute or two, her mind stirred. [I'm going to leave and go to sleep now,] she thought to him, and he felt her disengage.

When she was gone, he lay awake for a while. Remarkable, he thought. He'd heard of a few Iryalans—Masters like himself, and Experts—who could contact friends at a distance, perhaps on another continent, and might even meld with them. The T'swa of course had a long history of producing seers who could meld at a distance with almost anyone, as if distance didn't exist for them. But the entire population of Tyss knew the T'sel—or ninety-nine percent did, something like that—and had for millenia. They'd long since needed no procedures to gain it. And every T'swi who was born to Wisdom/Knowledge was trained as a seer. It wasn't terribly remarkable that some, a few of them, could find and meld with someone hundreds of parsecs away.

And now— His psyche quickened. Could Lotta learn

to? Learn to find the T'swa seer? Or even the Klestronu flagship and its captain? He'd have to look into this, even if it required slighting his work a bit as project leader.

Thirty-Six

Voker's commset chirped. He touched a key. "Yes?"

"Sir, Lord Kristal wants to speak with you."

"Thanks." He touched another key and the screen lit up. Kristal was sitting at a desk which, by Voker's criteria, was cluttered. "Good morning, Your Lordship."

"Good morning, Carlis. His Majesty and I have a plan. I want to run it by you before we decide on the details and implement it."

"Okay."

"We want to publicize the regiment. Judiciously of course. And later the Klestronu intrusion—and the teleport. The Klestroni will be used to make the teleport necessary and acceptable. It's touchy business of course. Some thirty percent of our population on Iryala, more than fifty percent in the Confederation as a whole, underwent a real Sacrament as children. And a lot of the rest are about as conservative, if less compulsively so. But circumstances seem to be forcing our hand. And if we handle it well, it will broaden the public tolerance of change.

"Varlik Lormagen's publicizing of the T'swa did wonders for us thirty-two years ago. So we've been screening feature journalists. Women, mainly."

"Emry," Voker interrupted, "a suggestion. Whoever it is should be in excellent physical condition. If she or he's going to follow these young men around effectively enough to get to know what they do."

Kristal nodded. "Good point."

And chances are, you've already considered it, Voker told himself. "Another thing," he added: "Any such person around here just now, or for the next two or three weeks, can't help but be aware of the Ostrak Procedures, and wondering what it is that involves so much time and activity. Are you willing for that to become public?"

"Obliquely, yes. Wellem suggested we call it 'special psychological drills to provide the trainees with T'swa calmness of mind. Very useful for fighting men.' Which is the truth, presented from a particular point of view. But we won't send her to you till the larger part of the activity is over with, and all the men have been processed to 3 and higher. Quite a few will be 5s by then, and done with."

"Umm." Voker cleared his mind for a moment, to let anything else come up that needed to. "And you're going to publicize the teleport too, you say."

"Yes. Assuming the Klestroni land in this sector in other than a properly peaceful, ambassadorial manner."

Which makes disclosure close to a certainty, Voker told himself. "What cautions shall I give the trainees? What shouldn't they say?"

"Wait till we've selected the young lady. I'll let you know."

Kristal shifted subjects. "Meanwhile Kusu's people are assembling a teleport for shipment to Tyss. We're sending it on a fleet supply ship, with a pair of technicians to operate it. They'll leave in four days if no complications arise, and it'll take fifty-one days to get there by hyperspace. Including a quick stop at Terfreya to deliver some new-model equipment to the cadets there."

"Why not send the teleport directly to Tyss, and send the cadets their equipment separately?"

"We'd only save four days that way. Iryala, Terfreya, and Tyss are as nearly aligned as any three inhabited worlds in this sector." Kristal paused. "Do you have some thoughts on that?"

The colonel looked at it, frowning. "I guess not. What time of year is it on Tyss?"

"What? Ah, I see your point. We've looked at that. At Kootosh Moks it's early winter." Kristal chuckled. "If I may use the term."

"How large are the vehicles it can teleport?"

"Small; almost the smallest. Light utility vehicles and armed scout floaters. It had to be something we could construct with components on hand or easy to make. Kusu's still designing the big one, the one we'll send the regiment's vehicles with. Although he has men fabricating parts already. It's quite a project."

Voker nodded. It would be, when most of the components couldn't be bought off the shelf anywhere.

"Oh, and Carlis," Kristal said, "your floater crews should arrive next Oneday morning. All with warrior profiles, you'll be glad to hear, and cross-trained for maintenance. And the eight-man regimental medical team you asked for. They'll all need Ostrak Procedures of course. Do you want me to tell Wellem?"

"No, I'll tell him. I'll be seeing him in a few minutes at lunch."

Having said everything necessary, they ended the conversation and disconnected. *A full contingent of floater crews with warrior profiles!* Voker thought. *Hmh!* He hadn't thought the army had that many warriors in its air branch. Not that six scouts, eight combat personnel carriers, and four gunships required a lot of personnel; mental arithmetic made it 120, with two crews per aircraft.

The sad thing was, their senior officers would be

glad to see most of them go. Well, he'd be glad to see them arrive.

He was very glad there'd be a teleport on Tyss. Although he still felt a little—uncomfortable about sending it by way of Terfreya. But a four-day delay wasn't going to mean anything when the war lodges wouldn't be graduating new regiments until equinox there, still a couple of deks away.

Thirty-Seven

Spring was on the verge of summer, even at Blue Forest, in the Subaustral Zone. The night smelled of things growing, and it was warm enough that Lotta carried her jacket as she walked through the gate into the compound. The new leaves were fully expanded, and the woods behind her sounded with the stridulations of small courting creatures, both insects and amphibians.

She'd found a place in the woods to be away from human busyness, physical and mental, a dry place where she could sit on the ground. She'd been going there at night after her last session. From there she contacted people she knew, people all over Iryala. Melded with them if they were sufficiently advanced and agreed to it, and occasionally if they were unaware and wouldn't be harmed by it. She was becoming adept at this by now, could have done it in her room with others present, but she liked getting away.

Entering the Main Building, she switched off her insect repellent field and walked briskly to the project dining room, where snacks were available for those who worked late. Meteen Kron was there; she'd finished reviewing the evening session reports. After drawing a cup of thocal, Lotta went to the table where Meteen was sipping joma, and sat down across from her.

"Been practicing?" Meteen asked.

Lotta nodded. "In the woods."

"Have you tried reaching anyone off planet?"

"I'm not sure I know anyone off planet. I suppose I do, but I don't know who they are."

"Did you know Kari Frensler? You were probably at Lake Loreen when she was still there."

Kari Frensler. Lotta recalled a tall, rather gangly teenager who'd graduated and left years ago, when she herself had been—nine; newly nine. "Is she off planet?"

"Nine parsecs off planet. She's on Sandhills staff on Rombil, with Jomar and me. Teaches history. It would be interesting to see if you could reach her."

Lotta felt a small surge of excitement. "Yes it would," she said. "Especially since I hardly knew her. We may have spoken all of three times. It would be a good test."

She and Meteen exchanged small talk then, briefly, and Lotta finished her thocal more quickly than usual. She'd go outside and sit on one of the benches—it would be quiet there, this late—and try the contact before she went to bed.

Thirty-Eight

It was the most promising-looking world yet—blue
and white, blue-green and tan—ocean and clouds, forest and steppe, and no doubt desert. At higher lati-
tudes, some of the white clearly was snow or ice, even
in the summer hemisphere. In fact, the instruments
insisted on it. They'd already reported temperatures in
the habitable range, though the mid-latitude summer
was rather cooler than one might wish. Nothing serious.

And the atmosphere promised to be breathable.

There was a complication though, of course: it had an
obviously sapient life form. Broad-band monitoring had
long-since found an object bearing a beacon, parked
outside the planet's radiation belt. Commodore Tarimenloku examined the object on the viewscreen. Considering its location 55,000 miles above the planet, he
told himself, it could be a processor for incoming mail
pods, a processor with a homing beacon. It was assuming a lot to think that a race out in this Kargh-forsaken
sector would have mail pods, but if they had hyperspace
generators, mail pods would no doubt have to be
invented.

There *was* radio here, there was no question about that, though only one broadcast source had reached the *Blessed Flenyaagor*. The voice even sounded human, and while that could be coincidence, the commodore was not addicted to coincidence as an explanation for anything. The words, of course, meant nothing to a son of Kargh.

That this object was here at all indicated a reasonably advanced civilization. If it was a pod processor, it indicated a multi-system civilization. And it was already clear that this was not a world with cities or the extensive use of powerful electronics—not a major planet. It would seem then to be a very minor world. Very minor.

Tarimenloku gave an order to pick up the pod processor or whatever it was; it should tell them something worth knowing about the technology here. He also gave an order to be alert for and destroy any missile sent up from the surface. These beings might detect them and send out either a war missile, or a message pod programmed to go to the nearest navel base, reporting an intruder.

Thirty-Nine

The sides of the tent were rolled up for light, and cadet Varlik Krellzo sat on a folding camp chair, at a folding table, figuring a food supply order the hard way, with stylus and writing board. His rolled-up sleeves exposed arms that were still slender but very sinewy. Varlik was nearly thirteen years old.

A command radio sat on the table, with a long-life power slug. It beeped a standard warning, and Varlik touched the record key, just in case.

After a moment, a voice spoke from it. "Attention! Attention! This is the Confederation Ministry at Lonyer City, with information to whomever it may concern." A sense of suppressed panic in the voice sharpened Varlik's attention. "This morning, at Lonyer City 0746:22, our systems monitor informed us that the pod processor's homing beacon had ceased to signal. At 0829:09, a shuttle lifted from the Lonyer City port to repair the processor. At approximately 0846:43, the shuttle crew reported two nonstandard ships—*repeat, nonstandard ships!*—one of them extremely large, parked in the vicinity of the processor's gravitic coordinates. The processor seemed to be absent. The shuttle crew undertook to return to the Lonyer City port and abruptly went off the air. It may have been destroyed by the nonstandard ships.

"We recommend that you leave your radio on for possible further information."

Varlik Krellzo was on his feet by that time, grinning. When the broadcast ended he tipped his head back. "*YEEEE-haaah!*" he whooped, then got on the radio to Colonel Jil-Zat. Young Krellzo had a definite feeling that he was going to be in a for-real war very soon.

Forty

Excerpts from "Terfreya," article in the *Standard Encyclopedia*, YP 748, Landfall, Iryala.

Terfreya, or Karnovir 02, is a trade planet. Local tradition has it colonized early in the prehistoric era, in the 15th millenium before Pertunis. There is abundant evidence that mining was extensive there for centuries and possibly millenia.

By the historical era, however, mining had ceased. A native spice, *kressera*, had become almost the sole export. It was popular throughout the sector, and Terfreya became or remained a prosperous world. However, in the 2nd century before Pertunis, a substitute "kressera," growable on many worlds, preempted much of the market. . . .

During the prehistoric era, probably in the early years of human settlement, Terfreya was nicknamed "Backbreak." This nickname is sometimes used in the literature, and was the vernacular usage both on Terfreya and Confederation worlds. Presumably it derived from the rigors of hard labor in Terfreya's gravity of 1.19 gee. . . .

The Terfreyan year contains 434.471 Terfreyan days, each day being 26.551 standard hours long, making the Terfreyan year 1.316 times as long as the Standard year. The orbit is somewhat eccentric, the maximum radius being 134 million miles and the minimum 118 million miles. . . . The axial tilt is 24.19, making the swing of the seasons almost as great as on Iryala, but as virtually the entire human population of recent millenia lives in the equatorial zone, axial tilt does not directly impact the lives of Terfreyans. . . . The relatively low solar constant makes Terfreya, overall, somewhat cold, but the temperature regime of the equatorial zone is comfortable year-round, if one disregards occasional chilly periods of winter rain. . . .

In YP 741, the planetary population was restricted almost entirely to a single region, and numbered only 87,911. It consists largely of farm families scattered in locales especially favorable for the cultivation of kressera. There are few villages. The administrative seat, Lonyer City, serves as the center for trade and services. . . .

General Kartoozh Saadhrambacoora* had been awake and mostly on his feet since landing on the planet with two of his four regiments at approximately 0830 local time. He'd gotten them bivouacked on farmland near the ridiculously small town which seemed to be the capital of this world. And harangued his officers with the importance of strict discipline. Troops were to stay within the hastily fenced base except as otherwise ordered, keep away from the local females, and in general avoid incidents.

A small crowd had approached the base to stare. And from the way the troops had ogled the women, you'd

---

*In the empire, the surnames of nobles have five syllables, with the stress on the first and fourth. Here dh is used to represent the sound of th in the; and c the ch sound in chew. Thus "SAADH-rahm-bah-CHOO-rah."

think they'd been conscious and dreaming of copulation the whole two years, instead of unconscious in stasis chambers. Or did they dream in stasis? He hadn't, but it was hard to be sure about peasants.

The women here *were* attractive, many of them: light-skinned, and either they had little hair on their arms and legs, or they shaved.

With a guard company, he'd personally marched to the most important-seeming buildings, taken the prisoners the commodore wanted, and sent them on a shuttle to the *Blessed Flenyaagor*, where DAAS would develop a translation program for their language and they could be properly interrogated.

At least he hoped DAAS would. The language here sounded more foreign than anything in the empire.

Now he sat down heavily in a camp chair, had his orderly pull his boots off, and his stockings. He wiggled his toes and regarded them with a certain glumness. It was easy for the commodore to say "no incidents." With 4,000 men on the ground, most of them peasants, it was something else to ensure it. But he would try. And Kargh take the soul of the man who caused one, for his head belonged to his general.

Forty-One

The stadium at Lonyer City had stands along both sides, and its benches, the general had been told, would seat more than ten thousand. Using the now-functional translation program, Saadhrambacoora had ordered a public assembly, requiring attendance by all male adults of the town and district, telling the local authorities to see to it. He'd helped compliance by telling them that the offending marines would be publicly executed there. And that if the stands were not full, hostages would be killed.

Standing with his guard detail at one end of the field, he eyed the now-packed stands. Hundreds more people, perhaps two thousand, stood behind the stands. And many of those attending were females; a strange people, these. The general did not doubt that there were concealed weapons among the crowd, but he did doubt they'd be used. There was a chance they would, of course—a chance that he would not live to eat supper, or pray again to Kargh. But the gunships circling overhead with beam guns and rockets—weapons he'd had demonstrated for the local authorities—militated

227

against an uprising. He was sure the gunships were far more intimidating than the two companies of armed marines on the field, a company along each sideline, facing the stands.

He let the crowd wait a bit, then spoke into his throat mike. Seconds later, two hovertrucks moved through one of the stadium's open ends—the far end— accompanied by two squads of military police on hovercycles, and stopped at what appeared to be the goal line. From his end, Saadhrambacoora now marched onto the playing field. He was flanked by aides, and by a hovercycle on which a translator was mounted. His guard section followed on foot.

The stands were remarkably quiet, and the general's hair crawled a bit, exposed as he was. But to keep the situation in hand, short of nuclear punishment, which the commodore would never consider, something like this was necessary. Almost at mid-field he stopped. From one of the hovertrucks, seven men were removed, seven marines, and marched in chains to the mid-field stripe, each accompanied by a pair of guards. When they were lined up along the stripe, they were ordered to kneel and bow their heads. In his Klestronu dialect of Imperial, Saadhrambacoora urged the seven to pray to Kargh.

After a minute he had one of his aides turn on the translator. Then he spoke to the crowd, the volume high so all could hear. "Inhabitants of the town named Lonyer," it boomed out, "and of its rural vicinity. The seven marines who kneel here are those who forcibly copulated with a young woman of your people. That was an act abominable in the eyes of Kargh, and a breach of military discipline. I will now punish them for it."

He stepped away from the translator, drew his large sword, ceremonial but scalpel-sharp, and walked to one end of the line of kneeling men. Peasants, each of them, except for the sergeant he now stood above. Saadhrambacoora raised the sword with both hands.

His eyes were open, almost bulging, fixed upon the nape, then he brought the blade down with all his strength. With a spray of blood, the sergeant's head fell free, his body toppling, and a collective sigh came from the stands as if from some giant who'd been holding his breath.

Grim-faced, the burly general went down the line. The seven had been treated with an obedience drug, but the dose had not been heavy. It had been necessary that they be alert enough to pray. Thus two of the men tried to avoid the stroke. One jerked his head up and back, so that the blade took him across the face, then split his rib cage. He clove the other's skull, adding crumbs of brain to the blood which by then had soaked the front of his own uniform. Of the other five, only three were beheaded cleanly, but all were very dead.

Beneath a moderate layer of fat, Kartoozh Saadhrambacoora was a physically powerful man. But when, sweat covered, he'd killed the seventh, he felt drained, his thick arms suddenly weak. The truck that had brought the prisoners came out onto the field, and bodies and heads were thrown into it. Then it left. Saadhrambacoora pulled himself together and walked to the translator.

"Yesterday," he said huskily, "five marines were murdered and nine wounded, by a cowardly ambush. We do not know what persons are guilty, but some of you do. Thus I declare that it is *your* responsibility to punish them, and the punishment must be death. The dead guilty people must be delivered at the gate of the military compound by midday the day after tomorrow. That is 1200 hours on Fiveday.

"We have hostages from you. If you are late with the delivery of those dead guilty ones, on the first day of lateness there shall be fourteen hostages executed, one for each of my casualties. And fourteen more on each further day of lateness. I have executed my guilty persons; I expect you to execute yours.

"This meeting is now finished. You will now leave."

*　　*　　*

Saadhrambacoora stayed where he was, watching the crowd move slowly down the aisles and out of the stands. He'd thought of mentioning that while they'd been there, marines had visited a school and taken 100 children hostage. But it had not seemed like the time and place to let them learn of it.

Forty-Two

General Saadhrambacoora crouched beside his dressing table in officers' white pajamas, listening, confused, to gun fire from the south and east, seemingly near the southeast corner of camp. He was suffering one of the nightmares of a general officer; that is, his troops were under attack and he had no idea at all what was going on.

First there'd been explosions, then gunfire—light automatic projectile weapons—then more explosions, different this time, as of mortar rounds. Right after that the gunfire had intensified strongly. Enemy gunfire, because his standard infantry weapons were beam guns, not projectile weapons. Someone had attacked his camp. And as the intensity of the racket seemed now to be lessening, presumably his people were either driving them off or subduing them.

With automatic weapons and mortars, it could hardly be locals unless they had a militia. Which seemed highly unlikely. The commodore would have learned of such a thing from his captive officials.

The bodies of six young men, locals, had been deposited with his officer of the guard at the gate, two days since. In recognition of the act, he'd released half his child hostages. It seemed to the general he had the beginnings of an amicable arrangement with local officials, and with the people here. They were commoners of course, but they did not seem to be peasants, so one might hope for rationality from them.

Going to a door, he pushed a flap aside to look out. His guards were there, guns ready. The projectile weapons *were* quieting; only sporadic racketing could be heard from them now.

A tall figure was trotting among tents toward him— Major Raspilaseetos, his aide. When the major saw his commander, he called to him. "General!" His voice was urgent, with an undertone of relief. Saadhrambacoora beckoned him in, letting the flap fall behind them.

"What is it?"

"Children!"

The general stared uncomprehendingly.

"The attackers! They are children!"

"Children!?"

"Those who saw them say so, and we have three bodies. They are children!"

Gooseflesh crawled. "What—kind of children?"

"Boys. Armed boys in uniform. They seem to be about twelve or thirteen years old. They attacked by stealth, moving about in the camp with knives, killing people silently!"

The general realized with a start that Raspilaseetos was trembling with emotion, which somehow calmed his own nerves.

"And— I'm told they killed men within a hundred feet of your pavilion! They must have seen it but not come to it."

Inside the officers' area then, despite the fence and guards.

"And the shooting?"

"Some were discovered in the Third Battalion area, but before anyone could do anything, they had disappeared. The tower guards heard the shouting though, and began to play their lights around. Then someone outside began to shoot at the towers with rockets, and put them all out of action. Right after that, some sort of high trajectory weapons lobbed explosives into camp, and projectile rifles began firing."

"How did they get access?"

"I don't know sir. I haven't had time to find out."

"How many casualties did we take? Approximately."

"Not known. I've seen several myself. It seems these children—" He paused, unnerved. "They preferred to kill two in a tent, then go on to the next. But I have no idea how many tents they visited. Or how many of our men were killed by the shelling and rifle fire."

While they'd talked, the general had put on his field uniform. Now he buckled on his side arms and strode from the tent, his guards falling in behind him, headed for his prefab command center. He'd send men outside the perimeter to hunt for enemy wounded they might take captive. And send for local officials, to learn what they knew. He needed information.

Forty-Three

As its senior officer, Tarimenloku was authorized to have alcoholic beverages aboard ship, but he didn't often use them. It was his observation that to drink more or less frequently meant to drink more and more frequently, which was not compatible with his responsibilities. This evening though—this ship's evening—he was having a *dharvag,* and would probably have another when it was gone.

His cabin was twice as large as any other on board, except for His Reverence's cabin; there was one of those, never occupied, or almost never, on every naval ship. Tarimenloku's cabin also had a window, more than a yard square and very expensive. Through it he could see Terfreya without electronic mediation. A beautiful world. Why in Hell did it have to be difficult down there? Cadets! If those were cadets, what must their soldiers be like?

Sooner or later the Confederation would learn he was here, though apparently no pod had gotten away. The prisoners who should know insisted that only one pod had been sent, and he'd destroyed that one outbound

before destroying the rest on the ground. His Chief
Intelligence Officer had assured him the prisoners had
told the truth; his instruments insisted they had.

He couldn't occupy Terfreya indefinitely. Didn't want
to, didn't intend to. His role was reconnaissance, not
conquest; he'd landed to get knowledge. The two marine regiments, the first two, he'd sent down for security, and to establish a posture suitable for an embassy
of the Sultan and of Kargh. He'd known it was risky
when he did it, but it had been necessary.

Now he'd learned enough that he could justifiably go
home, and he would if it weren't for those damned
cadets. They'd attacked his marines and continued to
harass them, thereby insulting Klestron and the Empire. If he ran away from the situation, His Reverence
the Sultan would have him impaled atop the palace
wall. While the emperor, the Kalif, when he heard,
would demand his bones and commit further indignities
on them.

Nor was nuking a solution. Kargh would never forgive nuking a planet in other than defense of the Faith.
While on another level, nuking might easily bring about
a hatred of the Empire that would make the conversion
and rule of this sector very difficult.

No, nuking was another way to earn a place on the
palace wall, decorating a long iron stake.

Responsibility!

As insurance, he'd sent off seven small pods of his
own, carrying the requisite reports to Klestron. It was a
hellish long way, and the standard error of arrival location accordingly large. DAAS had computed that five
should be sent, to be substantially certain of one arriving within beacon range of Klestron. He'd hedged his
bet with two extra.

Tarimenloku raised the glass to his lips again, sipped,
and gloomed down at the serene-looking world below,
visualizing jungle, and in the jungle, children. Boys
with sharp knives, boys too young to know a woman
yet, let alone shave. Children slipping among the trees

with projectile weapons in their hands and killing on their minds.

It would help to know how many there were. His prisoners knew little about them, their estimates ranging from five hundred to a thousand. The cadets didn't seem to mind taking casualties, though they'd left few enough behind. Their wounded fought to the death. They might lay seemingly unconscious, but with an armed grenade concealed, or a sidearm, then kill the marines who came up to them. So now his marines shot to rags any fallen cadet who wasn't conspicuously dead, orders be damned, and prisoners for questioning had so far been nonexistent.

Probably the salvation of the situation would be supply. The cadets had shown themselves frugal in their use of ammunition, a clear sign that their supply was limited. In time they'd run out, and landing the rest of the brigade had no doubt speeded the day.

He hadn't intended to, but Tarimenloku fell asleep over his drink, waking with a start, half an hour later, to the comm-buzzer on his wall. He reached, touched the acknowledge key. "Sir," a voice said, "we just registered emergence waves."

"Thank you. I will be on the bridge directly."

One damn thing after another! He sighed heavily. It was probably a merchant ship. He'd expect the matric disturbance of a mere pod emerging to be dissipated beyond the *Flenyaagor*'s ability to detect it. And there was no reason to anticipate a naval vessel. His information was that Terfreya received one regularly every ten Confederation years, and that the next one expected was four years away. Even the cadets, it seemed, had arrived on a merchantman.

The emergence waves traveled at light speed, but even so, the ship that had made them would be well on its way by now. And surely its captain had noticed that the homing beacon was missing. Would he be suspicious? Were merchantmen armed here? And there was always the possibility that it was, after all, a warship.

Tarimenloku went to the door and out into the corridor. He'd prepare as if it was naval, he decided, and wished that even one of his prisoners was informed on naval armament. He was confident that his own was superior to theirs, in general, but who knew what they might have, what one weapon, that he'd never heard of and wasn't prepared for.

How quickly would it know he was alien? Did they have a class of ships that resembled his? And the troop carrier? Would their instruments discern him before his discerned them?

Then a terrible thought occurred to him: *What if it was a warship from the hostile sector that had somehow tracked him down?* Irritated, he shook the notion off. The odds of it were zero, or nearly enough as to make no difference.

He'd be as ready as he could, and see what, in fact, happened.

Hours later his instruments picked up the approaching vessel. It showed no awareness of him, perhaps because it wasn't looking for him. Meanwhile DAAS, in its role as gunnery computer, tracked it. He weighed the relative risks of firing at too long a range, thus warning it, against waiting till it saw him, in either case giving it time to generate a shield. It was a computation DAAS couldn't make for him. Finally he fired, at a longer range than he'd have liked, and moments later the screen showed a vivid flash, an explosion. The strange ship came on, haloed by a cloud that disappeared almost at once. He fired again, and its forward end disintegrated. Again, and there was a massive explosion. Then there was no ship there; his instruments registered only debris.

He had his gunnery officer generate a shield, on the off chance that some piece of the debris might collide with the *Flenyaagor*, then ordered the stand-down from battle stations. He wasn't happy to have destroyed a merchant ship unwarned, but he'd seen no acceptable alternative. Kargh did not admire such acts, although he did not actually condemn them. And the Confederation ship could not have been allowed to land, or attack him, or return to hyperspace to notify the Confederation.

Forty-Four

Someone stepped through the door, and Voker's secretary looked up from his computer screen. The woman who'd entered was younger than he'd expected. In her early or mid-twenties, she was tall, honey blonde, and athletic looking—overall quite attractive. Her gaze was direct without being aggressive.

He stood up.

"I'm Tain Faronya," she said. "From Central News."

"Of course, Ms. Faronya. I'll tell Colonel Voker you're here." He bent, touched a key on his communicator. "Colonel, Ms. Tain Faronya is here to see you."

Voker's voice answered through his ear piece. "He'll see you now," the man said, and stepping to Voker's door, opened it. The young woman walked past him, smelling faintly of bath soap.

Tain heard the door close quietly behind her. Her gaze took in the colonel's office without conspicuously scanning. It was orderly in the military manner, but more personal than she'd expected. Shelves held books, some with bright covers, and on a small table, a fringed cloth was spread. Indigo flowers bushed out of a joma mug on his desk.

The uniformed colonel had gotten to his feet. He was a bit less than average height. His stubbly hair was gray, his face abundantly but not harshly lined. He was older, a lot older, than she'd expected, but he stood straight, his gray eyes calm and intelligent.

"Colonel Voker?" she said.

She's athletic all right, Voker thought. Somehow though, he hadn't expected her to be so good looking. "That's right. I saw you cross from the floater pad. What did you think of our reservation, flying over it?"

"If it started where the pilot told me," she said drily, "it's *very* big."

His use of *our* had offended, Voker realized, and her tone of voice suggested that the place was too big, a misuse of land. One of the new generation of journalists, he decided, that sometimes felt critical of government; sometimes even expressed that criticism. "It has to be big," he said, also drily. "It's an important field location for training officers, or was till we got it. They held major maneuvers here."

"Where are your soldiers?"

"They're out on a regimental exercise under their trainee officers, an exercise covering about thirty square miles of woods. They need experience in coordinated large-unit movements in forest, where the companies can't see each other and their regimental officers can't see any of them. Coordination is by radio and mapbooks."

"Why aren't you with them?"

"I'm a planner and administrator, Ms. Faronya. Their field training is supervised by a T'swa cadre under Colonel Dak-So. The main reason I'm here at all is that the T'swa aren't used to training young men of cultures and customs other than their own. And they're not familiar with our government and law. I am, and I'm also familiar with the T'swa; I was the army's liaison with them during the Kettle War. Beyond that, for a long time I was an advocate of this type of military unit, when almost no one else was. All of which the Crown knew. So when this job came up, they called me out of retirement and gave it to me."

He'd mentioned the Crown not only for effect, but also because the Crown was a central part of the truth behind the regiment. "Let me show you around the compound," he offered. "A barracks, a kitchen . . . These young men train extremely hard, and eat accordingly."

So he's a *changer,* she thought as they left his office, and realized then that her initial disapproval of him was really disapproval of his generation—a generation like hundreds before it which had refused change. She didn't, of course, know the reason for that.

She'd done an article on the army the previous summer for the Central News weekly magazine, spending two or three days at each of three army bases. Which she supposed had something to do with her getting this assignment. She'd never experienced anything more conservative than the army command there, nor had so little cooperation. Her interest in coming here had grown out of her editor's comment that this regiment was supposedly something quite different.

They talked as they walked, and her skepticism lost its edge. Voker seemed genuinely interested in her assignment, and answered her questions openly, or seemed to. These youths had been misfits, he told her, misfits in their schools and communities, in trouble for poor concentration in class, and for fighting. Here their behavior had become exemplary, their learning ability high.

"Colonel," she said, "you sound like a public relations officer. I'm afraid I'll need to observe them myself before I'll believe it."

Voker laughed. "Of course. That's why you're here, I presume. Otherwise you could have prepared your article by interviewing me over the comm."

Until evening though, the only trainees she saw were a few walking from their barracks to the Main Building. Colonel Voker said they were on their way to do psychological drills, to develop the calmness of the T'swa. She recorded his saying it, of course, but it didn't interest her. She'd been poorly impressed with the psychology courses she'd had at the university. To her, psychologists had too often been apologists for the status quo.

The messhall she looked in on did impress her. Three cheerful, well-fed cooks on loan from the army were beginning preparations for supper, helped by four flunkies also on loan. The flunkies, Voker told her, were misfits of a different kind, out here to separate them from liquor. They kept trying to make their own, but their various fermenting mashes kept getting found and confiscated.

The barracks were—barracks, orderly and clean.

She got Voker's written permission to eat with the troops, and that evening was taken to A Company's messhall. The first sergeant spoke with the mess sergeant, who set out tableware for her at the table assigned to 1st Squad, 2nd Platoon. Somewhere outside a klaxon sounded. Trainees started filing in, took sectioned trays, and were served by the kitchen crew. The mess sergeant inserted her into the line, and she went with the flow, startled at the size of the servings she was given—that all were given. The trainees looked too lean and hard to have been eating so much, and she wondered if the quantity of food was a ploy to impress her.

There was little talking at table; the trainees ate with dedication and apparent enjoyment. The one on her right was the best-looking youth she thought she'd ever seen: tall, tan, and muscular, his cropped brown hair showing the beginnings of curls. The name above his shirt pocket was *Alsnor,* obviously a last name, but it would have to do. "Excuse me, Alsnor," she said. "Is there a rule against talking at the table?"

He'd deliberately not been looking at her; he hadn't wanted to make her ill at ease. Now he did look. "Against talking needlessly, yes. If you want the salt though, or some joma, just ask."

She smiled. She wasn't above using her looks to get cooperation. "I'm with Central News. May I interview you after supper?"

"Me?" For just a moment he looked flustered, then grinned, showing strong white teeth. "Sure. I'll meet you outside after supper." Then he returned his attention to the food. Others at the table glanced at her now, also grinning, and suddenly she was self-conscious. Possibly even blushing; she hoped not.

She left first. Alsnor had emptied his tray before she had, but had gone for seconds. When he came out, he smiled without grinning. "Would you like to walk?" he asked.

"After a meal like that," she answered, "I need to walk."

He led off, sauntering across thick grass, through the long shade of frequent stately trees. Tain had her recorder on. "Where are you from?" she asked.

He told her, and as they talked, his troubled childhood and troublesome adolescence came out. She was surprised to learn that he was only eighteen. They passed the large swimming pool where a dozen trainees already cavorted, lean and muscular, ignoring the ancient warning to wait an hour, or two hours, after eating. The pool, she judged, was about two hundred feet long and half as wide.

"I'm surprised the army built such a nice pool here. Or was it intended for officer trainees?"

Jerym laughed. "Would you like to know how we got it?"

Eyebrows raised at his tone, she said she would, and he told her the story of 3rd Platoon, F Company: of the mugging of Pitter Mellis, the arson, the vandalism, and the hard core troublemakers of the detention section, who'd dug the pool with sledge hammers and chisels in the middle of bitter winter nights.

She stopped, looked hard at him. "You're joking."

Jerym shook his head. "See this?" he said, and pointed. His left eyebrow was bisected lengthways by a scar. "Our first night here, 2nd Platoon had a big brawl with 1st Platoon. That's where I got it." He laughed. "Anyone but the T'swa, the T'swa and Voker, would have sent us all back where we came from. Prison fodder, that's what we were. But they had faith in us, faith and patience, besides which they could whip any of us. Our 400 T'swa could have whipped all 2,000 of us at once, no problem. Colonel Voker fought the guy with the reputation of being the toughest in the regiment, Coyn Carrmak, and beat him easily."

"Colonel Voker did?!"

Jerym nodded. "That was last fall. He couldn't do it now of course, considering what we've learned."

That finished the interview; she excused herself and left. Despite the qualifications Jerym had added to his story about Voker, it seemed to Tain that he'd been lying to her all along. And she resented being made a fool of.

But afterward, alone in bed, she imaged his face, his smile, his keen friendly eyes and pleasant voice. His large strong hands . . . And decided that the rest of what he'd told her had probably been true—the part before the story about Voker. She'd get a better idea when she interviewed more of the trainees.

Jerym Alsnor had spent most of the evening at lectures: one on the use of diversions, the other on the dangers of bypassing subordinate commanders. He'd hardly thought of the woman journalist.

But that night he dreamed of her, her violet-blue eyes, her lips—her long legs. And woke up with heart thuttering, face hot . . .

Tunis but she was pretty! Even beautiful. He wondered if she'd dreamt of him. He hoped so.

Forty-Five

The squad had been lying in the woods, waiting. Then the word came and they got to their feet, Tain Faronya with them, and began trotting easily. She was as tall as several of them, her legs as long, and her pack much lighter. Her helmet camera was light too, its focus following the direction she was looking, its pictures approximating closely what she saw in the square on her visor. She was well-drilled in its use; her head movements showed it.

Through the trees she could see the opening where they were to show themselves. Though why they'd do that she didn't know, except that Brossling had ordered it; Brossling, the teenaged battalion commander. She'd heard it on her radio, through the descrambler she'd been issued. Now it was time. Someone in some other unit had reported an enemy gunship headed this way.

It seemed crazy to her, even if the gunship would be firing blanks. It made no sense to do things in maneuvers that you wouldn't do in combat, and ordinarily they'd been keeping carefully to cover thick enough to hide them from aerial observation. Now they were supposed to show themselves to a gunship!

In half a minute they were trotting down a short mild slope and into the opening. It was a wet meadow, about a hundred yards across, she decided, seemingly boggy near the middle. Quickly the ground turned springy underfoot—a little strange to run on. Someone called out and she looked around, saw the silent gunship overflying one end of the meadow, and ran faster. It swung their way. The trainees had begun to sprint, dispersing, and runner though she'd been, fit and lightly laden though she was, she fell behind. She heard the floater's heavy blast hoses, a sound shocking and harsh, making her heart speed wildly, and her legs. Her feet encountered bog, splashed water and muck; one foot hit a soft spot and she fell heavily, jarringly headlong.

Prone, she saw a trainee, Venerbos, with a rocket launcher at his shoulder. The sound of it was lost beneath the coarse frenzied roar of hoses firing out of synch, but she saw the flash when the rocket was fired. It startled her; the rocket was real! Which reminded her that the blast hoses were firing blanks. Abruptly they stopped firing, and the floater, rising, swung away and left. She got to her feet and jogged into the woods, reflexively wiping wet hands on wet shirt.

Her radio was tuned just now to F Company, to which this squad belonged. She could hear Third Platoon's two umpires talking to Mollary, the squad leader, and wondered how many casualties they'd charge them with—how they'd decide. They hadn't been with the squad. The decision would have to be arbitrary, which irritated her, but she supposed there was no alternative.

And there'd been a real rocket, which apparently had hit the gunship!

Several minutes later the umpires arrived, a big-framed T'swa corporal and a lanky army lieutenant. Tain wondered how they worked together, with such disparate ranks. Ground rules, she supposed, but even so . . . They painted each casualty with a red substance, sleeves, helmet, and face. Red for blood, but this blood would wash off and leave no scars. Both sleeves and both sides of the face meant dead; one sleeve and one side, wounded and unable to continue. There were no other casualty categories from this encounter. The squad had been "destroyed": seven dead, one WOA—wounded, out of action. Heavy blast slugs rarely produced light wounds.

"What about her?" the lieutenant said, looking at Tain. "Should she get off free?"

"She is not part of the maneuvers," the T'swi answered, then spoke to her. "Would you like to be a casualty?"

She stared at him, not sure what he was suggesting.

"It would have no practical significance," he added. "You would be free to continue. But if it would make you feel more a part of it . . ."

Part of it! She shook her head. Through her earplug she heard Third Platoon's leader telling the two able-bodied survivors to join the platoon when the umpires released them. The umpires in turn told the unwounded they could leave when ready. Venerbos said he'd stay to give aid to the wounded man, and catch them later.

Tain stared, hardly believing, feeling the growth of anger. They'd abandon their wounded as well as their dead! The other unwounded trainee was already trotting off through the trees, not crossing the meadow again. It was the T'swa corporal who answered her unspoken accusation, his large dark eyes holding hers.

"The regiment is in enemy territory," he said, "isolated, on the move, without means of evacuation. That is the predicated situation of this exercise.

"The casualties will, of course, be picked up by a floater, but not as a combat evacuation of dead and wounded. Simply because they're done with this exercise. They are out of the game now."

Then, without saying more, he trotted off with his army counterpart.

Out of the game now? What kind of game was this,

where men practiced being killed and wounded? What kind of people were these? She wanted to ask the umpires that, the T'swi, actually. But somehow, just now, she didn't have the will to follow them. Instead she went over and squatted down to watch Venerbos treat the "wounded" man. As if the wound were real. He'd already cut away a trouser leg, applied a tourniquet around the thigh, sprayed something on a hairy calf. He'd even snugged up the tourniquet.

"You fired a rocket!" she said.

Venerbos answered without turning to her, continuing to bandage. "Right. Scored, too. If that had been a live round, I'd probably have crippled the bugger, at least. The umpires on board must have agreed with me; anyway it quit shooting and left."

So the rocket had been an uncharged round, hitting without explosion. "Could it have damaged the floater?" she asked.

"Naw. These practice rounds are dummies and collapse on impact. It left a patch of orange though, to show where it hit. When the floater gets back to base, the umpires can decide whether it's a kill or not."

A kill.

She'd come to Blue Forest guardedly pleased at the assignment. It had sounded potentially interesting, and it could help build her career. For five days she'd mixed with the young men—more than kids despite their youth. Watched them train, hiked with them, even ran with them, though she'd run without pack or weapon. Had been awed at their fitness, and gained their respect, it seemed to her, by her ability and willingness to keep up.

Now her enthusiasm was gone. Entirely. This war game with the army's 8th Heavy Infantry Brigade was real enough that she suddenly realized what the regiment was all about. Its function wasn't hypothetical anymore, was no longer something less than real. It was the gunship attack that had done it, made her see it—that and the umpires painting the casualties. She'd heard shooting off and on all day. Once, quite a ways off, it had been heavy, insistent, tapering off only after half an hour or so. But this— This had been immediate and personal.

From Blue Forest, the regiment would go to Backbreak and train for a year in its jungle, probably its tundra-prairie too, and maybe its cold rainforest, in a gravity of 1.19 gees. After Backbreak there'd be a year on Tyss, with its terrible heat and its 1.22 gees. Then they'd go to some trade world or resource world, to die in a war that was meaningless, or get limbs torn off.

She'd thought about going to Backbreak with them for a few weeks, had planned to talk to Colonel Voker about it. Now, suddenly, the attraction had died of acute reality.

She squatted, attention obscured by her thoughts, then realized that Venerbos, his bandaging done, was reassembling his aid kit.

"And now we wait," she said.

"Not him. Us." It was Mollary who answered. "Dead" Mollary. "You can go with him or stay here with us casualties."

She sat groping for what she wanted to say, how she wanted to say it. "And if this had been real," she pronounced slowly, "real bullets, some of you'd be really dead by now!"

"Right. Maybe all of us." Mollary looked at her without his usual grin. Not, she thought, because the enormity of it had gotten through to him. It hadn't; she was somehow sure of that. But because he read her mood and realized that a grin would offend her. "And the gunship," he went on, "might be lying out there in the grass, smoking. Unless Venerbos had been one of the casualties too, hit before he could get his rocket off. The umpires decided he wasn't, probably the ones in the gunship."

Tain looked hard at him. "Do you know what you're really doing here?"

His eyes met hers calmly. "Maybe not. I thought I did."

"You're practicing dying."

"Not really. Dying is incidental. We're practicing war."

"You're practicing dying! And dying is not incidental!"

"Okay. I understand."

She stared, partly deflated by his reply. "Do you? Really?" Her words were part challenge, part question.

"I think so. You consider death the end of existence. That when someone gets killed, that's it. And that bothers you, pretty badly."

Her gaze, her perception, seemed to change, become dreamlike, as if her eyes had photographed him and she was looking at the print, a print with definition sharper, colors more vivid, than reality: sandy hair, blue eyes, his cheeks tan where the paint didn't cover them. "And you don't think so?" she heard herself ask.

"That's right," he said quietly. "I don't." Quietly as if, again, to soften the impact on her.

She remembered some of the trainees going to the Main Building in the evenings. When she'd asked about it, asked to accompany one of them, she'd been refused, almost the only refusal she'd received with the regiment. The drills, what the trainees did there, she was told, were personal and confidential. She'd gone to Voker then, hoping he'd overrule the refusal, but he hadn't. They were doing psychological drills, he'd repeated, to develop T'swa calm. *There's another way of putting that*, she told herself now. *They've been psycho-conditioning these kids with some technique they didn't tell us about in Psych A and B. Something T'swa that they probably don't even know about at school.*

A chill ran over her. "So," she said, also quietly. "What *do* you think happens when you die?"

"What are the possibilities? It's either the end or it's not. To me— I recycle. Maybe take a vacation first."

"And if you're wrong? If you don't?"

He shrugged. "If I don't, I won't know the difference

because I won't exist anymore. But that's not real to me."

What do you say to something like that? she asked herself, and getting to her feet, walked toward the opening, the meadow.

"Tain," Mollary said from behind her, "don't show yourself in the opening. A gunship might see you and waste his time strafing here when we're already dead. It wouldn't be fair."

Fair! His warning seemed to her an accusation, and she glared back at him without answering, then sat down a little ways within the forest edge, absently switching her recorder from *on* to *wait*. It would turn itself back on in response to any voice. Taking out her mapbook, she played angrily with it, hardly noticing what she did. Another matter surfaced in her consciousness: Why had they shown themselves to the gunship? To get an open shot at it? Would they sacrifice a squad for that? She couldn't think of any other reason, and the thought added to her anger.

She remembered the girl she'd met the evening before, on a late walk. Lotta. They'd strolled together, talking, and Tain realized now that while Lotta had learned a lot about her, she'd learned nothing about Lotta. The girl looked no more than fifteen or sixteen, but had to be in her twenties. They'd said goodnight at the reception desk—perhaps guard station was a better word—she turning off toward the guest section, Lotta turning in the direction the trainees went for their drills.

It occurred to Tain now that Lotta might know something about those "drills," and she determined to find and ask her.

Less than twenty minutes later, a floater landed. She boarded it with the casualties and it took off for the compound. By then her mood had recovered somewhat, to mildly aggravated.

*　　*　　*

The dispatcher wouldn't send a floater to take her back to the platoon. That would tell the "enemy" where troops were. Tain wasn't really disappointed. It was nearly supper time, and she'd been with Third Platoon, F Company, since daybreak. So she was tired, despite her hobbies, recent and not so recent—dance and gymnastics in lower and middle school, track in upper school and college, and since then, backpacking, orienteering, mountain climbing, ski touring. And the workouts she did semi-regularly to stay fit for the other four.

She'd eat and take a nap, she decided, then look up Lotta and see what she might know about the "psychological drills."

If Lotta would talk. And she would. Tain considered herself a good interviewer—one reason, she supposed, that she'd gotten the assignment. This was only her third year on the job, but she'd demonstrated more than once an ability to get people to open up to her.

Forty-Six

Tain's after-supper nap was deeper than she'd antici-
pated. It was nearly midnight when she woke up, woke
just enough to take off her clothes, stumble to the
bathroom, and crawl back into bed. She never even
thought of Lotta. And when she got up in the morning,
it was to shower hastily, eat hastily, and get shuttled to
the headquarters of the 8th Heavy Infantry Brigade,
"the real army," where she expected to experience the
maneuvers from the other side.

It was not a good day. Brigadier Shiller seemed irritated that she was there, and assigned a youthful officer, Lieutenant Bertol Gremmon, to be her escort.
Obviously with instructions to keep her out of the way.
Politely and perhaps even regretfully, he refused her
request to visit "the combat zone," and to ride a gunship on a sweep. It was, she was told, too dangerous;
"accidents were possible." Both arguments she considered asinine.

Instead she spent the day around the fringes of brigade headquarters, a meadow with enough tents and

command modules to house a battalion, it seemed to her. She saw officers coming and going, saw them consult, but was allowed to hear none of it. She was also refused permission to interview the brigadier or his executive officer, or any of their aides. They were "too busy."

She kept her pocket radio on at all times however, listening to it through her helmet receiver. The radio itself she carried in a shoulder bag. Voker, a referee and hence a neutral in this wargame, had given it to her that morning with two comments: it would access the brigade's command channel for her; and it would be best not to mention it to them. She kept the volume barely loud enough to hear and understand, and when something on it sounded particularly interesting, she reached inside the shoulder bag, adjusted the volume, and brought out a tissue to dab sweat from her face.

Much of what she heard was too cryptic to be very informative. There were too many shorthand terms, jargon she didn't understand, and an absence of contexts. She gathered impressions from it, but only a limited and fragmentary picture.

Gremmon didn't help much, evading or refusing any question that dealt directly with the maneuvers, till it seemed plain that Shiller didn't trust her not to tell everything she knew to the other side—the "mercenaries" as they called them, or "mercs." Gremmon ("call me Bertol, please") did answer more general questions though, and volunteered some background comments. For instance, the brigade was not at full strength. There were two regiments of mobile infantry, each with its scouts and utility floaters, gunship squadron, and squadron of combat personnel carriers. But the third regiment was armored-remote, and an armored-remote regiment was inappropriate to both the forest and the predicated "scenario" here. So its personnel, numbering about half that of a mobile infantry regiment, were being used as an over-strength infantry battalion, so the army's force here was more like a light infantry brigade.

But a single mobile infantry regiment, the lieutenant assured her, would be more than adequate. For one thing, the mercs were "undisciplined adolescent hoodlums." (Questioning brought out that they'd gotten this reputation within the army from the administrative and supply personnel who'd processed them in.) And secondly, the army's umpires would see to it that the T'swa did not direct the merc's actions.

The army would show those kids how professionals did it.

Tain was smart enough not to waste her time telling Gremmon that (1) the central purpose of the maneuvers was to exercise and test the "adolescent hoodlum" commanders, few of whom were as old as twenty and none of whom had as much as a year's service; and (2) that the "adolescent hoodlums" she'd just spent six days with had been open, poised, friendly, and intelligent. Albeit with some strange viewpoints.

By early afternoon, she and Gremmon were thoroughly tired of each other. She asked if there was material she could read on the brigade, and he was overjoyed to take her to a tent where several clerks sat at computers, writing into them occasionally, watching their screens, and monitoring something or other on headsets. Before he left her there, Gremmon provided her with a chair, a small table, and several manuals and handbooks, putting her on her honor not to leave farther than the nearby sanitary facility they'd set up just for her. He also told a corporal "not to let her get lost," and to see that she got whatever she needed.

The corporal kept her joma cup filled and hot all afternoon. If she'd tried drinking any large percentage of it, she told herself wryly, she'd have come through it bloated and waterlogged. Meanwhile she browsed the material Gremmon had given her, listened covertly to the brigade's command traffic, and thought how glad she'd be when the day was over. She wouldn't give Shiller the satisfaction of asking to leave early though.

On her radio she overheard an interesting butt-chewing. It seemed part of a conference at brigade headquarters, rather than intended radio traffic, as if a microphone was open which shouldn't have been. Tain inferred from things she'd already overheard that the brigade's plan was to catch the mercs, or the bulk of them, in the smallest block possible surrounded by roads. Then locate armored mobile gun batteries at frequent intervals, with troops dug in between them; clear fields of fire; sweep the area with gunships, hosing anything that moved; lay artillery and lobber fire into areas where merc concentrations were thought to be; and in general to pound on the merc while keeping him at arm's length. Meanwhile the merc would be living out of his pack, and had only the ammunition he carried on his person.

It made sense.

The butt-chewing occurred when someone suggested to Shiller that they airlift troops to engage the enemy in the forest, causing him to expend his ammunition much faster. Shiller exploded. Couldn't "the damn fool" remember twenty-four hours? From the content of the lacing Shiller gave the man, Tain gathered that they'd airlifted a rifle company in the day before to test the enemy in the forest, and within thirty minutes, umpires had counted the entire company killed. The [unprintable young hoodlums] had taken no prisoners.

She remembered the prolonged firefight she'd heard the day before, and supposed that was it. She also caught herself justifying the refusal to take prisoners: The regiment was operating in enemy territory as more or less separated units, without air or any other support services, and keeping to cover, with high mobility their only tactical advantage.

Through it all, her little audio recorder was power up, keyed on by every human voice and strong sound that reached it, either live or on the radio.

In late afternoon, at about 1620 hours, Gremmon returned to tell her that a floater was standing by to take her to the compound whenever she was ready. That, she told herself, would give her time for a relaxing shower before supper at 1800, and she accepted. On the short flight to the compound, she thought how odd it was, after yesterday, to be pulling so strongly for the regiment to win this war game.

After supper she went to Voker's office. Ford, his secretary, told her that Voker was gone, standing a shift as referee. She already knew that a team of four referees was over the maneuver area at all times, in a specially equipped floater, monitoring and evaluating the maneuvers and available to decide any disputes between umpires, the referees being senior. On each shift, two of the referees were ranking T'swa, or Voker and a T'swa, and two were senior army officers.

No, Ford told her, there weren't many disputes. Major General Thromlek, Lord Carns, had been selected by the Crown to assign the army's umpires. Thromlek had been a friend of Colonel Voker's, and was known in the service for his efforts to improve training and organization. His selections would be fair. The Crown itself had assigned the army's referees—younger officers from the general staff's staff. Colonel Voker was quite satisfied that both the umpiring and the refereeing were as impartial as could reasonably be hoped.

After supper she went to the Main Building and asked for Lotta, but was told that Lotta was busy and couldn't be disturbed. She'd probably be available around 2230. Briefly Tain wondered if the confidential services the girl performed might be sexual, then irritatedly rejected the thought. Out of curiosity though, she hung around the entrance to the Main Building for half an hour. Only a few trainees came in for drills—"casualties" home from maneuvers, she supposed. Then, in her room, she printed out and edited her recordings so far, adding commentary. She didn't try to contact Lotta again that night. She needed to go early to bed. Tomorrow would start at daybreak.

Forty-Seven

Outside her open window, black night had scarcely been tinged by dawn when Tain pulled on her field uniform. It was a strange-feeling morning, as if she'd awakened in a different time, in a world where the things that happened, and how they felt, were subtly different than she was used to. The birds sounded tentative, chirped instead of sang, as if unsure of the coming day.

Dressed, she went downstairs to a quick breakfast with the referee teams that would stand the day shift together: two T'swa Majors, Duk and Git-Ran, and two army colonels, Vornkabel and Dorsee. They did not speak to her; their name patches were all the introduction she received. Nor did the teams exchange greetings. The two T'swa murmured occasional quiet Tyspi; the two white colonels spoke to each other even less— quietly, tersely, the content obscure.

She did not look forward to her day.

After breakfast, they walked to the floater pad through an overcast dawn that was chill and breezy, like autumn ahead of time. She was glad to climb inside the referees' floater.

She found it surprisingly comfortable. There were three large window bulges on each side, for 180 observation; six swivel seats, contoured and padded; monitor screens that just now were black except for cryptic combinations of letters and numbers glowing patiently blue; and a small stainless steel restroom, sparklingly clean, which nonetheless she did not look forward to using. There was also a kitchenette, and two army orderlies, one for each team, to use it.

One of the orderlies had been assigned to orient her, which he did quietly and concisely. Each seat had a terminal; she was not to use hers. And there was a speaker over which relevant umpire traffic would be received; also a headset for each referee and one for her, that made them privy to the command traffic of both forces.

They took seats and the floater lifted. Apparently someone called for a situation update. The monitors lit up, rolling for them the events of an evening and night which had had little to report. As if, she thought, the opposing forces had recessed for darkness and gone home to bed.

In minutes their floater parked over the approximate center of the maneuver area, then the floater with the nightshift bobbed a salute and left for the compound. Somewhere down there, she told herself, was F Company, and what was left of 3rd Platoon. Taking out her mapbook, she called up the largest-scale quadrangle she was sure applied, locating landmarks she could see on the ground—ponds, a stream, small scattered bogs, a grove of dark and particularly lofty koorsas towering above the canopy of broad-leafed trees—and from these approximated her present position. From her window she could see two army recon floaters some distance off, parked at a similar altitude, no doubt with instruments and possibly eyes watching for movement below. She suspected that two more were visible from the windows on the opposite side.

There wasn't a lot of command traffic yet from either

force, and what there was was mostly army. The regiment's command channel had traffic only now and then. The army's dealt mainly with troops moving on the road, and gunship reports. As best she could, Tain related these to her map and to what she could see from her window, and with her electronic pocket stylus, began to add to the map the army's designations for different roads. Before long the radio traffic began to make more sense to her.

Something else began to take shape as the morning and the traffic went on. "Little A" was regimental headquarters, Artus Romlar commanding. "Big C" was 1st Battalion headquarters under Coyn Carrmak, "Big J" was 2nd Battalion under Jillard Brossling, and "Big K" was the 3rd. These she knew from her pre-maneuver briefing by Colonel Voker's secretary. But though there was occasional command traffic to Big C, Big C neither replied nor acknowledged. While Big K not only didn't send anything, regiment never sent anything to it! Tain found that exceedingly interesting. She knew that transmittal locations could be read by instrument, and it seemed to her they must be keeping radio silence to prevent brigade from determining where they were. Big J, on the other hand, did broadcast occasionally, presumably on the move to avoid the resulting gunship attacks on its points of transmittal.

Brigade headquarters plotted the two sources of merc command traffic and found them moving on more or less parallel courses. The major source baffled them. It tended to stay in one place till attacked by gunships. Then somehow it would show up somewhere else. After a bit, and to Tain inexplicably, an order came from brigade headquarters to discontinue gunship attacks on sources of merc command traffic.

Except for the early gunship attacks on regimental transmitter locations, almost the only action was attacks by "mercs" on hover trucks—hit and run affairs by platoons of 2nd Battalion—and gunship attacks *on* 2nd Battalion. Gunships responded rather quickly to ambushes on road traffic, hosing the woods in the vicinity. But having spent a day with F Company, she suspected the gunship responses weren't very productive; after a brief strike, the squads would have separated, loping off like wolves, and been well away from the ambush sites before the gunships arrived.

By 0820, vehicles on certain roads were being convoyed by gunships. Ambushes diminished, and what there were produced fewer casualties, as if made by squads or fire teams—half squads. At the same time, the ambushes having tied up gunships, gunship attacks on targets of opportunity were fewer than they'd been.

The more serious gunship attacks, more productive of merc casualties, were on targets of opportunity—mercs sighted from the air. The sightings were brief but the responses immediate; invariably they were followed by radio traffic between umpires on the gunships and those with the trainees on the ground, deciding on casualties. Twice it was decided that a gunship had been shot down, and twice more that one had been damaged. There was an appeal to the referees concerning one claimed "shot down." The referees compromised. It was badly damaged, they decided, but not shot down. It returned to its base and was henceforth out of action.

On Tain's map, and on the army's too she supposed, the sightings and ambushes built a clear picture of mercs moving westward. The line of march, or more properly the broad avenue of march, was centered on a creek and bounded by parallel roads two miles apart. But judging from the mercs' occasional, descrambled radio calls, this movement was apparently all by 2nd Battalion, something the army of course would not be aware of.

It occurred to her to wonder if squads of 2nd Battalion were letting themselves be seen, the way 2nd Squad, 3rd Platoon had that first day.

On the holographic photo-map, she thought she could see where the regiment—2nd Battalion anyway—was headed: If it kept going—big if—by evening it would come to an extensive swamp forest, much of it fairly dense, some of it sparsely timbered but thick with tall brush. Here and there were pools and small round ponds, looking black and bottomless on the map, though she suspected the water was shallow and only the muck beneath it bottomless. Frequent densely wooded humps marked low islands in the swamp, and there were no roads at all. It seemed to her that a woods-wise force would be almost impossible to root out.

But they'd have to cross two roads to get there. The first road was narrow, minimal, a straight, twenty-foot-wide track through the trees. They'd reach it in early afternoon, say 1300 hours, at their present rate of movement, which seemed to her uncharacteristically slow and cautious. The army would no doubt make a crossing expensive. The second road they might reach that evening. It was somewhat wider, and bordered almost continuously by the bare sites of old log decks, making it much more exposed.

About the time she'd put the picture together for herself, army radio traffic began to increase. Armored assault vehicles—hover vehicles—were being dispatched. Troops began clearing fields of fire along the two roads the mercs would have to cross. Tain began to have nervous stomach; emotionally she was definitely committed to the regiment.

At the same time, attacks of opportunity ceased entirely, and so did ambushes along the flanking roads. Second Battalion's radio traffic ceased too. Army command, concerned now that the mercs might change direction and break out across one of the flanking roads, intensified gunship patrols along them. It seemed to Tain, though, that her mercs would hardly make such a move. It would only put them in a different box. The obvious move, the one with most promise, was across the narrow road ahead of it to the west.

Under the circumstances, she forgot all about 1st and 3rd Battalions.

At 1215, hopefully with many of the army's people

sitting or squatting with mess gear on their laps, eating lunch, 2nd Battalion made its move to break across the narrow road. The attack was abrupt and intense, the racket of blank ammunition audible even in the referee floater a mile from the firefight. Umpire traffic was just as intense. Gunships swooped and circled like angry hornets. The major merc force—initially it was thought to be the entire force—was attacking one short segment of the road, but minutes later there were swift thrusts at two other points almost at the flanking roads, thrusts so quick, and by that time unexpected, that gunships didn't get there in time to play a role.

By 1235 it was over; 2nd Battalion was across at a cost of "201 killed and 42 wounded, out of action," including those "hit" by gunships after crossing. Tain found herself relieved that the cost wasn't greater, though 243 seemed a lot from one battalion. If it *was* just one battalion. Two hundred and forty-three "dead," really, assuming the WOAs would be abandoned. The army had lost 48 killed and 71 WOA on the ground, plus three gunships destroyed with their crews, and four severely damaged. All in all it clearly suggested that elite training did not balance off fire power, air support, and position.

She wondered how she'd feel if the losses had been real instead of hypothetical. Or if she'd been on the ground with F Company. Things seemed different, sitting in a referees' floater 4,000 feet above the ground.

Her thoughts went on to 1st Battalion. And 3rd. First had at least gotten some cryptic orders, even if it hadn't replied to them. Third had gotten none, at least by radio. Could the 3rd be operating with the 2nd, to make it more convincing in its apparent role as the entire regiment? Perhaps they'd both crossed the road. Or was it with the 1st, wherever the 1st was?

As far as she could see, the army had no way of knowing that Big C and Big K weren't on the air, unless they'd broken the merc's scrambler system. And it seemed to her that Little A must be using 2nd Battalion to mislead the enemy and occupy his attention, *while the rest of his force escaped, perhaps dispersed, trying to sneak free under cover.* Second Battalion would have to fight its way free, or try to. The regiment's objective definitely seemed to be escape. In fact, it seemed all they could hope to accomplish.

Not long afterward, Shiller himself was on the radio, demanding faster progress. *Progress on what?* Tain wondered. Probably on fortifying the final road, and maybe the flanking roads.

The referees' floater moved, circling at 2,000 feet the road-framed block of forest where 2nd Battalion was now. This block differed from the previous one. Not only was it quite a bit smaller; the land rose gradually from east to west, and the creek occupied a deeper valley, with side slopes that grew higher and steeper farther west.

The north road ran along the top of the slope, and near its west end was what seemed to be an army field command center. A dozen hover modules were parked along the road there, with trucks and armored assault vehicles. For half a mile, in the strip between road and rim, men and reaction dozers were finishing defensive positions overlooking the slope. Behind it were truck-mounted heavy lobbers, and many light lobbers. Flanking this line were lesser defensive positions all along the road. Shiller had something specific in mind for all this, Tain was sure, and had to remind herself that these were maneuvers, the ammunition blank.

After circling the block, the floater parked over the middle of it at 4,000 feet—centering itself among the four army recon floaters parked at the same altitude. Tain was glad to see them there. If she was right about Little A's plans, this meant they'd succeeded to the extent that Shiller was investing his full attention on Big J. Or seemed to be.

Brigadier Barnell "Barney" Shiller sat in his command module, his field operations center, which his troops referred to wryly as "the brain case." He was watching a battery of monitors. And not seeing much—mostly treetops from 4,000 feet, the input of his recon floaters. *Damn mercs aren't bad,* he admitted grimly. What sightings there were were momentary, and scattered widely enough that it seemed the mercs must have dispersed across almost the width of the block. Damn poor targets.

He was also impressed at how little the mercs used their radios. Their main transmittal source, presumably their regimental headquarters, obviously used narrow beam signals, hitting relays that converted them to 360 degrees. That took foresight, and superb performance by whoever was placing the relays. Their regimental commander could be sitting miles away if he wanted.

It was the accurate relay placement that most impressed Shiller and gained his grudging admiration.

And at the breakout, merc point men had worked their way between hose outposts almost to the road itself without being seen. They were only discovered when they began shooting up the outposts from behind. He'd expected a lot higher bag than the umpires' tally of 240. Five hundred would have been a lot harder on merc morale, and made it less likely that a significant number would break out of the sack he had them in now.

He cheered himself, though, with the thought that the final road they'd have to cross was wider, and his people more fully prepared there. He'd *wanted* the mercs to get across the first one; he'd simply intended that they pay a higher price for it. And they would have if he'd known when and where they'd attack.

Actually he'd rather expected them to wait till dark and try infiltrating across. His people had pretty much finished digging in by lunch, but they'd been less than ready mentally. Which was why the outposts had been hit from behind, he told himself.

But that was all water over the dam; he had them in his sack. Work was far along on clearing fields of fire along the west road. A mine layer was busy there, and the electronics were already being emplaced—a bit thinly perhaps, but Storker had assured him they'd do the job. And Storker was clever. Not smart, but clever. Setting a security field was the sort of thing you could trust him to do very well.

Things could always go wrong, of course. If he hadn't learned anything else in his fifty-seven years, he'd learned that. But you did your best, kept options open when you could, and moved with due speed once you'd made a decision. When it was clear that the mercs intended to try for the wild country, he'd known at once what to do.

And had left them with damned poor options. To try crossing any road would cost them. All his gunships were assigned now to road coverage. The least costly road to cross would be the flanking road on the south. But if the mercs decided to cross it, which would cost them, they'd be in a strip only three-quarters of a mile wide, backed up against the reservation's boundary with the Blue Forest Wildlife Preserve. Which was strictly off limits to them, a restriction the umpires would enforce adamantly. And westward on that narrow strip they'd be hemmed in by open bog impossible to cross without being chewed up from the air. As for crossing the north road— His eyes narrowed. He hoped they'd try. That would be the quickest and most satisfying.

Mentally he rehearsed scenarios. The mercs would scout the west road and discover his preparations. They'd probably try infiltrating it first, at night; then, after taking enough casualties, give up on it and try an assault. If they pressed it long enough, he'd butcher them. If they backed off, he still had them in his sack. If they tried the north road, they'd find out what real trouble was. Crossing the south road would be practical but costly, and then where were they? Between the hammer and the anvil.

And if they stayed inside his sack, they'd soon be hungry. Any time they let themselves be seen, his recon floaters and scouts would give the coordinates, and he'd lay lobber fire on them. Sooner or later they'd either surrender or commit themselves to a west road crossing. A few would probably make it into the wild district, but they wouldn't be a regiment or even a battalion any longer. The referees would call the game finished, and he'd have shown the Crown that T'swa-type forces were no match for well-led regulars, that they'd built their reputation on fringe planets—trade worlds and gook worlds—fighting ducal armies, militias, and untrained rebels.

And the general staff would notice who'd demonstrated it. When he retired, in two and a half years, maybe it would be as a major general instead of a brigadier.

"Corporal," said Tain Faronya, "how can I talk to Colonel Voker at the compound?"

"Ma'am?"

"From here, that is. He's a referee on the next shift."

"Yes ma'am, I know." The orderly stepped to the back wall of the compartment and touched a small grid. There was a small screen above it and a slanted keypad below. "Right here. I'll key it for you, if you'd like."

He tapped keys as she stepped over, and when the screen lit up, she found herself looking at another army corporal, presumably at the compound. He put her through to Voker's secretary, who, after a short wait, connected her to Voker.

"Colonel," she said, "I'd like to be out here with the next shift of referees. This afternoon that is. But— Is there any way I can? I suppose you'll be on station up here before we leave."

"Yes, there's a way." He paused, examining her. "Why do you want to put in a sixteen-hour day?"

The question took her off guard. "Sir, I don't know. It just. . . ." She shrugged. "How can I do it?"

Voker smiled slightly. "Each referee floater has a hatch in the top and one in the floor, in the utility locker. When we've picked a gee coordinate and parked there, if your pilot will let down to a foot or two above us, I'll have the top hatch open. You can climb out onto the top of our floater and get inside through the hatch."

He observed her expression. "It's safe enough, if you're not overly afraid of heights and if the wind's not blowing too hard."

She didn't answer for a half dozen seconds. "It sounds—scary, but if you'll have that top hatch open . . ."

"Fine. I'll see you in about an hour. Is that all?"

She nodded. "Yes sir."

"Good," Voker said, and disconnected.

She stood there for a minute, composing herself. Maybe the pilot would be unwilling, and she wouldn't have to do it. But she knew that if he refused, she'd give him an argument.

Jillard Brossling lay on his belly, peering through the branches of a fallen tree at the hill sloping up in front of him. He believed in looking things over personally when he could. The trees on it had been painted with orange rings at chest height, in lieu of actually cutting them down. Those of any size were marked with double rings, indicating they'd been dragged away as well. Standard war games procedure. Farther up the slope he glimpsed reaction dozers maneuvering their way uphill, pretending to drag away imaginary logs.

The army was thorough, or tried to be, Brossling told himself. That was for sure. Carefully he began working his way backward to rejoin his troops, half of whom should be napping.

It was dusk, edging into twilight. In charge of 2nd Platoon, A Company, Jerym Alsnor crouched in the woods, waiting. He'd never in his life felt this much responsibility.

The overcast had broken that afternoon, the liberated sun expelling remnant clouds. Seeren, more than half full, would light the first part of the night, which would help, even given the enhanced night vision provided by their helmet visors.

Jerym ignored the mosquitoes. Several times in early summer, the T'swa had left the trainees out all night without repellent fields. Repellent fields ran down in time, and while the trainees had been injected with antivenin so they wouldn't swell, they'd needed to develop a psychological indifference to being hummed around and bitten.

The T'swa had interesting ideas about psychological toughness. Once the regiment had been flown in to a slaughterhouse, company by company, and had had to crawl around in guts, roll in them, smear blood and slime on their faces. They wouldn't need that tonight of course, but if this were for real . . .

Jerym heard leaves rustle overhead—a bird perhaps, or an *oroval*. Now and then an evening *rast* trilled, like whistling down a tube with a pea in it, but somehow with a delicious sweetness. At school they'd said bird calls were challenges; this sounded like an invitation.

Pretty soon there'd be plenty of noise; enough to cover any sounds they'd make moving up. Even with all the practice the regiment had had that summer, it was hard to move around in the woods with no noise at all, especially after dark.

The dusk thickened. Then he heard the first shots from the enemy positions ahead, shots that quickly escalated into a racket of rifle and hose fire that drowned out the thumps of small caliber lobbers. Supposedly aimed the other way. To 2nd Platoon it was the signal to move forward, alert for pickets whom they needed to get past without disturbance.

Jerym started forward through the twilight, half crouched. Covering the hundred or so yards took several minutes that seemed longer, but finally, through the tress, he saw an opening. There were vehicles parked there. Apparently he'd hit close to their target; the vehicle park was supposed to be opposite the command center. Not half a mile ahead, the army poured gunfire down the hill in the direction of 2nd Battalion. Jerym turned down the exterior sensitivity of his headset and kept moving.

He didn't know if they'd bypassed any pickets or whether there simply were none. Romlar had said there might not be, a statement that had left Jerym skeptical. Reconnaissance had been sketchy, a walk-through by two guys in army uniforms stripped from soldiers jumped the day before. The soldiers still were held handcuffed—the only prisoners the regiment had taken, though technically they were dead.

To Jerym, the most impressive thing was that Romlar had known in advance what the enemy would do. Seemingly before the enemy himself could have known. It had been convincing enough when Romlar had gone over it two evenings earlier, giving the rationale, but to stake so much on it . . .

Standing, Jerym walked among the vehicles to the road. From there he could see no sign of defenses facing north, which fitted the report by the two scouts.

He scanned the other side of the road. There were several command modules down off their AGs, apparently resting on timbers to keep them level. One, the operations control center, was his personal target, but from where he stood, it was hard to tell which module that was. The scouts had said it was approximately in the middle, which would make it a hundred feet or so to his left.

They'd navigated it nicely, with Warden's guidance. Warden had come up with Romlar's talent for intuitive orienteering—for "going without knowing," as Esenrok had dubbed it. To Warden's amusement, Jerym had kept track of their progress on his mapbook, using compass and landmarks, just in case.

He hadn't broken radio silence for two days, nor did he now. After pivoting his visor to the top of his helmet, he stepped into the road and began walking eastward till he was opposite his target. There he stopped.

The roar of gunfire was extreme, even damped by the headset control.

A guard stood outside the operations control center, watching him, an anomaly in the scene. Jerym took out a pocket lamp, lit it, and waved its light conspicuously, signalling his men. Then he repocketed the lamp and began walking briskly toward the module.

The guard watched him approach through the twilight. Jerym seemed innocuous: He wore only side arms—knife and pistol—and behaved as if he belonged there. He was within five feet of the guard before the man began a double take, perhaps waking to the camouflage pattern on his field clothes, or the different, visored helmet. Abruptly Jerym's right fist struck him in the breastbone, the trauma paralyzing him, then struck him hard on the neck with a side hand. As the man slumped, Jerym supported him to the ground, then rolled him under the module.

No one had seen. Drawing his pistol, Jerym opened the door and stepped inside. Shiller, who'd been watching his monitors, pivoted on his chair to see who had entered. He started to rise, opening his mouth to yell, and the heel of Jerym's hand slammed him between the eyes. The chair went over backward, the brigadier hitting the floor like a bag of sand. His aide, a captain, grabbed for his own pistol, then froze his hand as Jerym's pointed at his face.

"I don't know what yours is loaded with," Jerym said, "but the blanks in mine would give you a bad burn. Might even blind you."

The army's umpire stared in consternation. The T'swi raised his eyebrows slightly. "Consider that I just shot them both to death," Jerym added, then gestured at the unconscious Shiller. "I couldn't have him raising an alarm. Just a minute; I've got another dead one outside." He stepped out and dragged the sentry in.

"This one we'll say I knifed," he told them. "Quieter that way." *Not*, he added to himself, *that it would make any difference out there in all that racket.*

"Very well," said the T'swi, "all three are dead. But—" he pointed at the radio. "The microphone is open. The shots might have been heard."

"Got it." Jerym was sceptical that they would have, but he raised his pistol and fired two blank rounds at the ceiling, then took an object from his thigh pocket. "This is a blast grenade. I'm about to cripple this place." He shut off the power to the computer-communication central, armed the dummy grenade, pushed its plunger, and laid it on the console, then ducked back out the door and under the module. *The grenade should be going 'pop' about now,* he thought, *and to the umpires that's as good as a boom.* He swiveled his mike to his mouth, then reached into a pocket and switched his radio to the regimental command channel; the need for radio silence was over.

"Little A, Little A," he said, "this is 2nd Platoon, A Company, Alsnor commanding. The enemy's commanding brigadier and his aide are dead. Their operations control center is crippled; I've destroyed their computer and comm central. Oh, and we encountered no pickets."

Acknowledgement was prompt. Then feet ran up to the center, hesitated for a minute outside the door. Someone opened it and stepped in, the other one following. Jerym rolled out and to his feet, and went in after them, gun in hand again, firing more blanks at the ceiling. "Two more dead!" he snapped, and turning, was gone again. One of the last two had been a full colonel; and he suspected he'd "killed" the brigade exec. Now it was time to steal some armored assault vehicles.

First Battalion, with G Company of the 3rd, moved through the woods as fast as feasible in the dark, toward the rear of the hilltop containment line. Shiller had taken no precautions at all against such a possibility. And in the noise and flash of their own gunfire, it never occurred to the brigade to look backward.

Meanwhile men from 2nd Platoon started a number of armored assault vehicles and sped down the north road a mile to its end, their two umpires following in a borrowed command car. The assault vehicles turned onto the west road, their heavy caliber hoses spewing blast slugs. They'd gone half a mile before the troops dug in there realized what was happening and began to shoot back. When finally they did though, their fire was heavy. The umpire channels were alive with traffic.

The augmented 1st Battalion didn't start shooting till they hit the north road, striking the brigade's forces from behind, "shooting hell out of 'em and taking no prisoners." Then some of them too started assault vehicles and headed west.

In the woods below the hill, 2nd Battalion's attack had never been more than a diversion. One company, thinly spread but guns blazing, had made a feint, then drawn back with heavy casualties. It had been enough to start Shiller's entire line firing downhill into the woods. Whenever the brigade's gunnery slackened a bit, a few remnant merc squads would start firing again, showing their muzzle blasts, and brigade gunnery took new life.

Then Little A informed 2nd Battalion that 1st Battalion had begun its attack, and also that the west road line had been shot up and disorganized near the northwest corner. With that, Brossling pulled his men back, and they started westward at a lope to make their breakout.

In the referees' floater, Tain Faronya, switching between command traffic and a buffet of umpire traffic, found it hard to keep from cheering.

Forty-Eight

It had been a long but jubilant night-march from the maneuvers area to the compound. Most of the brigade's personnel were picked up by big TTMs at their headquarters area and flown out, but now and then a convoy of army cargo trucks had passed on the road. Each time the hum of their approach was heard at the rear of the column, the word went by radio to Romlar, up front, and he gave the order to double-time. To the army drivers, it seemed that the mercs ran the whole twenty-odd miles back. Their reputation would not suffer from it, and in the soldiers' tellings, the distance grew to forty.

At the barracks, the previously evacuated "dead and disabled" had already been notified of the victory. They'd decorated the barracks with what they had on hand—toilet paper twisted and strung about. The cooks, army though they were, had gotten out more colorful paper to decorate the messhalls, and a feast was ready for the stoves and ovens when the word came of the approximate meal time.

The trainees arrived tired but happy. Shower rooms filled with steam and laughter. Evacuees, some of them, got dragged in with their clothes on. Then everyone dressed in clean field uniforms and trooped to the messhalls for a four-in-the-morning breakfast—a breakfast like none of them had seen before: sugar-cured ham, potatoes and gravy, buttered goldroot, green vegetables, hot rolls with butter, tart *rilgon* jelly, pie and ice cream. There were impromptu speeches, especially in A Company mess, which after all held the trainee regimental commander, the 1st Battalion's trainee C.O., and the man who'd killed the enemy general.

Afterward everyone went to their barracks and collapsed, being allowed to sleep almost till muster, which wasn't till 1300 hours. For most, the afternoon was dedicated to laundry and cleaning the barracks. After supper, they knew, there'd be assembly.

Each trainee officer and noncom, though, got a minidebriefing by his T'swa counterpart. At 1600, the T'swa met with Voker to give him anything particularly noteworthy that they'd been told.

Tain Faronya had returned well ahead of them, in the referees' floater with Voker and Dak-So. She was tired too, but the stress had been nervous, not muscular, and she wasn't sleepy. She'd looked up Lotta Alsnor, who it turned out was busy with one of the evacuees. So with her repellent field on, Tain went out for a long, solitary run on familiar forest roads, till she was physically tired. Then she showered and went to bed, her alarm set for the normal hour.

As usual she ate breakfast with Voker, his staff, and the battalion staffs, in the command dining room. The T'swa were amiable as always, but there was an added spark, a certain ebullience even, that she hadn't seen before among these scarred veterans of various wars.

She spent her day editing the hours of recordings— audio and video—that she'd compiled during the exercise; dictating draft commentary; and outlining a plan to get the additional material she deemed necessary.

Coming back in the floater, the night before, Voker had let her know there'd be an assembly in the evening, to review the maneuvers with the trainees. She was there a few minutes in advance, on her feet in the rear, a fresh power slug in both recorders, audio and video, her camera helmet conspicuous. At 2003 hours, the trainees began filing in, and while they were entering, she saw a number of civilians, two dozen at least, come in through a side door, the girl Lotta among them. They took seats in a separate row at the rear of the hall, seeming as happy as the trainees.

When everyone was seated, Colonel Voker got up from his chair on the podium, stepping front and center. "Good evening, men," he called out.

"Good evening, sir!" the regiment boomed back. The roar kicked in the volume modulator in Tain's audio recorder. It also kicked in a distrust of broad and enthusiastic consonance. The thought returned to her, from days earlier, of "drills" and psychoconditioning. Irritated, she shook it off. She knew these youths, and Voker, and liked them all very much. As she did the T'swa, foreign though they were.

"This won't take a lot of time," Voker went on, "and when we're done, you can stow the benches for a party. But first I want to congratulate you all for the great job you did in maneuvers. Give yourselves a hand!"

The place erupted with cheers, whistles, and the sound of strong, callused palms beating together in what quickly became a rhythmic unison. Voker let it go on for a minute or longer before he cut them off.

"And I especially want to congratulate—" He paused, let them wait a few seconds. "I particularly want to congratulate your regimental commander, Artus Romlar, for his ingenious, and more importantly his successful, strategy. Artus, stand up!"

Romlar did, and the place erupted again. After fifteen seconds, Voker, grinning broadly, once more waved them quiet. "Artus," he called, "come up here."

The big trainee, also grinning, hopped up onto the podium, ignoring the steps, faced Voker and saluted. Voker held something in one hand. He stepped up to Romlar, pinned it on the young man's collar, and stepped back. "The bronze fist of a subcolonel," he said. "Colonel Romlar is now your official regimental commander. Ranks and insignia will be presented to others at ceremonies later in the week." He shook hands with Romlar. "But the cadre and I still rank you, young fellow. Till your training is over. Take a seat now."

"Thank you sir," Romlar answered, and taking the steps down, returned to his bench.

"All right. Now for a brief review. I won't go into details, but starting with less than forty percent of your opponent's manpower and less than a tenth his firepower, lacking any support services, and threatened and harassed by his air support, you maneuvered him into an exposed position with his forces spread out and dispersed. And without his getting the least notion that he was being manipulated. You destroyed his operations control center, killed his commander and part of his command staff, took control of much of his hover stock, totally disrupted his operation, and inflicted substantial casualties—casualties somewhat heavier than your own. In the eyes of the army's own referees, you performed more than creditably; you won the game brilliantly and decisively.

"In fact, Major General Thromlek, Lord Carns, was in the referees' floater during the final shift, and he sends his personal 'very well done' to all of you. He was extremely impressed not only with Colonel Romlar's strategy, but with your mobility, your endurance, and your initiative and resourcefulness as individual units and fighting men. As well as your coordination as separated, sometimes widely separated units, mostly with only one-way communication. He plans to recommend that the army's infantry and officer training be reexamined in the light of what you accomplished out there."

Voker paused and looked his audience over. "Although the army doesn't have warriors to work with in any large numbers. On the Matrix of T'sel, most soldiers are at Work, not Play, and training and tactics have to recognize that. But on the other hand, units of soldiers well trained and led can be very effective. In the Kettle War, for example, a majority of the Orlanthan army was not warriors, but determined soldiers."

He paused and looked them over again. "You've noticed I didn't refer to the 8th Brigade as 'the enemy.' And I suspect that many of you could tell me why. They were your playmates, not your enemy. Just as Colonel Dak-So's old Lightning Regiment and Captain Tuk's Ro-Sok Regiment were playmates when they warred against each other on Gwalsey."

In the back of the hall, Tain Faronya stared, a numbness creeping along her spine as she absorbed what Voker had said about the T'swa. They'd killed each other for pleasure!

"Brigadier Shiller, killed in action at his operations control center, had no comments for us, even after being returned from the dead. For one thing, he was suffering from a concussion. I'm afraid that Trainee Alsnor, the warrior who killed him, slightly miscalculated the impact necessary to prevent the newly dead brigadier from raising an alarm before the umpires could make his death official."

The colonel paused, looked them over. "Incidentally, the umpires who witnessed the event agreed that striking the brigadier, while startling and unprecedented, was not unreasonable under the circumstances.

"Which brings me to another matter. The umpires and referees assigned from the army did a generally fair and unprejudiced job—and a competent job—in their part of the exercise. Although the army in general has not been friendly to the concept of elite forces like yours."

Voker glanced back at the T'swi sitting to one side. "Now I'll turn this meeting over to Colonel Dak-So, who'll look at the overall results with you and give them some perspective. Colonel?"

Dak-So stepped front and center. "Let me add my voice to Colonel Voker's," he said. "You all did very well indeed. I speak for your entire cadre in saying that; we are all very proud of you."

Dak-So's words, in his deep resonant T'swa voice, nudged Tain partly out of her numbness. Pride was something she empathized with, and she did not doubt the black colonel's sincerity. It occurred to her that the drills might actually have been just what Voker had said—something to develop in the trainees a T'swa emotional stability. Something had.

"You performed splendidly," Dak-So went on. "And consider the stated scenario of the game! You were a regiment without support, caught within hostile territory. The opposition sent a brigade to destroy you. You broke that brigade.

"But meanwhile—" He paused for emphasis. "Meanwhile you were running out of food. Your ammunition was seriously depleted, although you might have replenished it with captured supplies. You had lost more than twenty percent killed, and left wounded scattered over many square miles of forest. And you were still within hostile territory.

"The maneuvers were over, but in a sense the game was not. It was simply well begun. Very *successfully* begun, but just begun. You had reached, or were approaching, a time when your strategy and tactics would need to change. What changes you might have decided on would reflect circumstances not described in the scenario provided you."

He scanned the regiment. "I want you to play with these thoughts, and someday soon we will discuss what you might have done next.

"And now—" He stopped, grinned. "We T'swa have watched you grow and develop as warriors. At the beginning, we thought of you as 'the recruits.' Soon that changed, and we thought of you as 'the trainees.' Now, with this experience, this victory under your belts, to us you are more than trainees, though there is still a great deal you will learn. To us you have become 'the troopers.' "

He paused, then continued more slowly, to stress what he would say next. "It is the custom, in the Lodge of Kootosh-Lan, for the novice warriors to name their own regiment. Occasionally they change their minds later, and rename it when they've graduated. You may conclude that it is time to name yours. But until you do, your cadre has decided to call you by an informal name of their own selection. One we feel fits you." He paused again. "After your performance of the last three days, to us you are—" Once more he paused. "*You are now The White T'swa.*"

Tain wasn't sure what she expected. A concerted cheer, or possibly a palpable sense of embarrassment. What she got was a long moment of silence, and a sense of sudden sobriety that seemed could not be hers, must be theirs. Then Artus Romlar stood up. "Sir," he said, "we are honored." His big voice was tight with emotion. "And on behalf of the troopers of the White T'swa Regiment, I thank you for all you've done to help us become what we are—to help us fulfill our purpose."

Romlar stopped and looked around. His voice had been on the verge of breaking, and when he continued, it had lowered in both pitch and volume. "I also thank the Ostrak Project for all they've done. Project personnel, those of you still here, please stand up." He waited while they did, then turned to Dak-So. "Without them you could have made us warriors, but you'd never have decided to call us 'White T'swa.' "

Turning again, he raised both hands overhead, fisted, and his voice became a sudden trumpet. "Regiment! On your feet!"

They stood, and Tain, covered with chill bumps, could feel something building.

"Let's let our cadre and the project both know what we think of them!"

It wasn't instantaneous, but when it came, it was abrupt. The cheering that arose was wild and elemental, more emotional then anything Tain Faronya had ever felt or witnessed. Then the regiment left their places, stepping over benches, some headed for the T'swa, some for the civilians near her in the back. There were embraces, handshakes. The grins were unbelievable, many mixed with exuberant tears, and she stood apart confused, almost in shock, getting it all with her helmet camera, not understanding nor fully trusting, but deeply moved by what she saw and how it felt.

For just a moment their emotion shook Voker almost to tears of his own, and it troubled him not at all that the assembly had come apart as it had. This was needed. So much had happened in nine deks. Nearly two thousand young men whose dreams, whose drives, had been frustrated, had had their purpose validated here, had found themselves and felt their lives salvaged.

Several of them jumped grinning onto the podium, converging on himself and Dak-So. His hand was being pumped. He was hugged. After a moment the first troopers were off the podium again, but more were coming. Voker stepped quickly to the microphone—he'd need it to be heard—and spoke.

"Men, the assembly is over. When you've finished doing what you're doing, stack the benches and we'll bring the goodies in and continue from there."

Then he turned his attention to another round of embraces and handshakes.

Forty-Nine

The music was on cube, by the Garyan Quintet. Tain arrowed to Jerym, shaking off invitations as she went. His back was to her when she got there. "Want to dance, soldier?" she said to him suggestively. His head snapped around, and she laughed. He echoed it, reached out, and they clasped in the daring new style in which the couple dances close together.

"I have an apology to make," she said. "I've been staying away from you. I shouldn't have."

He tilted his head back, eyebrows raised. "Tell me about that."

"That evening we walked together," she said, "you told me some pretty wild stories, and I believed them all. Until you told the one about Colonel Voker beating some trainee, some kind of trainee champion, in a fight. And that sounded so far-fetched that it suddenly seemed to me you'd been lying all along, to see how much I'd believe."

"Ah!"

"I liked you at once, you know. Maybe more than I'd ever liked a guy before on first acquaintance, so it really

284

stung me." She paused, holding his gaze, wondering how he'd take such bold frankness. "Well, I just congratulated Artus Romlar on getting his subcolonel's bronze fist. And I said something like, 'How does it feel to replace Colonel Voker at age nineteen?'

"He said no one replaces Colonel Voker, and told me the same story you did. And that you—the regiment that is—owed Colonel Voker for everything you've become."

Jerym nodded soberly.

"He said you owed the T'swa, too, and the Ostrak Project, that you'd never have made it without all three, but that Voker was the one who guided it all. Is that how you see it?"

Again Jerym nodded. "Voker is our father, the father of the regiment. The T'swa are our teachers, and the project our— The ones who got us acting sane."

She nodded. "Anyway I'm sorry I doubted you. And stayed away from you."

She paused, started to ask him about the Ostrak Project, then didn't. It might sound as if her apology was a way of getting him to talk, which in fact was what she'd started out to do. Instead she danced closer, felt the warmth and hardness of his body. Reminded herself that he was eighteen and she was twenty-four, and that they had no future together. The music stopped, they stepped apart, then abruptly she stepped close again and kissed his cheek.

It startled her as much as it did him, and she almost fled, then got a grip on herself. "I'll only be here three more days," she said. "And I know you'll be busy. But I'll write to you when you go to Terfreya to train, and I hope you'll write back."

Then she turned and left, left Jerym, left the assembly hall, wondering what had gotten into her. Jerym was scarcely out of adolescence, and she'd only talked to him twice in her life, for only minutes each time; it made no sense at all. She couldn't possibly love him.

But she would write to him, she was sure about that.

She went to her room, wondering what Jerym thought about it. Had she seemed like a fool? Or had he been attracted to her the way she had to him? Was he downstairs at the party wondering? Feeling confused? Frustrated?

Perhaps she should go back down, find him, and take him to the woods or—to her room. The thought troubled her even as it attracted her. It would be cheap, degrading. Not to him perhaps—men were different—but to her.

She stayed for a while; tried to read, but couldn't keep her mind on the book. Perhaps she could go down and dance with others. Finally she got up from the bed and left her room, unsure of her motives or what she might do when she saw Jerym again.

From the hall outside her door, she heard trooper voices filling the main-floor corridor, spilling out into the night, as if the party was over. She went to the stairway and most of the way down, watching them leave. The girl Lotta flowed with them, Lotta who was part of the mysterious Ostrak Project.

Lotta moved out of the current, stepping onto the first step up, out of the troopers' way, as if waiting for them to pass. Tain went down and stood beside her.

"Waiting to take a walk?" Tain asked.

Lotta looked at her and smiled. "Yes, as a matter of fact. Want to come along?"

The place emptied quickly, and they left together. Seeren bulged lopsidedly white, and the breeze and chill of two nights earlier had been replaced by mellow stillness. The two young women strolled down the main road, its grass newly mown and blown from the right of way, its fragrance sweet around them.

"I'm afraid I'm not a party creature," Tain said.

Lotta nodded. "Me either. I enjoy them, but they're nothing I feel much attracted to. I generally prefer the company of a friend or two—or maybe half a dozen."

Dak-So had announced to the troopers that tomorrow they'd begin parachute training, Lotta said, and that was all it had taken to wind down the party. The troopers had been looking forward to parachute training. On less Standard worlds than Iryala, parachuting had long held a certain minor interest as a sport, but as a military technique, it was unique to the T'swa, who used it for covert infiltration, jumping from high elevations and at some distance from the drop zone, then body-planing in.

Tain decided it was time to turn the conversation to the psychological drills. "How old are you?" she asked.

"Sixteen."

"Sixteen?!" She peered at Lotta, honestly surprised. "I thought— You look about sixteen, but somehow you seem older."

"I suppose I do."

The road forked. They kept to the wider one, where more moonlight got through to light their way.

"What is it you do here?" Tain asked. "At age sixteen."

"I interview the trainees, the troopers that is, and take them through psychological drills. To improve their emotional stability."

Tain glanced sideways at her. "To give them the emotional stability of the T'swa. That's what Colonel Voker said. Tell me about the drills."

Lotta was tempted to *show* her. Find a good initial button, jump her into whatever opened up, and take her through it. That would really give her reality on it. But the journalist was not to know what the Ostrak Procedures really did. That was the word from Wellem— from Emry, actually. Besides, there were journalists, prominent ones, who'd grown up in The Movement and knew the T'sel. The Crown had brought in Tain Faronya instead, because they wanted an outsider who'd write from a viewpoint closer to the public's. To open her up, even just once, would alter that.

"There's really not much to tell," Lotta said shrugging. "We lead the trainee around"—mentally that is, she added to herself—"get him to look at things." Just don't expect me to tell you what kind of things. "I'm afraid it's not very interesting. It's a lot of repetition; quite time consuming."

Tain frowned. It didn't sound like much. It didn't sound like something that would do any good. "And these are drills the T'swa do?" she asked.

"No no. The T'swa are the way they are because of how they grow up. The philosophy they grow up with. Have you read Varlik Lormagen's book on Tyss?"

"I'm afraid not. But I've read his *With the T'swa on Kettle*. How do the drills make the troopers like the T'swa? Frankly, they don't seem much like T'swa to me, except as soldiers."

"They aren't. The T'swa are from another culture, a very different culture. They're even a different species. Their life experience has been a lot different, and these T'swa are twice as old as the troopers."

Tain nodded. *Three or four wars older!* she thought grimacing. "I spent the first day of maneuvers in the forest with 3rd Platoon of F Company," she said. "And heard some weird things there. Like, death is only incidental, and dead isn't really dead. Does that attitude grow out of the drills?"

Lotta laughed aloud, not only to mislead Tain but to reduce her seriousness. "It does sound weird, doesn't it? But you need to expect a different viewpoint from them. There's one way they're very much like the T'swa: They're inherently warriors. Their psych profiles show it—profiles of their innate personality. That's why they were recruited."

She changed the subject then. "We'd better go back now. I have to work in the morning. Want to run?"

They ran. When they reached the Compound, Lotta was much the more winded. At Main Building reception they said goodbye, each going to her own room.

As Lotta showered, she told herself that this had been her last conversation with Tain Faronya. The woman was too persistently inquisitive.

Interesting though that Tain had read *With The T'swa on Kettle*, and still had the questions she had about dying and death. Apparently what the T'swa had said to Varlik had seemed so unreal to Tain, when she'd read it, that it simply hadn't registered.

Tain lay down and turned off the light. As she composed herself for sleep, it occurred to her that she'd never really gotten an answer, a real answer to her question about the drills. Or had she? Perhaps they were nothing more than Lotta had said. Perhaps she was making too much of it. Apparently the psychs had identified these kids as warriors—or inherent warriors, whatever that really meant—and that could account for their peculiar views.

Interesting that the psych courses she'd taken at the university had never mentioned innate personality.

And if her talk with Lotta hadn't been very enlightening, at least she hadn't run into Jerym again, perhaps truly to make a fool of herself.

Fifty

It had taken twenty-eight days for the first report to reach Iryala about the arrival of the Klestroni at Terfreya. Twenty-eight days by mail pod from Tyss. After that they got a new report almost daily.

Master Tso-Ban didn't learn everything that went on with the Klestroni there, although he was spending as much as fourteen hours a day monitoring. For instance, he'd been out of touch when Tarimenloku destroyed the Confederation ship, and subsequently the encounter hadn't entered the commodore's conscious mind while Tso-Ban was melded with him. So the monk didn't know about it. But Tso-Ban sent word of the Klestroni landing, and later the capture and questioning of prisoners, the executions, and the attack by the cadets.

Nor had it occurred to Kristal that the supply ship might have been destroyed. Tso-Ban had said nothing about it, and the elapsed time made it easy to assume uncritically that the supply ship had already left Terfreya, continuing on toward Tyss, before the Klestroni arrived. A simple check of its scheduled arrival time would have corrected the assumption, but nothing happened that caused Kristal to look.

Originally it had been planned that the regiment would travel by ship to Terfreya, after the equinox, for a year of training there. Now the training plan and the transportation plan both were obsolete. For one thing, travel by ship was slow. And it seemed quite possible that the Klestronu flagship by itself was too strong for anything the Confederation could send to protect the regiment's troopship. Earlier, in the Garthid Sector, Tso-Ban had said something about the Klestronu ship having a force shield; the Confederation had nothing like that.

So clearly, the most promising way to get the regiment to Terfreya was to teleport it, with its equipment, as soon as the large teleport was ready. Assuming Kusu had developed adequate targeting procedures by then.

Meanwhile the assumption was that they'd soon have a teleport, with its technicians, on Tyss. The ship would leave a shuttle there as a suitable power source. And when the targeting procedures were adequate, a Crown representative would be ported there to expedite the hiring of a T'swa regiment.

Of course, if the war lodges had contracts for their graduating regiments in advance, as they usually did, they might very well refuse to bump one of the contract holders and give the Confederation priority. On the other hand, they might do it without being asked. Or they might put together a regiment or battalion of demobilized veterans.

We'll just have to wait and see, Kristal thought, and reached for his comm set to make his daily check on Kusu's progress.

Fifty-One

"Lotta Alsnor to see you, Colonel," said the voice from the commset.

Voker's eyebrows arched. "Send her in," he answered, then sat back in his chair. A moment later Lotta stepped into his office, and without asking, sat down facing him.

"We're done with the floater crews," she said, "but I hope you're not done with me."

"Wellem told me last night that you'd finished. What do you have in mind?"

"I want to go to Terfreya with the regiment."

"Oh?"

"As part of Headquarters Company. Intelligence Section. I have no doubt at all that I can meld with the Klestronu commander on the ground. And probably their commodore."

Voker was instantly interested. "Wellem told me what you were working on. I didn't know you'd made such progress." He looked her over. Five feet two, he thought, and ninety-five pounds. But then, she wasn't asking to be a lobber man. "What makes you so sure you can meld with him?"

"I've gotten so I can find people I've never met, if I know of them and have some idea where they are. And if I can find them, I can meld with them. I've done it, to make sure."

"Can you reach him from here?"

"Not yet. I should be able to—theoretically the distance shouldn't make any difference. But for some reason I haven't succeeded with anyone outsystem, except for a couple of people I know personally."

"What about language?"

"That shouldn't be any problem. One of the things I learned as a little kid, melding with animals, is that their minds deal with a surprising lot of images and even concepts. They don't verbalize them, but you can read them quite completely. Even people only verbalize some of their mental activity."

She laughed then. "I've been practicing on your cadre. They know it, of course; you can't slip into a T'swi's mind in secret. So I touch one of them psychically, and if it's all right with him, I meld. He can be reading or talking or meditating. And even when he's talking Tyspi, which I don't understand at all, the verbalization's no problem. I ignore it."

"Hmh! Headquarters Company may move around a lot on Backbreak. The way it did on maneuvers. Possibly on foot for security. Do you know the gravitational constant on Backbreak?"

"One point one-nine gee."

"And how much do you weigh? Here."

"A hundred and two."

"That much! Is that with boots on?"

She grinned. "That's wearing a smile and nothing more. I'm heavier than I look; my body's hard. I've done gymnastics and ballet most of my life, and I've made time to run and work out lately."

"That's a lot short of what these troopers have been doing for next to a year now," Voker replied. "As you well know. And on Backbreak, a hundred and two pounds of mass will weigh a hundred and twenty-one."

"Right. And Artus's 210 will be 250."

Voker laughed, shaking his head in appreciation. "Since the beginning of warfare, military commanders have been wanting intelligence officers that can do what you can. So I'll accept your offer on one condition: that Artus agrees."

"Thanks," she said, and got up.

"Does Wellem know about this?" Voker asked.

"He's known for deks that I've had it in mind. And he's got his students working on melding. It's good experience, even if they never go very far with it. Maybe you'll have more intelligence people like me in a while."

"If Colonel Romlar agrees"—*and I have no doubt he will*, Voker added mentally—"tell Captain Esenrok I want you running and hiking with A Company as much as you can, until you're ready to leave. With 2nd Platoon; you can buddy up with your brother."

She nodded, turned and left. Voker sat thoughtfully motionless for a few seconds, contemplating what the girl expected to do, then swiveled his chair to his terminal and began scanning reports again.

Fifty-Two

In the twilight, the big teleport gate seemed to loom above the instrument van, and Carlis Voker, standing by it, grunted softly at the strangeness he felt. Kusu Lormagen unlocked the van's rear door and opened it, a light coming on automatically inside. He motioned the other two men in—Voker and a middle-aged civilian—then followed them, leaving the door open.

The portly civilian, a one-time Iryalan trade official on Terfreya, exuded tension. Though he hadn't received the true Sacrament, to be in the presence of anything as utterly non-Standard as this, anything so conspicuously, technologically new made him distinctly uneasy.

While Voker watched, Kusu keyed the power on, then called up and briefly checked several subsystem status reports. Satisfied, he called up a holo-map, a globe, showing Terfreya's inhabited hemisphere, rotated it thirty degrees, moved the cursor to a point in the equatorial region, and called up a map of the district it covered.

It looked like a high altitude aerial holo. A black

thread of river crossed it, and locating the cursor on it, Kusu called for another enlargement. Now, near the top, Voker could distinguish an irregular, light-colored strip—open ground—with the river a slender ribbon curving through it. Kusu moved the cursor, the map recentering as he did. "This one looked good to me," he said, and called up another enlargement.

The open ground showed now as a valley bottom more than half a mile wide; a white line in the upper left corner provided scale. The bordering ridges were jungle clad and fairly steep. Voker guessed them at perhaps three hundred feet high; Kusu didn't call for contour lines.

Again Kusu recentered the cursor and called for maximum enlargement. Now they were looking "down" at tall grass—a variable stand ranging, he guessed, from waist high to taller than a man, and mostly sparse, with scattered denser clumps and patches.

Kusu looked at the third man, whose face was the color of bread dough in the artificial light. "What can you tell us about that?" Kusu asked. "As a site to put a regiment down on."

"That's tiger grass," the man answered. "It means the valley floods briefly now and then, during heavy winter rains and maybe after exceptional summer storms."

"Winter?" Voker said. "That's near the equator there."

"They call it winter. Things cool down planetwide in the long arm of her orbit. The solar constant gets down to point-seven-eight about midway between the winter solstice and spring equinox. It gets chilly, even at Lonyer City."

Of course. I should have realized, Voker thought. "What makes the tiger grass so sparse?" he asked. "Is the ground mucky?"

The ex-trade official shook his head with tight little movements, over-controlled. "No. It's probably covered with a layer of stones. Flat rounded stones about an inch or two across. That's what you find when the grass is thin like that. And tiger grass never grows on mucky ground. Or so I've heard."

Kusu looked at Voker. "Okay as the transfer site?"

Voker nodded. The year was halfway into Sixdek on Terfreya;* a flood was highly unlikely. "Considering the time factor," he said, "and what's likely to be happening to the cadets, let's get on with it."

He watched Kusu back off the magnification, move the cursor to where the grass was relatively sparse, and touch a key. Planetary surface coordinates appeared top-center, and Kusu touched another key, presumably entering them into the targeting equation.

"Now," said Kusu, getting up, "we tinker the equation and cut the error."

It was near midnight at the outgate site on Terfreya when the LUF—light utility floater—ported through well above the jungle's roof. It had two men aboard—a pilot and a T'swa corporal. The pilot parked the floater at 500 feet. All they could see below was forest; there was no sign of an open valley. After raising the roof hatch, he folded down a ladder from the overhead, climbed it, and took instrument readings on the sky. Then he climbed back down and fed them to the computer.

Their location within the planetary coordinate grid popped onto the screen. *Not bad,* he thought. *We're less than eighty miles off target.*

In Tyspi, the T'swi sent an open message pulse across the radio wavebands, a message which included their coordinates. Within seconds he had a narrow beam reply in unaccented Tyspi, from the cadet night CQ, getting the status of the war and all they knew about the locations of enemy forces and cadet units.

---

*In the Confederation, the calendar year for every inhabited planet begins with the southern hemisphere winter solstice. The southern hemisphere was chosen as the base because Landfall, the original settlement in the Confederation, is in Iryala's southern hemisphere.

The boy's voice broke a couple of times, but from puberty, not emotion. They were operating as short platoons, he said, had lost a third of their personnel. Their walking wounded—what there'd been of them—had been gotten to local farms, where the farm families were hiding them.

The T'swi told the cadet what to expect, approximately where, and how they'd arrive. A couple of deks earlier the cadet might have cheered wildly at such a scenario. Now he simply grinned. "All right!" he said in Tyspi. "Tell them our T'swa say it's as good a war as any they've seen since Kettle."

After that the LUF landed in a little glade, and the T'swi guided a small, AG-mounted teleport out the door. The pilot set the teleport controls on a reverse vector. The T'swi peered through, signaling till the pilot had gotten the outgate site on the ground. Then he stepped back onto Iryala, with a radio to let Kusu know the correction and Voker the war situation. And to get himself picked up, of course.

The second LUF arrived less than seven miles off target and flew to the open valley, where it examined the target site first hand before porting a second T'swa corporal back to Iryala for a final correction.

When Kusu had entered the second error report, he left the teleport site to its guards, troopers from the regiment, and drove back to the Lake Loreen Institute with Voker and the ex-trade official. He left the official with Wellem Bosler. The man had become visibly upset when the first LUF had ported out. Wellem would get him out of it.

Fifty-Three

The season seemed later than it was, with the peiok trees around the hayfield tinged purplish bronze by early frost.

It was obvious to Lord Kristal why Kusu had chosen this place. It was a level open field, secluded, and less than a mile from the Lake Loreen Institute.

Although it was none too large. He could see why Voker didn't have the whole regiment there at once; the place was already on the verge of being crowded. First Battalion was there, and Headquarters Company with its 158 personnel including floater crews and medical section. The regiment's floaters were parked at one end: four gunships, six scouts, and eight CPCs—combat personnel carriers that could haul two squads each with gear. Not much compared to army regiments, but for a T'swa-type regiment, unprecedented.

Kristal eyed the quiet troopers standing relaxed in ranks and wondered idly what it would be like to step from this rural, mellow, somewhat sylvan late summer landscape into equatorial jungle. What would the weather be like there today?

The focus of attention here was the teleport, looking much different than the small apparatus he'd stepped through on the roof of the Research Building, not so many deks earlier. It was wide enough for the floaters and seemed needlessly tall, a gate-like structure on a low platform. No doubt, thought Kristal, there was good reason for its height. On one side was a metal housing resembling a narrow shed or overgrown cabinet, presumably holding whatever made the teleport function. This in turn was connected by cables to an instrument van with the door open. He'd seen Kusu go inside. An assistant knelt on the platform, comm set in hand, seemingly waiting for something.

A small media contingent had been invited, had arrived with an eagerness grown in part from sharp public interest in the Central News series. In fact, they were the busiest-seeming people there, those from Iryala Video shifting around with Revax cameras on their shoulders. Two small camera floaters positioned and repositioned themselves, like hoverbirds over a flowerbed. The young woman from Central News had dressed in the camouflage uniform she'd been given by the regiment, wearing it like a badge as she walked quietly around, talking to one and another of the troopers.

Kristal himself didn't really need to be there, had no function there. But this was an important event, the climax of an activity that had held more than a little of his attention for over a year. He'd developed a considerable affinity with its young men, even though his knowledge of them was largely indirect. Very soon now—perhaps before this day was over—some of them would die. Probably many would over the next weeks, perhaps most of them. Presumably none with regret. For not only were they warriors; they knew the T'sel now.

He would not regret either, of course. Though he would miss Lotta Alsnor, should she die. To him she was a symbol of the future, and he'd been tempted to veto her accompanying the regiment to Terfreya. But he'd rejected the thought at once. One did not interfere with the self-chosen role of someone like her.

And in a few more generations, perhaps no more than six or eight, the people of Iryala and the Confederation as a whole would know the T'sel. They'd be comparable to the people of Tyss then, their children wise and playful.

Assuming there was no serious invasion from the empire. Conquest could not kill the T'sel, but it would doubtless throw the timetable out, and change the nature of the playing field, perhaps for a long time.

Carlis Voker rarely fidgeted, but he did now. And noticing, stilled it with a T'sel order to himself: "Turn around and look at you." In response he felt a brief wave of chills and a sense of unfocused amusement.

He scanned the assembled troopers again. This was incomparably the best regiment he'd ever been part of, and now it had a new commander—a commander still short of twenty years old. *And with more talent,* Voker told himself, *than I ever dreamed of having.* Too, the floater crews, a late addition to the Table of Organization, had fitted in beautifully. There was good reason to hope that the regiment would accomplish its objective: Chew up the enemy ground forces, and send the imperial ships home convinced that the Confederation sector was not a promising place to invade.

He was sending no T'swa advisors with the regiment, a decision that hadn't been easy to make. Dak-So had agreed though, without reservation. The regiment was good, very good, from top to bottom, and Dak-So said that, even by T'swa standards, Romlar was a tactical genius.

Besides, 2,000 new recruits would be arriving at Blue Forest at week's end, needing cadre to train them. This batch would average less troublesome than the first. The recruiters had used a much slower screening system to identify candidates—winnowing through many thousands of innate personality profiles, rather than starting with a preliminary selection by behavior records. For not all, or even most intentive warriors on Iryala were trouble-makers.

A command on the bullhorn broke Voker's thoughts, and his gaze sharpened, focusing on the port. One of the gunships had begun to move toward it.

Tain Faronya had found a good angle, where she could see the gunship float into the gate. And disappear! She'd been briefed on arrival, she and the video people—had been told what would happen. And she'd believed; it seemed to her some hadn't. But seeing it happen excited her in a way she'd never imagined. She felt suddenly eager, and at the same time queasy, her knees momentarily weak.

A slow-moving column of troopers followed the gunship, stepping onto the platform in two files, and she recorded the first few pairs disappearing. Then she took her eyes from them, looking around as if for another vantage or another shot. Climbing down off the hood of the hovercar where she'd been standing, she moved back along a column of waiting troopers, her helmet camera on their tan young faces as if to document their fearlessness, their eagerness.

When she came to the rear, she stopped behind them and looked around again. Her excitement manifested as a seeming need to relieve herself. As best she could, she ignored it. Here the personnel carriers were parked, loaded not with troopers but supplies. Their pilots were visible in their cockpits; other crewmembers were standing on top, where they could better see the troopers disappearing.

As casually as possible, and certain that everyone's eyes were turning to her, Tain went to one of the rearmost carriers, stepped up the ramp and inside.

The cockpit door was open, and she could see the pilot's right arm and shoulder. In the troop cum cargo compartment, there was hardly any room at all except for a narrow aisle between stacks of cases. The cases were of different sizes, and in several places there was room enough for a person to lay down on top of them.

She stepped quickly to one such place, grabbed a tie strap and pulled herself up, then squirmed sideways as far back as she could, all the way to the side of the floater. From there, all she could see were the ceiling and the tops of boxes.

Only then did she feel her heart thudding. She'd committed herself! Tunis only knew what they'd say when they found her, somewhere on Terfreya—wherever they arrived there. But they couldn't send her back, not through the teleport. The briefing had made clear that a teleport was a one-way gate.

Her wait seemed long; long enough that her heart slowed to something like normal, and she had time to imagine discovery scenarios—exposure scenarios, actually, with her coming out of hiding. Then the rest of the crew was boarding; it must be time! She had no doubt she'd know when they arrived: She'd feel the craft sit down, hear the crew talking.

It lifted. She felt it, barely, but she was sure. Felt it move forward, shift direction slightly, accelerate a little. She realized she was holding her breath. And then . . .

Fifty-Four

The scream so startled Flight Sergeant Barniss that his hands twitched on the control wheel, causing the floater to jerk forward, almost bumping the craft in front of it. He recovered instantly, though the screaming continued—repeated shrieks, inhuman and shockingly harsh. In the troop compartment, he heard Kortalno swearing loudly.

"What the fuck's happening back there?" he called over his shoulder.

"Sergeant, we've got a stowaway! A woman on top of the cargo, back against the side of the aircraft! She's coming unglued up there!"

"Oh shit," Barniss muttered. "Arlefer, go back there and help him get her down. And be careful. I don't want her hurting herself, and I damn well don't want her hurting either of you."

His copilot got out of his seat and was gone, while Barniss swung the floater out of line and to one side, looking for the nearest place to set her down. "Little A, Little A, emergency on CPC 4. Emergency on CPC 4. We've got a stowaway having a screaming fit on top of

304

the cargo, a stowaway gone psycho on top of the cargo. Get us a medic right away."

Troopers were getting out of his way, and he put down between two platoons. The shrieking hadn't changed; it was raucous, blood-curdling, and utterly mindless. *Already a damned emergency*, he thought, *and I haven't even had a chance to see what this world looks like.* When he felt the floater touch down, he hit the AG switch, swung out of his seat, and started back to help Kortalno and Arlefer.

Lotta was standing within eight feet of Romlar when CPC 4's emergency call sounded from the command radio, and she *knew*—knew who it was, though she hadn't seen her at the field, hadn't known she'd be there. She moved a stride behind the medics, running through coarse sparse grass as high as her chest. Troopers dodged out of their way.

As they approached the floater, she saw one of its crew standing disheveled at the head of the ramp, waving them on. The shrieks sounded as if they'd rupture the lining of the screamer's throat. On board, the crew had gotten Tain down from the cargo stack. One of them, angry scratches across a cheek, lay on her, arms around her hips, more or less pinning her legs with his body. Another, with a bloody lip, held her arms with his knees and hands. Dr. Orleskis had arrived with his belt kit open. Now he knelt, held her head still between his knees, and triggered a syringe against her cheek.

It took a few seconds before she stopped jerking, her movements reduced to feeble shudders.

"Is she unconscious?" Lotta asked.

"No more than she was. I gave her a tranquilizer; in large subcutaneous doses it's very effective for psychomotor convulsions. Is this the teleport shock I was told about?"

Lotta nodded, remembering the sorlexes. Sedation

had controlled their convulsions but they'd died anyway. "Get her on her feet," she ordered.

Orleskis frowned. "On her feet?"

"Support her; carry her upright."

The crewmen were already disengaging themselves from their stowaway. She stank; both excretory openings had let go. Two medics hoisted her to her feet. "Outside," Lotta said, and one under each arm, they carried the stowaway, her toes dragging, following Lotta down the ramp and into the tiger grass, here considerably trampled.

Lotta stopped them and took Tain's right wrist. "Tain!" she ordered, "lift your right hand!", then raised it for her to shoulder height. "Thank you," Lotta said, then lowered it, shifted to the left wrist and repeated the action. Next she turned the woman's face left, then right, always after the appropriate command, always thanking her for the enforced completion. Had her "go over to" the floater, the medics toting her, and providing both guidance and impetus, had her touch the side of it with one hand, then the other. All on command, all in a regular, unvarying format. After a bit, troopers relieved the two aid-men and carried Tain to the nearby forest, out of the way, where Lotta continued the procedure, using trees. Later other troopers replaced the first two. Within an hour, Tain was moving her legs a bit, as if trying to walk, and Lotta could feel her feeble effort to raise her arms for herself, though her eyes still were glazed.

Orleskis had left briefly to see to other things. Now he'd returned. "Want me to take over?" he asked.

Lotta shook her head. "It's working. Best not to change."

The doctor nodded and watched. After another twenty minutes, Tain was largely supporting her own weight, moving her own head, directing her attention as ordered. Her eyes weren't glazed any longer, though they were vague and she did not try to speak. After another ten minutes, her head was drooping as if she was starting to doze.

"Can we get her to bed somewhere?" Lotta asked.

Orleskis nodded, and turned to one of his aid-men. "Get ready to clean her up," he ordered. "In the aid tent." The man trotted off. The rest followed slowly, two of them supporting Tain.

"She's going to make it," Orleskis said. "No doubt about it. Where did you learn to do that?"

"I've been inside the minds of experimental animals when they were teleported, and got a sense of what they were feeling: incredible panic, and utter disorientation; not the most enjoyable thing I've ever experienced. The first time it bounced me right out.

"Later I read the reports of teleportation tests on trainees with insufficient processing. They'd described a feeling of having no control, of either body or environment." Lotta shrugged. "What I did back there just came to me—reestablish her control, even if only by proxy at first. It seemed appropriate."

Orleskis nodded. *Inside their minds!* he thought. *What a diagnostic tool!* If he got back to Iryala alive, he told himself, he'd see about learning to do some of these things, including the Ostrak Procedures.

Tain slept heavily without sedation. The medics, with Lotta standing by, had cleaned her up, then dressed her in army hospital pajamas. Orleskis had said that when she woke up, she'd be stiff and sore from the convulsions.

It occurred to Lotta that now she'd have a tentmate. And that she'd probably need to run some Ostrak Procedures on Tain, regardless of what the Crown might prefer. Such drastic teleport shock was bound to have severe mental after-effects. As far as that was concerned, the Crown had already gotten the main story it wanted from her, while the departure story had been covered by Iryala Video.

She wouldn't try anything ambitious with her, Lotta told herself; her intelligence duties wouldn't leave time for it. Just handle her through the zone that had been agitated and sensitized.

Fifty-Five

After Tain had fallen asleep, Lotta had taken time to find her way around Headquarters Company. Their outgate site was fifteen miles from the nearest farming district and probably somewhat farther from any area patrolled by Klestronu ground forces. But there seemed a risk of discovery by Klestronu aircraft, so the regiment was bivouacked in the forest. Even the combat personnel carriers had been maneuvered back among the trees.

It seemed important now that she find the Klestronu ground forces commander, meld with him, and learn whether he was aware of anything unusual happening. But camp held a lot of people and a lot of activity, some of it hectic. She'd learned back on Iryala that to make a first contact with someone she only knew *about*, and not much about, she needed freedom from distraction.

So she left camp and hiked far enough into the jungle that none of the activity intruded on her attention. Two troopers went with her as bodyguards; there were tigers, blue trolls, and other dangerous wildlife in these equatorial forests.

It took a few minutes to still her mind, after a day so eventful, but it was no real problem. There were a few seconds during which her body seemed to resonate like a harp chord—an occasional personal symptom of readiness. Then, eyes closed, she reached.

She was surprised at how easy it was. She was with him at once, and the meld was effortless. But not terribly informative. She stayed with Saadhrambacoora for half an hour. He was working intently on administrative matters, and apparently was not much given to ruminating on things other than business while working. But it seemed obvious that he hadn't an inkling of a new enemy force on Terfreya. If he had, it would have been apparent to her, even if his conscious mind had been engaged with other matters. It would have been just below consciousness, with a discernible unit of attention stuck to it unavoidably.

So Lotta had pulled her attention back and returned to Romlar's command tent to let him know that so far their secrecy hadn't been compromised.

That done, it was supper time—field rations—and by the time she'd eaten, it was getting dark. The troopers were retiring to their tents, and stillness was settling over the bivouac. She wore a visored helmet to find her way in the darkness. Romlar offered her a parked scout-craft, a small three-man floater, as a private place to sit while she sought and melded with the enemy commodore in his flagship.

The scout sat not many yards from the command tent, just within the jungle's edge. She chose the pilot's seat. From there she could see between trees into the open, starlit valley bottom. From somewhere came a distant, keening howl; perhaps a Terfreyan wolf, she thought. She felt very relaxed now, and the trance came easily. *Commodore!* she thought softly, and reached outward with her attention. *Commodore!*

There was brief darkness, a familiar sense of otherness, then of beingness that was not her own. The beingness ignored her; that was good—

*   *   *

Terfreya nearly filled the commodore's window, blue and white, blue-green and tan. The half that wasn't night-dark, for the terminator was creeping westward toward the ocean. Tarimenloku sat in his lounging pajamas, gazing out at it. He'd have liked a dharvag, but denied himself; he'd been drinking more than he should lately, and it was time, he'd decided, to assert his self-control.

By ship's time it was late evening. And so it was at the marine base, 55,000 miles out. Or down. The terminator had passed Lonyer City, leaving it in darkness, or twilight at least. Darkness didn't mean relaxation and inactivity for the marines down there, he knew. Stealth was the enemy's ally, and the child warriors, the cadets, were often active at night.

He'd gotten brigade's daily casualty report shortly before retiring: sixty-three—fifty-two dead plus eleven wounded and unfit for service. A bad day. More and more the cadets were using captured beam guns, which usually killed what they hit. Although the killed-to-wounded ratio had been surprisingly high from the beginning, reflecting the enemy's excellent marksmanship.

The day's reported enemy body count was 115, 113 of them cadets, and 2 large black men. Tarimenloku knew from his informants that the black men were the cadets' training cadre, and renowned fighting men. He also knew that they were mercenaries, and not numerous anywhere.

A body count of 115! If the body counts I'm given are correct. he thought wryly, *then we've killed a total of more than 3,000 cadets and cadre. And all from a beginning number estimated at 500 to 1,000! Remarkable!*

He thought about having just one drink, and pushed the thought away, focusing his eyes again on the world outside his window, a world on which Klestronu colonists could prosper and multiply. One of dozens of such worlds in this sector. Again he thought of disengaging—of going home with what he'd learned. But there'd be an evaluation, legal and military, and any claim that he'd been driven away by greater military forces would be uncovered as a lie. He was fighting a small force, a single battalion, mostly of children!

Considering the value of what he'd discovered, it was possible, though not likely, that he wouldn't be executed. But if death were all he'd have to face at home, he told himself, he might well start back tomorrow, or as soon as he could bring his people off that world out there. *Disgrace* was what he feared most, and disgrace there would be, for himself and his family, whether he was impaled or not. If he allowed himself to be driven away by forces less than clearly superior in numbers or armament.

The commodore realized he was sagging in his chair, and stiffened, straightening. Getting old, he thought sourly, old and pessimistic. With the entire brigade on the ground, and far better armed, surely his marines would outlast the cadets, who might in truth be nearing extermination. It seemed likely that, in a week or two, the opposition would melt, the ambushes and raids dwindle to nearly nothing. Then he could go home with honor.

Lotta Alsnor opened her eyes and stared out through the night forest toward the star-lit valley. She felt depression and shook it off; it wasn't hers.

She felt something else, too, and realized it was the T'swa seer who'd been melded with Tarimenloku when she had. Now, for a moment, he was with her, an amused but friendly presence. Inwardly she saluted him, felt a glow at his acknowledgement, and realized that now she could find and touch him at will—meld with him if she wished.

She opened herself to deep perception. At least that was what she intended; neither experience nor education had anything to say about the possibility of deep perception. But it seemed to her it was possible, and she wanted the T'swa seer to know as much and as quickly as he could.

Then the T'swa presence was gone, and it seemed to her that it wouldn't be back, that it was leaving surveillance in her hands. She got up and stretched. She'd report to Artus, then check on Tain. And then go to bed. It had been a long day.

Fifty-Six

Flight Sergeant Faron Gosweller sat in his LUF, LUF 1, wishing his computer had something interesting to read. He was parked at the edge of a half-acre glade, backed between two trees and concealed by the eaves of the forest. The last twilight had faded from what little he could see of the sky, and it was dark indeed.

It had been a long day, and he still hadn't gotten a call.

As far as Gosweller knew, the enemy wasn't aware of him. Even if they'd picked up his 360° call to the cadet force, the night before, that had been from two miles away and above the trees. The only investigation he knew of had been by local wildlife. Twice large herds of tiny deerlike animals had entered the glade to browse, stopping frequently in their feeding to look toward the floater. The herds had numbered twenty and thirty-odd; exact counts had been impossible because the animals moved around too much. There'd also been a band of much larger deer—an even dozen of them. Of these, the larger had three horns each—a central

314

pike flanked by two lesser, out-curved horns. The smaller wore only the central pike, a matter of sexual dimorphism he suspected.

Once a band of small piglike animals had entered the glade, where they seemed to be rooting up tubers or mushrooms. Then something like a big cat, black dappled with tan or gray, had rushed out and killed one of them. After momentary panic, the pigs had rallied, swarming at the predator, and the cat had escaped into a tree. After a little the pigs left, and the cat jumped down to reclaim its kill.

The cat looked big enough to kill a man, it seemed to Gosweller, and he'd decided not to go out unarmed. Or at night.

Too bad I couldn't have downloaded a book on Terfreyan wildlife before I left Iryala, he thought. Instead, everything not essential to his mission had been erased from his computer's memory, on the off-chance that the enemy might capture the craft.

But what they really didn't want the enemy to capture was the teleport, tricked up though it was. Sitting power-up a few yards outside his floater, and connected to it by a power cable, it was Gosweller's escape hatch. If the enemy threatened to find him, he was to run to it and press three switches in order: The first targeted the port on Iryala on a reverse vector; the second activated a destruct mechanism with a one-minute delay; and the third opened the gate for a single passage, after which the targeting program would revert to the default target, which was the teleport platform itself. If anyone tried to follow him before it destructed, they'd enter a loop and arrive at the same place and time as they'd "left." But in teleport shock, unless they'd been defused.

A tiny light began flashing on Gosweller's console, accompanied by a soft beeping. He reached, opening a switch, knowing who it had to be. His computer screen told him it was a scrambled message via a fifteen-

degree beam pulse transmission; the regiment knew, of
course, approximately where he was.

"LUF 1, LUF 1, this is Little A, this is Little A.
Bring your teleport to the accompanying coordinates.
Repeat: Bring your teleport to the accompanying
coordinates."

His computer copied the coordinates and he had it
read them into his navigator. Then he acknowledged
the message. And even as he pressed the *acknowledge*
key, he realized he'd screwed up. He was a civilian
pilot with warrior tendencies, who'd been called up
from the reserve for this project, and he'd brought
some civilian habits with him. He'd sent 360°; he should
have sent a narrow beam aimed at the coordinates. Or
not acknowledged at all.

He swore under his breath. Well, he'd hustle—load
the teleport and get away from there quickly.

The slowly cruising Klestronu gunship was alone and
it wasn't; a narrow carrier beam from brigade's comm
central was locked on it. The badly bored pilot, Flight
Sergeant Sarkath Veglossu, was expecting an order to
return to base; nothing had been heard of the enemy
radio source since the night before.

Instead he received a set of coordinates for a new
enemy radio source less than three miles away, and an
order to attack it at once. His computer gave the coordinates to its navigation program, and the gunship swung
around.

The teleport was on an AG dolly, which made it easy
to raise off the ground. Its mass and inertia were considerable for one man to handle though; otherwise
Gosweller might have had the rig inside the LUF before the gunship got there. As it was, one end was in
the door. He might even have gotten off the ground
with it—perhaps even gotten away. As it was, Veglossu's
high-intensity floodlight caught the Iryalan by surprise,
blinding him for brief seconds. Long enough that he

wasn't able to find any switches, let alone press them, before the gunship fired a concussion pulse that struck the side of the floater less than four feet from him.

Veglossu saw him fall, and put a crewman down to investigate, Sweating, heart thudding, the Klestronu private made his way to LUF 1 and the teleport by a series of short sprints, hitting the dirt after each of them. He had no notion that he'd make it alive. When he did, he found Gosweller dead.

Using his belt radio, the private let Veglossu know. Veglossu then radioed base to send out a floater and pick up the loot, whatever that consisted of.

Fifty-Seven

The tree stood some thirty yards back within the jungle's edge, but rose well above any others around it. Hensi Kaberfar, age thirteen, had climbed the lianas that laced it, and lay on an ascending branch thick enough to obscure him from the road nearly half a mile away.

The 300-acre piece of jungle he was in, he and his platoon, occupied a low bulge of quartsite, its soil shallow and infertile, bordered on two sides with fields and on the third, a road backed by scrub. On the same three sides it was surrounded by Klestronu marines. On the fourth, the north side, flowed the Spice River, eighty yards across, with extensive jungle on its opposite side. Gunships watched its brown current from a distance deemed relatively safe from cadet rockets. If the cadets tried to cross it, the gunships were to move in quickly and chop them up.

Hensi's tree was on the south side however, and from its height he watched the marine company deployed along the road. There'd be other companies on the east and west sides, he knew. Sooner or later the Klestroni would have to make a decision. Send a company into the jungle—maybe two companies—or sit around behind their electronic sentry fields and try to starve their quarry out. Starve them out or root them out. Odds were, Hensi thought, they'd called for armored missile trucks, each carrying a battery of launchers that could pour scores of ground-to-air rockets into an area in a hurry.

All for an understrength platoon—twenty-one cadets.

Just now Hensi's sniper-scoped rifle was cross-slung on his back, and binoculars occupied his hands. He wore no helmet, but a throat mike was clamped to his collar. The artillery would come up the road from the west, if it came, and he was to report when it appeared. The Klestroni were a light brigade, without any real artillery, and their missile trucks were not heavily armored. They tended to use them sparingly, in favorable situations. The idea was for this to seem like a favorable situation.

The plan had been for two platoons to ambush a company of marines on a road, by daylight, pour fire into them for half a minute, then take to "the bush," a district of mostly overgrown, abandoned farmland.

The Klestroni didn't have an endless supply of gunships either, so troops on the road usually rode unescorted in armored assault vehicles. A gunship, or more than one, could be sent in a hurry if called for.

The ambush had been a success. They'd holed some AAVs and killed maybe twenty or thirty Klestroni, then all but three guys had taken off into the young forest. The three who stayed were well separated and carried surface-to-air rocket launchers. A gunship was armored but not invulnerable, and given enough hits—a single hit if you were lucky—you could bring one down.

They'd hit the bugger all right, and although they hadn't brought him down, they'd sent him veering off, clearly hurt and no doubt radioing for reinforcements.

Klestronu scout floaters and two more gunships had arrived minutes later. And gotten glimpses now and then of a cadet or cadets moving through the scrub, glimpses most often deliberately allowed. One platoon had laid low, as planned, then slipped away unnoticed. It made no sense to expose both.

Hensi's platoon had been larger when the ambush was made; they'd numbered thirty-one then. When someone exposes himself to a gunship, there's a good chance he'll get his ass shot off, along with assorted other body parts.

Now Hensi saw dust. It was the missile trucks coming, he had no doubt, but he waited to make certain. When he was, he radioed. When they'd parked, gravitically locked to firing positions along the road, he radioed again. When they began to fire, he didn't need to radio; missiles slammed into the jungle with a ragged roar heard for miles. Hensi could easily have been killed then, but as usual he was lucky. And instead of scrambling back down, he sat tight; he wanted to see what happened next.

The launchers themselves were noisy enough that the Klestroni ignored the two gunships at first, even when they'd begun strafing. And when they became aware of what was happening, it was with disbelief, because gunships were their own—had to be. The cadets had none. So the response, briefly, was shock and indignation instead of returned fire.

The gunships passed over two hundred feet apart, the first giving its attention to the emplaced troops, the other to the missile trucks. They didn't make a second pass. Then lobber fire began to land on the emplaced marines from behind, lots of it, accurately. Someone had established the range in advance.

The missile trucks stilled.

Hensi slid to the first crotch below him, then went hand over hand down the lianas toward the ground. If the Klestroni reacted as expected, their gunships were already responding, leaving the river unguarded. The platoon would be concealed along the riverbank, watching for their chance, ready to drag their boats to the water, boats that locals had stashed for them. He'd have to run all the way or be left behind.

When the Klestronu artillery had begun firing from the south road, the two companies along the east road had been grimly pleased. Their rifle platoons lay ready and alert, watching mainly the jungle in front of them, into which their mortar platoons began to throw their own high explosives.

There were two companies on the east side because there was no longer any open field there, only the road, with forest in front of them and an abandoned field, more or less overgrown with scrub, behind. This was the side the cadets had come from, and these two companies were part of the force that had pursued them, "driven" them. Its marines had been nervous till now. The cadets had long since established their capacity for tricks, surprise, unpredictability.

But not from the air; the cadets had no air support. The regiment's gunships, having shot up the artillery along the south road, rounded the corner and surprised the two companies along the east. The result was more than casualties, though there were lots of those. It was also shock and utter confusion. Thus when 1st and 2nd Platoons, A Company, came out of the scrub to the rear, hoses and rifles blazing, the surviving marines, most of them clinging to the ground, hardly reacted. Grenades arced, roared.

Then Jerym Alsnor, the assault team leader, saw another gunship line up with the road. The regiment's were gone by then. He barked an order into his helmet mike, and barreled back into the scrub, Tain Faronya beside him. She'd recorded the assault. A dozen seconds later, energy beams—butcher beams, the cadets called them—slashed angrily through the regrowth, severing fronds and young stems. Then, for the moment, it was past.

Another hundred yards of running took them into

older regrowth, dense young woods sixty to eighty feet tall. There they pulled up, breathing hard, beside the streamlet that bordered it. There were more sounds of falling fronds and branches, as if the gunship was ranging over the scrub and forest shooting blindly.

Jerym had allowed for the gunship response. His assault line had been thin, its men initially a dozen yards apart. Thus fleeing through the scrub, they'd been mostly unseen and very scattered targets.

Again he spoke into his helmet radio, ordering the two platoons to their rendezvous. Fourteen minutes later he arrived at a cutbank above the Spice River with Tain beside him. There were stragglers—able-bodied troopers helping three wounded. After an hour, twelve of Jerym's eighty-plus troopers had not arrived and could not be raised by radio.

Hopefully 4th Platoon A Company had gotten away unscathed; it had been they who'd shelled the south road with lobbers.

Jerym moved his men out then, hiking through forest, upstream along the river. He'd given, and received, his first casualties—given a lot more than he'd taken. But now the excitement and exhilaration were past, and he lacked both the perceptivity of the T'swa and their deep calm. Thus he felt the deaths as personal losses. After all, the casualties were men he'd lived and trained with for more than a year.

Tain sensed his feeling and said nothing, felt it herself, though not as sharply as she would have expected. Nor was she angry or indignant. Her two sessions with Lotta had done more than help her over the lingering effects of teleport shock, and this was war. Fought at least on this side by warriors, men who warred by choice and did not fear dying.

Fifty-Eight

Igsat Tarimenloku frowned at the structure sitting in his conference room. It had been put there instead of in the Intelligence Section because the conference room door had been large enough to accommodate it. The thing looked a bit like a tubular metal doorframe without a wall, a doorway that went nowhere. A nearly square-topped metal arch, it stood on a base that reminded him just a little of a large platform scale. At one side, against one of the vertical tubes, was something like a cabinet or locker.

Strange looking. No function suggested itself, but presumably it had one. "And DAAS has no suggestion?" the commodore said to his chief science officer.

"None, sir. DAAS says its computer was wiped by the concussion pulse that killed the man with it.

"Hmh!" He scowled as if considering how he might coerce it, then turned to his CIO, his chief intelligence officer. "And the man was an adult white, you say, but in uniform. With a floater."

"Yes sir. And the floater has markings on it—numerals and letters—that could have been a military designation. Although it was unarmed. I'm told they had a different pattern than those observed on civilian equipment."

The commodore searched his mind for anything in the weeks of warfare that seemed to relate to a cadet use of floaters, or of reports of floaters, but nothing came to him. There were things that might be explained by air support services, but it seemed extremely unlikely that there'd been any. They'd surely have been detected.

Still, there was, or had been a floater in presumably enemy hands. Floaters had been few on Terfreya, but there may have been some, or one, not on the tax records, and thus missed during the impoundment sweep. As for a uniform—private clothing could resemble a uniform, or even . . .

A thought struck him then which seemed almost likely. Certainly it fitted experience on Klestron and probably every other empire world: smugglers and sometimes brigands. On a world as loosely managed as this one, there were sure to be some, and the dead pilot might very well have been one. He'd have his captives interrogated about the . . .

The security comm beeped, and the CIO flipped its switch. "Commander Ralankoor here," he said.

"Commander, I have a class one message for the commodore, from the general."

Class one! "Let's have it, Yilkat," the commodore barked.

The message shook him. Hostile gunships had hit a marine battalion surrounding a company of cadets in an outlying block of forest. The battalion hadn't been prepared for gunship attack, hadn't even realized at once what was happening. Then a strong enemy ground force had attacked the battalion and been driven off. Casualties had been heavy. A full casualty list and the enemy body count were not available yet, but the enemy casualties had been white adults.

Not cadets. White adults. Tarimenloku's skin crawled.

Uncanny! "How large was this enemy force?" he demanded.

"Sir, I was not told."

"Well damn it, you should have asked! Find out! Right now!" *Kargh* damn *people who take no Kargh-damned responsibility! You'd expect better than that of a senior lieutenant, especially of the Yilkatanaara family.*

He looked around at the others there: his EO, chief science officer, chief intelligence officer. "Gentlemen, I'm going to the command room." He gestured at the foreign machine. "Bavi," he said to his CIO, "I'm leaving this enigma to you. You will interrogate our captives about it, of course, and about this new enemy force. Let me know at once of anything you learn."

Tarimenloku stomped out into the corridor then. How big was this new force? he asked himself. Where had it come from? Why hadn't they run into it before?

His instruments and sentry craft hadn't reported any ships entering real-space, nor approaching this world from elsewhere in the system. And it was hard to believe anything could have gotten through undetected.

He shook his head, an angry, impatient gesture. Somehow he had no doubt at all that his captives would know nothing about it.

He decided he was no longer seriously concerned about the enemy machine. Not now anyway. But he'd *demand* some live military prisoners from Saadhrambacoora; they might know what it was. If they didn't, SUMBAA would have to work it out when they got home.

When they got home. Tarimenloku brightened a bit. *Maybe this new enemy force is big enough to justify leaving,* he told himself, *justify heading home to Klestron!*

Lotta's daytime "office" was a quiet place on top of a ridge, some hundred and fifty feet from camp, where she could sit alone, except for two bodyguards, and plug into the minds of the enemy commanders. Occasional spots of sunlight dappled the ground around her.

She'd been sitting in trance most of the time since breakfast, with a short break for lunch.

Now her eyes opened. She stood and stretched. It had been a good day and a bad one: Earlier, word had come of the successful assault on the enemy force surrounding the cadets, and of the cadets' successful escape without further casualties. First and Second Platoon's casualties had been moderate, and Fourth's zero. But both of the regimental gunships involved had been lost; the Klestronu gunships were faster, and their weapons more effective.

And now—now she knew why only one LUF had come when called last night. She started jogging along the ridge to Romlar's headquarters tent. She'd tell him what she'd learned, then come back and look in on Saadhrambacoora again.

Fifty-Nine

Once the battalions had moved into contact zones, regimental headquarters had moved too, to a safer location. A series of relay transmitters had been set up on high points, to which headquarters could radio its messages on a tight beam. The selected relay transmitter in turn sent them outward on a more or less narrow beam— from five to sixty degrees—toward the intended recipient unit or units.

Only 1st and 2nd Platoons of A Company were located with headquarters, as an air-mobile strike force. The rest of the regiment had no home; its battalions lived separated and on the move, supplied at night by floaters from one of several supply dumps.

The hills in which Headquarters Company now hid were the remains of an old plateau, not high but dissected by numerous ravines, mostly narrow and steep, all heavily forested. Just now it was located next to one of those ravines.

From a nearby patch of marsh, floaters could sneak up the ravine under cover, and park beside the creek in its bottom, cut off from the sky by overarching trees.

Just now, two scouts sat parked below headquarters on their AGs; most of the others were parked not far away.

It was preferred that the floaters travel by night. When they did travel by day, they moved largely in ravines, flying above the treetops but, where possible, below the hilltops. The headquarters, however, they approached only beneath the forest roof. The camp itself was on the broad and fairly level hilltop.

The CPCs carrying 1st and 2nd Platoons slipped up the ravine bottom, moving a few feet above the creek. The sun was newly down, daylight weakening, when they arrived below camp, parked on their AGs, and disembarked their troopers. The two platoon leaders climbed the hill to the headquarters tent. After a debrief, Jerym went to his own tent, stashing rifle and pack, keeping his sidearms with him, and his helmet, then walked to the larger tent assigned to his sister, and stood by the closed flaps. It was a little apart from any others, for privacy.

"Hello," he said quietly. "Anyone at home?"

"Come in." He recognized Tain's voice, and opening the flaps, ducked in, leaving his helmet on the ground outside. It was darker in than out, but he could see Tain half reclining, leaning on an elbow. He knelt beside her on the tent floor.

"I hoped you'd be here," he said, and realized it was true. "I—want to tell you how well you did today. That wasn't the safest place in the world."

"It wasn't, was it. It— I'm amazed I wasn't terrified. Nervous, yes. My stomach was in knots, and my pulse must have been going a hundred and twenty a minute. But it wasn't fear; at least it didn't feel like it." she paused, put her hand on his arm. "How about you?"

"Huh! I don't know. About my pulse, I mean. I don't think my stomach was all that nervous. My attention was on other things, I guess."

Neither of them said anything for a few seconds, then Jerym reached, put a hand on her shoulder. "Right now my pulse is going pretty darned fast though," he murmured. "If you want me to leave, tell me."

Tain's grip tightened. "I don't want you to leave, Jerym. I want you to stay here. Tomorrow you may be dead, or I may, or both of us may, and I want very much for you to stay."

He nodded, not thinking whether she could see the nod or not. "Lotta may come back," he said.

"Lotta left three minutes before you came. She was going to one of the scout floaters to—do whatever it is she does there. Spy on the Klestronu commanders."

She leaned toward him then and kissed his lips, brushing her hand down his arm to rest on a muscular thigh. When the kiss ended, she laid back. He kissed her again, fumbling at the buttons on her field shirt with a hand that, embarrassingly, trembled. A minute of tugging and twisting left both of them naked. He thought of telling her it was his first time, then decided it was best not to. They embraced, kissing, and it seemed to Jerym he couldn't breathe at all. Hands explored, caressed and fondled, but only briefly. Then she squirmed, got beneath him, helped him. His orgasm began at once, and he was done in seconds.

But Tain was not inexperienced, and he was young, his desire and recuperative powers strong. They made love over most of an hour.

When he'd pulled his outer clothes back on, he kissed her once more, tenderly. "I—think I love you, Tain," he murmured. "I really think so. And I know I'm the luckiest guy on Terfreya."

She nodded, eyes welling. *I hope you're lucky,* she thought. *So lucky, you'll come through this war alive.*

He didn't see the nod nor hear the thought, but he never questioned whether she felt the way he did. He touched her cheek gently, felt the moisture of her tears and was awed by them. He left his fingers there for a moment, then kissed her again and backed out of the tent.

He wasn't ready to go to his own yet though. Instead,

putting on his helmet and lowering the visor for night vision, he found his way down the hillside toward where the scouts were parked. A trooper squatted by one of them.

"Who goes there?" the man asked quietly.

"Lieutenant Alsnor, A Company. I'm Lotta's brother; I want to talk to her. Figured I'd wait here till she came out."

The trooper chuckled. "Pull up some ground and sit. I don't know how long she'll be. I guess you guys had some fun today, eh?"

It took a moment for Jerym to realize that the guard had the firefight in mind. His own attention was stuck on Tain and himself, and what it might mean. "Uh, yeah. It was good. I wish Sergeant Dao could have seen his old platoon. He'd have been all grin."

It had been good. His senses had never been so sharp, he thought, his reflexes so tuned. It occurred to Jerym that the guard might like to hear about it. But it also seemed that, talked about, it might not sound like all that much, so he said nothing more. And the guard didn't ask; they squatted there without talking further.

Jerym wondered if Romlar planned to rotate his head-quarters personnel into fighting platoons so guys like this guard could see some combat. They might see combat anyway, of course. The Klestroni might locate Headquarters Company and come with gunships and a force of marines. But it seemed unlikely. The Klestroni had never been able to pin the cadets down, and Romlar seemed to operate out of a level of subliminal wisdom that hopefully would keep him outguessing his enemy.

Romlar! The one-time dumb fatboy! And that's what he'd have stayed, except for the regiment. Except for Varlik Lormagen and Colonel Voker, and the T'swa and the Project.

And himself? He'd probably have become a jailbird.

He dozed off then, squatting near the scout, and woke up to Lotta's voice. "Jerym?" She wore a helmet too, to help her walk in the jungle darkness.

He grunted awake and got up. "Can we talk?" he asked.

She turned and gestured. "Will the scout do?"

"That'll be fine."

They got in, Lotta sliding the door closed behind them, and sat in the pilot's and copilot's seats. "What did you want to talk about?"

"I'm in love with Tain."

He paused. "I suppose that sounds strange. I mean, Tain and I don't know each other all that well, haven't talked to each other very much. But . . . We're attracted to each other. Pretty strongly. And I'm afraid I'll get polarized, lose my neutrality about living or dying. I've sure as Tunis lost my neutrality about Tain living or dying.

"And it could affect my performance as a trooper. Which is not okay, especially for a platoon leader."

"Ah. All right. In this life and others, how many times have you been in love before?"

The question took him by surprise, and for a moment he didn't answer. Then he grinned, the grin widening. "Huh! All right. Many times. Many many times."

"Care to say a number?"

He chuckled. "Not necessary."

"Okay. How many times have you been separated from a lover by death? Your death, your lover's death, someone else's death."

Chill bumps flowed; Jerym laughed. "Okay. Your point is made."

"Good. Now tonight you'll dream about dying, and about Tain dying, and it'll be all right. You'll also dream about both of you living a long time together."

"Can you do that? Make me dream that?"

"No. You'll do it. Although I might help a little."

They got out and hiked up the hill together with the bodyguard following. At the top they separated, Jerym going to his tent, Lotta to hers.

When she crawled inside, she could smell what had happened there. It made her a little horny herself. For

Romlar. It wasn't the first time she'd felt that way. But she'd given him no sign, and wouldn't. He was doing very well. To complicate his situation would be unwise.

Tain was asleep, her breathing slow and shallow. Lotta decided to help her dream too.

Sixty

Looking like some neoclassical sculpture come to life, Artus Romlar stood nude in the creek, washing off sweat. The sun was newly up, the air cool, but he'd just finished thirty minutes of stretching and gymnastics, and fifteen more of close combat drill forms.

Romlar's belt radio chirped at him, and he went to where it lay atop his neatly folded clothes beside the creek. "This is Romlar."

"Artus, this is Jorrie. We just got the pulse from today's supply drop. Bressenhem's on his way to his scout to go check it out."

"Good. Thanks."

The daily supply shipment from Iryala usually outgated at about sunup, on a hover truck. The general area used had numerous glades and small meadows to outgate into. When he was down, the driver moved his truck under cover, then took directional reads on regular Klestronu and Lonyer City radio sources to triangulate his location, and set his radio for a two-degree transmission beam in the direction of a relay. The relay location had been specified in the previous evening's regimental

333

report, teleported to Iryala via LUF 2's gate. The regiment's comm center, part of the regimental computer, would receive the truck driver's message pulse and extrude the outgate's coordinates on several navigation tabs. One for the navcomp in a scout and the others for combat personnel (cum cargo) carriers.

A scout would go check out the location and any possible dangers. Assuming all was clear, the carriers would follow, to pick up cargo and driver. The truck would be abandoned and its driver ported back to Iryala.

Romlar brushed water from his body, dressed, and hiked up the hill to his command tent. His executive officer, Jorrie Renhaus, and their sergeant major were eating breakfast out of ration cartons, using a crate as a table. "The female reporter left some cubes off to port back," said Renhaus. "Showing the assault yesterday. We played the video cube on the computer. Very good stuff. I'm glad you decided she could stay; it'll be good publicity."

Romlar opened a ration carton. "If she wants to stay, why not. She went through hell getting here. And we couldn't port her back without Lotta spending a lot of time working on her first."

Renhaus grinned. "Which reminds me: I've got an idea about the teleport the Klestroni captured. Leak word to them what it really is, and how to use it. Teleport someone into their base camp, so they'll take it seriously. And give them the coordinates for Iryala, for Landfall. Then they'll teleport a regiment there, figuring to capture the government, and the marines will land helpless and dying from teleport shock."

Romlar looked up from the fruit juice he was mixing, and cocked an eyebrow. "Jorrie, are you serious?"

Renhaus laughed. "No. But it's a funny thing to imagine. Actually, let the Klestroni know what the teleport is, and they'll take it and run for home. If they have any sense at all, which they must have."

Romlar nodded absently. Renhaus's weird humor had reminded him of a problem they'd talked about earlier;

the risk of a cadet or trooper being taken alive and giving up the information that the regiment had been teleported. Then the Klestroni'd probably suspect what the thing was that they'd captured.

Apparently it also reminded Renhaus of the problem. "What if the troopers were told to say they'd arrived by ship?" he said. "Say a ship with some sort of invisibility device; call it a cloak. Landed in the prairie tundra and they'd flown north in combat personnel carriers? Or if it was a cadet, he could say the troopers had come by personnel carrier, he didn't know where from. And they could say that the teleport is a device sent for the execution of any high-ranking Klestronu prisoners we might take. They're considered 'criminals responsible for the invasion of a Confederation resource world.'

"Presumably the port's on the default setting, right? So if they try it on someone, it'll execute him sure enough, very unpleasantly. Unless they try it on the prisoner, in which case it won't appear to have done anything."

Romlar looked thoughtfully at his EO. "Jorrie, write up that idea in the form of an order to be read to the regiment. And one for the cadets. I don't know whether one of them could get away with lying under instrumented interrogation—they probably couldn't—but if someone gets caught, he can try."

Sixty-One

Tain had been in on D Company's raid from the beginning—had been in the headquarters tent when the idea came up.

First and Second Platoons had been out on several raids since the one she'd been on, but Romlar hadn't let her go along. Too dangerous, he'd told her.

Jerym had been on each of them. It hadn't been easy, waiting, and when he'd returned safely, they'd had each other in the tent, or off in the forest away from camp.

Then this situation had come up. Romlar had heard about it via a cadet radio message; the cadets had learned it from a local, a kressera broker. A marine battalion was bivouacked in a large open area. Their headquarters seemed to be in an armored floater marked by abundant electronic bric-a-brac.

It was obviously intended as a very temporary bivouac: The marines had dug in, but just foxholes, nothing elaborate, and they hadn't fenced the area. There were two antiaircraft trucks on each side, in case of gunship attack, and they were sure to have electronic detection measures—sentry fields. It was the sort of display the Klestroni made from time to time, showing themselves in settled districts, conspicuously and in force. Presumably the idea was to keep the locals properly impressed and intimidated.

It was the sort of setup you couldn't approach undetected. But port in two men in black with satchel charges, next to the AA trucks on one side, and poke a pole charge through next to the armored headquarters floater, then blow all three, and the place would go frantic. Blow the HQ first, as a signal, and immediately afterward the trucks. The electronic detection measures would be centered on the headquarters floater of course, so that knocking out the HQ should knock out the sentry field. Then send in a company to raise hell in the confusion—hit, shoot the place up, then get out before the Klestroni could get gunships there. After which a lobber platoon could drop high explosives on the place.

It wouldn't be much better than a suicide mission for the guys with the satchel charges, but they'd make it possible to blow the AA trucks, which would save lives.

Second Battalion was nearest the Klestronu bivouac— only six miles from it.

Of necessity, the planning was thin; the opportunity would be brief. Romlar talked it over with Renhaus and his sergeant major, then by radio with Brossling, commanding 2nd Battalion. Brossling talked it over with the CO of D Company. They were all for it. Romlar began to give orders . . . .

Tain had talked Romlar into letting her go along, not as part of the assault, but to observe and video-record from a little distance. Now, watching from the scout in the moonless night, she had nervous stomach. Nervous colon, actually. A small ravine issued onto the open area, and the scout, the command post for the raid, was parked a little back from its mouth, nestled in the treetops. Given half a chance, a scout could outrun

Klestronu gunships; they'd learned that the exciting way.

She stood peering out the open top hatch, camera recording everything she saw. With the cam's state of the art night viewer, it was surprising how much she could see. Just now she was looking at the Klestronu camp nearly half a mile away. D Company, sheltered within the edge of the woods, was keeping back, out of her sight. No one knew how far out the Klestronu sentry field was set to operate. The troopers would move fast when the fireworks blew. Swiftly and quietly.

Then the first explosion roared, powerful enough, it seemed to Tain, to have turned the Klestronu headquarters into shrapnel. The two AA trucks blew almost simultaneously a few seconds later. This was the cue. The scout moved out of the ravine and over open ground at perhaps thirty feet, staying low to keep the hills as a background, instead of open sky. And now she could see D Company jogging along in a line on both sides of her, falling a bit behind.

Some kind of alarm horn was howling in the Klestronu camp.

Halfway to the camp, the scout stopped abruptly as a dozen, a score, a hundred sharp lines of visible light began lancing outward toward D Company. The sentry field was still operational, had to be! The scout began to lift, veering away, and a bigger beam, thick as Tain's wrist, sliced into its nose. The scout staggered, throwing her off her feet, off the small platform she was standing on. She screamed, smelled hot metal and burned flesh, felt the scout slipping downward, sideways, felt its heavy impact with the ground, and briefly knew nothing more.

She regained her senses gradually, vaguely aware of explosions that seemed to go on for a while, then of no more explosions. Her next awareness was of someone trying to open the scout's door, which wouldn't function. Someone from D Company, she thought blurrily, someone come to get her out. "I'm all right," she called—croaked—and got unsteadily to her feet. Her helmet was gone—she'd disliked wearing the chinstrap when she didn't have to. She staggered, although the scout was almost level, stepped back onto the platform, pulled herself up through the hatch and slid down to the ground. There were men around her.

"Tah rinkluta koh! Drassnama veer!"

The words froze her. Someone grabbed her from behind. Another stepped close, peering into her face from beneath brows bushier than any trooper's. His hands gripped her shirt and ripped.

"Hah! Rinkluta koh, dhestika!"

They began to laugh then, loud, ugly, a sound more frightening than anything she'd ever heard. She began to kick wildly, then a fist hit her hard in the stomach, driving the wind out of her. The man who held her threw her down. Other hands were on her, pulling at her belt, her waistband, her legs.

Suddenly there was a roar of command, an angry roar, a scream, and the hands were gone. She stared up from where she lay, at a man holding a sword, pointing with it, barking orders, another beside him with a ready gun. The other men were backing away, then reluctantly, growling, began jogging off into the darkness. One man lay across her feet, her lower legs, not moving, and she knew he was dead.

Watching them depart, the man with the sword blew a gust of relief, almost a snort, then looked down at her. She realized her shirt was off, except that one hand and wrist were still in a sleeve, and her brassiere was gone. Her field pants were down to her knees, along with her torn underpants. Her skin crawled beneath his gaze.

He stared long, gave an order. The man with him holstered his gun, bent, and dragged the corpse off her feet. She could see now that the dead man's head had been cleft like a melon.

The man with the sword reached down. She found herself reaching up, and he pulled her to her feet. She crouched, pulled up her field pants, rethreaded the

half-jerked-out belt through the loops and fastened it,
then pulled her shirt back on.

When she was done, the officer spoke sharply to her,
pointing with the sword again. The other man grabbed
her roughly by an arm, shoved, and they began to
follow the men who'd run off, toward the Klestronu
camp.

She was still somewhat in shock when they got there.
They walked her between foxholes, shell holes, and
shelter tents to a large tent, a line of weak light showing
faintly beneath overlapped flaps. Inside were men's
voices. The officer called quietly. The light was killed;
the flaps drew back and he entered. She heard him
talking. There was a pause, then a preemptory order in
another voice. The other man shoved her in ahead of
him. The light came on again, not brightly, a battle
lamp.

There were several men there, mostly officers she
thought, some seated at a folding table, others standing. They stared as she was pushed toward them. One,
a heavyset man, was clearly in charge, and he spoke to
her. She shook her head, not knowing how else to
respond. He gave an order and one of the men left. The
rest began to talk, their glances lascivious but not threatening. They were more relaxed now, even laughed. In
about a minute, the man who'd left was back with handcuffs, and her wrists were manacled in front of her.

The man who'd brought the manacles turned her
around, then walked out into the night ahead of
her while another pushed her after him. They walked her
among some tents and past a crater—where the headquarters had been, she supposed—to a small hover van
with barred windows, where the first man opened the
door, stepped in, and flashed a handlamp around inside. The other pushed her in after him.

Four thin narrow mattresses had been leaned against
a wall on their sides; a pail and jug sat in a corner. The
man with the light flipped one of the mattresses down
onto the floor with his foot, looked at her, and opened

her shirt to stare at her breasts from beneath hairy brows. The other, behind her, unfastened her belt and shoved a rough hand inside her field trousers. Then the first man snapped an order and the hand was removed. Pointing, he ordered her down on the mattress, and she obeyed, cringing.

But they did not molest her further, simply fitted a set of irons on her ankles, over her boots. That done, they left, closing the steel door behind them. She lay there and shook violently. It was several minutes before the shaking stopped.

Then she stretched out on her back, staring at the dim ceiling, wondering what was going to happen to her. And what had happened to D Company. She remembered the explosions she'd heard while semi-conscious; 4th Platoon, the weapons platoon, must have been laying in covering fire from the edge of the forest, she decided. Maybe they'd gotten away, some of them, most of them.

She heard a key, heard the latch turn, and faint star light came in through the door. A man stepped in, gave an order, and the door closed behind him. A lamp flashed on in his hand, settled on her exposed breasts, and she saw the heavyset commander looking down at her. She lay stiff as a board.

He spoke to her in his own language, not harshly, a question. She shook her head. "No. Leave me alone." The words came out quiet but intense. He looked a long minute longer, then left, switching the handlamp off before he opened the door.

With some difficulty she snapped her blouse shut. After a time she slept.

Sixty-Two

Tain awoke to faint dawnlight through the window. It seemed to her she'd dreamed continuously, dreams in part violent but not nightmarish. She couldn't remember their content. Crablike, she worked her way across the floor to the pail, after some difficulty relieved herself, then refastened her field pants and crept back to her mattress to sink immediately again into dream-filled sleep. When next she awoke, it was daylight, and someone was unlocking her door. As it opened, she raised her head to look.

A hard-faced man peered in at her, like the others bushy browed, his close-shaved jaw and cheeks blue against brown. He snapped an order over his shoulder in a voice as sharp as a laser knife, as hard as steel. Another man she hadn't seen before scuttled in to remove her ankle irons; her day jailor, apparently. When he'd put the irons in a pocket, he reached down, grabbed her wrist, and jerked her roughly to her feet, only to be lashed by the tongue behind him. Hand flinching away from her, he yelped his reply, then motioned her to the door.

She went, confused but not just now feeling threatened, feeling much better in fact than she would have imagined when she'd been brought there. The dreams had helped, she thought. She couldn't remember what they were, but she was sure they'd helped. She stepped outside into early-morning chill, though the sun was up. The hard-faced officer's uniform was tailored, its creases as sharp as his voice. He had an aide with him, his uniform less elegant but also sharply pressed. Low on both dark foreheads was a small laser tattoo, a tiny star artistic and precise, distinct by daylight even on their dark skins.

The officer spoke to her in Standard that was accented but easily understood, his voice brusque but not harsh. "I am here to take you to General Saadhrambacoora. You will there have an opportunity to bathe and eat." He examined her not quite insolently, his eyes taking in her long legs. "You will also inform the general if you were forced to copulate with anyone here."

She nodded, then shivered, this time from cold, and he turned to the man who'd freed her feet, his voice once more a whiplash. Again the man yelped a reply, and left at a run.

The officer led off toward a small floater parked in a nearby opening, surrounded by shelter tents that, from their size and appearance, seemed to be for officers. The aide steered her by an arm, firmly but not roughly. Before they reached the aircraft, the jailor had caught them with a jacket, which the aide draped over Tain's shoulders.

She found herself saying "thank you," and wondered why. The aide helped her into the staff floater, seated her, and moments later the craft took off.

When the radio message ended, Saadhrambacoora sat back in his chair with a grunt of relief. The prisoner was alive and seemingly sound, even though a woman. Or perhaps because she was a woman. He turned to a lieutenant who stood white-faced by the door.

"You realize, I trust, that if anything had happened to her, if she'd been killed or rescued, I'd have broken you to private, had you flogged, and assigned you to a penal platoon."

The general's words had been delivered quietly, coldly. The young officer felt faint. Penal platoons were used in the most dangerous situations, their men to be shot on the spot for any failure, or even slowness, to obey orders.

"As it is," Saadhrambacoora went on, "I am transferring you to the 1st Rifle Battalion for assignment as a platoon leader. Perhaps you will learn something about good sense there. If you don't, one of those little boys may cut your throat. Tell Sergeant Major Davingtor to prepare the transfer form. I will read and sign it."

He watched the man leave the room. *Idiot,* he thought after him, and turned to his computer with its accumulation of messages and reports. *After all the emphasis I put on obtaining a prisoner—with all the emphasis the* commodore *has put on it—to leave her overnight in the field where she'd be subject to murder, even conceivably to rescue . . . And all on the idiotic grounds that my* sleep *should not be disturbed!*

He shook his head. Families who raised sons to such uselessness, then used their influence to get them staff positions, were no longer noble, and should be stripped of title and land. But in this day and age . . .

He focused his attention on the screen, on the work awaiting him. It would be a few minutes before she arrived; then allow an hour for her to bathe and eat. A prisoner of such rarity and value, of such interest to the commodore, must be delivered in good physical and mental condition—as good as possible. But he had no doubt at all that Major Thoglakaveera was handling things properly.

He'd keep his own questioning brief, and find out what if any punishments to battalion personnel were called for. And what *rewards* were appropriate; she was, after all, alive and ambulatory.

*   *   *

Lotta sat in the jungle with her legs folded in a full lotus; she'd been like that for hours.

She'd awakened from sleep abruptly, the night before, aware that something had happened to Tain, and had found and melded with her without leaving the tent. Then, when Tain had gone to sleep, Lotta had withdrawn and gone back to sleep too. She had to be asleep herself to help someone dream; so far as she knew, there was no other way of doing it. The next time she woke up, she remembered little about the dreams, any more than if they'd been hers. She only knew she'd been there, guiding.

Briefly she'd melded with Tain again, then with Saadhrambacoora. Now she was with Tain once more, accompanying her outward 55,000 miles.

As reflected by his three-syllable surname, Bavi Ralankoor's family were gentry, not aristocrats. An exceptional record in secondary school had gotten him into a professional college. Where, given the conservatism of some professors and academic administrators, he'd had to be very good to pass, much better than if he'd been noble. And his opportunities for advancement in the fleet had ended at lieutenant commander. He was proud of what he'd accomplished though, and seldom troubled by the limits which birth had laid on him.

Still it made him a bit nervous to have the commodore watch while he worked, particularly with this prisoner, from whom much was hoped for. Strapped to the interrogation seat, she'd said nothing at all out loud, though she'd given him some interesting monitor reads. He could always, of course, apply a drug. And while neither responses nor readings were reliable under the drugs, they could provide valuable leads for further questioning, and in the long run rather exact information. To get explicit answers, pain or the threat of pain, with punishment for lying and rewards for the truth, were often quicker. Or so the manual said. But an occasional subject became tenaciously recalcitrant under such treatment. While a few were said to show an impressive ability to lose consciousness under pain or even the threat of it, a sort of escape mechanism.

He'd probably end up using a drug on her, he decided, but there were a few more questions he wanted to ask first.

He turned to the commodore. "Sir, I'd like to take her to the conference room and question her about the apparatus there."

The commodore nodded without speaking, his broad face expressionless, and they all left together, a mixed procession. Ralankoor led, his two assistants wheeling the interrogation chair with the prisoner still strapped into it, the two marine guards walking alongside. The commodore, his aide and orderly brought up the rear. An elevator took them two levels up.

When Tain saw the teleport, the monitor betrayed her reaction. Ralankoor turned to Tarimenloku. "She's afraid of it," he said, then looking at her again, keyed on the translator and pointed. "Are you afraid of that?" he asked; the terminal spoke the question in Standard, in a decent facsimile of Ralankoor's own voice.

Again she said nothing, but the monitor screen did.

"Do you know what it is?" he asked.

She shook her head, her first voluntary response.

"My instruments tell me you do," he said, and the reading of fear became stronger.

Fear. Of what, specifically? Deviating from standard interrogation procedure, Ralankoor took a shortcut, a shot in the dark. If it didn't work, no harm would be done; if it did, it could save considerable time. "If you do not tell me everything we want to know," he said drily, "I will have you wheeled onto it, and turn it on."

Again the monitor responded strongly. Tain turned to the man and for the first time answered him, her words issuing from the terminal in Klestronik. "You're playing with me," she said. "You know if you put me on it, you'll learn everything anyway."

He looked thoughtfully at her, then at the teleport. "Of course we will. But it is painful. I give you an opportunity to tell us without it."

His attention was on her face now, instead of on his instruments. Her expression showed distrust. "Painful?" she said. "Why do you play with me like that? What can you gain from it? The truth machine is not painful."

"Commander," Tarimenloku interrupted, and turning to look at him, Ralankoor put the translator on hold. "Can you operate it?" the commodore asked.

"I have read the labels—those that are complete words: *Power. Activate.* That's all."

"Put her on it!"

"Yes sir." Ralankoor felt vaguely ill at ease, and thought of trying it on a crewman first. But the commodore did not tolerate having his orders questioned. He eyed the mysterious "truth machine"; the cumbersome interrogation chair was clearly too wide for the platform, so after activating the translator again, he took a small, palm-sized instrument from his belt and held it in front of her.

"Do you know what this is?" he asked.

She shook her head.

"It is a neural whip." He thumbed the setting, pointed it at her, and squeezed the trigger. She yelled, recoiling at the pain. "And now," he said, "you know what a neural whip is. At its lowest setting. It can be much worse. My assistants are going to release you and place you on the truth machine. If you do not cooperate, I will show you what a high setting is like, and then we will tie you and you will go on the truth machine anyway."

He released her restraints himself, then his men helped her to her feet and walked her to the apparatus, gripping her arms. She stepped onto the platform, holding back a bit, her face ashen. At the control panel,

Ralankoor pressed *power*. A small red light came on. He wasn't sure what it meant; sometimes apparatus required time to reach full operational status, and often this was indicated by a light coming on, or changing color. After some seconds the red light went off and a green light came on. He looked at the prisoner; she was staring at it, trembling visibly. He pressed the *activate* switch, and the red light began to flash. She started to moan, to shake more strongly. Admirable! Clearly she had a very strong ethic not to tell what she knew.

"She is holding back, sir," said one of his assistants. "She doesn't want to go."

"Force her!"

They pushed, and suddenly, taking them by surprise, she lunged forward into the gate.

And went berserk, bounding from the platform with a wild coarse howl, crashed blindly into the commodore's aide, sending the man sprawling, then charged into the conference table, rebounded, still howling, staggered, lunged, and fell over a chair onto the deck, where she lay thrashing and kicking. Ralankoor, recovering partly from his shock, ordered the security detail to hold her there, then strode to the comm to call the chief medical officer.

Holding her wasn't easy; his assistants had to help the two marines. Tense, avoiding the commodore's eyes, Ralankoor could only wait helplessly for the doctor to get there. The howling had changed to shrieks, which were worse. The prisoner's body arched and writhed, her limbs jerking in the grasp of the men who held her; they had all they could do to control them. The reek of her made Ralankoor ill.

It occurred to him to shut the apparatus off, but when he turned to the control panel, its lights were dark. He pressed the switch anyway, his hand shaking a bit. In the three minutes it took the chief medical officer to arrive, the prisoner's violence hardly slackened. The CMO administered a sedative, and when the prisoner had gone slack, looked at Ralankoor as if to ask what in Kargh's name he'd done to her.

Then the commodore stalked out without a word, followed by his shaken aide. Ralankoor wondered what this would mean to his career.

An hour later, in the clinic, the CMO stood observing the prisoner's vital signs on his monitor panel. She would probably survive, he decided; he'd been uncertain for a while. He wasn't at all sure what she'd be like when she regained consciousness though.

It was evening. The sides of Romlar's command tent were rolled down, and a field lamp was on low, lighting it dimly.

For Lotta it had been a long day, a long night and day, and she'd given her report slumped in a canvas folding chair. "Apparently something went wrong with the teleport after they used it," she said. "Even its power tap seems to be dead."

Romlar nodded. "You mentioned the flashing red light. That's a warning—of what I can't even guess. Maybe not to use it without a program cube; something like that."

She nodded. "I disconnected from her when she decided to do it; being melded when she looped through was not something I wanted to experience. Then I melded with the intelligence officer. Didn't think about it, just did it. I'd never realized I could switch like that without coming back to my body between times."

She stood up and rotated her shoulders. "After they sedated her, I melded with the commodore for a while. He's scared to death of the teleport now, though he'd never admit it, even to himself. He's glad it's out of order—had it hauled to a storage compartment where they keep a lot of broken down components of this and that. Told his chief engineer not to touch it, that SUMBAA would take care of it. SUMBAA's a computer on Klestron; apparently some kind of master computer."

Her eyes focused on Romlar again. "Next I melded with the doctor. He thinks she's going to come through it. Then I melded with her, and I think he's right. Probably it's partly having recovered from it once before, and partly the work I did with her afterward, the sessions we had."

Lotta got up. "I'm going to go check on her again. Then I'm going to catch some sleep."

Romlar got up too. "Sounds good. Give me another report in the morning."

In the clinic on board HRS *Blessed Flenyaagor*, Tain Faronya awoke from nearly eighteen hours of unconsciousness. Awoke stiff, sore, and hungry, but surprisingly cheerful, as if something good had happened. She didn't remember that she was Tain Faronya, or where she was or how she'd gotten there. Wasn't even aware that anything was missing. It was almost as if she were a clean slate. Even quite a bit of her vocabulary was gone, although she hadn't missed it.

Lotta stayed in her mind for a time. Then, with a sense of loss, she withdrew and went to bed.

Sixty-Three

Lotta no longer had bodyguards. No predators at all had been seen in the vicinity, or their tracks or scat. They seemed to be staying well away. Thus she was alone by the creek, washing her clothes—soaping them, then beating them with a stout stick, the sound of it dull and soggy.

"Sis."

She looked up. "Yes?"

"I'd like your help."

"Can it wait till I've rinsed these and wrung them out? Rinsed them anyway. I'm about done."

"Better yet," Jerym said, squatting beside her, "I'll help."

He began rinsing and wringing while she finished washing, his powerful hands and wrists squeezing things drier than she could have. When they were done, they stood, she coming about to her brother's chin. Together they climbed the hill and draped the wet things on saplings near her tent.

"I guess you miss your tent-mate," Jerym said.

"Yes, I miss her. But not as much as you do."

351

"That's what I've come to you about. I've got this feeling of vengefulness, and I'm afraid it'll warp my judgement—endanger my missions and men. We've lost thirty-four in 1st and 2nd Platoons, with me cool-headed. It's been a couple days since we've been out now, and Romlar's bound to give us another mission tonight or tomorrow."

"Okay," Lotta said. "Let's find us a log and sit." Not far from the last tent, her tent, lay a log, mossy and mouldering, too far gone for the local equivalent of ants. "Sit," she said pointing to it, and he sat. Then she sat on the ground in front of him, in the lotus posture, back straight, head up.

"Okay. This isn't going to be an Ostrak Procedure. It's just you and me, talking like brother and sister." Her eyes had settled on his face. "So. You want to revenge yourself."

"No. I want to avenge Tain."

"Okay. For what?"

"For— Their taking her away."

"Ah. How do you suppose she's taking it? Being away."

He frowned thoughtfully. "Well, you say she doesn't remember anything. So I suppose she could be taking it all right."

"Actually, more than all right. She's happy. She remembers how to talk and take care of herself, and she's learning about the world around her, the only world she knows. The Klestroni aren't mistreating her at all; they plan to take her home with them—see if their medics there can get her memory back for her—and find out what she knows, of course. They've even assigned a female crew member as an attendant. So I'd say vengeance isn't needed; not by her."

Jerym frowned. "It's as if she's dead, not remembering like that, not knowing."

"True. It's a little as if she'd committed suicide to save the secret of the teleport. But instead of being reborn as an infant, she's been reborn as an adult." She shifted focus a bit. "Do you feel as if you need to avenge Bressnik? Or any of the other guys you've lost?"

He shook his head. "They were warriors."

"And?"

"Warriors expect to die. It's as if you're already dead but the timing hasn't been settled yet."

"That's true of everyone, Jerym. Everyone dies, over and over. Warriors just tend to die younger. Do you worry about dying, when you go out?"

"No. But I've had the Ostrak Procedures. I know it's not the end. Just a change."

"Okay. Tain didn't worry about dying, either—not then. Even if she hadn't remembered dying before, and living again. I was with her, remember, experiencing her thoughts with her. She was intent on what she was doing, and she carried it off. Took a lot of guts; a *lot*. In a way she was a warrior just then."

Lotta studied Jerym. His focus was elsewhere. "What are you thinking about?" she asked.

He half grinned. "Don't you know?"

"I could. But I'm asking, instead."

"What you just said reminded me of—things. Tain and I loved each other. And when I'd come back off a mission, we'd—we'd get together. You know. Make love."

She nodded.

"So I had something special to look forward to, and you'd think I'd have had attention on getting back alive. Not just to see Tain, but to make love with her. But— When I was out there, all I had on my mind was the mission. I'd start to think about Tain again when we were flying home from the rendezvous."

Lotta laughed. "Okay! That's a warrior! A warrior will sometimes give up his warriorhood if things happen just right. Or just wrong. But you didn't.

"It probably helped that you were T'swa-trained and had the Ostrak Procedures. They'd both give you a sense of perspective on Confederation-type cultural beliefs, beliefs that are fine for people at Job and Compete, and to some extent even Fun. But not so good yet for Wisdom/Knowledge, unless you get picked up by one of the Institutes. And it's not good at all for Warriors."

Jerym nodded thoughtfully.

"With these things looked at, d'you suppose, on your next mission, you'll have attention on vengeance?"

"Umm, probably not. I'm not sure, but probably not."

"Good. Medreth would have showed you a diagram before one of your sessions with her, probably not long before she went back to Lake Loreen. Remember? It was called the parts of man."

"Yeah. I sort of remember."

"Tell me about them."

"Well, a person—not the body, but the part that survives—has parts that do different things, like body parts do different things. And most of them come as a set, like bodies have a set of arms, a set of legs . . . Pairs. One pair deals with the role, like the warrior role or dancer role, or what *you* do, for example. I suppose they have to do with keeping you defined. And another pair has to do with the script, you could say." Jerym frowned slightly. "I kind of pictured it starting out with a script, and then revising it to current situations, trying to keep its integrity at the same time, keeping it in line with the role as far as possible. And that's as far as I can go, talking about it. That's as far as I understood it."

Lotta smiled. "Those are the basics. So Tain has all those too, right? Had them and still has them."

Jerym nodded, sensing now where Lotta was taking this.

She eyed him knowingly. "Anything you want to say about that?"

He grinned at his sister. "You know I do. Tain came out here to Terfreya in spite of the fact that stowing away wasn't the kind of thing you'd imagine her doing. And she talked Romlar into letting her go with D Company, when he started out saying no." He paused, his expression changing. "Although I'm not ready to say she scripted being captured by the Klestroni."

"Okay. Anything else?"

"Well— I suspect her script people have done a lot of rewriting the last couple of days."

Lotta's laugh was a light arpeggio. "Big brother," she said getting up, "I hereby declare this discussion at an end. Unless there's something more you've just got to say to me."

He stood too. "Just one thing. I'm sure as Tunis glad you're my sister."

She laughed again. "I am too, Jerym, I am too."

Sixty-Four

Lotta was at the command tent and the sun newly risen when Romlar walked in, his hair still wet. He grinned at her. "How's my favorite intelligence specialist?"

She stuck her tongue out at him. "Big praise! I'm your only intelligence specialist. The rest of your information comes from scout flights and cadets, and the locals the cadets keep in touch with."

He laughed. "Don't knock praise. Especially from the regimental CO. What've you got for me today?"

"The general's worried about his diminished supply of gunships. Your guys wrecked another of them yesterday, beyond repair, which leaves him with only eight. And the nearest replacements are more parsecs away than he cares to think about."

"Mmm."

"That's right. You might want to think about reducing them further. With your replacements, that could give you a huge advantage."

Romlar nodded thoughtfully. "I wouldn't bring in more gunships; I don't want air superiority that way. I want to drive them off with inferior numbers and inferior weapons; that'll stamp us with the mystique we want them to remember the Confederation by. But it would save us a lot of trouble and lives if we could wreck *their* gunships; gunships have given us probably eighty percent of our casualties. They're hard to kill though. They're better armored than ours, and even when we shoot one of them down, they usually haul them away afterward. To repair, or cannibalize for parts."

He paused, lips pursed. "Tell you what. You've made me relook at the situation. It's going to cost some guys, but I think I see a way to thin them out. I mean *really* thin them out!"

When Lotta left the tent, she hadn't fully recovered from Romlar's reaction to her report. She'd long known, intellectually, what warriors were all about, and hadn't questioned it. She understood the function of war and warriors in the real world of acquisitive rulers and merchant princes, of grudges and greed, threats and responses, rivalries and hatreds. And for the better part of a standard year now, she'd lived and worked among warriors, been around their activities, seen their mental images, even been inside their minds.

But when he'd said, "It's going to cost some guys, but I think I see a way . . . ."—and with enthusiasm!—it had struck her as something totally foreign. Those "guys," after all, were his friends, even if they were warriors.

As she walked to the supply tent for her day's rations, she contemplated the matter. Then it struck her—the side of the matter she'd overlooked, obvious though it was: Every gunship destroyed now meant lives not lost later.

She regarded herself with wry amusement, this sixteen-year-old woman, seer, spy, and mental therapist. *My wits*, she thought, *where were you hiding? In war, a commander, when he has a choice, invests his resources. Some perhaps in actions that promise modest payoffs at low risks, and maybe others in higher risks for bigger payoffs.*

Maybe, she thought, *I need to find my big brother and have him repeat what he told me. And this time listen for my own self.*

It was the zone between afternoon and evening, still full daylight but with the sun lowering in the west. Standing back within the edge of a dense second-growth forest, Jerym looked out between trees and across nearly half a mile of open pasture and field to where the Spice River flowed. The weather had been dry, the river relatively low, the banks consequently high.

On the other side of the river was forest.

Four miles west, a Klestronu battalion was setting up bivouac in open ground between the river and a road, a bivouac designed to look assaultable. In fact, the Klestronu general intended it as bait in an enticing deathtrap.

It had taken several days of waiting to get a set of factors this favorable.

The Klestroni, Lotta had said, would have a scout overflying the area constantly, watching hopefully unnoticed from two miles up for indications of cadets or troopers. If it spotted any, the bivouacked battalion would be warned. If it spotted a large enough concentration of them sufficiently vulnerable, a flight of four gunships was standing by, six miles west, ready to fly immediately. They could be over the field in front of him within three or four minutes.

Jerym peered out again at the sun. The boats, he thought, should be putting in the water within minutes, a little way upstream—carrying the whole of H Company, sweating in camouflage ponchos. Not that they'd be trying to hide themselves; they wanted to be seen. The ponchos were to cover what they were carrying.

Getting the boats had been easily the most difficult and dangerous part of the mission so far. At the request of a cadet—the Terfreyans loved the pint-sized warriors—the boats had been gathered by locals twenty miles and more upstream the day before. And been transported

by floater at night along the river—as much as possible
under the sheltering eaves of the bordering forest. The
risk of detection and destruction had been considerable.

The cadets had been in position since dawn, one
platoon in the woods across the river, another under
the dense brush that overhung the bank on this side.
Each cadet had a stubby surface-to-air missile launcher
and five small, wicked rockets. Under their ponchos,
each of H Company's troopers had the same. As did
several of the twenty-eight troopers in 2nd Platoon.

Timing was important but not absolutely critical. When
the boats launched, they'd let him know. When they
approached a point opposite him, they'd let him know
that, too.

Lotta had learned of the Klestronu plan the day
before, in the morning, but that had simply provided
the details of where and exactly how. Romlar's general
plan had been made six days before, and the request for
additional rockets and launchers sent to Iryala. When
Lotta's mind-spying had provided a specific situation,
Romlar had had a hurried day and a half to set things
up. The cadets had timed the current, clocking floating
wood over a quarter-mile section of river. If everything
went more or less as planned, Jerym thought, they'd
have a real coup. Otherwise— That would depend on
what went wrong.

So far the regiment had had only one disaster, a
semi-disaster actually, when D Company had lost 62
troopers, two scout crewmen, the company commander—
and Tain.

Jerym waited calmly, looked for the sun again, saw it
squatting red and swollen on the horizon. A moment
later he got the radio pulse that told him the boats were
in the water. He called to his platoon directly, main-
taining radio silence. Each man knew they had about
six minutes: Romlar's best guess-timate of how long it
would be before the boats were observed by Klestronu
aerial surveillance, plus time for the gunships to arrive.
If the gunships arrived later, things would be awkward;

sooner, and things could go very badly. If the gunships
didn't arrive at all, which was possible, the mission
would be scrubbed.

So far, with that one exception, Romlar's judgement
had been very good, and as far as Jerym was concerned,
that had been more than chance.

They waited, Jerym at last feeling tension. The second radio pulse beeped with no sign of gunships, and
he moved the platoon westward, out of sight within the
forest's edge, moving at a rate intended to match the
boats' speed. They hiked for several minutes before
he heard a rocket explode, then quickly another, and 2nd
Platoon moved closer to the forest's edge, to see.

There were four gunships over the river. Three were
rising and presumably also firing, their silent gun beams
invisible in the daylight. The fourth described tight,
climbing circles, tail up. Two more rockets struck it,
and it began to fall slowly, spiraling now, while rockets
exploded against two other craft without apparent effect.

The crippled ship disappeared behind the high bank
while the others continued to fire from higher up. For a
moment there were no further hits, then another was
struck three times within as many seconds. It staggered
and began to settle slowly, moving toward the open
bank. It was hit again, twice more, but its rate of fall
remained the same till it was over land. Then it sat
down heavily in a kressera field.

During all this, 2nd Platoon crouched motionless, as
if frozen by the sight.

Of the remaining two gunships, one was hit again and
began to climb sharply as if damaged and trying to get
away. That concentrated the rocketeers' fire, and quickly
it was hit twice more. It slid down and to one side, then
plummeted, the splash visible above the bank when it
hit.

Jerym wouldn't have been surprised to see the other
run then. Instead it seemed to intensify its attack,
diving, swooping, its guns surely slashing at targets.
Rockets struck it without apparent effect, and it dou-

bled back as if determined to wipe out the boats and men below. Almost it disappeared behind the bank, then rose abruptly, seeming to labor, swerved, took another hit, and came down in the same kressera field, plowing dirt.

"Now!" Jerym bellowed, and 2nd Platoon ran out into the field. The rocketeers led off, and at closer range fired rockets into the motionless targets. Then the hosemen took over the lead, firing short bursts at the gunports, in case anyone aboard still lived and tried to man their guns.

They didn't. While everyone else stayed back a hundred yards, two troopers ran up to each of the two craft, planted satchel charges, then trotted back, and the charges were detonated. High explosives roared, gutting the armored gunships.

Jerym led the platoon to the riverbank. From there he saw no sign of the other two floaters, nor of any boats beached. What he did see was some floating boat wreckage not yet out of sight downstream. There were no floating bodies; they'd been too loaded with equipment. A few troopers stood or lay on the far bank, some being administered to by cadets and other troopers—perhaps twenty troopers in all—but it seemed to Jerym that H Company was no more.

Other cadets were trotting downriver on his side, from their bypassed ambush upstream, and Jerym went to meet them. They'd have seen where the two other gunships went down, and he'd have men dive to find them. They could plant charges and blow them under water, so there'd be no chance of salvage.

The Klestroni were down to four gunships now, apparently, but at the moment he didn't feel like rejoicing.

Sixty-Five

They never did blow up the sunken gunships. Even before Jerym had a chance to question the cadets, hover vehicles came into sight down the road: a column of armored assault vehicles loaded with marines from the Klestronu bivouac—apparently two companies of them.

Second Platoon and the cadets, totalling fifty-four men and boys, went over the rim of the riverbank, fired their remaining STA missiles at the enemy, then threw weapons, equipment, helmets, and their remaining satchel charges into the river in order to swim for it. They were neither situated nor equipped for a serious fight with a force like that. The unexpected intensity of their brief rocket attack, though, plus Klestronu caution, allowed them to get across the river without being closed on. Then they separated again, cadets from troopers, into the jungle, into the evening, the troopers to find their way to places where floaters could pick them up.

One cadet went with 2nd Platoon. Their mapbooks and radios were at the bottom of the Spice; his radio

and local knowledge would help them get picked up.
Also with 2nd Platoon went H Company's thirty-two
survivors; five of them, wounded, were carried on make-
shift stretchers. The early part of the night they slept in
the jungle; without their visors, it was too dark beneath
the forest roof to travel. Later, when a moon came
up, they pushed on, along the river bank where visibility, if poor, was not impossible. Jerym wished he had
eyes like a T'swi's.

It was close to dawn when they reached another
farming district. Two CPCs waited at the back edge of a
pasture, and the troopers crowded aboard. The cadet
left them then, to trot to one of the farmsteads where
he could get a meal and a few hours' sleep in the hay.

On their return to Headquarters Company, 2nd Platoon slept much of the day. When they got up, they
mustered beneath the trees with 1st Platoon, along with
H Company's unwounded survivors. The wounded had
been ported back to Iryala already. Romlar assigned
thirteen H Company troopers to 2nd Platoon, bringing
it to full strength, and the other fourteen to bolster 1st
Platoon.

Then he dismissed them, except for the two platoon
leaders. Romlar took them to the command tent, where
Jorrie Renhaus and a T'swa major were waiting, the
T'swi being Colonel Jil-Zat's EO from the constantly
moving cadet HQ. Major Dho-Kat had arrived the night
before in a scout floater.

"Jarnol, Alsnor," Romlar said to the platoon leaders,
"something's come up, and we're planning a major action. The Klestroni aren't what you'd call innovative,
but their flagship's engineering section is modifying a
pair of shuttles for ground attack purposes. Lotta found
out last night. Their idea is to instrument one of them
as a stratospheric observation platform. And to modify
both of them for dropping bombs.

"If we let them pull this off, we'll be up against a
weapon we can't get at. This whole region will be under

constant surveillance, and it'll be a lot harder to conceal our movements and positions.' "

The teenaged colonel looked over his people, his friends, then went on as calmly and casually as if he were talking about a proposed ball game.

"I expected that if we reduced their gunships enough, we could move around more openly, maybe get them to bring troops into the jungle after us, where we could whip them good. I also thought it just might break their commodore's will to persist. But according to Lotta, he's developed a kind of grim resolution to leave Terfreya only on a victory. Which is just the opposite of our purpose.

"They seem to think the modifications won't take long—a week, maybe two or three if they have problems —and they've already flown marine ordnance officers back up to help design the bombs and get them built.

"So now's the time to do something decisive. To run them off. Here's what I've got in mind. . . ."

Six days later, his strike teams were ready. His plan was three-faceted but not intricate. Any one of its three operations could shock and hurt the Klestroni, regardless of the success or failure of the others. If all were successful, they'd hurt him critically.

Preparation had required considerable floater traffic, and with less than usual caution, for supply hauls to headquarters from the outgate sites. More combat personnel carriers were ported in.

Now it was night in the jungle. Handlamps, pointed more or less groundward and on low intensity, moved here and there to light the final preparations. There were several troopers with pole charges, and seventy cadets who'd been flown in to Romlar's headquarters. Fourteen cadets, selected for prepuberty voices and features, were dressed as girls, in party clothes provided by farm families. Their wigs, customized in Landfall on one-day's notice and teleported, were held to fresh-shaved scalps by a theatrical adhesive.

Preparation had been as careful as time allowed. The fourteen had had very little opportunity to observe teen-aged females, so Coyn Carrmak had been flown in from 1st Battalion to help Lotta inspect and coach them. According to a couple of troopers who'd known Carrmak in their days "outside," he'd been somewhat of a ladies' man. He and Lotta drilled the pretenders in appropriate walks and mannerisms.

The other skills they'd need on their mission they already possessed, very highly developed.

In their shoulder bags, beneath cosmetics, mirrors, and tissues, they carried automatic pistols and spare clips, with blast slugs. And one fragmentation grenade each, in case capture was imminent. Two carried additional grenades.

The other fifty-six cadets wore black uniforms especially dyed and ported in for this night mission. A number of them carried rocket launchers and rockets, and several had blast hoses. The rest carried rifles.

When the cadets were ready, Romlar went into his command tent, where a photomap at maximum scale already occupied his computer screen. At such a short distance, teleport targeting was highly accurate, but in this case the target had been built after the map photography was done, and was shown on the map only in a pen approximation. So Renhaus knelt on the platform of the small teleport, peering through, ready to coach Romlar's targeting.

Romlar hit it almost at once, then gave the word, and the "girls" went through the gate. When the last had stepped through, he retargeted and sent the other cadets through.

Again he retargeted, one of the troopers signalling as if greater precision was needed. The trooper raised a hand to halt him; then they waited, Romlar's eyes on his watch, for several minutes. Finally, "Now!" he said. The trooper activated the fuse on his pole charge and shoved it through the gate. On the headquarters side they couldn't hear the explosion.

Over the next several minutes they repeated this
with several more pole charges. Then Romlar got up
and rotated his shoulders, swung his arms. Uncharacteristically he'd gotten tense. There'd been a lot of
details to handle, and he'd been hurried.

Now the first two teams were committed, the first
operation well underway, and all he had to wait for was
the rising of the lesser moon to start the next.

In the darkness, twelve combat personnel carriers sat
hidden by trees in creek beds, waiting for orders to take
off. Each held two squads of troopers, fully manned up
and wearing parachutes and arm webbing.

Shortly after the White T'swa arrived on Terfreya,
the Klestroni had established two regimental field bases
about twenty miles from their main base near Lonyer
City. One northeast, one southeast. Miles from any
sizeable jungle as well, these were fenced and had
sentry fields, bunkers, minefields, and anti-aircraft batteries. One of the four remaining Klestronu gunships
was stationed at each; the other two were at the main
base.

Romlar had assigned three manned-up platoons to
attack each compound. When the order came, the troopers would jump, body-glide over the compounds, and
open their chutes at low elevations. Every second man
carried a blast hose, the others rifles, all supplied with
blast slugs instead of the solid rounds preferred in
jungle fighting. Every man's grenade pocket held fragmentation grenades.

Waiting, they didn't talk much.

The men of 2nd Platoon sat or lay around near Romlar's
command tent, waiting for the word. With their H
Company survivors, they numbered forty-two, including Jerym and his platoon sergeant, Warden. The T'swa
major who'd arrived with the cadets was squatting in
the darkness outside the tent, and Jerym squatted down
next to him.

"Do you T'swa ever get nervous?" Jerym asked.

The major chuckled. "Occasionally. When neutrality slips a bit. There are things we do then to calm ourselves."

"Such as?"

"A momentary transfer of attention to the 'I' outside this universe usually provides the necessary perspective."

"Outside the universe. The Ostrak people call it the balcony," Jerym said.

The T'swi chuckled. "That is a suitable way of talking about it."

"They taught us to do that too," Jerym said thoughtfully. "'Look at the 'I' in the balcony. Turn around and look at yourself,' they say. But it's easy to forget—for me, anyway. Till about a year ago I usually felt lousy— mad, resentful, guilty, hopeless—take your choice. What I feel now, when I'm not feeling good, is only a shadow of how it used to be, so I don't always remember to do something about it."

He paused. "We were supposed to get a lot more training when we got to Tyss—training in the T'sel, including meditation, as well as in military know-how. Maybe we will yet, when we're done here."

Dho-Kat gazed mildly at the teenaged Iryalan. "May I evaluate your troopers for you?"

"Sure. Go ahead."

"You do very well indeed, both as warriors and as human beings. I have associated closely with the people of several worlds—allies and adversaries belonging to various cultures and subcultures. With the exception of the cadets, none of them were your equals, or even approached you, as warriors or with regard to sanity. Or general happiness."

Jerym contemplated that for a few seconds, then asked, "How far are we from being T'swa? Really?"

Jerym felt more than saw the smile. "Speaking strictly," Dho-Kat said, "T'swa is a word used to describe human beings of a particular planet with a particular history and culture. But the beings in this universe who are being T'swa, who are playing the role of T'swa, are of precisely the same nature as those who have taken the role of Iryalans. Or of Klestroni. Those who, by intention or default, play the role of victim, do not differ in their nature from those who have taken the role of hero.

"You are Iryalans, the *new* Iryalans. At last the Iryalan culture is changing, and that change is accelerating. I suspect it approaches the point beyond which it cannot be defeated by internal factors. And if The Movement succeeds, as seems probable, the result will be beyond even that which Kristal visualizes."

It seemed to Jerym that the T'swi was talking as much to himself now as to his listener, examining his perspectives as he voiced them.

"Culture on Iryala and in the Confederation as a whole will take forms which ours on Tyss cannot. It will grow a new richness and splendor. In future lives, if you choose, you will take part in that, as I may." He laughed softly. "Or you may decide to spend a quiet life in a monastery on the backwater world of Tyss. That could be pleasant."

He squatted silent for a few seconds while Jerym waited. "By the circumstance of birth, you will never be T'swa in this lifetime," Dho-Kat finished. "But you have no need to be. You are truly exceptional warriors, tested and proven in combat. Think of yourself, if you wish, as 'honorary T'swa'; those of us here on Terfreya would agree without hesitation."

Jerym peered at the powerful black man squatting in the jungle night, and shook his head admiringly. "Major," he said, "you are something."

"As are you, Lieutenant."

"But suppose—even if we send the Klestroni home with a bloody nose and his tail between his legs—suppose they lead an imperial fleet back here in eight or ten years. A fleet that can destroy ours thirty times over. What then?"

"What indeed? If that should happen, perhaps they

will land on Iryala and conquer it, and from there rule the Confederation. But the T'sel would not die, not on Tyss and not on Iryala. Eventually it would conquer the conqueror. Meanwhile for a time, perhaps a long time, lives would be less comfortable, their roles perhaps less free. But they would be very interesting."

Someone stepped into the door of the tent, and Dho-Kat got to his feet. "But that is at most a future script which may never be played," he went on. "Meanwhile you have the now, the present to enjoy—this night, this war, this world. Within the hour you will go into battle leading men who know well how to fight and take joy in it, against opponents who are better than many you might encounter.

"Go into combat with the thought that you are already dead, that it simply has not happened yet, and enjoy the battle."

The man in the door stepped outside then, and with a handlamp started off down the hill toward the scouts, Dho-Kat following. Jerym too got up, limbered his knees and joined his troopers, digesting what the T'swi had said.

One part especially had stayed with him— "Go into battle with the thought that you are already dead. . . ." Considering 2nd Platoon's assignment for the night, it seemed a realistic assumption.

Sixty-Six

The cadet sergeant in charge of the "party girls" gated into the Klestronu officers' recreation compound and promptly stepped out of the way, looking around as he did so. He saw no one except the next two cadets, the third, the fourth, and at last the fourteenth. It was night, but not very dark there. The cadets were in shadow behind a squad-size tent with a raised floor, one of a large circle of them, their sides rolled down for privacy. In the center of the compound, unseen from where they were, the dance pavilion sent lanes of soft light between the tents. And music, foreign and rollicking.

They knew the layout, from a diagram and from a crude scale mockup on the Regimental Headquarters hill. Lotta had visited the recreation compound in the mind of young officers three times in the preceding days. She'd come to know them through her meld with their general.

When all fourteen cadets had gated in, eleven followed their sergeant between two of the lesser tents, remembering to walk like teenaged girls. The other two began to circle the tent ring from behind.

The brightly lit dance pavilion was centered in a space of grassy ground, and its sides were rolled up, giving a sense of openness and a free flow of air. Inside, the twelve could see couples dancing. Four of the cadets would stay outside. They separated from the others, moving in pairs to two opposite corners of the pavilion. The pair at the front corner stood as if talking, looking past each other, hands in their shoulder bags. Those at the back corner knelt as if hunting for something dropped, to keep out of the line of fire.

Meanwhile the others, regardless of the open sides, walked to the front entrance of the pavilion. A couple passed them, headed for one of the encircling tents—a Klestronu officer and a local girl who might have been sixteen. She was giggling. Her skirt was hiked up to her waist in back, and the officer had his hand in the rear of her underpants. Neither of them paid any attention to the newcomers.

Two guards stood casually at the front entrance, the only guards in sight. They gave the new "girls" little more than perfunctory glances as they filed in; obviously the recreation section had found more who were interested in a good time and a wad of requisitioned local money.

The cadets didn't worry about the guards. The two at the left front corner would take them out. The eight who went in sized up the situation as they distributed themselves across the front: The pavilion was crowded, girls in short supply, and a number of officers danced with each other while waiting.

The cadets wasted no time. Their hands came out of their shoulder bags with guns in them, and they began at once to shoot, first at the officers who already had started eagerly toward them. The flat blasts of their shots were mixed with the uglier sound of blast slugs exploding in flesh.

After the briefest moment, the screaming began, and the stampede. The cadets kept shooting, pausing only to eject an empty clip and slap in a fresh one. Bodies littered the dance floor. Several Klestroni tried to reach them and died. Most fled, scores of them ducking under the rolled-up sides; many of these fell to gunfire from the corners.

Except for the two door guards, the gate detachment and tower guards, the compound's security troops were posted in two large tents, side by side, from which they were to issue if called upon by whistles. So far they'd never been called on. Their shift lieutenant had arranged to be visited by one of the "hostesses," and had gone with her to one of the "rest" tents. Whereupon his men had brought forth a pair of bottles, passing them around to help shorten the shift.

When the firing began, there was a moment of stunned bewilderment. Then they dropped bottles, scrambling for their guns. At that moment, at each tent, a "girl" stepped into the entrance, threw a grenade, then another, and hit the dirt outside, below the floor level. The first grenades exploded almost at once, the second a long moment later. The cadets reappeared then, and darted in to pour blast slugs into the sprawled bodies. One wounded Klestronit managed to draw his own weapon, and one of the cadets died, but no guard escaped either tent.

The other fifty-six cadets, those uniformed in black, lay dispersed but ready along both sides of the road between the rec compound and the headquarters compound. But much nearer the rec compound: some one hundred yards outside its high barbed wire fence, and somewhat farther outside its fifteen-foot concrete wall. They felt exposed, lying there, and in fact they were. Harrowed every week, the field was smooth and bare of growth, while near the fence, floodlights bathed it, their light spilling farther, diffusing and thinning.

The fifty-six heard small caliber pistols begin to fire. So far, so good; their turn would come. The gunfire thickened. About a minute later there was a roar as the

armored cab on one of the guard towers blew apart—
one of the towers in front. The other blew a minute
later.

The floodlights and spotlights had been mounted on
the towers, and their destruction had left the cadets
cloaked in darkness. Now, like furious badgers, the
boys began to dig quick shallow holes, something to lie
in. Meanwhile a gunship appeared from the direction of
the headquarters compound, and circled the rec compound well above the wall. Its spotlights walked about
inside, but its beam guns did not fire. This continued
for a minute, then a tower cab blew on the back wall,
and the gunship climbed higher, not knowing what had
caused the explosion.

The cadets gave the gunship little attention. They too
wore the new helmets now, visors down, watching as
a column of twenty armored assault vehicles moved
down the road from the headquarters compound. The
fourth and final tower burst; they heard its roar. As
the column approached, the cadets on the north side of
the road opened fire on it with rockets. The AAVs
stopped, turrets pivoting. Beam guns came to life, lancing across the field, firing mostly too high at first. More
rockets hissed, slashed, exploded. Marines piled out
the hatches on the off side, the south side, and as they
did, rockets hissed from that side too, into the open
hatches, while blast hoses and automatic rifles poured
blast slugs into the marines. Fire from most of the
turret guns ceased, but marine rifles sent scores of
wire-thin beams sweeping and crisscrossing toward the
cadet muzzle blasts in a deadly, well-drilled pattern.

Meanwhile the gunship, unsure at first what to do,
sallied out to hit the cadets in the field. Two rockets
exploded on its armored bow, and its pilot swung away
to fire from a distance, as if not wanting to risk his
craft.

Another powerful roar blew the gate and gatehouse,
and the cadet riflemen, those who were able, began to
pull back, leaving the blast hoses to hold the marines'

attention. The marines advanced on bellies, knees and elbows, stopping only to shoot or die. Grenades roared. The hose fire thinned, stopped.

The combat personnel carrier slowed almost to a walk. "Visors down!" the jump master ordered quietly, and twenty grins dimmed behind face shields curved and tinted.

"Gloves on!" They pulled on warm gloves; it would be cold outside.

"Stand up!"

They got to their feet, the two rows of men dovetailing to form a single line. They wore no reserve chutes and no field packs. Their rifles were snapped diagonally across their harness in front; their magazine pouches were full.

The right-side door slid open to the night and cold.

"Stand in the door!"

The front men shuffled forward, spreading the line a bit. Their platoon leader stood with the toes of his boots over the edge, looking at the Klestronu field base, recalling Romlar's orders: "Aim for the middle—the muster field." Headquarters and officers' country—the primary killing zone—were immediately east of it. "Kill the head, and the body's in trouble," he'd said. For an outfit like the Klestroni especially.

And these troopers knew the base well, from aerial holos provided by a high overflight two nights earlier, had "drilled" their platoon and squad assignments on a crude scale mockup.

The jump master watched the computer screen beside the door. It showed the Klestronu field base 12,000 feet down and 2,300 feet east of their line of flight. The red blip on the screen was their floaters; white blips were the others. The red blip led.

The CPC's computer integrated atmospheric pressure, air movement, the lateral momentum that would be imparted to the jumpers by the floater's slow forward speed . . . A light above the screen lit green, and the jump master slapped Varns on the shoulder. The lieutenant dove, the line of men behind him following quickly out into nothingness. The jump master followed the last of them, leaving the troop compartment empty.

Jerym stood at the head of 2nd Platoon, watching as Renhaus and Romlar targeted the teleport.

"There!" said Renhaus. "Looks good!"

Romlar went and looked briefly for himself, then turned to Jerym and his men. "Okay. You'll gate into the exec messroom, as planned. Right now, as far as I can tell, there's no one there to see your mode of arrival, but don't depend on it. And remember, when you gate out, the entrance you'll be facing is at the south end, toward the operations area."

Lotta had provided a lot of "eye witness" information for them, including sketches, from "personal" observation during melds. And they'd "drilled" repeatedly their individual and unit actions on a crude scale model, mocked up on the ground outside Romlar's headquarters tent.

There were a dozen last minute advices Romlar could have given, but they weren't needed, and he knew it. "Any questions?"

No one said anything. Teeth showed. Eyes gleamed.

"All right. Alsnor, lead off."

Jerym jogged through the gate . . .

. . . and into the Klestronu exec messroom. He moved to one side and turned to face the rear, the kitchen area, while the rest of his platoon gated in trotting, running softly. He saw no bogeys, and speaking quietly, sent two men to check the staff officers' messroom on the far side of the kitchen area. Then he moved quickly to a window by the door, where Warden, his platoon sergeant, was already peering out.

He'd barely had time to look when there was a shot from the other messroom. The platoon, already distributed around the walls, turned; one fire team slipped into the kitchen, rifles ready. Seconds later, a trooper came back in to report there'd been a messman there, apparently checking an urn and platter of cakes for staff officers who might come in, perhaps after or before a shift. He'd run for the door and been shot.

Jerym nodded curtly, reminded by this that they might have very little undisturbed time here. He looked at his watch and pressed a button on it. "Team leaders here!" he said quietly, and they moved to him. "That shot's been heard, must have been, but they're not likely to nail down the direction of an isolated shot like that. And with all the emergency radio traffic they must be getting now, they don't have much attention for anything else. If they don't hear any more shooting right away, they'll likely assume it was an accidental discharge by some security detail. Remember, their internal security uses projectile firearms too.

"So we're going to sit quiet till I order otherwise— two minutes—and let their attention get back fully to what it was on before. Then you'll move out and hit your targets. Now take positions by the doors you'll move out of."

He turned back to his window then. The area was lit by lights on poles, not brightly, but sufficiently for seeing. A hundred feet away, by the door of the Klestronu command center, a guard stood on the small porch. Before, his rifle had been slung on a shoulder; now he held it in his hands as he scanned the neighborhood, though overall his demeanor still seemed casual.

Jerym looked at his watch. Most of a minute had passed since he'd set his timer. He waited half a minute longer, then swiveled his mike. His radio was set to transmit at minimum power. "Platoon listen up," he said. "The signal to move out will be a single shot from just outside the east door. Klefma!"

"Yes sir."

"Have Barkum go out the east side door and take cover behind the porch. There's a door guard at the entrance to the command center. I want Barkum to kill him with one round. And I don't want the guy to yell. Bang and he's dead. Then we move out. Barkum will join you when you leave. Questions?"

Barkum's voice answered: "Bang and he's dead. Then I go with my team."

Jerym grinned. "You got it. Start."

He watched then, eyes intent. Seconds passed quietly, ten, fifteen. The shot sounded and the guard fell at the same moment. "Go," Jerym barked, this time not using his mike, and men began moving out the doors. The team assigned to destroy the command center itself moved past him out the south door, followed by the teams assigned to the other prefab buildings of the operations area: the communications center, the briefing center, and the dispatcher's center.

Warden, the platoon sergeant, with Desterbi an interval behind, trotted toward the command center, slowly enough to mistake for marines going to report. They mounted the steps, then paused to let the strike men of the other hit teams—two from each—trot to their own targets. Their buddies stayed behind to give them fire support if needed. Warden bent and shoved the dead guard off the porch, while Desterbi put the basket bomb down, out of the way to one side.

So far, Jerym told himself, *so good.*

He'd hardly thought it when automatic weapons fire burst out north of the messhall, where four of the sweep teams should have been waiting for their cue to begin their kill sweep of officers' country. Across the way, Warden pushed open the command center door and stepped in, Desterbi right after him. Jerym could hear the racket of their rifles on automatic, and bare seconds later Desterbi was outside again, his back against the wall, waiting for Warden. From the nearby communications center, a basket bomb roared, followed a second later by another from the dispatcher's center, and almost at once by a third from the briefing center. With the particular explosive used, anything that might have survived the blasts would have been seared by heat flash.

The nearer yard lights had been shot out, and Jerym lowered his visor to see better.

The nearby gunfire was gaining intensity as the sweep teams spread into officers' country. Four or five long seconds passed before Warden backed out the command center door, dragging an inert body that had to be the Klestronu general. As Warden backed down the steps, Desterbi picked up the basket bomb, but before he could throw it through the open door, he fell, shot. For an instant Jerym held his breath, turning away to protect his night vision from the expected blast, waiting for the bomb to go off, to wipe out Desterbi, Warden, and the general.

There was no blast; Desterbi had been shot before he could flip the time fuse. Warden was crouched beside the porch. When nothing happened, he raised up enough to see, and there was Desterbi, motionless, and the bomb. Warden sprang up beside him, snatched the bomb, and jumped down again. Gunfire yammered, and from somewhere, a Klestronit swept a rifle beam across the area. Warden fell. Still the bomb didn't go off.

"First and 2nd squads!" Jerym snapped into his mike, "do whatever's necessary to suppress that enemy fire. Move out if you have to."

"First squad moving out."

"Second moving out."

"Mellis!"

"Yes sir!"

"When I say 'go,' get over there and throw that Ambers-damned bomb in the door. Then take care of the enemy CO."

"Got it!"

Jerym waited. Gunfire erupted seemingly at the other end of the messhall. "Go!" he ordered.

He watched Mellis dash in a low crouch, hit the ground, roll, scramble, dash, hit the ground . . . In

short seconds he was beside the porch and the body of
Warden. He bent, straightened, threw, hit the ground
again. Again Jerym averted his eyes. Three seconds
later the bomb roared, and he looked. There was a glow
inside the open door as things flammable began to
burn. Mellis was pulling off the general's shirt. It came
free, and he crouched over the form again, working
furiously, fell, got back to his knees, then pitched forward on his face. The automatic weapons fire increased.

"Shit!" Jerym swore, and went out the door. There
was no one else to send. He ran as Mellis had, dash, hit
the dirt, roll, scramble, dash . . . He rolled Mellis off
the general and quickly finished removing the general's
trousers and shorts. *Hairier than a bear*, he thought.
Three times hairier than Carrmak.

Then, still oblivious to the gunfire, Jerym slipped off
his light combat pack, drew out a small spool of det
cord, and in what shelter the porch offered, he hog-tied
the general.

Done, he crouched beside the porch, looking around.
In close, the shooting was only sporadic now, but it was
furious nearby in officers' country. Three troopers ran
toward the messhall from the direction of the ruined
briefing and communications centers. The floaters would
land at the muster ground north of the messhall, if they
were lucky enough to get through. Jerym bent, grabbed
the general under the arms, and dragged him into the
open, away from the building. Then he turned and
sprinted for the cover of the messhall.

Not far from Lonyer City, three combat personnel
carriers, widely separated, held back as if spectators.
They carried no troops, only their pilots and copilots,
who watched three gunships exchange fire a mile away.
The fight was brief, the two that fought with rockets
and hoses shooting down the one that fought back with
beam guns. By that time, one of the victors was losing
altitude, angling off toward the city as if its pilot hoped
to take refuge there.

When the Klestronu gunship went down, anti-aircraft guns began at once to fire, beams slicing the sky, seeking the enemy craft that remained. Instead of trying to escape, the gunship challenged them, thinning them, its descending tracers a delicate, hypnotic stitchery in the darkness, before it fell abruptly in a flurry of coruscating lights.

The sky went quiet, and the three CPCs moved in low and fast, at first undetected, drawing no fire. Then small-arms fire stormed first at one, then at a second. Their flight paths converged toward the center of the enclosed base, and the muster ground there. They slowed abruptly, pressing their pilots against their straps, then landed. Their doors shot open.

Men sprinted for one of them, several falling as they ran. Others, in a cluster, sprinted toward a second. The first group clambered in, and the floater launched while her door was still closing. She accelerated sharply, keeping low, barely clearing the tents in front of her, and with scarce feet to spare passed over one fence, another, beams slashing at her, then sped off across a field pursued by only random fire. Behind her, the second took a different though similar course. But the men who'd boarded her were marines. One threw a grenade into the cockpit. It roared, and skidding, the craft took out a row of tents, hit an antiaircraft emplacement and somersaulted. The third had risen last and without boarders, climbing vertically to decoy attention and fire. It was hit, staggered. More antiaircraft beams stabbed and sliced, till it plummeted, hit the ground heavily and broke in two.

In the first floater, Jerym got to his knees, then to his feet. Hot metal reeked. Around him in the rear of the troop compartment, other men picked themselves up. There'd been no time to belt down or even sit, and abrupt acceleration had sent them sprawling.

He counted heads. Eleven including himself. Eleven out of forty-two. Not enough to feel like celebrating, but eleven more than he'd had any right to expect. And the platoon had ravaged the Klestronu ground command structure—officers and equipment.

Crouching apelike against possible manuevers, he went forward and congratulated the pilots. The copilot grunted the only acknowledgement; their attention was fully occupied, intent on monitors, instruments, and what was visible in the night through the scorched and spalled armorglass windshield.

Appreciation delivered, Jerym went aft and belted himself into a seat. He was alive. *How many of the original 2nd can say that?* he thought. *Romlar and Carrmak, but they haven't been exposed to combat. And probably Esenrok; company commanders don't get exposed all that much either. But of the guys who've been in the thick of it, there's Presnola and Markooris, wounded and ported back to Iryala; and maybe half a dozen more. Add the H Company survivors and we've maybe got a squad and a half.*

Why me?

He'd almost given himself up, back when the Klestroni had rushed them. Well, maybe not almost, but for an instant he'd felt an impulse to crawl beneath one of the tent floors, then turn himself in when the fighting had stopped.

It had been brief, like a sort of mental hiccup.

It seemed to him that he must have known then what had caused it, though he'd had no time to look at it. Beneath that impulse had been the hidden idea: *Get taken prisoner, taken up to the flagship, and be with Tain. Somehow be with Tain and help her remember, help her be Tain again. Go to Klestron with her.*

Crazy! They'd have questioned him and learned about the teleport, and how they'd been beaten—the tricks and tactics and technology used. Guys had died to keep those things secret. Tain had, in a way.

He hadn't come close to doing it, of course. But he'd had the impulse. And it had soiled him. *I'll talk with Lotta,* he thought, *have her clean me up.*

Or am I making too much of this? Everyone's flawed in some way.

Then a question struck him, one she might well ask: What good is a flaw? What can you do with it?

He didn't have the answer, not consciously, but for some reason—some strange, but welcome reason—asking the question lightened him and brought an unexpected chuckle to his throat.

The trooper next to him looked at him curiously. "What's funny, Lieutenant?" he asked.

"I was just thinking how weird it is that here I am, still alive."

It wasn't a true answer, but it had the ring of truth, it could have been true, and it served. The trooper grinned at him. "Yeah. Some of us seem to be wired to duck at the right time. I don't know whether it's our script writer or maybe our props man."

There were other chuckles around them, and Jerym realized that he was feeling a *lot* better, extroverted again. He'd tell Lotta what he'd felt, he decided, but he wouldn't ask her help. Tunis! He hadn't even exercised what he knew to do, hadn't turned around and looked at himself yet!

Romlar sat in the dark at his radio. Beneath the jungle roof, the night was black as tar. All he could see were the tiny red power lights of radio and computer.

He could have pulled his visor down to see, of course, but just now the dark was comforting. The evacuation floaters should be headed back, he thought, those that could, but they were keeping radio silence. Apparently at least one of the Klestronu gunships was still alive, possibly two.

But of the survival and evacuation *status*, he knew nothing except for the cadet operation. Three of the "girls" had gotten out of the rec compound and reached the evacuation site, along with seventeen of those who'd made their escape possible by ambushing and engaging the relief column. That made twenty of seventy. There weren't many cadets left—a hundred maybe, and half as many cadre. He was prepared for even heavier casualties among B and C Companies, who'd dropped into the Klestronu field bases.

As for 2nd Platoon—if any got out alive, that would make it a really special coup. But then, the version of 2nd Platoon that went out tonight held nothing but survivors. The remaining originals had been through more tough missions than perhaps any other platoon in the regiment, while the guys who'd been assigned from H Company . . .

It was a regiment to be proud of, and he was proud. But at the moment he was depressed. *Sure it's unreasonable,* he told himself, *and sure the T'swa wouldn't feel like this. But it's how I feel.*

He'd talk with Lotta about it after she made her report. Whenever that was. It seemed to him she could handle his mood with two or three questions.

Just now, thinking of her, he felt horny, which surprised him, and he pulled his thoughts to the operational situation, so far as he knew it. The regiment was still formidable. And the Klestroni had so few gunships left—probably one, maybe two—that even if they got their new surveillance ship up, their responses would be badly limited. He—he and the regiment and the cadets—had hurt them badly. The question was whether they'd hurt them badly enough to drive them back to Klestron.

Sixty-Seven

Igsat Tarimenloku's back was straight but his morale had slumped. The bridge crew stayed as quiet as possible, moving as little as possible, as if someone in the room was dying. He'd come there from the chapel, where he'd prayed first to Flenyaagor for His guidance. And when, with that guidance, he'd made his decision, he'd asked Flenyaagor for His support with Kargh. Finally he'd prayed to Kargh himself, something he hadn't had the courage to do since his over-bold youth. And it seemed to him that when he'd finished, Flenyaagor had breathed His Divine Breath upon him, as if telling him to be of good faith.

He had not asked Kargh for mercy. Only for His blessing on what he must now do.

Back in his command seat, Tarimenloku had called onto the screen a holo of the marine base, magnified to look as if seen from 10,000 feet. It wouldn't look much different now, from 10,000 feet. No heavy weapons had been engaged. It hadn't been devastated. One could easily miss that a disaster, even a calamity, had struck there.

Would it have been different if he'd had a heavy brigade, with its tanks? He didn't think so.

Things had seemed so simple when they'd set it up. This was a backward world, seemingly without an army, its population scant and scattered. Control the small capital, learn about them, milk them of their information about the rest of the sector, and then leave. It was a Kargh-sent opportunity involving no apparent major risk, requiring no great haste. Eight thousand marines had seemed more than enough; the initial 4,000 he'd sent down had seemed ample.

Even now, nearly 5,500 officers and men were still alive, more than 5,000 fit for duty. But of the 615 marine *officers* who'd landed, only 283 were alive, only 241 fit for duty! Almost no senior officers were still alive: one colonel and three majors! And Saadhrambacoora of course, but more than his leg had been broken. Almost no one left down there had ever commanded a unit larger than a company, and even at the company and platoon levels, the officer shortage was severe.

You could not operate a brigade without qualified officers. To raise company commanders to battalion commands invited worse disasters than they'd already suffered, and who then would command the companies, the platoons? Peasants lacked the self-discipline, nor would they accept other peasants as their officers. It took more than insignia.

Even the remaining officers had lost authority. He knew it without being there, had heard it in Saadhrambacoora's voice. What a diabolical thing to have spared the man, thought Tarimenloku, deliberately leaving him alive among the dead, like the drunken Thilraxakootha on the Eve of the Battle of Klarwath. Even peasants would see the parallel; the man could never command effectively again.

Tarimenloku shook his head. *How could they know us so well?*

The commodore didn't ask himself another question:

how the enemy might have done what he'd done. It never occurred to him; defeat gripped him too tightly. In a voice as hard as ever but somehow flavored with apathy, he gave the order he'd decided upon in prayer: He ordered Saadhrambacoora to prepare his marines for withdrawal. It was time to return to Klestron.

When Lotta emerged from her trance, she did not at once get up. A unit of her attention was stuck on one of Tarimenloku's thoughts: *How could they know us so well?*

In a meld she knew the other's conscious thoughts, and felt—got the taste of, the sense of—the layer of active unconsciousness just beneath them. But she didn't go deeper. Couldn't, as far as she knew. So she'd never gotten the insights, personal and cultural, that Artus seemed to have, the insights implied in the actions he'd ordered.

How *had* he known?

She was reasonably sure that he couldn't have voiced those insights, but at some level he knew. The wisdom was there.

She thought she'd seen what Artus was, and almost certainly who he'd been—one of the whos—even though he hadn't recognized it himself. And Wellem had agreed with her appraisal. But that was no explanation for what Artus had done here, or it didn't seem to be. There was something deeper, but she was *not* going to poke around hunting for it. And she doubted that Wellem would either, when they got back to Iryala. It could throw Artus into something not even Wellem was prepared to handle.

She got to her feet. Time to report what the commodore had ordered.

Again Romlar sat in the inky dark alone. Lotta had reported to him, and when she'd left, he'd wanted to go with her, to spend what was left of the night with her, if she'd have him.

Artus, he'd told himself instead, *don't be a jerk. You want to use her to help you hide.*

So. Hide from what? Tonight he'd sent 411 personnel on what amounted to suicide missions. Ninety-two had come back; only 92, though that was more than he'd thought there might be. But deaths weren't what was bothering him. Tonight had broken the Klestroni, and if lives were the issue, tonight may well have ended the killing here. Tonight had saved lives, both Iryalan and Klestronu.

He grunted. It was true. And recognizing it hadn't helped at all. So something else was the problem.

Who'd died? Guys he'd known and guys he hadn't. On his side almost all of them warriors. All but some of the floater crews; the replacement crews hadn't been warriors. But they'd had the Ostrak Procedures, and not one of them had tried to weasel out of a mission. They were at Work, at Service. They couldn't truly be warriors but they could be soldiers, and they'd been good ones, laying their lives on the line and being effective.

Which shows me something, he told himself. *The operational difference between warriors and soldiers isn't necessarily courage or will. Soldiers, some of them, a lot of them, have all the courage and will you could want. The operational difference is talent—the kit that comes with being born a warrior, especially a cleaned-up warrior: the inherent attitudes, the inherent responses, the luck. And in most cases the reflexes and strength.*

Lotta reached her tent and ducked inside. Artus had had a cloud hanging around him, but it felt like something he wasn't ready to have handled. *If I went to sleep and he went to sleep, we could probably cook up some dreams to ease it,* she told herself, *maybe lay it to rest awhile, but the big oaf won't go to bed.*

She skinned out of her clothes and lay down on top of her sleeping bag. Maybe *he* wasn't going to sleep, she told herself, but she was.

But when she closed her eyes, it seemed to her that she was feeling what he was. Opening them, she sat up irritatedly, not used to being affected by things like that. Then, without a conscious decision, she reached.

[Artus!]

[Yes?]

To that she had no answer, didn't know why she'd reached. All she could think of was that a meld might help, and she had no reason to suppose it actually would. She hadn't been melding with him on Backbreak. He might be in conference, or on the radio, and going in person to headquarters was less intrusive than touching his mind.

[The meld sounds good,] he thought to her. [Let's try it.]

For a minute they sat, she in her tent, he in a canvas folding chair in front of his computer, while nothing happened. Then, [why don't I come over there?] he asked.

She didn't have an answer to that either, in words, but felt her body quicken. She was with him every step of the way, electric, and three minutes later he was outside her tent flaps, taking off his boots. Belatedly it occurred to her that she was naked, and somehow, for a moment, the realization alarmed her.

She heard as well as felt his chuckle. [I suspect,] he thought to her, [that for a couple of virgins, we won't do too badly.]

Lotta was breathing quietly, asleep; Romlar had been right. Just now he lay beside her with his hands behind his head, not sleepy a bit, feeling very good indeed. He had a semi-erection again but felt no need to do anything about it. Somewhere up above, in the top of the forest roof, he heard a bird chirp. Seconds later it was answered.

They must be seeing dawnlight, he thought. *Better get out of here before people start moving around.*

Carefully he felt about him, found his shorts, pulled

them on, his undershirt, shirt, field pants. He was glad
he'd issued the women a four-panel tent; it made dressing a lot easier. Then, sitting on the ground in front of
it, he put on his boots. Already a little dawnlight was
penetrating the leafy roof, so that the darkness beneath
was no longer absolute. The bird calls had changed
from tentative chirps to phrases, snatches of songs. *In a
minute or two they'll be a chorus,* he told himself, and
got to his feet.

*And today— Maybe today we'll organize an evacua-
tion of our own. We'll see.*

Sixty-Eight

It was an overdue rain, a badly needed rain, and it had been coming down hard for half an hour. At first almost none of it had penetrated the forest roof; now drip from the leaves pattered arhythmically, abundantly on Lotta's tent. But where her attention lay, it would never rain. She was with Commodore Tarimenloku in his office adjacent to the bridge of HRS *Blessed Flenyaagor*. It was a facility he didn't use a lot, but just now he wanted privacy on duty.

The marines were back aboard the troopship, and in stasis except for a few who needed medical treatment first.

The commodore sat watching his comm screen. He'd just ordered his chief intelligence officer to prepare the prisoners from Lonyer City for their return to the planet. The man's acknowledgement lagged for three or four seconds.

"Yes sir," he said at last. "Does that include the female soldier who was captured?"

"The prisoners from Lonyer City," the commodore repeated testily, then with a held breath calmed his

temper. "The female soldier we will retain. She is a prisoner of war, and the war is not over."

"Yes sir." The CIO's expression was troubled as he said it.

The commodore noticed, and touched the *record* key. In the empire, even in this time of infrequent wars, the repatriation of prisoners was a subject stressed at the academy. A sensitive subject wrapped in imprecise legalities, with significances cultural and religious as well as political and military. And while nothing he might do now was likely to save his life and honor, he would not abandon propriety or integrity. "Commander," he said, "would you care to speak for the record as the Conscience of the Prophet?"

"If you please, sir."

"A moment then. I will have the chaplain witness." He tapped other keys. After several seconds his screen split, a middle-aged face and shaven head sharing it now with the chief intelligence officer. Briefly the commodore explained the situation to the chaplain, then returned his attention to the lieutenant commander.

"So. As the Conscience of the Prophet, speak."

The younger man's face was even more serious than usual. "I have spoken with the chief medical officer about the female prisoner. She remains deeply amnesic. So profoundly so that he feels she will never recover her past while she is with us. Therefore . . ."

"I am aware of the chief medical officer's *opinion*," Tarimenloku interrupted, then wished he hadn't. "Continue."

"Yes sir. Assuming the chief medical officer's opinion is correct, and it *is* the most informed opinion available to us, she will never be of value as an intelligence source. He also thinks that she probably would recover, in time, if she were back among her people."

The commodore's expression did not change. "I have discussed this with the chief medical officer myself, with regard to her potential for successful interrogation. He admitted to me that he has only opinions. Amnesia, he tells me, is little understood."

He glanced at the chaplain, then looked back to his CIO. "For your personal information and for the record, I will point out that I too have considered, briefly, the matter of her repatriation. There would be some grounds for it if she were noble, but she does not bear the mark."

"Sir, as you know, I have interrogated the civilian prisoners extensively, to develop a picture of Confederation government, society, customs, and values, as well as their technology. The Confederation, at least its principal worlds, has its nobility. But—" the CIO chose his words carefully now—"they stress its importance less than we, thus noble families do not mark their children. The female prisoner, while bearing no mark of it, could easily be noble."

Tarimenloku grunted, a hand moving inadvertently as if to rise and touch the time-dulled, polychrome star on his forehead, a mark less than half an inch long. *A strange nobility*, he thought silently, *without sufficient pride to mark their offspring*.

"What evidence have you seen, if any, that suggests she might be noble?"

"Her action, sir. She saw a means of avoiding interrogation, and she was willing to die a gruesome death to keep it from us."

"Hmm. True. Well certainly she's no peasant. But she lacked not only the mark but the demeanor of nobility. The apparency is that she's gentry.

"And what is more relevant, Commander Ralankoor— sometimes even nobles are not repatriated until after a treaty is made. Usually there is at least a formal truce."

Tarimenloku's gaze had intensified, and when he paused, Bavi Ralankoor knew that, one, this refusal would not be reversed; and two, his superior was not done talking.

"Now. What do you suppose she feared we might learn from her? When we are back on Klestron, it is possible that SUMBAA will find out for us. And the information may be highly important to Klestron and the Empire. Therefore I have no choice but to take her with us."

He turned his eyes to the chaplain. "Unless Pastor Poorajarutha finds something seriously amiss with my reasoning."

The chaplain's expression betrayed no emotion. "Not at all," he said.

The commodore went on. "Nonetheless, Commander Ralankoor, as the Conscience of the Prophet you have made a case, albeit not a strong one, for her possible nobility. Therefore, have her moved to a cabin appropriate to noble rank. And see that she learns our language fluently.

"But before you do that—before you do anything else—have the civilian prisoners prepared for departure. Which will be at 0815; that gives you less than thirty minutes. They're to be delivered safely at the square in Lonyer City. Have Ensign Sooskabenloku accompany them in the shuttle. He's to be back aboard ship at not later than 1150 hours; make sure he knows that.

"We will leave these parking coordinates at 1200."

The chief intelligence officer voiced a rather subdued "yes sir; by your leave sir," and his face disappeared, allowing the chaplain's to occupy the entire screen for just a second before he too disconnected.

The cleric had had nothing further to say. They'd known one another for twenty years, he and the commodore. And he knew what Tarimenloku faced on Klestron. He knew also that any sympathy he might show, even silently, would only trouble the commodore's soul.

Tarimenloku looked at the clock. *In four hours and seven minutes I will turn my back on this accursed world. Kargh forgive me, I wish I could leave it in smoke and mourning, but I will not.*

His lips thinned, tightened. *But we'll be back. Not I, nor any fleet the sultan could send. And maybe not soon. But we will be back.*

And it will be an imperial fleet. With an imperial army, armed not merely to control uprisings, or repel unlikely incursions by other sultanates. A real army, unconstrained in its armaments. Then we will see how this confederation fares!

Sixty-Nine

The regiment's 1,178 troopers, along with the 106 surviving cadets and their remaining 47 T'swa cadre, had been gathered at several locations to be sent back to Iryala through the small teleport. Equipment larger than man-carried was stored at the Lonyer City landing field for later pickup. A single light utility floater stayed with the regiment, moving the teleport from one departure location to the next.

Headquarters Company would be the last to port home—Headquarters Company and what was left of its two attached rifle platoons. It hadn't yet struck its tents; its hour of departure wasn't certain, and neither was the weather, which had changed from persistently dry to sporadically showery. Lotta, after withdrawing from a trance a little earlier, had found Jerym. Now, together, they explored the creekbed above camp, mainly for something to do while they talked. Both carried sidearms. Neither wanted to be killed by some tiger or blue troll—certainly not on the day, the eve at least, of going home to Iryala.

The creek had swollen somewhat but was still small, bridged here and there by fallen trees in various stages of decay. Its pale amber water, still clear, ran mostly knee-deep now, or deeper, and four to eight-feet wide, in places striped with green water plants waving sinuously in the current. Mostly though it showed gravel bottom. Small fish swam in place, or disturbed, darted for cover under bank or log.

"If Tain was still with us," Lotta was saying, "what would you two do now?"

"I don't know. Why do you ask? She's probably half a parsec gone from here and getting farther fast. The chance of our ever seeing each other again is exactly zero."

Lotta bellied over a fallen log overgrown with what resembled a fine-leaved turf or coarse moss. "Right," she said. "But it might be useful to look at it with someone."

Jerym shrugged. "If Tain was still here . . ." He examined the question. "Romlar says we'll probably be sent back here in a week or two to continue our training. Not here in the jungle probably—I think we know jungle fighting pretty well now—but to the steppe, or the tundra prairie. Or maybe the coastal rainforest; I hear that's a lot different from this. Meanwhile Tain would be sitting here waiting for a ship." He turned and looked at his sister. "Unless you stayed and ran Ostrak Procedures on her so she could port back."

Again he shrugged; the matter was moot. "If we decided to be together, either she'd have to be with us here somehow, on some basis, and then go with us to Oven, or I'd have to leave the regiment."

"So what do you think you'd decide, the two of you?"

He shook his head. "It wouldn't be much of a life for her, with the regiment. I think she'd be too smart to try it. To be honest, I'm not sure she actually loved me; she might have just thought she did. It might have been a matter of the danger, of my going out every day or two to maybe get killed.

"No, if we were going to be together, I'd have to leave the regiment."

"Could you have done that?"

He stopped, looking thoughtfully at his sister. "I think so. One of the things the Ostrak Procedures do is make a person less compulsive. Right? You get more control over your decisions and actions. And look at the T'swa: When one of their regiments finally gets so shot up that it's down to a company or so, maybe understrength at that, the survivors get shipped back to Oven to do other things." He turned and led off again. "They stop being warriors," he added over his shoulder. "Our cadre weren't being warriors. They were being teachers.

"Maybe I could have become part of a training cadre. We're going to need cadres. The Klestroni might not come back, but I wouldn't bet on it, and His Majesty won't either."

"So," Lotta said, "as it is, what are you going to do?"

"No question. I'm staying with the regiment. It'll have to be my family." He used the word for marital family—spouse and children—then stopped again to look at Lotta.

"How about you? And Romlar? Anything developing there? I know he was interested in you, back on Iryala."

"We've had a strong mutual affinity from early on," Lotta answered. "I think it's scripted. Whatever; it'll have to wait. I'm going to tell Wellem I want to develop a program for training seers. Seers like the T'swa have. I intend to port to Tyss and train at the monastery of Dys Tolbash. Artus and I can get together later, when the regiment's disbanded."

Jerym's gaze was direct. "If Artus comes through alive."

"Right. If he comes through alive." *And I'd bet on it*, she added silently. *I am betting on it*.

HISTORICAL CHART
of the Human Species during and after the Great Annihilation

This chart outlines the histories of the three known human sectors. In different places and at different times, different calendar systems have been used. In this chart, year lengths are Confederation Standard years, but numbered from the emperor's decision to launch the Great Annihilation.

The history of the different human sectors are sketched in separate columns in the chart.

At this time, the sector called Haven has only one inhabited world.

The Home Sector

Year 0— In the Kron Empire of 53 worlds, which would later be termed "the Home Sector," the Congress of Constitutional Government meets to protest the Imperium's prolonged disregard of the constitution. They issue a position paper that includes a virtual ultimatum to the Imperium: Align your policies with the constitution or face rebellion.

The emperor orders construction of the HIMS *Retributor*.

Year 3— Plans approved for the *Retributor*, a gigantic, highly automated warship reputedly with the power to destroy planets. Actual construction begins.

Year 4— Coordinated rebellions break out on 17 worlds.

Year 6— Rebellions have spread to most worlds. Imperial fleet forced to concentrate on a limited number of worlds at one time. Two squadrons of the Imperial fleet mutiny, join the rebels.

Year 7— The *Retributor* is launched with the mad emperor as her master and with a psychoconditioned crew of fanatics. It reduces two rebellious worlds to orbiting rubble.

Further units of the Imperial Fleet declare for the rebels.

398

Year 8— Some worlds have fought themselves into collapse. The *Retributor* continues to "punish" (destroy) worlds for their rebelliousness.

Year 9— The surviving planets of the empire are devastated and in utter chaos. The emperor continues to destroy planets.

Year 10— Civilization has collapsed within the empire. More planets destroyed.

Year 12— The emperor suicides by destroying his ship. Of the 53 worlds previously inhabited, only 11 remain intact. The human species is nearly extinct.

Years 12 to roughly 100— On 8 of the 11 planets, the remaining humans, if any, succumb to severe conditions. On the remaining 3, one or more groups survive in extreme primitivism.

Years 100 to roughly 10,000— Hampered by the inaccessibility of fossil fuels and certain minerals, sulfur for example, and tin, the human advance out of primitivism is very slow.

Year 12,000— The sailboat has appeared on the seas of the planet Varatos.

Year 16,114— The calculus is invented on Varatos.

Year 18,349— First space flight to the moon of Varatos.

Year 18,517— Interstellar exploration ship from Varatos discovers the nearest other inhabited planet, Klestron. Exploration accelerates.

Year 18,619— The last of the 11 surviving habitable worlds is discovered. Within a century, further exploration ends with no further habitable worlds found.

The sciences begin a decline that will be broken only occasionally and briefly.

Year 20,008— The Varatosu Empire becomes a religious empire, the "Karghanik Empire," with 10 semi-autonomous planets, sultanates, under the rule of Varatos and its Kalif.

Year 21,491— The Sultan of Klestron sends a flotilla to seek habitable worlds at whatever distance. The objective is eventual colonization.

Year 21,492— The Klestronu flotilla encounters a Garthid patrol ship, engages it, then escapes into hyperspace.

In a later encounter with a Garthid patrol, the exploration flotilla loses a ship to enemy fire.

Year 21,493— The flotilla successfully emerges from Garthid space and begins to reconnoiter systems adjacent to the Confederation sector.

Year 21,494— Chodrisei Biilathkamoro becomes Kalif of the Karghanik Empire.

The Klestronu exploration flotilla lands marines on the Confederation trade world Terfreya (Karnovir 02) and captures Lonyer City, its capital. They are soon engaged in jungle warfare.

The marines are driven from Terfreya. The Klestronu flotilla leaves the Karnovir system for home without victory but with much information.

Year 21,497— The Klestronu flotilla arrives back in the Karghanik Empire and reports on the habitable world it found, part of a sector with many habitable worlds. The evidence is that the Confederation fleet is smaller and technologically inferior to that of the empire.

Year 21,500— A Karghanik invasion of the Confederation of Worlds is defeated.

Year 21,507— A powerful Garthid invasion of the Karghanik Empire is met by Confederation intervention. The Confederation is not nearly a match, militarily, for the Garthids, but it turns the Garthids back with a new approach to warfare.

The Confederation of Worlds

Year 4— Fleeing the impending megawar, a convoy of eight large merchant vessels refitted as refugee ships quietly departs the planet Renyala. Its ruling committee intends to look for a new home well outside known space.

Year 5— The refugee convoy from Renyala enters the previously unknown Garthid Sector and encounters a Garthid patrol ship. It is allowed to proceed through the sector but warned not to stop again within it.

Year 6— Psychiatrists with the refugee convoy develop "the Sacrament," a psychoconditioning procedure designed to prevent megawars in the new civilization they hope to found. The basic premises used in developing the Sacrament are (1) that men will fight each other; and (2) that research and highly advanced science are necessary for the development of megawar technology. Thus the Sacrament suppresses the type of mind which might otherwise pursue scientific enquiry. An additional effect is a tendency not to question authority.

Five subcultures (septs) among the refugees refuse the Sacrament and are segregated from the rest and from each other. The rest of the refugees are psychoconditioned, and the Sacrament will be delivered to all their children as they come along.

The refugee convoy leaves the Garthid Sector and finds a marginally habitable world deemed unsuitable to the unassisted development of technological civilization. Three of the five septs which had refused the Sacrament are offloaded onto it.

Year 7— The refugee convoy finds several further habitable worlds. It offloads the remaining recalcitrant septs on one of the most marginal.

Year 8— The refugee convoy lands on a highly suitable world, names it Iryala, and begins the work of making it home.

Year 117— One of the refugee ships leaves Iryala to explore the sector.

Year 798— The Ruling Council on Iryala, concerned over what they regard as dangerously innovative technology, passes the Standard Technology Act, which severely restricts the right to employ technological elements in new configurations. This virtually freezes technology in its existing form.

Year 892— The first new emigrant ship is sent out from Iryala to colonize another planet. This begins nearly fifteen thousand years of sporadic colonization.

Years 900 to 14,824— Thirty-six planets are colonized.

Year 14,916— Amberus is crowned emperor of what had been the Confederation of Human Worlds. A shrewd megalomaniac of remarkable charisma, Amberus regards history as a personal insult, and prohibits teaching it. He has the calendar years numbered from his coronation. After careful, covert planning, he has all historical libraries, collections, and archives destroyed, public and private, and all historical matter erased from computer banks except for administrative data directly necessary to government. Historians, professional and amateur, are hunted down and killed. This continues throughout the 27 years of Amberus's reign, ending with his assassination.

Currently, history prior to Amberus is known very largely from later reconstructions by seers on the trade world Tyss.

Years 14,944 to 15,690— Period of additional exploration and colonization. The planets Orlantha and Tyss, colonized long since by the off-loaded recalcitrants, are rediscovered. The manner of their settlement is not known.

Year 15,697— A decree prohibits further colonization, on the grounds that a larger empire will be impossible to administer. The empire continues in more or less efficient stagnation under the force of the Sacrament and Standard Technology, reasonably safe as long as no major perturbation occurs.

Year 20,750— After a brief revolt overthrows a later, so-called Thomsid Empire, the Iryalan general staff crowns Pertunis of Ordunak King of Iryala and Emperor of the Worlds. Pertunis promptly declares the empire dissolved, formalizing the actual state of affairs. He then proceeds to build a loose economic and administrative network of worlds with Iryala (as always) the central world.

Year 20,787— The Confederation of Worlds is ratified by 27 planets, with Pertunis as Administrator General. He then delegates most of his administrative duties and spends much of his remaining life developing a theory and structure of Management intended to rationalize and stabilize government, business, and personal life. At his death, this compilation of principles and policies is proclaimed "Standard Management." It provides a new level of understanding and efficiency, but also further calcifies human thought and action in the Confederation, leaving little room for innovation of any sort.

The love and respect accorded Pertunis results in the calendar years being numbered from his coronation.

Year 20,832— Barden Ostrak, Lord Heriston, becomes the first Iryalan to investigate the T'sel, the philosophy of Tyss, one of the two marginally habitable worlds on which the recalcitrant septs were offloaded. The Sacrament is not given on Tyss.

Year 20,834— Merlan Ostrak, age seven, becomes the first Iryalan child to live and train on Tyss under T'sel masters. He is joined within three years by two more Iryalan children. Being reared in the T'sel overrides the Sacrament.

Year 20,851— First covert T'sel academy founded on Iryala, on the Ostrak country estate. It appears to be an ordinary private academy.

Year 20,878— The so-called "Movement" is established by alumni of the Ostrak academy. A second academy is opened, the beginning of an expansion.

Year 20,913— Prince Jerym enrolls at the Green Plains Academy.

Year 20,949— Prince Jerym is crowned King of Iryala and Administrator General of the Confederation of Worlds, as Consar II. From that point, all Iryalan princes are covertly trained in the T'sel.

Year 21,439— Covert disarming of the Sacrament is begun on Iryala to break the Confederation free from the long technological stagnation.

Year 21,460— The Kettle War starts. [See *The Regiment*.]

Year 21,462— The Kettle War ends. The role played by nonstandard T'swa metallurgists and mercenary regiments is used by The Movement to crack Standard Technology. [See *The Regiment*.]

Year 21,487— Training of selected Iryalan children as warriors begins with the "cadets."

Year 21,493— An experimental regiment of adolescent Iryalans, "intentive warriors," begins training under T'swa veterans.

Year 21,494— A teleport is successfully tested with human subjects. The personal attributes for survival of teleportation are defined.

The Karghanik exploration flotilla lands marines on the Confederation Trade World Terfreya (Karnovir 02), and captures Lonyer City, its capital. The marines are soon engaged in jungle warfare by the 12-yr-old cadets in training there.

Their black T'swa cadre dub the Iryalan regiment-in-training "the White T'swa," following its highly successful graduation maneuvers.

The white regiment is teleported to Terfreya, and in company with the preadolescent cadets, drives the Klestronu marines off of Terfreya.

Year 21,497— The Klestronu flotilla arrives back in the Karghanik Empire and reports on the habitable world it found, part of a sector with many habitable worlds. The evidence is that the Confederation fleet is smaller and technologically inferior to that of the empire.

Year 21,500— A Karghanik invasion of the Confederation of Worlds is defeated.

Year 21,507— A powerful Garthid invasion of the Karghanik Empire is met by Confederation intervention. The Confederation is not nearly a match, militarily, for the Garthids, but it turns the Garthids back with a new approach to warfare.

Year 21,516— An exploration ship from Iryala finds and visits Haven. Diplomatic relations are opened with the sapient life forms there.

Year 22,002— A fleet—an enormous "funnel ship" with squadrons of powerful scouts and escorts—approaches the neighborhood of Haven, to steal its ocean. This force, or some force with a similarly inexplicable desire for water and a technology for translocating it, had visited this part of the galaxy some two million years before and transformed Tyss into a desert planet. The Confederation has had no serious wars for centuries, but with the four sapient species of Haven they prepare to meet the threat. In a slugging contest they'd be far overmatched, and the invading fleet seems to be entirely automated, with no biological entities present to negotiate with.

The invading fleet is turned away by techniques that are not military, with the help of a non-human ally from the Karghanik Empire.

Haven

Year 5— The merchant ship HS *Adanik Larvest* flees the empire with a crew of 15 and a cargo of 600 pleasure droids in stasis. (The droids were engineered from human genetic material; they are essentially human.)

Year 6— The *Larvest* too enters the vast Garthid Sector, encounters a Garthid patrol and is allowed to continue.

Year 7— The *Larvest* emerges from the Garthid Sector into a sector far distant from that entered by the refugee convoy.

Year 8— The *Larvest* is in serious need of an unavailable overhaul and has to put down somewhere. It finds a suitable planet and names it Haven. Circumstances dictate offloading the droids on a continent apart from the crew which colonizes a large archipelago. Thus human genetic material is introduced in two separate parts of Haven.

Year 37— The *Larvest*'s backup power system dies, leaving no means of entering the ship from outside, and the settlers on Haven are cut off from those ship systems that had remained functional. [See *The Lantern of God*.] Their settlement, hit by exotic diseases, has almost no one left of the original crew, and has already been declining toward primitivism. This new misfortune will send them the rest of the way.

Years 8 to 21,000— The two human populations develop civilizations in isolation from each other. Technological development is particularly slow because of a lack of known fossil fuels, the absence of intercultural stimulation, and, on the archipelago, because of periodic plagues.

Year 21,302— The entire archipelago has been colonized. It is brought under single, imperial rule under the dominion of the largest and first settled island of Almeon. This empire will fragment and be reunited repeatedly.

Year 21,386— Access is gained to the ancient hull-metal hulk of the derelict *Adanik Larvest*. Work begins on deciphering the captain's log, the language of which is now unintelligible.

Year 21,414— The captain's log from the *Adanik Larvest* is translated. It provides the Almaeic Empire with the story of the colony's origin, and tells of the dumping of the droids on a continent far to the east.

Year 21,417— A steam-driven exploration ship from the Almaeic Empire discovers the Droid Continent, finding there a technologically inferior civilization.

Year 21,478— The Almaeic Empire launches an invasion of the Droid Continent. The invasion fails, the huge invasion fleet is destroyed, and the oppressive Almaeic government falls. [See *The Lantern of God*.]

Year 21,516— An exploration ship from Iryala finds and visits Haven. Diplomatic relations are opened with the sapient life forms there.

Year 22,002— A fleet—an enormous "funnel ship" with squadrons of powerful scouts and escorts—approaches the neighborhood of Haven, to steal its ocean. This force, or some force with a similarly inexplicable desire for water and a technology for translocating it, had visited this part of the galaxy some two million years before and transformed Tyss into a desert planet. The Confederation has had no serious wars for centuries, but with the four sapient species of Haven they prepare to meet the threat. In a slugging contest they'd be far overmatched, and the invading fleet seems to be entirely automated, with no biological entities present to negotiate with.

The invading fleet is turned away by techniques that are not military, with the help of a non-human ally from the Karghanik Empire.

JOHN DALMAS

John Dalmas has just about done it all—parachute infantryman, army medic, stevedore, merchant seaman, logger, smokejumper, administrative forester, farm worker, creamery worker, technical writer, free-lance editor—and his experience is reflected in his writing. His marvelous sense of nature and wilderness combined with his high-tech world view involves the reader with his very real characters. For lovers of fast-paced action-adventures!

THE REGIMENT
The planet Kettle is so poor that it has only one resource: its fighting men. Each year three regiments are sent forth into the galaxy. And once a regiment is constituted, it never recruits again; as casualties mount the regiment becomes a battalion . . . a company . . . a platoon . . . a squad . . . and then there are none. But after the last man of *this* regiment has flung himself into battle, the Federation of Worlds will never be the same.

THE GENERAL'S PRESIDENT
The stock market crash of 1994 made the black Monday of 1929 look like a minor market adjustment . . . the rioters of the '90s made the Wobblies of the '30s look like country-club Republicans . . . Soon the fabric of society will be torn beyond repair. The Vice President resigns under a cloud of scandal— and when the military hints that they may let the lynch mobs through anyway, the President resigns as well. So the Generals get to pick a President. But the man they choose turns out to be more of a leader than they bargained for . . .

FANGLITH
Fanglith was a near-mythical world to which criminals and misfits had been exiled long ago. The planet becomes all too real to Larn and Deneen when they track their parents there, and find themselves in the middle of the Age of Chivalry on a world that will one day be known as Earth.

RETURN TO FANGLITH
The oppressive Empire of Human Worlds, temporarily foiled in *Fanglith*, has struck back and resubjugated its colony planets. Larn and Deneen must again flee their home. Their final object is to reach a rebel base—but first stop is Fanglith, the Empire's name for medieval Earth.

THE REALITY MATRIX
Is the existence we call life on Earth for real, or is it a game? Might Earth be an artificial construct designed by a group of higher beings—a group of which we are all members, and of which we are unaware, until death? Forget the crackpot theories, the psychics, the religions of the world—*everything* is an illusion, everything, that is, except the Reality Matrix! But self-appointed "Lords of Chaos" have placed a "chaos generator" in the matrix, and it is slowly destroying our world.

PLAYMASTERS (with Rod Martin)
The aliens want to use Earth as a playing field for their hobby and passion: war. But they are prohibited from using any technology not developed on the planet, and 20th-century armaments are too primitive for good sport. As a means of accelerating Earth to an appropriately sporting level, Cha, a galactic con artist, flimflams the Air Force Chief of Staff into founding a think-tank for the development of 22nd-century weapons.

You can order all of John Dalmas's books with this order form. Check your choices below and send the combined cover price/s to: Baen Books, Dept. BA, 260 Fifth Avenue, New York, New York 10001.*